I0779325

FRAZZLED MOMS VS. WILD

Stephanie Paige King

For Brent and my mom. Your obsessions with camping
have given me enough stories to write volumes.

Acknowledgements

I'm deeply grateful to everyone who cheers me on and gives me the opportunity to write. To my Team Barnabas friends—Paula, Allison, Douglas, Mary, and Sara Meg—thank you for making me a better writer. I learn from you every week, and I'm awed by how beautifully each of you uses your words to tell stories.

A huge thank you to the ever-patient Cynthia Hickey for giving me a place at Winged Publications and for the unforgettable suggestion that a crab claw could be a deadly weapon. Kristen, your advice, edits, and the headshot that makes me look young and unwrinkled have been invaluable. Thank you. Christina, I have the utmost gratitude for your willingness to help the words do their thing, even late at night when I can no longer make sense of my own sentences.

Mom, thank you for reading countless renditions of The Frazzled Moms and for always being my biggest fan.

Brent, I couldn't do any of this without you. Thank you for feeding me—literally and figuratively—and for holding my feet to the fire when I'm easily distracted. You and our children have given me the gift of finding beauty and humor amid chaos, and I wouldn't have it any other way. Collin, Alisha, Kailyn, and Carter, you and the endless string of pets that have come into our house have kept us from ever having a dull moment. If the King house had been a boring place, I never would have found something to write about.

And as always, all glory to God for every good and beautiful thing in my life.

Chapter 1

Dana

Dana Harding had run out of creative ways to kill people. The clock was ticking, and if inspiration didn't strike soon, she'd be the one on the chopping block. She gnawed a hangnail, willing her anxiety to cough up one more deliciously twisted method of extermination.

"Hey Mom, where's my—"

Dana slapped her laptop closed. Her cheeks flamed, and she plastered on an overly bright smile. "Whatcha looking for?"

Nate, her middle child and elder son, narrowed his eyes. "You first." He nodded at the laptop. "Do we need to have a talk about inappropriate uses of the internet, Mom?"

She drummed her fingers on the computer. "The usual research. Who knew murder could get so repetitive?"

"I still say you should go with my idea about stabbing someone with a snow crab claw."

"I don't like this side of you, son. Besides, I already ran it by my editor, and she vetoed it." Hashing out the details of her crime novels with a fourteen-year-old might not be the best idea. There was a decent chance it would stunt his emotional development.

The doorbell rang, eliciting a bark from the giant Bernese Mountain Dog, Harvey, who lay in a furry heap at Dana's feet. The old guy didn't bother to get up.

"I'll get it!" Adam, the ten-year-old, sprang down the

stairs and hurdled a long box blocking the entry way to get to the front door.

"Expecting someone?" Her youngest never rushed that efficiently when she called him to dinner or to take out the garbage.

"The guys might want to play basketball or something." He opened the door as the engine of a truck revved and then faded away. "A little help, please." Adam wrestled with the delivery, but he couldn't get it through the doorway.

Nate stepped over the first box blocking his path and helped his brother bring in the next one. "*More* camping gear? You can't even get to the living room because of all the boxes."

Dana swiveled the barstool that doubled as an office chair to face the living room behind her. "One of them is a tent. Those over there are hiking packs. Or maybe they're the sleeping bags your dad ordered." She'd never been camping before, but surely her husband Will was going overboard for their big family adventure. There was no way pretending to be homeless required a sporting goods store to take over their residence box by box.

She rubbed her temples. "I'm scared to open any of it. Unless there's a hotel with running water in that big one, I don't want to know."

Adam ripped a flap off one of the boxes and pulled out a backpack. "This trip is going to be epic!"

Epic wasn't the word Dana would have chosen for sleeping on the ground. Will and the boys had somehow convinced her and seventeen-year-old Leah that camping would be the trip of a lifetime, the best way for them to bond as a family and really experience God's creation. More like a way to meet God in person, if you asked her.

"I hope we see a bear," said Nate. "That would be so cool. I know the bears in Colorado aren't giant like the ones in Alaska, but wouldn't that be amazing?"

"*So* amazing." Dana made a mental note to order bear spray. She really was excited to take in the crisp mountain air scented by pine trees. Colorado's views of snowcapped mountains would be a welcomed change from the flat, dusty West Texas plains. But why couldn't they bask in the scenery and breathe fresh air from the balcony of a mid-priced hotel?

Nate nudged the box in the walkway with his shoe. "Come on, Mom. Where's your sense of adventure? I bet you could come up with all kinds of new serial killer tactics in the great outdoors."

She leveled him with a withering glare.

Adam stiffened, and his eyes grew wide. "Are there really serial killers where we're camping?"

"No. Your brother's kidding." Eager to divert his attention, she changed the subject. "Any homework?"

He shook his head. "We won't have homework for the rest of the year."

"Notes in your bag you should have given me?"

He squinted at the ceiling. "Oh yeah. There's one about the end of school party." He pulled his backpack from beneath the kitchen counter and produced a wadded sheet of paper. He pushed it across the counter to Dana. "Mrs. Dickens said any parent who only brought paper goods to the Valentine's Day party *must* bring a food item this time. She said they *can* be store-bought, but you have to doublecheck that whatever you bring complies with the class allergy list."

Dana scanned the note. "Yay. I get to track down or make gluten-free, dairy-free, sustainably-sourced chocolate cupcakes."

"As long as they don't have Red Dye 40," he said.

She pursed her lips. "Super."

Nate leaned against the counter playing a game on his phone.

"Didn't you come in here looking for something?" she

asked.

"Oh yeah. Have you seen my football? Coach said to practice our ball handling before training camp starts in July."

Adam facepalmed his forehead. "Bruh. You're a lineman. You don't get to touch the ball."

Nate darted around the counter. "Then I guess I better practice tackling." He wrapped his arms around Adam's waist and laid him out on the tile.

With little more than an hour before the family had to be out the door for Wednesday night Bible study and her mentor moms' group at church, Dana couldn't afford to waste any more time. She opened her laptop once again as Harvey heaved himself up to investigate the commotion. "Don't get blood on my clean floor before we leave for church."

Chapter 2

Josie

Josie Caraway was unloading the dishwasher when out of the corner of her eye, she spied one of her triplet two-year olds dragging a disembodied head by its hair.

"Come here, you little thief." She flipped her dark red braid behind her shoulder and chased Connor down the hall. "Mommy's head is not a toy." She cornered him and pried his fingers out of the mannequin's hair.

He screamed and lunged for the head. "Mine!"

Josie held it out of his reach. "This is not yours. It's mi—" She stopped short of saying the word the toddlers used no less than a combined eight hundred times a day. "It's Mommy's school project."

Connor threw himself down and wailed. Josie stepped over him and delivered the head back to its home in the rolling case amid her cosmetology supplies. She wheeled the bag to the garage and stowed it in the trunk of her red Honda Odyssey, the only place still safe from the toddlers' reach.

She drooped against the van and pressed the heels of her hands against her eyes, relishing the solitude of the garage for a beat before trudging back into the lion's den. Tomorrow's Parents Day Out couldn't come soon enough.

Josie stepped into the playroom just in time to catch

Olivia tip over the last toy bin that hadn't already been dumped out. Across the room, Ben stood triumphantly atop the bookcase, arms raised like he'd conquered Everest. Josie rushed over and plucked him down before disaster struck. "Bookshelves are not for climbing." How many times in a day did she repeat that phrase?

The triplets tore through the house, giggling as they dashed into the living room. Josie took the opportunity to scoop up handfuls of toys, tossing them into their bins. She had barely made a dent when a loud thud sent her sprinting toward the commotion.

Ben landed on the couch with a victorious bounce, having launched himself from the coffee table. Olivia, not to be outdone, had one foot on the table, ready to follow. Josie swooped in, planting her daughter onto her hip before she could take flight. Her patience hung by a thread, and she was fresh out of energy to referee yet another round of toddler parkour.

"Alright, you daredevils. Let's get out of the house before Mommy has a stroke. How about we go for a ride?" She clapped her hands, overselling a walk around the block with the enthusiasm of a cruise director. "Come on, boys." Josie carried Olivia to the entry way and buckled her into the Peg Perego triple stroller she'd dubbed "Peg."

Peg's best feature was her toddler-proof harnesses, protecting both the children from harm and everything in their path from further destruction.

"Next." She repeated the process, strapping Connor, then Ben into their seats.

Josie pushed the monstrosity off their cul-de-sac and down a side street.

The kids shrieked and pointed at birds and squirrels along the way. "Mama, yook. Kicken!"

"I see it, but that's not a chicken. It's a... regular bird." She really should beef up her bird-watching skills.

"Kicken. Bawk." Connor's attempted clucking was

adorable, though far from authentic.

Josie's shoulders loosened, amusement replacing the stress that had knotted them. She pulled out her phone. Tonight was the last meeting of her mentor mom group before summer break. If the kids stayed out of trouble until then, she might have a shot at picking up the house and starting dinner before her husband, Hunter, got home. At least then, she wouldn't feel so guilty about leaving him to put the kids to bed on his own.

Josie wheeled Peg through the front door, maneuvering the stroller into position in front of the TV. With a click of the remote, the opening tune of a preschool show filled the air. She backed slowly out of the room, careful not to spook them.

The state of the playroom nearly made her turn around and walk out. Blocks, stuffed animals, and plastic food covered every inch of the floor. She cracked her knuckles. Restoring some semblance of order, even temporarily, always renewed her hope that the terrible twos wouldn't last forever.

She dove in, flipping bins upright and sorting toys with the efficiency of a woman who had done this a thousand times before. Cars in one bin, blocks in another. The carpet slowly reemerged, and Josie sank onto the multicolored rug, pulling out her phone for a quick check-in with the adult world.

Vacation pictures flooded her feed. Two of her old college friends sipped cocktails in Cancun, their sun-kissed faces grinning beneath wide-brimmed hats. Josie's stomach twisted with envy. She hadn't kept up with anyone from those days well enough to plan a getaway like that. Even if she could convince some of the women from her mentor group to go on a trip, she didn't have the heart to leave Hunter alone with the triplets for that long. They'd eat him alive.

"Mama, gimme down. Want out." Ben's demand was

immediate, insistent.

Before she could move, the others caught on.

Chaos erupted.

So much for a quiet escape.

"Mama. Mama. Mama."

The sounds of little feet kicking against Peg's footrests mirrored the throbbing in her temples. She sent a text to her neighbor Dana.

I'm going to take my own car tonight so I can stay out until I know for sure the kids are asleep.

"Maa-ma!"

Josie dropped her chin to her chest. "I'm coming." She stood, tucked her phone back in her hip pocket, and dove back into the fray.

Josie paused at the doorway by a poster that read, "Welcome M.O.M.s (Mothers on Mission)." The sign had been the same for over a year, and she missed the old days when their leader Serena made a cheesy new one every week, like the photo of a hammock with the words "rest for the weary mom's soul."

She had voted for them to be called the Village People, given how often Serena emphasized they were a village for one another. But that probably would have been a hard sell with the church deacons.

Josie glanced around the room, where women greeted one another with hugs and laughter filled the air. Since the group's inception, she had witnessed God working through a handful of weary moms, drawing in women from all walks of life. While many were church members, some came from different faith backgrounds, and a few had none. Over late-night texts, emergency babysitting swaps, and tearful prayers in the Target parking lot, they had become more than just a group. They had built a sisterhood, a safety net, and a village in the truest sense.

Anita Steen approached from another hallway with a warm smile. They'd been table mates from the start, and Mrs. Steen had become a mother figure to Josie. "Come sit by me and tell me all the fun things the triplets are doing this week."

Josie followed her to their assigned table and sank into her seat. "Well, they think all birds are chickens, and my entire house is a jungle gym, so that's fun."

"Wearing you out, are they?" Mrs. Steen put her hand on Josie's arm.

She threw her head back. "Like you wouldn't believe. I love them to pieces, but I look forward to my class just for the break. Learning to cut hair alongside girls barely out of high school might not seem like a reprieve, but at least they aren't climbing on tables, screaming at me, or pouring milk into the couch cushions. And not once have I had to wipe a classmate's nose or rear end."

"Hang in there. It won't be like this forever."

"No, summer break is about to begin, and I won't have Parents' Day Out or class as an escape for three months."

More women trickled in and found their seats. Josie turned to Mrs. Steen. "What about you? Are you glad to get your peace and quiet back?" Her son and grandchildren had been living with her for over a year and recently moved out.

"You know, it's funny. I'm so thankful my son and his wife reconciled, and they're doing the work to rebuild their family, but I had just gotten used to the noise and messes when they moved out again."

"I can drop my kids off any time you need some noise and a mess to keep you company."

Mrs. Steen leaned into Josie and gave her a side hug. "I would love that. Any time you need a break, just let me know."

Her neighbor Dana slid into the seat next to Mrs. Steen. "You're always welcome to bring them to my house, too. Or text me, and I'll come over."

Josie had lost count of how many times she'd hauled the kids over to Dana's. She honestly didn't know what she'd do without her neighbor across the cul-de-sac. But Dana had just as much on her plate, maybe even more, juggling her family and a publishing contract.

"I know you have a book deadline, and I don't want to distract you," Josie said.

Dana waved a hand dismissively. "Distract me anytime, please. I can't get any writing done anyway with this camping trip looming over me."

"Are you afraid of the great outdoors?" asked Mrs. Steen.

"Yes." She ticked off a list on her fingers. "Bears, bugs, snakes, oh, and outhouses. More than all of those, I'm deathly afraid of the lack of outhouses when they're needed."

Mrs. Steen folded her arms and turned her body toward Dana. "Are you telling me that in forty-something years, you've never used a port-a-potty or peed outside?"

"I try not to, and since we don't do many outdoorsy activities, it's been pretty easy to avoid."

Josie snickered. "Have you ever even been camping?"

Dana threw her hands up. "No, and I don't understand why I have to start now."

Josie's older sister was a nature enthusiast. They'd gone backpacking together once in the Lincoln National Forest— eating freeze-dried meals, munching on granola bars, and giggling all night at silly stories. "It'll be fun. You'll see nature in a new way. Life's simpler out there. You might even want to do it more often."

Another mom took her place across from Josie. "Is someone going camping?"

Josie pointed her thumb at Dana. "Her family. Rachel,

tell her, how great it'll be."

The newbie grinned. "Just think of all the quality time you'll get without phone signals in the mountains. Your kids are going to be so much better for it."

Josie nodded enthusiastically. "So true."

Dana cast a pointed look at each of them. "What I heard was 'you won't have a way to call for help in a wilderness emergency.' This just keeps getting better and better."

The women laughed.

"What is it you church ladies say? It'll give you a stronger testimony," said Rachel.

As the gathering wound down, Josie lingered, chatting with a few women and deliberately stalling her walk to the parking lot. Eventually, with no more excuses to stay, she stepped outside into the breezy evening air.

Dana rolled down the window of her Tahoe and called, "I can't leave until Nate and Leah get out of youth group, but what's your excuse for being here so late?"

Josie walked over. "Today was so rough I cried just thinking about making the kids' lunches. If they're still awake when I get home, I don't know what I'll do."

"Aww, Jos. You need a break. I wish you would let me help you more."

"I can't come running to you every time I'm having a tough day. You'd never get that book written. Besides, two-year-old triplets cause early aging, and there's no reason both of us should look like the Crypt Keeper." Josie stooped to examine her face in Dana's side mirror. "Look at these crow's feet. Got those bad boys from my kids."

Her neighbor raised a skeptical eyebrow. "You're like thirty-five. What do you know about the Crypt Keeper?"

"It's from *Freaky Friday* when Lindsay Lohan wakes

up in Jamie Lee Curtis's body."

The older Harding kids jumped into the car.

"If Leah drove the boys, you could be home by now," said Josie.

"What? No." Leah leaned over her mom. "I have to pay for my own gas. We aren't taking my car."

"Let's go to dinner Friday night," said Dana. "A double date. My kids can watch yours. We'll have adult conversation and take the night off from cooking."

Josie and Hunter were long overdue for a night out. "You had me at 'let's go.'" She said goodnight to the Hardings, slid into the minivan, and called Hunter as she backed out of the lot. "Is the coast clear?"

He chuckled. "Livvie's still singing to herself, but I bet she'll crash before you get here. Just to be on the safe side, you could pick us up a couple of tacos on your way home."

That man knew the way to her heart.

Chapter 3

Dana

Dana opened her father's front door without knocking. "Dad, I'm here."

His little mutt Patch Johnson greeted her with full body wags.

"You're such a good boy. You don't even jump on people anymore. I'm so proud of you. Where's Dad? Or is he 'Edward' to you? Go find Edward."

Her dad strode in from the kitchen with a treat and coaxed the dog into his crate. "Do you think he knows me by my first name?"

"How would I know? You call *him* by his full name."

He crouched to fasten the latch. "Patch is a common dog name, but he's the only Patch *Johnson* at the dog park."

"You could call him PJ for short."

"Now you're being absurd," he said.

Gauging Dad's mental faculties proved harder than it should have been. Dana surreptitiously scanned the room for signs he was still taking care of himself. Immaculate kitchen. Did that mean he'd washed his breakfast dishes already or skipped the meal entirely? "The place looks nice. I take it you like the new cleaning service?"

"Nope. Told them not to come back after the first day."

"Oh? What happened?" Dana braced for another of his hairbrained stories. Sometimes he had moments of skewed perception or memory lapses, which might have led to him firing the cleaners.

"Slow as molasses. They paid more attention to their phones than to my floors."

On his good days, he was perfectly capable of keeping the small house tidy and handling a few chores. However, Dana liked having someone else handle the deep cleaning to keep him from overexerting himself and to alert her to any oddities that might indicate a decline in his condition again.

She shifted her weight from one leg to the other, racking her brain for a diplomatic response. "You're doing a great job around here, but I can find someone else. I mean, if you want."

"The couple who moved into Rita Brewer's old place across the street recommended their cleaning lady, Maggie. She's efficient and quiet, and she doesn't mind Patch. She also makes me sandwiches. And if you don't have any further questions, maybe we can get to my doctor's appointment on time for once."

She squelched the urge to roll her eyes. They were always on time. But to Edward Johnson, unless you were fifteen minutes early, you were late.

"I have a feeling, Dad, that Dr. Leyva is going to say the same thing she says at every check-up." She gulped down the lump threatening to choke out her words and give away her true feelings. "'Keep doing what you're doing, and we'll see you back here in six months.'"

As Dana said it, she prayed it would be true. Even though her dad's mental health was stable, and he'd been having far fewer bad spells in the last couple of years, she always breathed a little easier after getting another good report from the neurologist.

She squirmed in the exam room chair and jiggled her foot. Dr. Leyva asked more questions today than usual and was spending an eternity reviewing her dad's charts and medications. Finally, Dana's impatience won out. She clasped her hands in her lap and cleared her throat. "Is everything alright?"

The doctor peeled her eyes from the computer screen and smiled. "Looks that way. I'm making sure there's been no relapse that would indicate a need to increase Mr. Johnson's dosage. Sometimes after being on the same treatment plan for a while, it becomes less effective. But so far, I don't see any indication that we need to make changes."

Dana heaved a sigh of relief.

Her dad met her gaze with mock consternation. She raised her eyebrows in silent question, but he said nothing. Once they were back in the car, his stare bored through her, practically drilling a hole in her head.

She turned to face him and brushed away a strand of hair that had stuck to her lip balm. "What, Dad?"

"You're so tightly wound every time we go in there that I'm pretty sure if Dr. L. ever gives us bad news, you'll faint or have a panic attack."

"That's ridiculous. I don't have panic attacks."

He gave her a placating pat on the arm. "Well, you need to lighten up."

She tugged her earlobe, and her voice came out an octave too high. "What are you talking about? I'm light as a feather. I go with the flow. Totally chill."

Her dad harrumphed. "Whatever you say."

The rest of the ride to Mesquite Village was silent. Dana didn't think of herself as uptight, but sometimes she probably came off that way. Between juggling her family's endless needs, a fledgling writing career, and her dad's health struggles, she never had a moment to herself. She had to keep a tight schedule to fit it all in, and if one piece fell out of place, the rest would crumble right behind it.

When they pulled up, she declined his perfunctory invitation to come inside for tea. "Can't. Adam's school lets out in half an hour, and I still need to run by the house and grab my laptop."

The publisher who bought her first crime novel, about a mom willing to do anything to procure organ donors for her dying son, had contracted her for a second book within a year. Thus, she had learned to write in stolen moments—waiting in parking lots, sitting through practice, anywhere she could squeeze in a few words.

Just as Dana pulled up to the curb, taking her place in the pickup line, she got a call.

"Mrs. Harding, this is the head trainer for the athletic department."

This wouldn't be a write-in-the-car day after all. Dana's chest tightened as she braced for bad news.

"We have Leah in our office, and I believe she has sustained a scaphoid fracture."

He might have said more, but Dana's own thoughts were too loud. Wasn't the scaphoid a skull bone? Soccer players were prone to concussions.

"Mrs. Harding?"

She snapped to attention. "I'm here. Just tell me what I need to do. Is she conscious? Is the ambulance on the way?"

"Ma'am. The scaphoid is a small bone in the wrist. We don't usually call for an ambulance unless a bone is protruding through the skin. I've splinted it, but she needs to be seen by a doctor to get cleared to return to practice."

Soccer was the least of her worries. Dana slumped against the driver's seat. The *wrist*. Not her head. Perhaps she should add some anatomy lessons to her to do list.

Dana's instinct was to rush to her injured child, but her Tahoe was stuck in the fifth-grade pickup line. Will would have to get Leah while she grabbed the boys.

He answered on the first ring. "Hey, honey."

She filled him in without returning his greeting. "So, you'll need to take Leah to get x-rayed while I get the boys. Then we can go back to get her car—"

"Dana, stop. I just left Amarillo. I'm a hundred miles away."

She muttered a mild expletive. Will's job had come with the promise of limited travel, but "limited" was proving to be a relative term. He drove to Midland and Amarillo every other Thursday, each two hours from Lubbock. "I forgot. I'll figure something out. Call you later, okay?"

The bell would ring in ten minutes, and she couldn't desert Adam. Josie was out of class by now and picking up the triplets from Parents' Day Out. If a better option with fewer cranky toddlers didn't materialize first, she would call her neighbor to help.

She leaned her forehead on the steering wheel and prayed aloud. "Lord, what do I do?"

A tap on her window startled her. She jolted upright, spotting her friend Kathy from their Wednesday night mom's group chuckling outside. Kathy's son was a grade above Adam and attended the same middle school as Nate.

She rolled her window down.

"I didn't mean to scare you." Kathy pointed to the car ahead of her. "I saw you in the rearview mirror."

"Hey, what are you doing here?"

"Picking up my nephew." Kathy nodded her chin at the line of cars. "I forgot how brutal elementary pickup can be. You okay? You look upset."

Dana told her about the fracture and Will's location. "Any chance you have a cloning machine in your trunk?"

"Afraid not, but I'm already here and heading to the middle school next. Why don't you let me get the boys for you and drop them at your house? You go take care of your daughter."

It was too good to be true that help showed up at exactly the right time. Kathy was her answer to prayer. The Wednesday moms who'd become her village had a unique way of showing up when all hope seemed lost.

Dana pulled the lime green laminated sign reading "Adam H./ Dickens" from her dash and handed it to Kathy. She called both boys' schools to alert them of the emergency change in plans as Kathy inched forward to give her room to get out of line. After an arduous process of backing, pulling up, cutting her wheel, and repeating seven times, Dana finally extricated her Tahoe and made her way to Leah.

They left urgent care with a referral to an orthopedist. An x-ray confirmed a scaphoid fracture below Leah's left thumb. She climbed into the passenger seat and shrank into a sullen ball staring out the window.

Dana's heart ached for her child. "Does it hurt a lot, sweetie?"

"Kind of. I guess." She flipped down the visor and examined her sleek ponytail in the vanity mirror. "How am I supposed to fix my hair with one hand?"

Dana smiled, taking in Leah's naturally sun-streaked hair and blue eyes framed by unfairly perfect lashes. "I'll help you."

Leah's gaze swept over her mom's brown, shoulder-length hair, routinely dyed to mimic the vibrancy of its youth. Dana squirmed under the weight of disdain in her daughter's eyes.

"No offense, Mom, but hair really isn't your thing."

She kept her eyes on the road and resisted the urge to swat at her mouthy child. Mostly because the closest arm was the one in a splint. "You know, prefacing an offensive remark with 'no offense' doesn't make it less offensive."

"I'm sorry, but I'm under a lot of pressure right now."

Dana pursed her lips and willed herself to say nothing.

"There's only like a week and a half until the end of school, and I'm not going to be a starter my senior year if I spend the whole summer on the injured roster." Leah wailed as only a teenage girl could. "What if my broken arm ruins the camping trip?"

"I didn't realize you were so excited about that. If you aren't up to it, we can stay home and let the boys go on their own." Dana hadn't been thrilled about it herself, but now that the possibility loomed that Leah couldn't go, her heart sank. Her proposal evoked more wailing.

"Mom, no. I *have* to go. I told everyone we were going backpacking, and my friends are all jealous. My Instagram is going to blow up on this trip." At least Leah had her priorities in order.

"Oh good. Here I was worried you might miss out on family bonding."

Leah whined, "Don't try to make me feel worse than I already do. What if I need surgery?"

Dana patted her leg. "Let's wait to find out what the orthopedist says before we worry about that. The urgent care doctor didn't think it was displaced. You might need a cast for a few weeks at the most."

"A *cast?* How am I going to shower? I'll miss out on swimming all summer."

Nothing Dana said right now would placate Leah. She'd learned over time the best antidote to her daughter's emotional spirals was to avoid eye contact and provide sustenance. She pointed to the Sonic up ahead. "Boy, tots and a chocolate milkshake would really hit the spot right now. You interested?"

"Are you even listening to me? I can't eat junk food. Since I can't work out with the team, the only way I'll look fit for my Instagram photo series is to diet."

Dana pinched the bridge of her nose with the arm propped on her window. If there was one thing that might be worse than an injured, surly teen, it was one who was also dieting.

She had abolished carbs herself many times in her adult life, and the meager pounds she lost weren't worth the agitation it caused. Will called it "Carb-ageddon." Her dieting wreaked havoc on everyone in the family in her pursuit of the sleeker body she'd lost a decade ago.

Carbs were the epicenter of her bliss, her inner happy place where the nice words came from. Leah may not have inherited her mother's flailing metabolism, but if she went off carbs cold turkey, there would *be* no camping trip. Only the most foolish of men would dare get into the car with her, much less venture into the wilderness where there were no witnesses.

Leah posed for a selfie with her splint. "I'll take a healthy fruit smoothie with chocolate protein powder instead."

The smoothie place was just a block down from Sonic, so Dana pulled in. The nutrition information on the menu proved Leah's healthy smoothie had a similar sugar content to a chocolate shake, but Dana refrained from pointing it out.

She let out a slow exhale as she received the smoothie through the drive-through window and passed it to Leah. Carb-ageddon—the junior edition, was a false alarm.

Will met them at the garage door. "How's the patient?"

Dana hugged him and whispered, "Patient is such an ironic word for the infirm. Your daughter is anything but."

Leah edged herself out of the Tahoe cradling her splint. She'd suddenly lost the strength in her good arm to cart her backpack or even her smoothie cup.

Dana counted to three in her head. "Here, sweetie. Why don't I carry your stuff for you?"

Will gingerly looped his arm around patient zero. "Sweetheart, I heard what happened. Come here."

She fell against his chest. "Everything is ruined now. We won't get to go camping, and I might need surgery. What if I can't play soccer my senior year?" She sobbed into his shirt.

"Let's wait and see what the orthopedist says before we jump to the worst-case scenario."

She sniffed and wiped her face with her sleeve. "Thanks, Dad." She disappeared into the house.

Hadn't Dana told her the exact same thing? She passed the backpack to Will and reached for the melted smoothie remnants. "How come you get to be the favorite parent, the one they listen to?"

He smirked over his shoulder. "Maybe because I'm not sending them home from school with strangers."

"Adam told you that, didn't he? Well, if you'd been in town, I wouldn't have had to resort to friends from church at the last minute."

They deposited Leah's stuff on the kitchen counter and retired to the living room sofa together. Harvey lowered his massive head onto Dana's lap and licked her hand.

"At least this one still likes me."

Will pecked her cheek. "You're *my* favorite too, and if you must know, I won't have to take any more day trips until July. That means the only travel on the docket is the camping trip, provided the wrist gets the greenlight."

"Okay, I know a few hours ago I didn't even know what a scaphoid was, but I did a lot of research in the waiting room. I doubt surgery will be necessary. I've also looked up outdoor activities with a wrist fracture, and I think she can still do all the things. She just needs a few days to adjust to the inconvenience of having half her arm immobilized."

"That's a relief. It'll be great to get out into nature and get a break from urban life for a while."

Dana had never considered their small city particularly urban. Sure, Lubbock was home to a D-1 university and the largest medical facilities between Albuquerque and Fort Worth, but in many ways, it was still a small town.

Will fished his phone out of his pocket and pulled up a website of a campground with picturesque mountains mirrored on the surface of a lake. "I reserved us a site here for the week after school gets out. There's running water and electrical hookups, so we won't have to rough it too bad."

She halfheartedly pumped her fist.

He patted her leg. "How enthusiastic of you. You're dreading this trip, aren't you?"

Of course! "I'm sure it'll be great. Camping just seems messy, uncomfortable, and dangerous. And if Leah could break a bone doing the sport she's been in for eleven years, there's no telling what injuries await the boys exploring the mountains." She scratched Harvey behind the ears. "And what about this guy? He's not getting around as well as he used to. Hiking may be too much for him."

"Dana, we aren't trekking the Himalayas. It'll be a relaxing vacation." He leaned away from her and studied her face. "I still can't believe you've *never* been camping before."

She shrugged. "I guess the Johnson family just never saw the point in roughing it."

His eyes lit up like a kid on Christmas morning. "It's the greatest thing ever! You'll see."

"Uh huh. Then why is this our first foray into the wilderness?" If it was as fun as Will wanted her to believe it was, he wouldn't have waited until the kids were half-grown to suggest it.

"I took the boys to the state park that time, but we're

too busy to go more often. Now, we only have one more summer after this before Leah goes off to college, and I want us to make the most of it and do all the things we never got around to."

If that wasn't a gut punch, nothing was. How were they down to two last summer breaks? Dana didn't want her kids to look back on a long list of adventures they never got to take because their parents were too busy. She vowed to make the most of this summer vacation. Besides, Will had already promised if she happily embraced camping, she'd get to pick where the family spent Labor Day weekend. It would definitely be somewhere with a spa.

Chapter 4

Relief washed over Dana when the orthopedist's office called the next morning to squeeze in Leah, sparing them a weekend of waiting for answers.

The doctor pointed to the x-ray on the monitor. "The good news is you don't need surgery. The bad news is you're going to be in a cast for the next four to six weeks while the bone fuses."

Leah slumped and blinked back tears. "This is going to ruin my whole summer."

"Not at all." The doctor pulled up a website featuring a neon lattice sleeve. "We have a new type of cast that's completely waterproof and outdoor-safe. Less irritating and easier to remove than a traditional fiberglass one, too."

The teenager brightened. "Do I get to pick the color?"

"Of course! That's the best part of having a cast." He handed her a lollipop from a jar on the counter.

A technician led Leah and Dana to the casting room and slid a flexible transparent sleeve over the fractured wrist. Leah made her color selection, and the tech injected liquid resins into the sleeve's lattice tubes, activating the hardening process and molding it to the arm.

"You're lucky," said the tech. "So far, wrist fractures are the only injuries we can set like this."

Dana didn't agree that the break was lucky at all, but the turquoise contraption did look cool. Leah would return to school Monday with her futuristic cast and a modified workout plan for soccer. So why was Dana still so stressed?

That afternoon, she left Leah home to rest and met her writing group at a coffee shop. Usually, the whir of the grinder and aroma of roasted beans centered her. The tension of the day would drain out of her upon entering this sacred space where the caffeinators and wordsmiths participated in the ritualistic exchange of holy brown nectar for creativity. Today though, the coffee beans were no match for the gnawing anxiety that had settled in her gut.

She waved to the group already huddled over laptops with pages of copy spread between them. Their leader was Carlos Ruiz, the disheveled English professor who taught the creative writing course that brought them together a while back. He wrote high-stakes heists, real suspense. Beverly was a former journalist-turned-stay-at-home-mom writing speculative fiction, and Peyton, a rookie history teacher with a penchant for young adult fantasy, wrote about fairies and dragons.

Most writers likely had critique partners who wrote in their same genre, but somehow Dana's group with their different styles just meshed. They made one another better storytellers.

"I like how the killer faints at the sight of blood," said Peyton. "The irony is hysterical."

Carlos flipped back a page in a stapled stack of copy paper. "I must have missed that. Makes sense now why she always resorts to poison or asphyxiation."

A passing customer's eyes got wide as she scurried out the door.

Dana smirked and scribbled notes in the margins of a page. "Maybe we should try and find a less public location to critique lest someone report us for being unhinged."

"Where's the fun in that?" asked Peyton.

Beverly peered over the top of her reading glasses and wagged her finger at Dana. "As much fun as all this murder talk is, I want to know why you look like you're carrying the weight of the world on your shoulders."

Dana tapped her pen on the table. "I'm fine."

"Sugar, your eyebrows have been pinched together ever since you walked in. What's eating you?"

Dana's hand flew to her face, ironing out the wrinkle above her nose. "I have to provide cupcakes with very specific criteria for my son's end-of-year party, and my daughter just broke her wrist."

"Is she okay?" asked Bev.

"More or less. It's a minor fracture, but everything feels serious when it's happening to your child, you know?"

Bev and Carlos nodded.

"We're also getting ready to go on this big camping trip. It's overwhelming." She described Will's growing collection of gear taking over their living room and her anxiety about sleeping on the ground with nothing but a piece of canvas protecting her family from wild beasts.

"It won't be that bad," said Carlos. "I take my sons camping every year, and they love it."

"I'm not worried about the boys' enjoyment. They don't have the same dependence on running water that Leah and I do."

Peyton sipped her iced latte, even as the annoying gurgle signaled her straw had pulled the last remaining drops of liquid. "What about a camper? You could rent or borrow a camper trailer. That would give you more shelter and peace of mind, not to mention running water and a bathroom." Anything with hard sides would be better than a tent, especially since the mountains might be cold and rainy.

"Do they come small enough to tow with our Tahoe but large enough to sleep our family of five?"

"Doesn't hurt to check," said Beverly.

An alarm on Dana's watch vibrated. "Oh, I have to go." She closed her laptop and stacked her typed pages on top of it. "Same time next month?"

Carlos loaded his belongs into a backpack that had seen better days. "Unless the bears get you."

She narrowed her eyes at him. "You're so helpful."

Dana's dad's Buick blocked both spots in the driveway, leaving her to park next to the curb behind Leah's car. She walked in through the garage, where Will's car was in its space. Every vehicle in the family was there, yet she entered a silent, empty house. "Guys? Anyone here?"

Harvey lifted his head from his bed and gave a lazy bark in greeting. She bent down to pet him. "Where is everyone?"

Muffled voices drifted in from the backyard.

She dropped her purse and tote on the counter. "Such a big help, Harv. Thanks."

Out back, she spotted the five human members of her family wrestling with a red blob of nylon.

Dana planted a peck on Will's cheek. "You know we have dinner plans with the Caraways tonight, right?"

He glanced at his watch. "Yeah, this will only take a minute. Leah, read the next step." He shook out a section of fabric while holding a bendy rod in one hand.

"You have to thread the pole through the channel thingy," Leah said.

Dana walked around the perimeter of the tent. "Do y'all know what you're doing?"

"We're not idiots," her father retorted. "We watched a YouTube video." Since when was the seventy-six-year-old an expert on internet tutorials?

"How long did the video say it takes to set this up?" Dana peered at the instructions over Leah's shoulder. "And why now?"

Will squatted to slide the flimsy pole into a sleeve

stitched into the seam. "We need to practice and see how everything is going to fit inside." He looked across the sea of nylon at Adam. "I'm going to push it to you, and then you poke the metal peg into the bottom of the pole when it comes out."

She was about to point out that he had only answered half her questions, but Leah spoke up. "It says two people can do it in twenty minutes, so we should be able to knock it out in about eight." Her mood had perked up considerably since earlier in the day.

"And how long has it been so far?"

Leah shuffled the instructions to see her phone. "Thirteen."

Dana shook her head. Imagine if they hadn't watched the YouTube video. She turned to walk inside. "We're leaving in forty-five minutes, so find a stopping point that gives everyone time to get ready."

"Hey, Mom." Adam pried the end of the rod onto a metal pin at the base of the fabric, creating an arch. "Can me and Nate sleep out here tonight after we finish babysitting?"

"Sure. It'll be good practice for next weekend." What was the alternative if the boys hated sleeping in the tent? Maybe it wasn't too late to return all the gear and head to the Mayan Riviera after all.

As Dana put on her dangly date-night earrings, Adam ran inside calling for her to come look at their finished product. It had only taken the five of them a half hour to put it up.

She ducked to step through the zippered entrance into a screened-in porch and through a second zipper to the main quarters. It was more spacious than she'd expected. Two curtains could be rolled down to divide the space into separate rooms, giving the illusion of privacy.

"What do you think, Mom?"

Dana flashed Adam her most convincing smile. "It's

great. I'm sure with bedding in there, it'll be downright cozy." She pinched the fabric wall and gave it a tug. Internet videos of tents being picked up and blown away by strong winds flashed through her mind. This one likely wouldn't withstand the force of a hard sneeze, let alone a gale-force wind. She pulled out her phone and added "allergy meds" to her packing list.

Nate tossed a sleeping bag through the opening. "Do you want to camp out with us tonight?"

"No." She answered too quickly and cleared her throat to cover her tracks. "I want to wait until the actual trip to get the full experience." Until then, she would enjoy her air-conditioning and adjustable bed.

Dana warned Leah to protect her wrist and let her brothers do the bulk of the physical labor while babysitting the triplets. "Don't be a hero. If you need us, call."

"I'll be fine, Mom." She was a different girl from the one who had trudged in from urgent care last night.

Several minutes after the Harding kids crossed the street to babysit, Hunter and Josie scurried to the Hardings' side of the cul-de-sac and hopped into the Tahoe.

Will glanced at them in the rearview mirror. "You two rushed over here with grins more in line with a team celebrating a big win than two adults going to dinner with their neighbors."

"We don't get out much." Josie ran her hand over the leather. "Wow, a car with no baby seats. This is new for me."

"Did Leah seem nervous about her wrist?" Dana asked. Despite Leah's repeated insistence that she was fine to babysit, Dana couldn't shake the worry that her daughter was pushing through discomfort and taking on more than she could handle.

Hunter shrugged. "Not at all. The kids asked her about her cast, and they all wanted to touch it. I didn't even know casts like that existed. I would have lost fewer pencils trying to scratch my itchy arm if I'd had one like that when I was a kid."

"I'm so excited to get to eat a hot meal for a change," said Josie.

Dana remembered those days well. When the kids were little, she often ate over the sink after they went to bed. By the time she'd gotten everyone settled and fed, her own plate had long turned cold, and her appetite was gone.

Josie leaned forward, wrapping her arms around Dana's shoulders from behind in a quick hug. "Do me a favor and eat slow, okay? I want to revel in adult conversation as long as possible. Sure, I talk to grownups at school—well, quasi-grownups. But half of them say 'like' and 'O-M-G' so often, I have deeper conversations with the triplets."

Will turned onto the main thoroughfare. "You go to Moms on Mission with Dana. Those women are all adults."

Dana gave him a sidelong glance. "Most people like to have conversations more than once a week." Communication wasn't Will's strong suit. He used up his words at the office and had few left for her at the end of the day. At the very least, she prayed their upcoming trip would give the two of them time to reconnect and have fun together for a change.

Chapter 5

Dana slid into the steakhouse booth and set her menu aside without giving it a glance. She always ordered the same dish here, and after the stress of the last few days, tonight would not be the night she stepped out of her comfort zone.

Josie peered over the top of her menu. "I've been looking forward to this for two days. Although I expected y'all to cancel after Leah's accident."

"Soccer has made her tough, but I think she's also relishing the attention that cast gives her."

"Why did she get such a high-tech arm gadget?" asked Josie.

"Kids are notoriously hard on traditional casts, especially in the summer months. When Leah asked the doctor if she would still be able to go on the family camping trip, he recommended this style. Said it would be perfect for the wild." Dana had kind of hoped the broken scaphoid would give them an excuse to stay home, but no. The way Leah's face lit up as the doctor approved her Instagram adventure, Dana knew she'd better start breaking in her hiking boots.

"I'm a little jealous of y'all," said Hunter. "I grew up camping and can't wait to take our kids. There are so many life lessons and memories to be made in the great outdoors."

"Come with us." said Will. We can take the whole cul-de-sac crew to Colorado."

Josie had just taken a drink of water and sputtered. "What? How did I get roped into this?" She wiped her mouth with her napkin. "Besides, we can't put our kids in a tent. They can work zippers, and they'd escape."

"Or worse," said Hunter. "They'd have the whole campground destroyed in two minutes flat."

Dana buttered a roll. "A lady in my writing group suggested we rent a camper, so we'd have a bathroom and a sturdier structure for weather protection." *Bear protection.* "Y'all should do that."

"That's cheating," said Will. "You don't get the full experience when you're literally packing the kitchen sink."

"Losing a two-year-old isn't part of the 'full camping experience,' is it, Will?" Josie made mocking air quotes.

Dana gestured at her friend across the booth. "Right, and does the full experience involve hypothermia or contracting cholera from the lack of hygiene?"

A waiter appeared in a long apron and crisp, white button-up. "Ooh, cholera and hypothermia. Y'all are planning quite the party."

Dana pressed her lips into a thin smile. "Yes, a recreation of the Donner Party."

The waiter's eyes darted to the rest of the group.

Will put his hand on Dana's shoulder. "Ignore my wife. She's being dramatic about camping."

"Ah." The waiter shrugged one shoulder. "Well, we don't have frozen carcass on tonight's menu, but I do hope you'll find our specials to your liking." He winked at Dana and proceeded to recite the evening's offerings.

"That kid is rethinking his career choice," said Josie after he'd taken their orders and retreated.

Everyone chuckled.

Will pulled up a photo on his phone of the kids and their Pops standing in the tent, their outstretched arms indicating its spacious interior. "Look how happy they are. We *could* return this bad boy and rent a camper, but look at their excited faces."

Dana smiled, but didn't respond. How was she supposed to accept responsibility for crushing her boys' dreams of sleeping in the wilderness? Even though it terrified her, she didn't have the heart to ruin their plans. However, if tonight cured them of wanting to camp, she'd be fine with that.

Hunter leaned across the table to see the photo. "Is that a screened-in porch?"

"Yep," said Will. "We'll put a doormat out there and keep muddy shoes out of our pristine living space." There was no pristine living space anywhere on the planet that included two teenagers, a preteen boy who hadn't yet recognized the value of deodorant, and a giant hairy dog, especially not one that only measured 137 square feet.

Josie took Will's phone to get a better look. "Is Edward going with y'all? What about his cute little dog?"

"No, we're all set on dogs and grumpy old men." Dana nodded her head at Will.

"Hey, I may be grumpy, but I'm not old," he said.

"Dad's going on a trip with his senior adult Sunday school class in a couple of months while we dog sit for him. That's about all the excitement he needs for one summer."

Her dad had been known to get lost in the town he'd lived in most of his life. On a particularly harrowing afternoon stroll, he'd even tried to unlock the wrong house and ended up getting a ride home in the back of a police cruiser. The mountains would be too much for him. Edward Johnson in the mountains? Definitely too much for Dana.

"I'd pick wrangling two-year-old triplets in the wild over keeping up with Edward and Patch Johnson," said Will.

Hunter cocked his head. "You call the dog by its first and last name?"

Will rubbed the back of his neck, his tell when embarrassed. "Habit, I guess. Once Edward yelled for Patch at the dog park, and another senior citizen accused him of trying to lure her dog away. So, he's trained his pup to answer to his full name to keep little old ladies from clocking him with their purses."

Dana patted Will's arm. "We just go with it."

When Dana and Will got home, the boys had already taken over the middle section of the tent, a queen-sized air mattress and sleeping bags filling the space.

Dana eyed their handiwork. "You're going to share an air mattress?"

"We're workshopping the layout." Nate stood at the far end and gestured like a contractor presenting blueprints. "If you and Dad put your big one over here, Adam and I can share this one…"

"In our own sleeping bags, of course," Adam interjected.

"And Leah can use a twin mattress over here." Nate stepped to the other side. "That way, we'll have plenty of space for Harvey and our luggage. But if we hate it tonight, you can return the queen and get two smaller beds instead."

An amused grin played on Dana's lips. Not only had she never heard Nate use the term *workshopping*, but they'd invested far more thought into how to use the space than she had imagined possible. Her strategy was going to be to wing it and hope for the best. "Did you leave your sister to fend for herself with only one good arm against the triplets?"

Nate made a "tch" sound with the side of his mouth, the disgruntled cousin of the teenage eyeroll. "We did everything over there. She bossed us around while we cleaned up the babies *and* put them to bed. They were asleep when we came home."

"Are you going to let her camp out with you tonight?"

Adam sprawled on the bed with his gaming device. "We already offered for the malevolent dictator to sleep out here, but she doesn't feel like it. Her arm aches."

Dana's stomach knotted with guilt. Letting Leah do too much today had been a mistake. "Nathan Harding, stop teaching your sweet baby brother to call your sister that." There was no way Adam had come up with such an eloquent moniker on his own. She walked in the back door just as Leah came in the front. "How's the arm? Do you need pain meds?"

The teen shrugged and continued heading to her room. "It was fine until a little bit ago. Do you think it'll stop hurting before the trip?"

Dana trailed behind her. She'd never broken a bone, so she had no clue. "We'll pray it does. The doctor did say kids heal more quickly than adults." He'd also said Leah's growth plate had fused, so her bones had already reached adulthood, but that information would only stress Leah out.

She pulled a box of craft supplies from under her bed. "Will you help me decorate my cast?"

After Leah's hurtful reaction to her offer to help with her hair yesterday, Dana was caught off guard—and touched—by her daughter's request. She tried to keep her expression neutral, but the corners of her mouth twitched upward on their own. "Of course I will, sweetheart."

She followed Leah's instructions and looped monofilament around a section of cast just above the knuckles. Leah added a crystal bead and had Dana loop it again. She alternated sparkly beads with the letters of her name until the turquoise mesh across Leah's hand was adorned to her liking.

Dana furrowed her brow as she tied the ends of filament and secured the knots with clear nail polish.

Leah poked her mom between the eyes. "You shouldn't make that face. It's giving you wrinkles."

"And you shouldn't say that to the woman who just spent a half hour beading your cast.

Leah raised her arm and inspected the product. "Looks good, right?"

"I love it." Dana smiled and put away the craft supplies. "You know, when I saw that you weren't getting an old-school cast for people to draw on, I was worried. No one has ever tested the healing process of a broken bone without artwork on it. I can rest easy now that you have found a workaround and will heal properly."

Leah was already posing for selfies. If she heard Dana's attempt at humor, she ignored it.

"I'll leave you to it then. Let me know if you need anything." She kissed her daughter's head and went to her own room.

Will was stretched out on their bed propped on one arm. He patted the mattress beside him. "You've got to see this." The TV showed an episode resembling *House Hunters,* except every home had wheels.

He waved the remote toward the screen. "Take a look at that camper."

She sat cross-legged on the bed and studied the marble bathroom with a spa tub and touch screen controls. "That's a camper?"

"I know, right? The kitchen is nicer than ours."

The motorhome even had a spiral staircase leading to a loft. At the end of the tour, its seven-figure price tag flashed on the bottom of the screen.

Dana's jaw dropped. "Talk about glamping for the rich and famous."

He angled his chin at the couple pursuing motorhomes. "The guy is like a nature photographer or something, and the wife is a travel blogger. They're planning to live in it fulltime with two kids."

"I'm clearly writing in the wrong genre." Dana stared wide-eyed. "Who knew blogging could be so lucrative?" She watched the rest of the episode with her mouth hanging open. "Where do you even park a thing like that? And do you need a CDL to drive it?"

Will shook his head in slow motion, his face a mirror of her own astonishment. "Can you imagine waking up every day to the incredible beauty God created all over this country?"

A knot formed in Dana's belly. Will's fascination had less to do with the exorbitant price tag and a bit more to do with wishful thinking. She studied his face. "Are you considering quitting your job and moving us into a motorhome?"

He tore his gaze from the screen. "What? No, of course not. But you've got to admit, that would be an exciting way to explore America. All the luxuries of home, but you can take it anywhere you want. What do you think, should we rent a rolling Hilton after all?"

She waved toward the window. "It's a little late for that now. The boys are already living their best life in the tent."

He put his hand on her shoulder and jostled her playfully. But you and Leah would prefer to stay in an RV like that, wouldn't you?"

"Who wouldn't?"

Their eyes locked, and they answered the rhetorical question in unison. "Adam."

The conversation with Nate from earlier in the week came to mind. Dana held up a finger. "Although, his brother has him worried about serial killers in the woods, so something with a locking door might look pretty good to him now."

"Let me show you the campground again. Maybe it'll get you as excited as the boys are," Will said.

Doubtful, but she vowed to try and work on her attitude. After all, she did agree to this before the gear began arriving on their porch.

He pulled up the website for the campground which boasted "modern facilities" and a game room. The photos showed kids laughing at a ping pong table while an older couple played checkers in front of a fireplace behind them. Amenities included fishing, biking, and hiking.

There were no pictures of the so-called modern facilities, but one sentence stuck out to Dana. "Primitive campsites have vaulted toilets." She pictured high, pointy ceilings in the restrooms, but that was an odd thing to mention in the same sentence with 'primitive.'

She pointed to his phone. "What are primitive campsites?"

The corners of his mouth turned up. "It means no running water or electricity." He must have sensed Dana's mounting panic because he quickly added, "I reserved us a campsite with hookups. There will be a water faucet and a place to plug in an extension cord."

Her pulse rate slowed. "Then I take it vaulted toilets aren't architectural eye candy?"

He chuckled. "Definitely not."

Chapter 6

Josie

Josie pulled her phone from its permanent home in her hip pocket and texted Dana. OMG, I am so breaking up with you!!!

Her phone pinged a reply right away. What did I do?

Hunter and Will perched on opposite ends of the sofa. Their eyes were glued to the screen like a tied Super Bowl was in its final seconds. But it wasn't a game that had them on the edge of their seats; it was the Outdoor Channel.

Hunter hasn't shut up about camping since last night. And now he and your husband are watching an RV show together like they're trying to find out who gets the last rose on The Bachelor

Ever the resolute planner, Josie liked her lists and started packing days, if not weeks, ahead of every trip. Now Hunter was bent on the idea of them tagging along on the Hardings' camping adventure, or at the very least, taking one of their own. There were only a couple of weeks left of spring cosmetology classes and Parents' Day Out. She didn't have time to plan a vacation with the triplets, never mind pack for one. What would they even need for spending a week in the middle of nowhere?

Her phone rang.

"I'm sure they're just doing the guy version of flipping

through bridal magazines like we did back in the day," said Dana.

Had Josie ever picked up a bridal magazine? Pinterest boards, sure—but this wasn't the moment to bring up their age gap. "I hope you're right."

"What happened to 'it'll be fun. Blah blah blah, quality time without phone signals?'" Dana's voice morphed into a nasal mocking one.

"Those were Rachel's words, but I stand by them, for *your* family. Your kids are older and can run away from bears. Mine are snack-sized. This will not end well for us."

"Try not to think about it. I'm sure it's all talk."

Josie shook out her hands and rolled her neck. She was probably getting worked up over nothing. Dana was right. "We already have plans to visit all the grandparents this summer anyway, so I don't know about adding another trip to the docket."

"Oklahoma City, Albuquerque, *and* Los Angeles? Wow, you've come a long way since the first time you took the triplets out of state."

Careful not to wake the babies, Josie eased a dining chair out from the table and sat. "We haven't come that far. I have separate packing lists for when we visit Hunter's family versus my mom. And we won't go to LA. Dad said he and Alana would get a hotel in Albuquerque and meet up with us when we go see Mom. I guess that's progress."

A couple of years ago, her dad had been sick and not bothered to tell his daughters. Since then, they'd tried to have a more transparent relationship, but he was destined to always be a hands-off dad and grandparent.

From the living room, Josie heard Will say, "Check this one out. It's available the same week we're going to Colorado."

"Okay, that's it. I don't think they're looking at bridal magazines anymore. I've gotta go." Josie ended the call and stood between the men and the TV. "Playdate's over, gentlemen. I have an early day with the terrible two-year-olds."

They men stood and clapped each other on the backs. Josie waited with her arms akimbo until Will had crossed to his side of the cul-de-sac before she confronted Hunter. "What do you think you're doing? You're planning a vacation for the five of us—scratch that, the *ten* of us—with your buddy without even discussing it with me first."

He closed the distance between them and took both of her hands in his. "Come on, Jos. It's not like that. Will came over to borrow our cooler and fishing gear for their trip, and we just got to talking about how great it's going to be. For them."

She studied his face. "Right. So, the camper that's available the week the Hardings are going to the mountains was for *them*? Because you seemed pretty sold on the whole joint vacation thing Will was pushing."

Hunter led Josie to his recliner and pulled her into his lap. "I admit, I don't hate the idea of us taking a camping trip. And if we did have a motorhome like the one Will showed me to take care of the kids in, it would be a lot easier than roughing it." He pulled up a website with camper photos. "Take a look at this. It has everything."

She leaned into him and swiped through the images.

He zoomed in on a bedroom at the back of the RV. "That queen bed would be a great spot for the kids to sleep. They'd be contained and safe there while we slept up front on the sofa bed. We wouldn't have to worry about them escaping or pulling the parking brake and rolling us off a cliff."

She glared at him.

"What? They're a little bit feral." He wasn't wrong.

"I guess maybe it would be fun to go with good friends. Extra hands and eyes on the kids couldn't hurt either." What was she saying? She pressed her fingers to her temples. "This is ludicrous. I can't believe you have me considering this."

"Just close your eyes and picture waking up to sweatshirt weather. Sipping your coffee wrapped in a cozy blanket under the pine trees."

She opened one eye and peeked at him. "And what will our three toddlers be doing while I'm sipping coffee in this blanket?"

She would have sworn he sat up two inches taller. "I'll turn on *Bluey* while I scramble eggs. I don't know. Bundle them up and strap them into the stroller, and they can watch me cook over a campfire. That sounds more magical, doesn't it?"

Fire in the same sentence as her three children sounded anything but.

"Look at this." He pulled up another website on his phone, Silver Mountain Campground.

The home page showed snowcapped mountains and a crystal-clear lake surrounded by trees. Hunter tapped on a gallery showing families fishing together, eating at picnic tables, and playing games in front of a large stone fireplace. It did look cozy.

Josie missed the mountain views she grew up with in Albuquerque. Lubbock didn't even have hills, let alone mountains. The locals joked that on a clear day—meaning one when the dirt wasn't blowing—the land was flat enough to watch a tumbleweed blow all the way to Amarillo.

"It looks amazing, babe. It does. But maybe in a couple of years when our kids are slightly less rambunctious, okay?"

He switched off his screen, but the glint in his eye told Josie the conversation was far from over.

After church on Sunday, Josie's phone rang with a call from her mother. She reflexively looked around before answering as though Marie Saldana might be able to detect her messy house through the airwaves.

"Hey, Mom." She tucked the phone between her cheek and shoulder and righted the sofa cushions the boys had been using as trampolines.

"Josefina, how are you?"

"Good, the kids are eating lunch, and I'm undoing the damage they caused while we were making their food. What about you?" Josie braced herself for the reply. Her mother would have Facetimed to see the grandbabies if this were a mere social visit.

"I'm ready to get started on the next chapter of my life." She paused, her silence inviting a response.

"Congratulations, I hope." Josie had no idea what that chapter could possibly be. She closed her eyes and bit her lip. *Please don't say 'dating.'*

"Of course. I thought I would work until I die to keep my mind active, but I'm ready to retire."

Retirement would give her mother time to travel, see the aunts, maybe take up a hobby other than nitpicking Josie about her housekeeping.

"What would you think if I sold my house here in Albuquerque and moved to Lubbock to be near you and *mis nietos*?"

Josie froze. "M-moved to Lubbock?"

"Yes, what's keeping me here once I quit working?"

Her eyes darted around the living room as if the answer were held somewhere in its haphazard décor and toddler toys. "That would be great, Mom, but what about Laurel?" She pressed her fist to her mouth. Did she just tell her mother it would be great if she moved here?

"What about her? Your sister doesn't live in Albuquerque."

"Well, uh," Josie's brain short circuited. She waved her hands trying to come up with the words that eluded her. "You're like halfway between us now. What will she think if you move here?" In the past, tension had flared between Josie and her older sister when Laurel assumed their father was favoring Josie. Thankfully, they'd gotten past that misunderstanding, but surely there would be another one if their mom moved to Josie's town.

"Laurel and Jefferson are never going to have kids. Their lives in Boulder are busy, and they travel all the time. They don't need me. *You*, however, are going to need a lot of support when you graduate from cosmetology school and start working at a salon. I would *love* to get to spend more time with my grandkids."

Josie sank onto the edge of the coffee table, her legs buckling under the weight of her mother's words. When the triplets were babies, she and Hunter had welcomed her help anytime she was able to come to town. They were still grateful for it, but cleaning the house in preparation for her visits was next to impossible. Lately, Josie's mother had also grown critical of what she perceived as Josie's lackadaisical parenting.

There was no end to her mother's critiques and suggestions. *Mija, you should set stricter boundaries and keep the kids from climbing on the furniture. Mija, why don't you enroll them in gymnastics and give them a structured outlet for their energy. Why don't you wash the dishes as soon as you put them in the sink, so they don't pile up?*

"I'm planning to come out the first week in June and meet with a realtor to get a jump on house hunting. I'll plan to stay four days—"

"You can't!" Josie grimaced. She loved her mother, but

dealing with her the first week of summer break was out of the question.

"Oh? Do you have other plans?"

Hunter poked his head out of the kitchen and mouthed, "What's wrong?"

"We're going camping in Colorado that week." Josie clamped her hand over her mouth. She didn't know what came over her. Desperation maybe?

Hunter's face formed a silent question.

"That's right, Mom. Of course we're taking the kids." She held up an empty palm and shrugged.

A grin spread over Hunter's whole face. He wrapped his arm around her waist and pulled her to him. He nuzzled her neck until a clatter in the kitchen made them both jump.

"Mom, I've gotta go. I'll call you soon, okay?"

She ended the call, and they both entered the kitchen to find three kids looking over their highchair trays and Connor's plate on the floor.

Olivia pointed down. "Uh-oh, Mama. Mess. Mama. See?"

She saw. For once it would be amazing if they could get through a single meal without a mishap. "Connor, are you finished, or do you want more?"

He used a toddler derivative of the American Sign Language signal for "finished." "Want down."

Josie stared at her son and the remnants of his lunch scattered all over the tile, then glanced up at Hunter, who was doing the same. "I don't think we should reward him for this. If we get him down, he's teaching the other two that the way to be excused from mealtime is to toss their food."

Hunter scratched his chest. "I agree. Man, I wish we had a dog to clean this up for us."

"I have another idea." Josie bent over eyelevel to Connor. "Throwing your plate is not okay. You are going to clean up your mess now."

"No keen. I pay." He kicked his feet against the chair.

"You cannot play until your food is picked up." Josie unbuckled him and lowered him to the floor. She turned the plate upright and modeled picking up scattered green beans and chicken bites and putting them on the plate. "Now it's your turn."

Connor squatted and pinched a green bean off the floor. Josie turned her attention to the two still in highchairs. She unbuckled Olivia while Hunter extricated Ben from his seat, and they both lowered the kids to the floor in time to witness Connor dutifully carry his plate to the garbage and drop it in.

"Awe keen," he announced and ran out of the kitchen.

His siblings scampered after him.

Josie dropped into a chair and rested her forehead on the dining table. "Why is everything so hard with kids?"

Hunter was elbow-deep in the trashcan fishing out the plate. "Jos, you just told your mom we were going to Colorado. Are we really?"

She grabbed a broom from the pantry. "Oh, we're going all right. Otherwise, I just lied to my mother, and I do *not* lie to my mother." She swept up the mess, envisioning exactly how much work taking toddlers camping would be.

He set the plate in the sink and washed his hands. "We're actually planning to drive those kids to the wilderness and set them free like rehabilitated animals?"

She emptied the dustpan and sagged against the counter. "I feel sorry for the wilderness. But hey, if you can rent that motorhome you and Will were drooling over, we might stand a fighting chance of keeping them out of trouble."

"Good because with what it'll cost to rent that RV, we won't be able to afford fines for destruction of a national forest."

Josie peeked her head through the doorway to the living

room, preparing to yell at someone to get off the coffee table as usual. Instead, all three kids were playing nicely on the floor for a change. "I don't care what it costs. Take it out of their college fund. What are the odds they're all going to need it anyway?"

Hunter's eyes widened. "Josie!" After a pause, he smirked. "Okay fine, the plate thrower will probably need the money for bail instead." He crossed the room to her. "We don't have to go."

Her eyebrows rose, and her jaw tightened. "Oh, yes, we do. Marie Saldana will check with the forestry service to make sure we did the thing we told her we were doing." She pointed toward the living room. "And we're doing it with all of them."

"Maybe it won't be so bad. We'll just put ankle weights on them to slow them down."

"Ankle weights? Like athletes do to condition themselves to be stronger and faster? Good plan." Josie rubbed her forehead. "I guess you can contact the RV rental place, and I'll start researching what to pack. Consider this trip your birthday present."

"Don't worry, babe. We'll make the best of it. You'll see." Hunter kissed her and dashed out the front door. She would have sworn he skipped, but she appreciated that he tried to curb his enthusiasm and at least didn't squeal as he ran off to tell Will the good news.

Chapter 7

Dana

Dana waited her turn at the door to Adam's classroom as his teacher Mrs. Dickens inspected each party offering and grilled parents on compliance with the allergy list. Dana kicked herself for not thinking to make homemade popsicles out of nothing but orange juice like Pax's mom did. That would have been so much easier than enduring the teacher's scrutiny.

"From where was the chocolate in these cupcakes sourced?" Mrs. Dickens eyed Dana with the suspicion of a defense attorney hoping to catch a witness on the stand in a lie.

The lady taught fifth grade, not Shakespeare, and could have simply asked, "Where did the chocolate come from?" Dana bit her tongue and smiled, just a bit smugly. "Actually, there's no chocolate. They're made from carob, the pods of which are sustainably sourced in California." She held her breath and prayed her mention of California wouldn't count against her.

The teacher's lips turned up at the edges, but it wasn't quite a smile. "Very well. You may place them on the snack table."

"Thanks for the cupcakes, Adam's Mom," said a kid Dana was sure she'd never seen before.

"Don't thank me until you try them," she muttered.

A mom she recognized from previous class functions was arranging a fruit tray across the table. She glanced up with a wry smile. "That allergy list is nuts, am I right?"

"Shh. Don't say 'nuts,'" said Dana. "That's at the top of the banned foods list. Just above flavor and enjoyment."

The mom laughed. "The nut allergy I actually understand." She lowered her voice. "But are we really saving the rainforest by not buying chocolate cupcakes from Walmart? I mean, come on."

Another mother snagged a carrot from a vegetable platter. "Look on the bright side. Next year we won't have to worry about class parties, and there won't be any of this food red tape."

Dana recoiled like she'd taken a punch to the gut.

"You okay?" asked the carrot-munching mom.

"Yeah, it just hit me that this is my last school party ever." Middle school was a different ballgame altogether. She didn't miss the days of running between classrooms to attend parties for multiple Harding children at one time, but reaching the end of an era stung a bit.

The first mom put her hand on Dana's shoulder. "Girl, enjoy the break because once senior year hits, you'll be so busy with all the parties and sentimental events that you'll be wishing to go back to the fifth-grade farewell."

Dana's chest tightened. Where had the time gone? Soon her kids would be on their own and not need her or her baked goods anymore. She pressed her hand to her heart. Starting now, she would be more present and savor the time she had left with the kids, even if it meant embracing the camping trip she dreaded so much.

While the students were engrossed in the festivities, Adam's teacher pulled Dana aside. She hugged a red folder to her chest as she spoke. "Every parent gets a portfolio of their child's best work from this year." She patted the folder. "But I wanted to see your face when you read Adam's piece de resistance."

Dana held out her hand to receive the folder with more than a little trepidation. There was no telling what her third child had come up with that his teacher found worthy of a live reading.

Mrs. Dickens held out the folder but laid her hand on its cover, halting Dana from opening it. "A couple of months ago, the students had a homework assignment to write an informative essay to present to the class."

Dana nodded slowly. She had Algebra and Physics to worry about with her older kids. She didn't specifically remember the essay in question or giving Adam any guidance on it.

"One student described how to get past a dragon on a certain level of a video game. Another gave information on what to see and what to avoid at Disney World. A couple of them discussed the steps to bake cookies."

Surely if Adam's report was as scandalous as the teacher was making it out to be now, she'd have gotten a call or an email sooner. Right?

"And then we rounded out the informative speeches with this." Mrs. Dickens removed her hand from the folder and gave Dana a nod.

She hesitated a beat, then opened the cover. The first page of notebook paper fastened within the brads was emblazoned in Adam's scrawl, "How To Sir-vive In The Wild." She glanced up at the teacher, who was studying Dana's face. Will used to look at her like that when he'd experimented with a new recipe and wanted to see her reaction to the first bite. It made her squirm.

My dad and ~~me~~ I like to watch a television show called <u>Man verses Wild</u>. It is about a man named Bear ~~Girls~~ Grills who teaches people how to not die if they get lost in the wilderness. He was a soldier in the Navy I think, but he talks with a british accent, so he was probly in a different Navy then ours. His job must be very dangerous since he has been in so many life threatening situations and learned how to keep himself alive. He gives many good tips to help people not die which made me want to learn more sir-vivel tips too. I have made a handy guide that I will now share with you.

1. Always carry a knife because it can save your life. (But not to school because you will get arrested and you are not in the wilderness).

2. You can find plants to eat in nature. But first test them for poison by swishing them in your mouth and spitting them out. Then see how you felt. feel. If your mouth doesn't feel weird, try eating a little bit, but do not drink water (or urine but not if it is super yellow) with it so you know if you need to throw it up. If you do not get sick in a few hours, you can eat some more—this time with water or urine if you do not have water. I think it is super important to know that the urine might be what makes you throw up, so be careful. Only drink it if you are desperit.

Dana snickered, much to the delight of Mrs. Dickens, and turned the page. "I don't know what to say."

Mrs. D. had one arm folded across her body supporting the other elbow. Her chin rested in her hand. "Keep reading."

3. Mark your trail so you do not get lost. I am not talking about the way animals mark their trails. I mean with rocks and suck such. If you do get lost, get high. Oops. I mean get UP high where you can see what is around. (say no to drugs) You might see something that you reconize and can find your way. If not, light a fire and smoke out so anyone who is out looking for you will see it.

Dana suppressed another chuckle.

4. Drinking still water can be dangerous and make you sick. If you have diarea, you will get more dehydrated and be in more danger than if you do not poop at all.

"He can spell 'dehydrated' but not 'diarrhea?' Or

'desperate?'" As a writer, her child's atrocious spelling reflected poorly on her. Maybe she could have coached Adam on this assignment if she weren't so wrapped up in her writing career.

"Or 'survival.' I've already added them to next year's spelling lists. You're almost halfway." Mrs. D's hand covered her twitching mouth.

5. It is a very good idea to always keep a water filter in your posesion in case of emergency, but sometimes a sock can be used to filter dirty water before you sterelize it over fire. (the water. Not the sock) Because of this, wearing sandals in the wilderness is not recomended. If your socks are both filthy, it's a good idea to wash them off in different water then what you are about to drink.

6. Also try not to sweat if you are lost because this will make you dehydrate even faster. Walk slow and do not freak out. Try to find shade and get wet if you are hot. Do not get wet if you are cold. (we will get to that)

7. When you make a shelter for yourself, make the opening point away from the wind. You can test the direction of the wind by licking your finger and holding it up. (I learned this from Michal Scott on the Office)

When had he watched *The Office*? She started to tell Mrs. D. that Adam wasn't permitted to watch that show, and she was mortified, but the teacher's shoulders were racking.

8. If you get cold and wet, you are more likely to die. Always wear layers and keep them clean and dry so they are safer. I do not know what the layers have to do with staying warm ecsept that you are wearing more clothes, which is always warmer.

9. Keeping snacks in your pockets can save your life. I have began doing this just in case of emergency, and it is the best sir-vival tip I can recomend. Chocolate, nuts, and

raisins or other dried fruit give you energy, but nuts are not allowed in most places. Raisins are gross, and chocolate will defiantly melt in a pocket. I have found that Cheetos and gummy bears will last in a pocket all day.

Dana tried to recall the last time she'd checked pockets before washing laundry. She prayed he wasn't practicing his survival skills now.

10.   Wild animals might see you as a threat or as food. It is hard to know which sometimes. Make lots of noise so animals will be scared of you. And if you get too close to a bear, keep an eye on it but back away very slowly. If it seems like it wants to attack you, be big and loud. This is also where your knife can save you.

As you can see, the wilderness can be a dangerous place if you are not prepared. However, a little bit of planning (knife, socks, snacks, something to make fire with) can save your life. If we have to give another speech, I will look up ways to build a fire to share with you. I also highly recomend watching <u>Man Verses Wild</u> and other shows that teach you how to stay safe out there.

Dana looked up. "That's quite an essay."

"You should have tried keeping a straight face while he read it to the class. I think I pulled a muscle trying not to laugh. I thought you might get a kick out of it, and some day you can show it to him when he wants to explore nature."

Dana closed the folder and held it up. "It may come in handy sooner than you think. We're about to go on a family camping trip, so we can review Adam's tips together."

Mrs. Dickens grinned. "Please pack extra socks." She returned to the party chuckling to herself.

As Adam goofed around with his friends, Dana was struck by how much he looked like Will. He had the same light brown, wavy hair and blue eyes. He had shot up three inches since school started in the fall and reached that gawky phase that always reminded her of a Great Dane puppy—all legs and ears, clumsy, and full of energy.

Would he still think survival skills in the wilderness were cool in a few years, or would he become more like his mom and decide avoiding the wilderness altogether was the best survival skill of all?

Adam cocked his head back and laughed at something she couldn't hear, but watching him made her giggle. She had the sudden urge to wrap her arms around him and beg him not to grow up.

After the party, Dana tucked the cupcake container under one arm and draped the other over Adam's shoulder, expecting him to shrug away from her affection. Instead, he stayed by her side as they walked to the parking lot.

"Thanks for coming to my party, Mom. I feel bad for the kids whose parents can't come."

She swallowed the lump forming in her throat. "I wouldn't have missed it for the world. And I'm proud of you for thinking of other kids' feelings." She ruffled his hair.

"And *I'm* proud of *you* for changing out of your writing clothes and fixing your hair before you came." He ducked out of her embrace before she could swat him on the back of the head like he deserved. The teenage years were going to be delightful with this one.

On the ride from his school to Nate's, she asked, "What was your favorite thing you did in fifth grade?" She glanced at him in the rearview mirror as he tapped his chin.

"That's a tough one. I liked playing games and going to recess. The talent show was pretty fun."

Adam had been a stagehand. He moved gymnastic mats and cued music. His talent was enjoying whatever was happening in the moment, and she loved that about him.

"Tomorrow is only a half day, and we get to watch movies in our pajamas, so that will probably be my favorite thing."

She vowed in her heart to give Adam the best wilderness vacation imaginable so he would carry the memory with him into middle school. And she would soak up every moment of it or die swishing poisonous plants in her mouth.

Chapter 8

Josie

The big trip was only three days away, and Josie still hadn't made a dent in the packing. Trying to make progress with three toddlers under foot was worse than bringing home her cosmetology supplies expecting to get in any hair styling. The triplets undid her efforts with the practiced skills of a demolition team.

She'd put snacks, flashlights, and extra batteries into a storage tub, and they climbed in and threw the supplies out. Most of them anyway. They managed to squish a bag of marshmallows until it popped and ate half of them in two minutes flat. The pile of toddler clothes she'd stacked in the nursery to pack had become the victim of a category three tornado known as the Caraway children.

Josie called in reinforcements, hiring the Harding kids to keep the triplets busy for a couple of hours while Dana helped her pack. Her friend who had been her closest companion throughout the bedrest portion of her pregnancy would have helped no matter what because she was thoughtful and selfless. However, Josie sweetened the pot by bribing Dana with a pan of homemade chicken enchiladas, ensuring the vacation went off without a hitch.

Josie pulled two clear plastic tubs out of the closet and into the center of the room. She patted herself on the back for her forward thinking. Clear bins would be easier to navigate in the camper than a bulky suitcase that required space to unzip and lay open. "I still can't believe we are doing this."

"Which 'we' are you talking about?" Dana pointed between herself and Josie. "You and me—coffee-drinking, online shopping, non-outdoorsy we, the five Caraways 'we,' or all ten of us going on this great American vacation?"

Josie waved a pair of toddler sweatpants in her hand. "All of the above. I couldn't believe it when you said y'all were going camping. It was so out of left field. Then the deliveries kept showing up to your house, so it was either really happening, or you were doing something weird to make the delivery guy keep coming over."

Dana knelt on the floor and loaded toddler clothes into one of the storage bins. "Well, *I* got suckered into camping because the boys begged and begged, and Leah and I were outvoted when we said we wanted to go to Cancun. But why did *you* agree to go? You still have a little time before your kids get a say."

"Right? If they had their way, we'd be spending a week in a fast-food restaurant with an indoor playground." Josie held up a hoodie and checked the label. The kids had outgrown all their winter clothing, and they were relying on hand-me-downs from another mom in the Wednesday mentoring group to get them through the chilly mountain temperatures.

She folded the shirt and added it to the bin in front of Dana. "Actually, I'm the reason we are going."

Dana paused her meticulous sorting. "I'm shocked. I know your sister is super into the outdoor lifestyle, but I never figured you for a nature enthusiast."

"I'm not." Josie's voice cracked. She pressed her palms against her flushed cheeks. Her pulse thudded in her ears as she stared at the floor, unable to meet Dana's eyes. The words spilled out, each one heavier than the last. "I lied to my mom. I told her she couldn't visit next week because we were going with y'all to Colorado."

"I thought you liked having your mom's help."

Josie fanned the heat from her face and busied herself with stacking blankets and bedding on top of a box of diapers to put in the camper the night before they rolled out. "I did. I mean, I do." She scratched her forehead. "It's just that as the kids have gotten older, she's become more critical. She thinks we should have established a better routine or learned how to keep up with the house by now."

"I get it," said Dana.

"You do not. All I've ever heard about your mom is what a saint she was."

"My mom was great but far from perfect. She didn't approve of me putting Leah in three-year-old preschool. She was also quite vocal about formula versus breastfeeding, and we had differing opinions on the subject. I had to tell her to butt out a time or two."

Josie put the lid on the bin of clothes and slid it next to the diaper box. "But did you ever have to go on a trip that completely terrified you just to make good on a lie you told her?" Her chest tightened and her palms turned clammy. She took a deep breath and counted backward from ten.

"Jos, you okay?"

"I'm just a little anxious. I don't know what's freaking me out more—the trip, or how I feel about my mom right now." Josie wiped her hands on her jeans. "I'm ashamed that I lied to her. But in that moment, I was more willing to sleep in the woods like a mountain man than tell her the truth and let her stay with us while she house-hunts to move to Lubbock."

Dana folded her arms, nodding as things started to click into place. "Ah. That explains a lot. I get why you lied, even if I don't approve."

"You can?" The pulsating in Josie's ears lessened somewhat.

"Of course. You're anxious about your mom living here. And if she's retiring, then she will be even more in your business."

Josie leaned back against a crib with her hands on the rails. "So, I'm not freaking out about losing one of my kids in the woods or wild animals attacking them?" She pointed to her chest and inhaled deeply again. "You're saying all of this is because Mrs. Clean, the woman who punished me when my bed-making lacked proper hospital corners, is going to be able to pop by whenever she wants?" She put her hand on her pounding chest and focused on slowing her heart rate. "Okay yeah, that sounds about right."

Confessing to Dana didn't bring the crushing shame Josie had braced for. Instead, a fragile sense of relief crept in. She closed her eyes as a silent prayer formed. *Lord, this is too much. Please, help me fix it.* The tension in her chest began to ease, her pulse settling into a calmer rhythm.

"I know you're nervous about taking the kids camping." Dana nodded toward the backyard. "But my kids are great with them, and we'll all be there to help. You're not doing this solo. Except at night, when you're cozy in your bougie RV and I'm freezing on the ground in a tent."

Josie laughed. "Since the guys are the ones who wanted this so much, maybe Hunter should sleep in the tent with your boys, and you and Leah could join the babies and me in the heated camper."

A loud commotion and screaming from outside cut off Dana's reply. The moms abandoned packing and beelined outside.

Josie scanned the yard for injured children, but there were none. Olivia waved from the top of the toddler slide. "Mama, see me?"

"I see you, Livvie." She noted her happy daughter with Leah by her side and the four boys kicking a ball all over the yard. She turned to Dana who shook her head and shrugged. "What was the crash?"

"Sorry, Josie." Nate jogged over. He mopped the sweat off his face by pulling the neck of his tee shirt over his nose. "I kicked the ball too hard, and it hit the window. Adam knocked over a chair trying to block it."

"And the screaming?"

"It was Ben," said Adam. "The chair falling scared him, but nobody got hurt."

Ben wrapped his arms around his mother's legs. "Da chair kwash."

Josie patted his back. "The chair crashed?"

"Yeah. Adam funny."

Connor shrieked with delight as he kicked a ball to Adam. Everyone was safe and having a good time.

Josie met Dana's eye and smiled. She'd totally overreacted, and her kids were in great hands with their neighbors. The trip was going to be fine.

Chapter 9

Dana

Camping gear filled every bit of living room floor space and was piled into towers on the coffee table, sofa, and armchair. If the entire neighborhood fell into ruin, and everyone needed temporary accommodations, Dana was sure there were enough supplies here to set up an REI-themed shanty town.

She had no idea where they were supposed to store it all when they got back from Colorado, and more than that, there was no way it would fit in their Tahoe along with five people and a giant dog.

She stood with her hands on her hips as her husband constructed a sandwich at the kitchen counter, like the mess in the living room wasn't bothering him at all. "William, this is too much stuff. It'll never fit in the SUV."

"I'm one step ahead of you." He sucked a blob of mustard off his thumb and jutted his chin toward the armchair. "See that black vinyl bag?"

She started to walk toward a black thing by the chair, but too many obstacles blocked her path. She was afraid she would end up in a cast like Leah if she scaled the piles just to get a closer look. "I think so."

"It's a rooftop cargo bag. We'll put all the lighter, bulky items in it. It's waterproof and straps to the top of the car, freeing up space in the cabin." He took a bite of his sandwich. "That box over there?" He nodded toward the heavy one the boys had propped against the wall last week. "It's a metal rack that attaches to the trailer hitch. The ice chest and supply box will go on that thing so it's also outside the car."

Her eyes swept the space, landing on a heavy-duty plastic trunk with a padlock on it. "I take it that's the supply box."

"Yep." He swallowed the bite. "Dry foods, cooking utensils, camp stove, all of that will go in there. It'll be fine. You'll see."

"Where's all this supposed to live once we get back from Colorado?"

"That's a problem for two weeks from now." Will's brow furrowed as his gaze landed on something in the living room. "What's that yellow and black thing on the coffee table?"

Dana straightened, her chin lifting slightly. "A solar rechargeable mini generator. My contribution to the camping supplies."

Will shook his head and frowned. "Dana, you're throwing money away. We have an extension cord, and I already told you the campsite has electricity."

They didn't need any of this gear. An all-inclusive beach vacation at a resort with indoor plumbing and real mattresses cost the same as everything he'd bought preparing to sleep in the woods.

"I still have a book deadline, and you promised me I would have time to write on this trip. I'm not trusting my electrical needs to a campground that brags about having vaulted toilets like they're a big selling point. If the power goes out, we'll at least have a solar backup."

The vacation she pictured included lounging by the pool, the sound of her kids splashing blending with the faint rustle of pages from her paperback. Maybe she'd tap out a few chapters of her crime novel as she sipped frozen drinks under the shade of a cabana, then spend the rest of the time mentally unplugged.

Instead, she faced the reality of assembling their own shelter and braving a grimy community bathroom or an outhouse several times a day.

The generator was hardly a splurge, but Will's attitude prompted her to reconsider Josie's suggestion. She'd much rather share the luxury camper and leave the guys to the flimsy nylon dome of doom. Speaking of, it was the one item missing from the stockpile.

"Where's the tent?"

Will pointed his sandwich at a large gym bag under the coffee table. "In there."

"But it came in its own carrying case."

He shrugged. "After the boys slept in it, we couldn't fold it back small enough to shove it back in."

She ran her fingers through the sides of her hair and clasped them behind her head. "If we can't even fold up a tent right, our chances of surviving in the wild are very low."

Leah shrieked and bounded into the room. "You're never going to believe this."

Dana glanced between Leah and Will, waiting for their daughter to deliver the unbelievable news. She lost patience with the dramatic buildup. "We're never going to believe what, sweetie?"

"I've been posting selfies with my cast at school and soccer practice and talking about our trip."

Without missing a beat, Will said, "Oh, I believe it."

"Anyhoo." Leah raised her eyebrows, indicating she was not amused. "The company that manufactures the cast DMed me and they want me to be a brand ambassador for them. I will document our trip taking selfies with the cast and tag them in my posts. And I get paid for it." She squealed, which drove Harvey out of the room. "Wild, right?"

Since when were medical devices trendy? And what would an orthopedic supply company hope to gain from one teenager with a broken wrist and a few hundred followers?

"That's great. Let me take a look." Will read the message on Leah's phone. "I don't see any harm. Just don't give them any sensitive information."

Leah skipped back to her room.

"Shall we start loading some of this stuff into the car top thing?" asked Dana.

"No, we have to mount it on the roof before we fill it. There's a whole process."

A low rumble from the driveway interrupted him. Will peeked through the blinds. "The camper's here. Let's go check it out."

Dana joined him outside to find a truck with "Minnie Winnie" emblazoned on the side, blocking the front of the Caraways' house.

Hunter jumped out of the driver's seat. "Come take a look." He ran around to the other side as Will and Dana trailed behind.

The Caraways' front door swung open, and three small children bolted out as their mother held it for them.

"Dana." Ben held his arms up to her.

She lifted him into a bearhug. "Benny, I'm so happy to see you. Let's go look at this camper." She shifted him onto her hip.

Hunter opened the side door and pulled down a set of steps. "Let me give you the grand tour." He hoisted Olivia and set her inside the Winnebago.

Josie stood at the back of the line as adults and toddlers climbed into the RV. "Watch her, Hunter. That thing's not childproof."

Will helped Dana climb the steps with Ben in tow and set Connor inside behind her. Dana lowered Ben to the floor, and the triplets ran to the back and climbed onto the bed. To the right of the stepwell was the cutest little stove and sink Dana had ever seen. Across from it was a U-shaped dining banquette and table. She stepped a few feet back to where the kids crawled on a queen bed walled in on three sides and opened a door to a tiny bathroom. The shower was so small a person would have to tuck in their elbows to shampoo their hair. She turned to get a view of the rest of the camper. Cabinets lined the top edges, and a ladder behind the driver's seat led to a loft bed above the cab.

Sure, the Winnie offered more space than their tent, but the walls pressed in around Dana. "Let me step out so someone else can take a look back here." She edged past Josie.

Hunter sat at the banquette to give her room to pass, and she stepped down into the stepwell with her back to the open door.

"What do you think, Jos?" asked Hunter.

She turned a circle in front of the bathroom door. "I foresee an issue. The kids have claimed their bed, and I think that's the obvious choice. You and I can share the dining room slash bed, or I'll take it, and you can sleep in the loft. I however will not be climbing a ladder to squeeze into a crawlspace."

Dana wouldn't have either. She would most definitely sprain an ankle getting up in the night to go to the bathroom or give herself a concussion trying to sit up in bed.

"For safety's sake, we should remove the ladder to keep the kids from climbing up there and use it for storage and our bedding when we need the dining area for eating."

Josie rubbed her forehead. "We have to take apart the bed and redo it every night? That's a lot of work."

Hunter swept his arm toward the loft. "It's either that or we sleep up there."

Josie wore the hollowed-out expression of a weary mom who wanted to be anywhere except in a camper with her family for a week. Dana's heart went out to her. Family vacations caused more work for the mom than staying home, and a camping trip would likely quadruple the load.

"Fine. We remake the bed. And where are we going to change diapers? Where we sleep?"

The four adults scanned the camper as if a suitable changing station would materialize from a hidden corner. Except there were no hidden corners. Surely confronting Marie with the truth would have been easier than this trip was going to be.

"I vote we put the changing mat on their bed. And if the weather is nice, we can eat outside and leave the dining area a bedroom." Hunter slid out and lifted the bench he'd been seated on. "There's storage down here and outside. The owner showed me all the things."

Will took in the scene with a dreamy look on his face. "What kind of things?"

"How to hook up to a water and electrical supply and turn on the heater. How to drain the sewage tank. The cockpit features." He put his hand on Josie's back. "Don't worry, babe. I videoed the whole thing in case I forget anything."

By now the kids had grown bored of bouncing on the bed and ran up the narrow aisle.

"Do you guys want to go play outside?" asked Josie.

"Yay!" Connor jumped, shaking the whole camper.

Dana opened the door and helped the little ones exit. "Stay in the grass, okay?"

She and Josie stood in the yard watching the kids play while the guys explored more gadgets in the camper.

"Tell me this is going to be great, Dana."

She opened her mouth to reassure her but closed it because one lie had gotten Josie into this mess in the first place. A second one might sink them both. "It's going to be one for the books, I know that." She balled her fist and gave it a half-hearted pump. "Woo hoo, we're going camping."

Josie muttered something in Spanish, her tone laced with frustration.

Dana didn't understand her, but she sympathized with the sentiment. She wasn't too sure about this either, and her kids were at least old enough to pack their own bags and be helpful at the campsite, she hoped. "Want me to take the triplets on a walk so you and Hunter can load up some of the stuff?"

"Yes please." Josie's shoulders relaxed, the tension visibly lifting from her posture. She dashed inside and returned pulling the giant stroller.

"Hey, are you gonna take Peg to Colorado?"

Josie peered behind the cargo door Hunter had unlocked. "There's no way she'll fit in here even folded up. We'll have to bring umbrella strollers instead."

As they lifted toddlers into the seats and strapped them in, Dana said, "Sometimes it creeps me out that you personify the triple stroller. Disturbs me how you talk about folding her up and shoving her in a trunk."

"Says the crime writer." Josie stood and shook her finger like an idea had just come to her. "You could write about a creeper lurking in the woods. Or a killer who transports his deceased victims in the cargo hold of his camper and deposits them where wild animals will dispose of them."

Dana's eyes bulged. "I can't believe you talk like that in front of your children."

Josie grinned and swiped away Dana's criticism. "They don't know I'm being morbid." She tapped the side of her head. "But it's good stuff. You should use it."

Maybe Nate and Josie could get a group discount on the therapy they clearly needed for their criminal musings. "Okay, you get to loading up now while I sing little kid church songs to the babies so they don't have nightmares from their mommy's twisted conversation."

"Take your time." Josie waved over her shoulder as she disappeared into the house.

Dana heaved her weight against the stroller to get it going. She'd pushed Peg many times before, but the kids were the biggest they'd ever been. She would be worn out in a few blocks. Besides, as much as she wanted to give Josie a break to get things done before they left in the morning, she hadn't finished her own packing either. Hopefully twenty minutes would be long enough for Hunter and Josie to make headway on loading some of their gear.

"Yook, kickens." Olivia pointed to a cluster of birds on a lawn.

"Those are doves, not chickens," Dana panted slightly. Maybe the Caraways could put a dent in loading the camper in fifteen minutes because she wouldn't last for twenty.

Olivia was undeterred. "Bock bock bock."

Dana stopped the stroller and leaned over the handle. "Shh. If you listen, you can hear the doves say 'coo.' Do you hear them?"

"BOCK!" Connor's shrill impression of a chicken sent the doves into a tree. "Bye kicken."

The three kids waved at the tree.

Dana missed that age. Her children might be able to clean their own bodies—relatively well anyway. The boys were still hit or miss with hygiene, but the older they got, the bigger their problems, and the more she worried about them.

Leah sparked the most parental concerns. She was driving, and that alone was a constant threat. Add to that an entire parking lot of teen drivers before and after school, and every day held the potential for catastrophe. Physical dangers like driving and sports injuries barely scratched the surface of the concerns that came with being the mom of a seventeen-year-old.

Dana forced the stroller forward again. "You guys just stay little forever, okay?"

"I not yitto. I big boy," Ben asserted rather loudly.

"Yes, you are. All of you are big." She struggled to maneuver Peg around the corner. The thing was longer than she was tall, and its turn radius was about the same as a super cab truck. They strode a few more blocks before Dana's legs had endured all of Peg they could handle.

When she trudged back up the Caraways' driveway, the triplets oohed and awed pointing at the Winnebago, as if they forgot they saw it fifteen minutes ago.

"Yook at dat big twuck."

Josie hopped down from the Winnie's steps. "Hey guys, did you have a good ride?"

"I'm not saying you should have them tested or anything, but your kids are oddly obsessed with chickens," Dana said.

"I know. It's weird, right?" She unbuckled Connor and set him on the grass.

"Meh, if they still think all birds are chickens when they go to kindergarten, then it'll be weird." She lifted Olivia out of the stroller. "Did you get much done?"

"Yeah, we put everything that would fit under the dining bench, and we installed their car seats." She thanked Dana for taking the toddlers off her hands and wished her luck with her own vacation prepping. "We ride at dawn!"

Dana helped Josie herd children into the house. "That may work for Hobbits, but we'll be lucky if we get on the road by eight."

"We ride at eight!"

Chapter 10

Dana stood at the base of the stairs and called the kids out of their rooms. "Has everyone finished packing?"

A chorus of "Yes" echoed back, but the history of half-packed bags left her skeptical.

She grabbed a copy of the neatly typed packing list she'd made for each of them and held it up like a scroll of commandments. "Let's go through it."

She read each item aloud waiting for verbal confirmation before moving to the next, not unlike a flight attendant reviewing emergency exit row procedures. "Socks?"

Adam scratched his head and looked everywhere but at his mother's face. "Yes."

"Shoes?"

"Yes."

By the end, their guilty fidgeting told her everything she needed to know about the state of the kids' bags.

Dana laid the list on the edge of the breakfast bar. "Don't come crying to me when you run out of clean underwear."

Leah huffed and tried to cross her arms but settled for tucking her good arm under the other elbow. "Is this necessary? I'm technically a senior in high school now. I can pack my stuff without you micromanaging me."

The kids had turned 'micromanage' into a weapon, hurling it at Dana whenever they didn't like being told what to do. Every time they said it, Dana's blood boiled. "You were sure wishing I had micromanaged you last winter on our ski trip when you left your snow boots here, weren't you?" She swept her hand over the gear flooding the living room. "We've never gone camping before, and it would be a problem if you forgot something important like warm clothes and extra socks. We also won't have laundry facilities, so if you fall in the river and didn't pack enough, what're you going to do?"

"Fine, Mom. We get it."

Dana took a cleansing breath. Rather than punish her daughter's insolence, she tasked her with packing the camp towels and extra blankets into a single moving bag. Ordering the moving bags had been Leah's suggestion as they were all the rage on Instagram for students leaving for college. Their uniform shape and backpack straps made them easy to both carry and stack.

Leah held up her turquoise mesh arm. "How am I supposed to zip it?"

"Just fill it. Then call me." She told the boys to pick out some games for the trip and walked down the hall to her and Will's room. She closed the door softly behind her and slumped against it.

"Kids causing problems?" Will's voice so close to her made her jump.

"Where'd you come from?"

"Throwing the rest of my stuff together." He encircled her waist. "I can't wait to get on the road. I'm so excited."

Dana's pursed lips formed a smile that didn't reach her eyes.

He pulled back to study her face. "You're still not even a little bit excited?"

"I'm trying to be for the kids' sake. After I read the informative essay Adam's teacher gave me, I realized how important this time with the kids is for all of us. I *want* to be excited, but I'm so terrified."

Will took her by the hand and led her to the edge of the bed. "What are you afraid of?"

"Something bad happening. Bears. Injury. Getting lost. Bug and snake bites. Freezing to death. I don't know how to do any of the stuff we're about to do. A million things could go wrong."

"Sure, but a million things could go right, too. This week might be our best vacation yet."

"I kno—"

A burst of static cut off her words. "Captain. Come in Captain. This is Iron Robot."

Will grinned and pulled a walkie-talkie out of his pocket. "This is your captain speaking. Come in, Iron Robot."

"We're having a disagreement here about whether to pack Monopoly. Over."

Dana couldn't help laughing. "Those are quite the nicknames you have."

"They're call signs." He put the device to his mouth and pushed the button. "Eighty-six Monopoly, Iron Robot. Let's stick with small games with few pieces. Cards, dice, etcetera. Over."

"Roger that, Captain. Over." Adam yelled something to Nate with his finger still on the talk button before the radios went silent.

Dana ran her hand through Will's hair. "Alright, Captain. If Adam's Iron Robot, what's Nate's call sign?"

His eyebrows furrowed. "Shoulder Pads. He'll probably change it when he finds out his brother came up with that."

"Uh huh. And what are mine and Leah's?"

"Girls don't get call signs. Besides, you have phones. These are mainly to keep track of the kid who doesn't have one and is most likely to wander off."

She pushed his back onto the bed and tried to wrestle the walkie away from him. "Girls don't get call signs? Are you sure about that?"

He stretched his arm out of her reach. "It's not a toy. It's a safety device."

Dana poked him in the ribs, and Will reflexively pulled his arm down. She made a grab for the radio. "So, you're lecturing *me* on worry, and this whole time you've been nervous about Adam getting lost."

He pulled her down beside him. "It's just a precaution. Like that giant first aid kit you packed with enough stuff to stock a field hospital."

Dana relaxed into Will's side. She wasn't the only one concerned about the children's safety, even if he didn't openly admit it like she did. She patted his chest. "I have a confession."

"You want a walkie-talkie of your own? You're in luck. I bought two sets just in case we hike somewhere without a cell signal."

She laughed. "Yay, but I'm picking my own code name, and it'll be better than Shoulder Pads." She gave him a sheepish shrug. "I may or may not have bought an AirTag to slip in Adam's pocket. You know, for the same reason you got the two-way radios."

"Smart, but we might be taking the protective parent thing too far. Let's promise each other we will trust God to safeguard our kids and stop making contingency plans, okay?"

"Fine. But we're still taking the safety supplies we already bought, right?"

Static crackled again, and Nate's voice came over the radio. "We will also be eighty-sixing call sign Shoulder Pads. Deciding between 'Hulk' and 'Thor.' Over."

Will grinned. "Roger that, God of Thunder."

Loading the Tahoe took much longer than anticipated. The rooftop cargo bag, which Will had assured Dana was the answer to all their packing problems, should have come with a warning that installers must be eight foot tall or have access to stilts. Hunter jogged over to lend a hand just in time to wrestle the zipper closed while Adam laid on the bag, squishing the top and bottom together. Will and Dana stood in the open back seat doors to fasten it to the rack. It did hold a lot of gear though, and so far, the roof hadn't even caved in. She prayed it would withstand highway speeds without ripping open or flying off.

Anchoring the storage container and ice chest to the hitch hauler was also problematic. The box was wider than the expanded metal it was supposed to rest on. They'd used no less than twelve bungee straps to batten it and the ice chest in place.

At last, all five human Hardings and one fluffy dog were loaded and ready to go, a half hour behind schedule.

Will pushed the starter, and nothing happened. He patted his pockets and turned to Dana. "Do you have my keys?"

"Clearly not, or the engine would have started." She dug through her hot pink belt bag. "I must not have mine either. Kids, fan out and find both sets of car keys, or else we'll be taking this camping trip in the backyard."

Will cocked one eyebrow. "Both sets? More contingencies?"

She opened her door. "Yeah, you're a dropper. If one set falls in the creek, we'll still have mine to get us home."

Chapter 11

Josie

The Minnie Winnie was loaded and ready to roll right on schedule. Josie buckled the babies into their seats and queued a preschool show on her tablet while Hunter ran across the street to help Will secure their load to the Tahoe.

Small wheels rattling and scraping against asphalt announced his return. He pushed a large purple suitcase underneath the dining table and took his place at the helm of their rented land yacht. "Leah's luggage wouldn't fit, and this was easier than spending another half hour trying to strap it onto the ice chest."

Josie looked back at all the open space in the Winnie. They'd stashed stuff in the wardrobe and in every cabinet and drawer. The exterior cargo hold held fishing gear, lawn chairs, and other miscellaneous items, but there was room to spare.

"Should we have offered to put more of their stuff in here?"

He started the ignition. "I think they've got it. I told them we were going to get a head start since we will probably have to stop more than they will. We'll be lucky if this thing gets ten miles to the gallon."

Hunter maneuvered the RV around the circle at the end of their cul-de-sac.

"How is it? Do you feel like you're driving a tank?" Josie asked.

"It's not much different than my truck. You can take a turn if you want."

She did want to try it out, but she would let Hunter have his fun first. He hadn't stopped beaming like a kid on Christmas morning since he drove it home yesterday. "Tell me about your family camping trips growing up."

He regaled her with tales of their adventures in New Mexico in a tent and then in the pop-up camper his dad bought for Mother's Day one year. "Mom was not a happy camper. Pun intended."

Josie had trouble imagining her mother-in-law bothered at all. She was an easy-going boy mom, and nothing rattled her. "Why was she upset? Wasn't it practically luxury glamping compared to sleeping on the ground?"

"That's what Dad thought. But there's a learning curve to the pop-up. The process of setting it up with all the moving parts is tedious and can cause damage if not done correctly."

Still, that sounded like a step up from tent camping.

He was quiet for a minute before continuing. "Honestly, I think Mom liked that we boys did all the work setting up the campsite and the tent. She got to be a passenger princess, and she made Dad stick to campgrounds with modern facilities. But when we got that camper, she had to help set it up to keep things from falling apart, and we went to more off-the-grid locations." He kept his eyes on the road and chuckled to himself. "She wasn't a fan of the cartridge toilet right by the camper door. It had a shower curtain around it, but there wasn't any privacy."

Poor Emmaline. "I can see how trying to use a toilet with four boys in the same room would be a drawback." Josie had a newfound appreciation for the bathroom door in the Winnie.

By the time they crossed the Texas-New Mexico border, the kids had grown antsy. Hunter pulled into a grocery store parking lot to let them loose for a bit.

Josie pulled a soda out of the fridge. "Can I drive?" She raised her voice to be heard over the pounding of six little feet running up and down the length of the Winnie.

"Be my guest."

She held up two fingers. "Two minutes, guys. Then you get back in your seats."

Olivia countered by holding up all ten fingers. "No two. Dis many minutes."

"Sorry, sis. We'll never get there at that rate." He scooped her up, blew a raspberry on her belly, and set her back on the floor.

"Let's just tell them their time's up and get this show back on the road," said Josie. She was anxious to get her turn behind the wheel, but more than that, she dreaded the thought of traversing mountain roads in the dark.

Hunter's mouth dropped open. "You would lie to our kids? Wasn't it your lie that got us here in the first place?"

"Yeah well, you *wanted* to take this trip, so you're welcome for my lie." Guilt settled into Josie's gut as soon as the words left her mouth. She pulled out her phone and checked the time. "Fine, we'll give them their full two minutes, even though they don't know the difference."

Hell hath no fury like three toddlers restrained against their will. They kicked their seats and screamed for the next fifteen miles.

With her arm propped on the driver's window, Josie massaged her forehead. "Babe, I can't take it anymore. I'm going to find a place to pull over."

"And do what? Leave them on the side of the road?"

She flashed him a wistful smile.

"Josefina Camille Saldana Caraway."

She reflexively stiffened at hearing her whole name. Only her mother ever used it. "What? I wouldn't really leave my babies." Unless a very nice family stopped for them.

He put his hand on her shoulder. "I'm sorry I went full Marie on you. Just for that, I'll go back there and see what I can do." He unbuckled his seatbelt and climbed through the opening in between the cockpit and living area. "Daddy's here. Y'all want a snack?"

Olivia pounded her shoes against the underside of the table. "Yay, snack!"

Josie glanced in the rearview mirror at Hunter rummaging through the cabinets. He grabbed bowls and shook rattly, dry food into them, likely cereal or goldfish crackers.

She saw the railroad crossing at the last second and barely had time to brake before the Winnie rumbled over it at sixty-five miles per hour. A Hunter-sized thud echoed through the camper as bowls of snacks clattered to the floor.

"Sorry, babe. You okay back there?"

"Daddy fall." Olivia announced. "You okay?"

"I'm okay. Easy on the bumps, Jos."

The crying stopped.

Josie stole another look in the mirror to see Hunter picking up scattered goldfish crackers and dropping them into melamine bowls. "Are you feeding my babies off the floor?"

"Hey. You're the one who sent the food flying. And it's probably cleaner than our floor at home, which they eat from all the time."

When they finally pulled off the highway into the campground, the sun kissed the mountaintop, casting long evening shadows over the valley. A log cabin next to the parking lot served as the visitor center. It had a patio out front with two bistro tables, a red sun umbrella, and a flagpole flying both the American and Colorado flags. A sign by the door, staked in a whiskey barrel planter of geraniums, welcomed guests to Silver Mountain Campground.

Josie hopped out of the passenger's seat and inhaled the crisp air. She shivered as goosebumps trailed her bare arms. They would have to locate warmer clothing for the kids before they got out of the Winnie. She jogged inside.

A kiosk on one wall overflowed with brochures advertising every imaginable outdoor activity Colorado had to offer. Opposite it stood a coffee station with an empty pot so stained she was sure even fresh water from it would carry the aftertaste of burnt coffee. A vintage Smokey the Bear poster graced the front of a tidy metal desk, incongruous with the rustic charm of the building itself.

"Hello?" The desk needed a bell. Beyond it was another, slightly larger room. Josie took a few cautious steps and peeked inside, hoping it wasn't someone's living quarters—that would certainly be awkward. Instead, she found a general store complete with souvenir racks of shirts, keychains, and toys bearing the campground name. Shelves held groceries as well as camping supplies and what she could only assume were parts for RVs.

The door she'd just entered swung open. A petite senior citizen with cropped, white hair greeted her. "Evening. You must be a Caraway. Checked in the rest of your group about ten minutes ago."

Josie stuck her hand out. "Yes ma'am. Josie."

The woman wiped her hand on her ruffled apron before shaking Josie's. Her grip was shockingly firm for a woman of her stature. "I'm Frances. My sister Bonnie and I are the proprietors. You'll have to forgive my state. I've been whipping up some chocolate chip cookies." She pulled a form out of the desk and passed it to Josie. "Fill this out, please. By the time we get business taken care of, Bonnie should be back to lead you down to the campsite. She'll show you where everything is and help you with your RV hook ups if you need it."

Josie thanked her and filled out the form.

When she handed it back, Frances's eyes grew round. "You have three two-year-olds with you?"

Josie gave a polite nod. Saucer eyes and dropped jaws were the common response to finding out she had triplet toddlers. "They're in the Winnebago with my husband."

"Well, I reckon they're going to be glad to get out of there. When you get settled, you walk them up to my cabin and let those babies get a chocolate chip cookie. It's the only other cabin besides this office, so you can't miss it."

Josie thanked her and turned to leave.

"Tell those big kids I've got plenty of cookies for them, too."

Josie hopped into the passenger seat rubbing her bare arms to infuse some warmth into them. "We're supposed to wait here for Bonnie to escort us to the campsite. She'll show us the ropes, and then her sister invited us to bring the triplets to their cabin for C-double-O-K-I-E-S."

Hunter's eyes moved as if he were spelling it out in his mind.

"Are you still trying to figure out the word?"

"No. I was wondering if it's a good idea to take our kids to a stranger's cabin in the woods for cookies. How do you know it's not a Hansel and Gretel situation?"

She popped his arm with the back of her hand.

"Cookie? Want cookies," said Ben.

"COOKIES," echoed Connor.

Josie rolled her eyes. "Seriously? Why do you think I spelled it? You set them off, so you can walk them back over here for their treat, Hansel."

One side of his mouth turned down, and he shook his head. "You're hurtful after a nine-hour road trip."

"It was closer to ten. You forgot about the time change."

"Somebody needs a snack," he muttered.

She opened her mouth to protest that her grumpiness had nothing to do with hunger, but a golf cart approached and pulled next to Hunter's window.

Another senior woman in a straw cowboy hat waved. "You folks meeting some tent campers?"

"Yes, ma'am," said Hunter.

"I'll circle around, and you can follow me." The golf cart moved at a snail's pace. She stopped and pointed at the sign indicating the speed limit in the campground was seven and a half miles per hour.

"I guess Bonnie would like you to know they're serious about the speed limit," said Josie.

"This thing idles faster than that."

"Then you better ride the brake. If you rear end her, there's no chance they'll let us stay, and we'll be stuck in here for ten more hours." Maybe Hunter had a point about her irritability. She'd never been a fan of long trips, especially on winding roads. But traveling with toddlers was worse—even with a rolling kitchen and bathroom to take the edge off long stretches of sitting still.

About a quarter mile down a gravel road, Bonnie pointed at an open driveway next to a fire ring and a picnic table. The Harding boys waved. Dana and Will were unhooking the straps from the back of the Tahoe, wearing intense expressions.

Josie spotted Leah in the fading light walking toward them from up the path. Her good arm was pulled into her tee shirt, and her shoulders hunched inward, teeth chattering.

Josie leaned out the window. "Where's your jacket, girl?"

"In your dumb camper, remember?" Oops. Leah's tone indicated she wasn't in any better spirits after the drive than Josie.

Bonnie directed Hunter on the best positioning for the RV and pointed out the water and electric hookups. "The dump station is located by the bathrooms." She indicated the direction from which Leah had come.

Hunter scratched his head and gave her a sheepish grin. "We're first timers. Any idea how often we'll need to uh, dump the tanks?"

Josie stifled a giggle. She didn't even want to think about how the wastewater went away, but Hunter's discomfort amused her.

Bonnie, on the other hand, was unphased. She sized him up and glanced at Josie. "Every couple of days, depending on your bathroom habits. It will help if you shower in the bathhouse up the road and conserve water when you wash dishes." She adjusted her hat. "Just keep an eye on your levels. And when you do drive over there to dump, be sure you detach the electrical and water connections and put the awning away. You wouldn't believe the number of first timers who drive off with their hoses still screwed to the spigot or tear up their awning because they leave it out." She wagged a warning finger at them. "We charge for damages to the campsite. Hop out and let's get you hooked up."

"Go on and hook up, babe," Josie snickered.

He handed her the keys. "You're a child."

Meh, better a child with an immature sense of humor than an irritable mom. She unlocked the main door and ushered Leah inside. Together, they freed the purple suitcase from its spot under the table.

"Gimme out," demanded Ben.

Olivia implored her teenage babysitter to free her. "We-uh, help."

Leah unbuckled Ben and then Olivia with one hand and helped each of them climb down from the dinette. "It's too cold to go outside without a jacket. Let me find mine, and then I'll help you put yours on."

Josie wrapped her arms around Leah, her attempted full-frontal hug settling itself against a bony teenaged shoulder. "You're my hero."

Leah leaned out of the unreciprocated embrace and awkwardly patted the arm pinning her in place. "Okay. Connor still needs help."

Josie finally understood what Dana meant when she said showing affection to her daughter was much the same as hugging a cactus. She pulled the top off the bin of triplet clothes she'd stowed in the wardrobe and found three little hoodies.

At last, everyone was ready to leave the camper. Josie opened the door, pausing to admire the sky, now glittering with millions of stars.

Over by the Tahoe, the Hardings wrestled with their supplies.

"Point the flashlight at the straps, not in my eyes," Will barked.

Adam groaned. "When are we eating? I'm starving."

In a barely muffled tone, Bonnie warned Hunter, "We do get bears and the occasional mountain lion in the campground, so it's a good idea to peek around before you let the littles outside. Make noise and such."

Josie paused mid-step and shut the camper door. Maybe going outside wasn't the best idea right now after all.

Chapter 12

Dana

Dana hadn't spoken to Will for the last couple of hours, and she wasn't planning to start as they rolled into the campground. After lunch, she'd swapped seats with Nate, letting her lanky teenager stretch out in the passenger seat, while she squeezed into the cramped third row next to Harvey.

Later when Will stopped for gas, Dana ran inside the convenience store to use the restroom. Her stomach dropped as she returned to the parking lot in time to see the Tahoe pulling onto the highway access road. She couldn't even call Will to yell at him because her phone was conveniently stowed in the third row cupholder. If Nate hadn't spoken up—albeit at the last possible second before Will pulled onto I-40, she might still be stranded in front of a gas station in Santa Rosa.

She shot a cold, hard glare at the back of his head as she reclaimed her spot amid the bags that had been shoved into every open space.

"I said I'm sorry." Will turned to meet her stare. "You should have told someone you were exiting the vehicle."

Did she need to tell the ten-year-old she'd literally climbed over getting out? Or her daughter whose hair she'd accidentally pulled during her clumsy escape from the third row? It wasn't like her departure had gone unnoticed—the entire family, plus the strangers in the car gassing up next to them, had witnessed her dramatic exit. Everyone except Will, apparently. Maybe her anger should've been directed at the ones who failed to speak up for her.

After that debacle, Will declared there would be no more stops, insisting they would arrive any minute. Leah's requests for a bathroom break and Adam's increasingly theatrical complaints about his lack of car snacks and imminent starvation were summarily ignored.

By the time they arrived, Harvey was the only Harding in good spirits. He raced around camp, sniffing everything and getting under foot. Dana hated to do it, but she tied his leash to the picnic table to keep him safe and out of the way until the tent was up.

Nate and Will set the ice chest on the table while Adam and Dana followed with the supply box.

"You folks be sure not to leave any food out. That's what draws the bears," said Bonnie, the campground proprietor. She'd offered helpful instructions upon their arrival and was doing the same for the Caraways, but Dana wished Bonnie would head back to her cabin. She was nice enough, but her critical eye made Dana uncomfortable.

The guys determined the best spot to set up the tent, far enough from the fire ring to avoid sparks on the fabric, but still close enough to the power for the extension cord to reach.

Adam clutched his belly. "How much longer? My stomach is really growling."

"For crying out loud," Dana mumbled. She used her phone's flashlight to find a suitable snack for him amid the dry goods. She handed him a box of vanilla wafers. "Eat a few of these to tide you over until we can get a fire going."

Will called for all Harding hands on deck. He stood in the open door of the second row unhooking the straps on the cargo carrier. "I'll take stuff down and y'all pass it into the back seat until I reach the tent. Then we'll set it up and move everything into it."

"And then make dinner?" asked Adam.

"Oh, for heaven's sake," snapped Will. "Have we ever made you skip a meal? Have we?"

Adam tore open the box of vanilla wafers, but the inner plastic bag wasn't giving in without a fight. His face squinched as his elbows pointed in opposite directions, muscles straining against the bag's seal.

Dana was about to suggest he hand it over and let her help when his efforts paid off. At the same moment the cookie package succumbed to Adam's brute force, Will unzipped the rooftop carrier. A sleeping bag careened off the Tahoe and knocked the cookies out of Adam's hand. Two more sleeping bags tumbled out.

"Seriously, Dad?"

Will yanked the zipper closed to stop the avalanche. "Sorry. I forgot the golden rule of opening overhead bins. Items may have shifted during the flight." At least his sense of humor was returning.

A disgruntled Adam bent over and picked a vanilla wafer from the top of the pile on the ground, blew on it, and popped it into his mouth.

"Son! There's no five-second rule in the wilderness," Dana said.

He glared at her and shoveled in another cookie without blowing the dirt off it.

Dana shook her head. "Don't come crying to me when you get sick later."

Will poked his arm into a small opening in the zipper. "Look out below. Tent incoming." The kids cleared the drop zone as he tugged free the duffle bag that held their shelter for the week. "Okay gang. It took us thirty minutes the first time. Let's see if we can cut that in half."

Dana hadn't been involved in the backyard practice or bothered with the tutorial video, so she stuck to holding the flashlight and staying out of the way while her "expert crew" handled the assembly. Setting up the tent took longer in the dark than it had at home in the daytime. Nate and Adam argued over which set of poles belonged where. Forty minutes later, their home away from home was operational. Good thing they'd worked out all the kinks before the trip.

Adam's complaints about his empty stomach returned with gusto and were echoed by his siblings who joined his moaning.

Josie emerged from the camper, possibly after feeding her children—or more likely, hiding from the Harding-induced chaos. "The owner invited all the kids to come up to her cabin for fresh-baked chocolate chip cookies. Why don't I walk up with the kids while y'all finish setting up?"

Josie tugged Hunter's sleeve and demanded, "Stay here and help them," through clinched teeth.

"You told me I was Hansel, remember?" Hunter whispered about as inconspicuously as Adam did in church.

Josie narrowed her eyes at him and turned on her heel.

"It's a little late to visit the neighbors, isn't it?" Will asked.

Dana consulted her watch. "It's eight-thirty, and they were invited." She turned away from Will. "Kids, go with Josie, and be polite."

Their parade set off on foot in search of cookies.

Hunter cupped his hands and blew into them. "I'm here to help. What can I do?"

Dana pointed to the Tahoe. "Let's haul the bedding from the car and run the electricity. I'll set up the beds while you two get a fire going so the kids can roast hot dogs when they get back."

She spread out the air mattresses and began inflating them one by one. The whir of the electric pump shattered the peaceful evening, an invasive species among the gentle sounds of nature. Hopefully, it was still early enough that the neighbors wouldn't complain.

A shiver ran through her at the thought of the dropping nighttime temperatures. They might not have packed enough blankets to combat the chill, but at least she'd had the foresight to tuck a small space heater into her suitcase. The paper-thin walls offered no insulation, and she silently applauded herself for keeping her family from succumbing to frostbite.

By the time Dana finished setting up the beds, the scent of burning wood drifted through the air. Outside, a fire crackled, casting flickering shadows as Will and Hunter arranged their well-worn soccer chairs around it. A pot of water steamed on the camp stove, promising hot chocolate, a welcome comfort after a long day.

Footsteps scraped up the gravel road as golden beams of flashlights danced in the dark. The Harding kids bounced into camp, with a Caraway toddler clinging to each of their backs.

Josie brought up the rear and lowered Connor from Leah's back to the ground. "You missed out. Frances and Bonnie are something else."

Olivia put her hands up like claws and showed her teeth. "Bear sca-wee."

"Yes, Livvie, the bear was scary." Josie put herself between her curious children and the blazing fire. "They have a taxidermied bear in their cabin."

Dana imagined shuffling down the hall for a drink of water in the middle of the night, bleary-eyed and half-asleep, only to come face-to-face with a predator. Seemed like a dangerous conversation piece for two ladies of their age.

"And they have a pet racoon named Sully," said Adam.

Dana's mouth dropped open. "Who *are* these people?"

Josie flipped her hair over her shoulder. "It's not a pet, per se. Just an overly friendly wild racoon who lives under their porch and trades pinecones for fruit. They're a couple of sweet old ladies who are a tad eccentric."

"Does eccentric mean weird?" asked Adam.

Leah struggled to poke a frank onto a roasting fork while Ben clung to her leg. "Yeah, but like good weird." Will stepped in to take over for her, and she sat in a chair. "Bonnie was a pilot and a sharpshooter. According to her sister, she was a big deal in the military in a time when women weren't allowed to have the most dangerous jobs. Isn't that cool?"

"Yeah," said Josie, "and Frances raised four kids with her husband before he died. That's when the sisters bought a dilapidated campground and refurbished it into the beauty you see before you."

"You got all that over chocolate chip cookies?" Dana regretted staying behind to set up the tent and missing out on the fascinating visit.

Josie pulled Ben onto her lap. "I get the feeling they wear each other out and appreciate the chance to visit with new people."

Where were Frances's kids? As an only child, Dana wouldn't have a sibling to keep her company if she outlived Will and her kids moved away. But at least she wouldn't have to open a campground with anyone either.

Leah posed for a campfire selfie, showing off her bejeweled cast. "*Noooo!*"

Dana's head swiveled, but there was no visible danger. Leah's distress might have indicated anything from a toddler getting too close to the fire to a pimple in her photo. "What's the matter?"

"I have no bars." Her voice rose, and her breath quickened. "There's *literally* no signal. How is this possible?"

"Calm down, sweetie," said Will. "That's pretty typical in the mountains." Just what every woman wanted to hear when she was upset.

"I don't need to *calm down*. I need a Wi-Fi password."

Dana pulled out her own phone and confirmed what Leah had already announced. The AirTag wouldn't work for tracking Adam after all. "That's not how it works in nature, sweetie."

"Then why did we come here?" Leah's hysteria was scaring the triplets, and they'd just come from a stranger's house with an actual bear.

Josie leaned toward Dana and whispered, "I think this is our cue to call it a night." She, Hunter, and the toddlers made the twenty-foot trek to their camper and disappeared inside.

Will stood over Leah. "Can you really not go a few days without your phone?" His stern countenance might have made his employees wither, but Leah was oblivious.

"Uh no. I'm supposed to be documenting my cast in the wild, remember?"

Dana met Will's gaze in the flickering fire light. They'd created a monster—a beautiful siren with a petrified net on one arm and a cellular device fused to the other. After a lengthy debate, they managed to convince her the effect would be the same if she posted them when she had a signal. No one would know the difference if she chronicled her wilderness journey a week after the fact.

Will reached out, offering Dana his hand to help her out of the camp chair. "We should turn in early, too. Let's fold up the chairs, smother the fire, and head up to the bathrooms." He made it sound like a quick task, but another hour went by before they were settled into their sleeping bags.

Dana and Will squirmed, trying in vain to get comfortable. The so-called king-size air mattress was noticeably smaller than their bed at home, and every tiny movement threatened to send one of them rolling off the edge.

The boys' frustrated mutterings indicated they were in the same boat.

"Be still."

"You're gonna knock my pillow into the floor."

Leah shushed them, but the annoying rustle of air mattress against the canvas floor lingered for several minutes. At last, the tent settled into silence, and the sounds of nature took over. Crickets chirped in rhythmic cadence, and the gentle rippling of the creek behind them grew louder with each passing second.

"Is that going to go on all night?" Leah sat up in a huff.

Will threw his hands up. "It's nature. What do you think?"

More rustling ensued, and Leah's form towered over Dana in the dark. "All the running water sounds mixed with the cold air are making me need to pee again. You have to come with me because I'm not getting kidnapped or attacked by a bear going to the bathroom by myself."

Dana wriggled out of her sleeping bag. "You'd rather we get attacked by a bear together."

Harvey's metal food bowl scraping across the ground cut short her complaint.

Will mumbled a mild expletive. "How did we forget to bring in Harvey's bowl?"

The boys argued about which one of them had been assigned the task of moving it inside.

"We're going to die in this tent because you two can't follow simple instructions," Leah screeched. "And I still have to pee." She grabbed the flashlight from a mesh pocket in the wall of the tent.

Her fear of walking to the bathroom alone had clearly been replaced by irritation with her brothers. She unzipped the window and shone the light in the direction of the bowl. "It's just a racoon. Probably the same one Frances feeds." She stomped to the door, unzipped it, and aimed the light at the racoon. "Bad Sully. No."

The racoon scurried away.

Leah retrieved the food bowl and put it in the tent.

"Some guard dog you are, Harvey."

The rest of the family sat motionless, silent witnesses to Leah's sudden take-charge moment. Then, out of nowhere, Dana was blinded by a tractor beam aimed directly at her eyes.

"Mom. Are you coming?"

Dana got up and pulled on her shoes. "You scared off a racoon, so I didn't know you still needed me to walk you to the bathroom."

"It's like a block away."

"Just use the outhouse across the road," said Nate. "It's right on the other side of Winnie the Minnie."

"*That's* the outhouse?" Dana asked. "I thought it was a well or something."

Will laughed. "That's your standard vaulted toilet. Give it a try. It's clean. Just close the lid after you use it so the smell vents out the chimney."

Dana followed Leah outside. "Let's use the vaulted toilet, okay? It's closer and I'm freezing."

They crossed the road behind the camper and stood stock still in front of the little building.

Leah pushed Dana forward.

As the adult, it was her job to go into the dark, scary room first, but they only had the one flashlight. "Let's go together. I'll open the door, and you shine the light inside."

"Okay," Leah whispered. She clutched the hem of Dana's jacket with her casted hand. The flashlight shook in her other one.

The building was deceptively larger from the outside. Inside, there was not enough room for the two of them without an uncomfortable amount of closeness.

Dana entered, hoping that a preemptive toilet visit now would save her from having to get up and go at two a.m. "I guess I'll go first. Just stand here with the door cracked. Keep the beam steady and then we'll switch, alright?"

The light bobbed as Leah nodded. "Hurry up. I'm the

one who needs to go. You were just supposed to be my bodyguard."

Dana took a step back. "You want to go first?"

"What? No." Leah ducked behind her. "I don't want to touch the lid."

After each of them took their turn and doused their hands with ice-cold sanitizer, they hustled back to the tent much faster than they'd trekked to the outhouse. Dana couldn't wait to burrow into the warmth of the covers.

"Well, Mom." In a rare show of affection, Leah slipped her arm through her mom's and rested her head on Dana's shoulder. "We conquered your number one wilderness fear. We're practically mountain men now."

"Bears are still my number one fear. After watching you scare off the racoon though, my new plan is to stand behind you if we see one." Her daughter had shown courage she wasn't sure she could match. A silent prayer formed in her mind: *Lord, please don't let me have to find out this week.*

Leah unzipped the tent and sidestepped the suitcases to get to her bed. "Too bad we didn't capture my heroism for Instagram."

Chapter 13

Josie

The Winnie's dinette wasn't the cozy bed the internet photos had made it out to be. Halfway between a twin and full-size bed, it proved to be the wrong option for two adults. Josie's arm prickled with pins and needles and her legs throbbed from being in the same position for too long. She'd spent the night pressed against Hunter to avoid falling off the front edge, warm to the point of overheating. But now, as she peeled herself free and stretched, a blast of cold air made her shiver. The camper was downright frigid.

She checked the thermostat, which showed forty-eight degrees. Mercifully, the queen bed's inhabitants were still asleep, sprawled every which way under a thick quilt. She tucked the covers over Connor's leg and tiptoed back to the dinette bed.

"Hunter," she whispered. He didn't budge, even when she jostled his shoulder. "Wake up."

She ripped the covers off him, jolting him awake. "Why is it so cold in here?"

"You tell me." Josie cocooned herself in the down comforter. "You paid attention to all the camper instructions, right?"

He fiddled with the thermostat, unplugged his phone from the charger in the cockpit, and scurried back to bed.

Josie enveloped him in the comforter while he scrubbed

through a video of camper instructions.

"There's nothing here to explain why the heater's not working."

She nudged him. "Hurry up and google it before Dana's irrational fear of hypothermia becomes a reality for our kids."

"There's no signal, Jos." He pulled her down beside him and tucked the comforter around them. "I'm sure the kids are fine. It's probably warmer in the alcove."

"This bed's way too small."

"Let's just try to sleep a little and figure it out in the morning." He nuzzled her neck.

"Think of it as a nap on the sofa."

This was their penance for the lie Josie told her mother—sleep deprivation while twisted into a pretzel on a toddler bed in a walk-in Winnebago refrigerator.

Despite her discomfort, Josie drifted off and roused to icy little fingers poking her face.

"Hi, Mama. Go aside, kay?"

Her eyelids fluttered against the morning light. "Good morning, Ben. You can't go outside until you get dressed and we check for wild animals." There was a sentence she never imagined coming out of her mouth. "Babe. Your kids are awake." She patted Hunter's face. "Up and at 'em."

Josie unfurled herself from the bed and pulled Ben onto her lap. "Gimme those cold fingers."

He shrieked and giggled as his mom clasped his hands in hers and pretended to eat them.

Josie craned her neck to see if Connor and Olivia were still asleep, but the queen bed was empty. She set Ben next to Hunter and crossed the camper in two steps. "Hunter, the kids are missing."

He bolted upright. "What are you talking about? Ben's right here."

She checked the bathroom and the wardrobe. Her hands trembled and tightness gripped her chest. "Connor?

Olivia!"

Hunter leaped up and jiggled the locked handle on the door.

A voice from the front of the Winnie pulled them from their search. "Yook, Mama. I jiving." Olivia bounced on her knees in the driver's seat clutching the steering wheel while Connor applauded her from the passenger's side.

Josie's posture relaxed as fear loosened its stranglehold. She and Hunter each lifted a toddler out of the cockpit. "I thought you said we would avoid them driving us off a cliff if we slept up here."

Hunter plopped Olivia next to Ben on the bed. "You'd think the cold would have at least slowed them down."

Wishful thinking. The high altitude and frosty temperatures had the opposite effect, charging them up like athletes on steroids. Josie shook her head. "Someone warn the wildlife— the Caraway triplets are about to be unleashed." Silver Mountain Campground wouldn't know what hit it.

Josie carried Olivia to the campfire to join the Hardings warming up before making breakfast. "Did y'all sleep alright in the tent? No one froze, I see."

Hunter sidled next to her and scrolled his phone.

Will put his arm around Leah and pulled her into a side hug. "We slept like babies after our warrior here scared off a racoon and rescued the dog's food bowl."

"One of us had to do it." Leah wrinkled her nose but didn't shy away from the embrace. "Dad and the boys weren't even trying to get out of their sleeping bags."

"Not fair." Will dropped his arm. "You were already out of bed and handled it faster than anyone else could have."

Leah looked over Hunter's shoulder. "Do you have a signal?" Hope edged her voice higher.

"No, I'm looking for the video of the camper owner explaining how to work the heater. It didn't kick on last night."

"Between the broken heater and the two of us sharing a twin bed," said Josie, "it's a miracle we got any sleep at all."

Olivia patted her chest. "I jived."

Josie lowered herself into a chair and recounted Connor and Olivia's cockpit caper for the Hardings. Will and Dana's laughter masked the sound of the approaching golf cart.

Bonnie waved. "Doing morning rounds. Everything go okay last night?"

The men nodded, offering brief affirmations.

Josie, however, took a cue from Leah's boldness with the racoon. "Actually, we have a small problem. The heater in the Winnebago isn't working, and we can't look up the solution without a signal out here. Any thoughts?"

Bonnie turned off the cart and stepped out. She sported a multicolored southwest print jacket with a sherpa collar and the same hat she'd had on last night. "I assume you have a full propane tank. Did you have hot water?" She didn't wait for a reply as she walked to the driver's side of the Winnie. "Pop the door and let's check your tank."

Hunter hopped up and followed her.

Josie remained by the fire to supervise the kids. "What were we thinking? We should have just come clean to my mom and stayed home. We're going to end up on a podcast about how we met our demise in the woods." She pointed to Olivia. "Probably at the hand of our own toddlers."

Dana sent the boys to unload the food box and ice chest from the Tahoe and turned to Josie. "You're going to give your children a complex. They're angels, aren't you, Livvie?"

The toddler giggled.

"Well, why don't you take this angel and let me see if Hunter and Bonnie have a solution to our heat problem?" Josie handed Olivia to Dana. "Boys, don't get near the fire. I'll be right back."

As she approached the camper, Bonnie rounded the front end. "Let's take a look at the control panel and your fuses."

Josie held the side door for her and followed Hunter inside. Bonnie punched some buttons mounted next to the microwave and knelt in front of another plastic panel below the wardrobe. Josie marveled at the lack of effort it took for Bonnie to get that low. She was far more agile than her age and heavy frame suggested.

"Aha. Here's your problem." Bonnie held up a tiny object. "Blown heater fuse. Happens a lot. We've got some up at the store, which opens at nine. Come by and we'll get you fixed up."

Josie glanced at the clock on the microwave. How was it not even seven a.m.?

"There's also satellite Wi-Fi up there, when the sky's clear," said Bonnie. "And there's a phone on the side of the building that'll connect you to emergency services if needed."

Josie shuddered. What kind of emergencies did they have up here?

Hunter and Josie thanked Bonnie. She might have just saved their vacation, or at least kept them from freezing to death.

The woman turned to leave. "If you folks need anything else, you let me know."

Josie pointed at the alcove with the queen bed. "Any suggestions on how to keep three toddlers from getting up and climbing into the driver's seat?"

Hunter raised his eyebrows at her. It wasn't quite a warning look, but his disapproval was loud and clear.

Bonnie peered into the master sleeping area and at the unmade dinette-bed. She poked up the brim of her cowboy hat. "Are you telling me you put the babies on the long bed and you two slept on the dining table? What are you, both about six foot?"

They nodded in unison.

The older lady's eyes widened in surprise. "Oh goodness. Did either of you get any sleep?"

"Not much," grumbled Hunter. "And it didn't even keep them contained. They still snuck past us."

She stepped to the front of the camper and surveyed the car seats stowed in the loft. "What if you piled the baby seats in the cockpit to block their access? I might even suggest giving the loft bed a try tonight. It's bigger than that bed back there, and it's got quite a bit of head room."

Josie wasn't convinced. Room to stretch out would be nice, but there wasn't enough space to sit up. Besides, if the kids could sneak into the driver's seat right under her nose, they would definitely climb the ladder and get hurt. "We'll test it out."

"I better get on with rounds before the day gets away from me. Don't forget about your fuse, now."

Hunter exited and held out his hand to help Bonnie step out safely, but she glared at him and descended of her own accord. They thanked her again as she returned to the golf cart.

The elderly proprietor pointed up the mountain behind the campground. "There's a waterfall about a mile and a half up Summit Trail if you're looking for something to do with the older kids. Follow the signs and stay off private ranch land."

Hunter and Will teamed up to cook toast and scrambled eggs with sausage for their group of ten. By the time breakfast cleanup was done, Josie was ready for a nap. Unfortunately, it was only eight a.m., and her vacation companions were eager to explore.

"Let's go down to the lake," suggested Nate.

An eon passed while the guys readied the fishing gear.

Dana offered to load the triplets into the single and double umbrella strollers.

"No," Josie said a little more emphatically than she intended. "Make them walk. In fact, let's hike to that waterfall just before bedtime so they'll be too tired for early morning shenanigans tomorrow."

They followed the road back to the visitor center, then turned right toward the lake. The narrow valley between the mountains widened into a meadow, bordered by trees on three sides and the road leading back to the campground on the fourth. A wooden fishing pier stretched over the water, where the Harding boys had already claimed spots, lines bobbing in the lake.

Nearby, Leah snapped selfies, angling her phone to highlight her weird cast.

For their part, the triplets climbed on rocks and chased a chipmunk until it disappeared into a hole.

A figure stepped out of the tree line across the way. Her unmistakable southwest print coat and straw hat drew Josie's attention.

She tugged Dana's sleeve and nodded toward Bonnie. "I wonder what she's up to out there."

"She's toting a rifle, so it can't be anything good."

The women watched until Bonnie left the clearing through another grove of trees near the road they'd walked to get here.

"She's an interesting character. Last night she was standoffish and disengaged while her sister was the one who did all the talking and served lemonade and cookies."

"Yook, Mama. Dis pink."

Josie knelt to examine the pebble Olivia held out. "It does have some pink in it."

"I caught one!" Nate's pole arched toward the water. He struggled to wind the line as the dads ran to the pier to help.

"Lord, please don't let it be something we have to clean and eat," Dana prayed aloud.

"Not a fish fan?"

"Only when it comes from a store or a restaurant."

"Come on guys, let's go see what Nate caught." Josie gathered the triplets, taking each of the boys by the hand while Dana took Olivia, and together they hurried toward the pier.

A mechanical thwack of rotary blades drowned out the rippling of the creek. The trees at the far end of the lake began to sway violently, though no wind stirred the valley. Both families, momentarily forgetting the fish on the line, turned their attention to the commotion as a chopper rose from behind the tree line. They watched it ascend and veer to the east over the shorter of the peaks flanking the campground.

"What do you think that was all about?" asked Dana.

Josie raised her eyebrows. "I bet it has something to do with Silver Mountain's resident Annie Oakley."

Chapter 14

Dana

Dana sat at the picnic table, fingers poised over her keyboard, her focus everywhere but on her manuscript. Her eyes flitted from the screen to the camper, where the triplets' screams punctuated their battle against afternoon naps. If the noise in the Winnie carried all the way out here, then any loud tent conversations would also drift into the camper—something to file for later.

Will and Leah had gone to the visitor center in pursuit of Wi-Fi, promising to check on Dana's dad. At the edge of the campsite, Nate and Adam wrestled with a hammock, struggling to string it between two trees. The downtime should have given Dana a perfect opportunity to squeeze in some writing, but her thoughts kept returning to Bonnie.

Clearly, the proprietor hadn't gone to the visitor center to open shop after completing her rounds, so what was she up to in the woods with a rifle? There was no way the helicopter ascending from the very spot where Bonnie slipped into the forest was a coincidence.

Dana would never find words to write until she satisfied her curiosity. "Boys, I'm going to walk the dog. Don't wander off." She and Harvey retraced the path they'd taken this morning to the lake. They angled left past the clearing, heading toward the tree line where Josie first spotted Bonnie.

Sunlight filtered through thick foliage, casting eerie shadows and filling the forest with a sense of foreboding. She took a few tentative steps into the grove and scanned the area.

Yesterday in the car, Leah strong-armed Dana into listening to a true crime podcast about a girl who vanished in the woods. The haunting tale led to Will and Dana spending the next hour hammering safety guidelines into the kids, like never wander into dark, creepy woods alone. Yet here she was, breaking her own rule.

She patted Harvey. "You'll protect me, won't you, boy?"

He panted and licked her hand.

Strapped to a tree several yards ahead was a rectangular camouflage box with a lens. A trail camera that would capture Dana eyeing it like a nosy Nancy.

Her hand flew to her head. She swept a rogue strand of hair out of her eyes, hoping she wouldn't be mistaken for a disheveled sasquatch whenever the camera's owner eventually checked the footage. She then backtracked into the clearing and trekked to the far end of the lake where Bonnie slipped away this morning.

Beyond the clearing, a thin line of trees was all that separated the lake from another meadow. This one featured a metal building, an empty helipad, and a windsock fluttering lazily in the breeze. A small parking lot contained a handful of cars and a larger golf cart than the one Bonnie used for her rounds. How many golf carts did one campground need?

A paved road extended from the helipad to the highway, branching off toward the campground. Curious, Dana followed it, confirming that it connected to the visitor center parking lot.

Will waved from the patio, but Leah never looked up

from her phone.

"Hey hon, where did you come from?"

She leaned in close and spoke in a stage whisper. "Did you know that road leads to a helipad?"

"Not surprising since we saw a helicopter take off from there this morning. Are you procrastinating writing by snooping?" Will stood and offered Dana his seat, which she declined. "They're two nice old ladies. Leave it alone and get back to work."

She told him about the trail camera. "Do you think Bonnie was hunting out there with that rifle?"

Will wore an even expression. "I don't know what's more incredible—that my city slicker wife identified a trail cam or that she recognized a rifle a hundred yards away."

Even though Dana had never seen a trail camera until today, she'd googled them after a recent news story credited one with a missing child's discovery. "I'm writing a crime novel. Do you really think I haven't researched every firearm there is?"

"I think we need to clear your browser history." He smirked. "Your dad and his goofball mutt are fine, by the way."

"Oh good. Did you ask him about the new cleaning lady?" Dana fished for her name. Maddie, was it?

Will tapped on his phone screen. "Didn't occur to me, but I'll ask."

She looked over his shoulder and tilted her chin toward the log cabin. "Are the sisters working?"

He shrugged. "The small one came out and offered me coffee, but she left and went next door. I don't know who's minding the store now."

Dana put the end of Harvey's leash in Will's hand, crossed the patio, and entered the cabin.

A woman wearing heavy-rimmed glasses looked up from the book she was reading at the desk. "How can I help you today?"

"My family is staying in site number twelve, and this morning we saw a helicopter take off from right over there." Dana pointed in the direction of the helipad.

"Ah yes. That would be my Aunt Bonnie."

"Right, I heard she was a pilot."

The woman slipped a bookmark in her place and closed the cozy mystery bearing a catchy title. "She's a retired naval aviator. Flew in the Persian Gulf War. There's not much Aunt Bonnie hasn't done."

Dana darted a glance around the cabin. "I wouldn't have guessed a campground off the highway needed helicopter access." She bit her lip. Bonnie's niece would have been well within her rights to tell her to mind her own business.

"You're right—the campground usually runs quietly." The niece gathered a stack of papers, tapping them against the desk to straighten the edges. "But choppers are a lifesaver when hikers get lost or injured. Bonnie flies search and rescue all over southern Colorado."

Dana's breath hitched. "Oh no! Is someone in danger?" Warmth crept up her neck. She felt like a heel for suspecting Bonnie of nefarious acts while she was out saving lives.

"No, everyone's fine." The niece winked. "The chopper also comes in handy when my aunt has business up in Grand Junction or Colorado Springs."

"I'm Dana, by the way. Nosy vacationer extraordinaire."

The woman stood and walked around the desk. "I'm Valerie. I live in town and come to help out and keep an eye on my mom and Bonnie a couple of days a week."

Dana smiled and shook Valerie's hand. "Your mom must be Frances. She fed my kids chocolate chip cookies last night."

"That's her. But don't let the baking fool you. She's as much a spitfire as her little sister. They keep me on my toes."

Dana chuckled. "I know a little something about that. My dad is every bit the handful my three kids are."

Valerie's gaze settled on the window looking onto the patio. "Did he come with you this week? Maybe we should introduce him to my mom so they can keep each other out of trouble." Did she think Will was Dana's dad?

"He's back in Texas. Probably grateful for a break from us. He coaches my youngest son's robotics team, and helped teach my daughter how to drive. Comes to all her soccer games. We have a lot of together time." She left out that a good portion of their together time was spent in doctor's appointments.

Dana had planned to wrap up the conversation and return to the campsite, but since she was already prying, she might as well go for broke. "Do people hunt in the woods around here?"

Valerie folded her arms. "We don't allow it on this property, and it's too early for game hunting season anyway."

Dana bit her lip, trying to work out her word choice. "It's just that…well, I saw a trail camera out past the lake."

"Oh." Valerie waved away Dana's concern. "You have nothing to worry about. We have a few trail cameras around to monitor wildlife, but it's strictly for safety reasons. If bears or wildcats get too comfortable coming into camp, they pose a risk to the guests. Could also mean someone is feeding them or being careless with their food storage."

Nothing about that put Dana's mind at ease. She scratched her head just behind her ear. "Should I be worried that Bonnie was carrying a rifle across the meadow to the helicopter?"

A flicker of alarm crossed Valerie's face before a reassuring smile replaced it. "I'm sure it's nothing. Aunt Bonnie likes to be prepared. Military training and all." She shoved her hands in her back pockets. "Anyway, we're glad you're here. Let us know if there's anything you guys need."

Dana took that as her cue to say goodbye. She stepped onto the patio and joined Will and Leah for the walk back to the campsite. "Why don't we get the boys and hike up to that waterfall Bonnie mentioned?"

As Will rounded up Nate and Adam, Dana tapped lightly on the door of the Winnie. A bleary-eyed Josie answered.

"I don't guess now's a good time for y'all to join us on a hike up to the waterfall."

"Thanks for the offer, but my lunch didn't agree with me." Josie clutched her abdomen. "I know what I said earlier, but I'm not in the mood to herd my feral cats up the side of a mountain after all."

Dana touched her friend's arm. "Want me to bring over the first aid kit? I brought meds for every conceivable ailment."

"Not yet, but I may hit you up later if it gets worse."

"Feel better. And if we're not back by dark, send Hunter to the visitor center to form a search party." She winked, only half joking.

Adam struggled to pull his backpack onto his shoulders. He bounced to get the straps up and staggered backward.

"Son," said Will. "That's too heavy for you to wear hiking. What have you got in there, rocks?"

The youngest Harding gave his dad a cold stare. The angst of adolescence was fast approaching with this one.

"Dad, it's common sense that you don't go into the woods without basic survival gear."

Dana tugged the pack off Adam and set it on the picnic table. "True, but if you overpack, you're going to get hurt. Let's see what we can redistribute or leave behind." She emptied the contents onto the table.

He'd packed a first aid kit that almost put hers to shame along with a water filtration straw, two pairs of socks, a survival knife, and compass. The family could eat for a week on the food he'd brought. He had taken his school essay to heart and planned for every contingency.

"It's a three-mile hike, round trip, so let's leave the paracord here." Will pushed aside a bundle of cord about the size of a skein of yarn and held up a road flare and a heavy-duty Maglite. "Where did all this come from?"

Adam shrugged. "Mom's computer. It's always logged into her Amazon account."

"What?" Dana turned to Will with a raised eyebrow. "I thought you were the one who ordered all the survival gear."

Leah threw her hands up. "Are we doing this or not? The light will be all wrong for photos by the time we get to the falls if y'all don't hurry up."

"Why don't you get a head start, and we'll catch up in a minute?" Dana suggested as she continued picking through Adam's stash.

"No." Adam shook his head emphatically. "We stick together. That's the rule."

Dana opened his first aid kit and removed two bandages and an antiseptic wipe. "Let's just take these. If someone does get hurt, we will be close enough to camp to come back and get the big kit." She put the three items into the backpack. "We also won't need that compass on a marked trail."

Adam grabbed the filtration straw.

"We have water bottles, and three miles isn't far. Let's leave that here, too."

Adam glared at her defiantly. "The straw goes where I

go." He shoved it into his bag. "Same for the Firestarter kit and mylar blanket." He pulled the backpack on once more, now several pounds lighter, and hooked a walkie-talkie onto his waistband. "Channel two?"

Will checked his radio. "Roger that."

Dana raked the discarded contents of the backpack into the dry-goods box. "Think it's okay to leave this out while we're gone?"

"Better safe than sorry." Will hefted up the box and loaded it into the back of the Tahoe. Then he flung his arm over Adam's shoulder. "Fall out, Iron Robot."

Leah rolled her eyes and marched up the hill. "Boys are so weird."

Nate overtook his sister when she stopped to pose for a selfie. Will and Adam kept to the middle of the pack, while Dana and Harvey brought up the rear.

Dana had done nothing to train for hiking uphill at 10,000 feet and regretted suggesting it. Fifteen minutes in, she peeled off her hoodie and tied it around her waist. Her lungs burned, and she fought to hide her panting whenever they met other hikers coming down. No way would strangers hear her gasping for air.

After an hour, Nate stopped in the middle of the trail. "Shouldn't we have reached the waterfall by now?"

"Well, we stopped for Mom to take a water break twice," said Leah.

Dana put her hands on her hips to cool her armpits and slow her heart rate. "Hey. Hydration is important for all of us."

Will surveyed the area and pulled out his phone. "Still no signal. Could we have taken a wrong turn in that clearing?"

Everyone shrugged.

"Man, I wish I had my compass right about now," said Adam.

So did Dana. Maybe they could angle the reflective

blanket toward the sunlight and send a signal for help.

Then again, maybe not. A cloud passed in front of the sun, draping the mountainside in muted grays. She was no meteorologist, but it looked like a summer shower might be headed their way.

"The waterfall must be close. We're probably just moving slower than we thought." Will turned to Dana. "Think you can pick up the pace a little?"

She scowled and tugged the leash. "Come on, Harv." Indignation proved to be a powerful motivator as she held the lead for several minutes. The path cut through a meadow where she sidestepped a cow patty and stopped. "Do cattle run freely in the national forest, or are we trespassing on the ranch land Bonnie mentioned?"

Will turned a circle as he surveyed the meadow. "I think we should assume we've entered private property, or else she wouldn't have bothered bringing it up."

"Why are there no signs up here?" asked Leah. "It's like the mountain *wants* us to get lost."

The only sign Dana had seen since they left the campground was a trail marker at the one-mile point. "I think we should backtrack."

Leah clicked a pouty selfie with her casted hand holding her empty water bottle upside down. "I'm thirsty."

Adam shimmied out of his backpack and dug through it. "Here." He handed a water bottle to his sister. "Give me your empty." He shook the pack to make room to zip it. He'd obviously refilled the bag with most of its original contents when Dana wasn't looking.

Retracing their steps meant a temporary reprieve from the uphill climb. The stabbing in Dana's lungs subsided, but her relief was short-lived as aching settled into her knees. She opened her mouth to request another break when they came upon an overgrown fork in the trail. Two wooden arrows partially concealed by shrubbery indicated Summit Trail to the left and Beaver Creek to the right.

Dana braced herself against a boulder and stretched her quadriceps. Harvey collapsed on the dirt path panting.

Will scrutinized each trail and scratched his head. "This must be where we got off course. To the falls we go."

Dana nudged Harvey back up. "Yay, uphill again."

After another grueling stretch, they reached a slender stream of water dribbling over a two-story ledge. Dana hadn't expected Niagara Falls, but what a letdown after the work it took to get there. Craggy rocks and overgrowth prevented them from getting a closer look, but there wasn't much to see.

Will slung his arm over Dana's shoulder. "It's a bit underwhelming, isn't it?"

She nodded. "You wanna be the one to tell Bonnie she sold us a false bill of goods?"

"Definitely not. It's probably the running camp joke. All summer she talks flatlanders into trekking up here, and no one will admit that it wasn't what they expected, so the legend of Summit Falls lives another day."

"Colorado's tourism conspiracy." Dana looked across the mountainside into the valley below. Columbine, paintbrush, and fireweed peppered the landscape in bursts of purple, white, and red. "The scenery really is pretty though. I'm glad we didn't miss this view." A cool breeze sent a shiver through her, prompting her to pull on her hoodie again.

Will pointed out the gray clouds building in the distance. "If we'd taken another wrong path, we would have missed it all." He cupped his hand around his mouth and called to the kids, who were scaling rocks and taking photos, "Let's head out before we get wet."

Dana reached down to reassure Harvey who pressed against her leg. She glanced at the deepening charcoal sky. "And make it quick!" A droplet struck her cheek, then another.

Lightning illuminated the ridge followed by a rumble

of thunder that all but drowned out Harvey's whimper.

And just like that, Dana unlocked a new level in her ever-growing list of camping fears.

Chapter 15

Nate balanced on a cattle guard. "I'm pretty sure I would have remembered crossing this thing on the way up."

"Are you kidding me?" Leah threw up her hands. "How are we lost again?"

Rain pelted them, and the wind whipped up the side of the mountain.

The trail grew slick, and Dana stumbled several times. "Let's find shelter until the storm passes or else we are never getting off this mountain."

The family huddled in a thicket as Adam fished through his pack. He produced the mylar emergency blanket and unfolded it. "We can use this as an umbrella while we wait." Adam's resourcefulness was the only thing keeping them from being the feature story on tomorrow's evening news.

Dana and Will held the edges of the mylar, shielding the family from the deluge as best they could while she mentally kicked herself for not tucking rain ponchos into that backpack.

"This thing isn't going to attract lightning, is it?" Leah asked as Harvey licked rivulets of water dripping off her cast.

Adam scowled at her. "It's plastic, not metal. But you can go stand out there if you're worried."

Dana stifled a laugh and silently prayed that Leah

wouldn't punish her little brother later for challenging her. Before long, her shoulder cramped from holding up the plastic sheet and bracing it against the wind.

Finally, the rain let up. Darkness had settled in, turning the muddy trail into even more of a challenge. Adam flicked on a headlamp from his trusty pack, its beam cutting through the gloom. He rummaged inside and pulled out a dry pair of socks.

"Why are you bothering to change your socks when your shoes are soaked?" Leah asked, her cutting tone honed to perfection over her seven teenage years—though some days, it felt more like decades.

He scowled as he traded his wet socks for dry. "The wetter the socks, the bigger the blisters."

"Is that true?" Nate peered into the backpack. "You got another pair in there for me?"

"Mom took 'em out." Adam sent his mom an accusing glare.

"You thought of everything, didn't you, son?" Will used the flashlight on his phone to illuminate the trail.

Adam hitched the straps back onto his shoulders. "You know why people die in the wilderness? Because they underestimate nature and don't plan ahead. How am I the only one who gets this? I'm ten."

Dana bit back a retort, properly chastened. If they made it back to camp in one piece, the next time they ventured beyond the tent, she'd prepare like her children's lives depended on it—because they did. Despite all the careful packing at home, this hike had caught her completely off guard. She swept her phone light over the uneven ground. "How can we be sure we're back on the right path?"

Will shone his light ahead. "Since the trail slopes downward, we're more or less heading in the right direction."

"It's the 'more or less' I have a problem with," said Dana.

"No! This can *not* be happening," Leah moaned. "My battery is literally dead. I can't see anything now."

Wordlessly, Adam pulled a glowstick from his bag, snapped it, and handed it to his sister.

Without warning, Harvey lunged in pursuit of an unseen threat, knocking Dana off balance. She skidded on the slope, breaking her fall with one hand while keeping a death grip on the leash with the other.

"Mom!" Leah shrieked. "Are you okay?" She took the leash and scolded Harvey. "Bad dog. Look what you did."

Blood oozed from the heel of Dana's searing hand. Debris clung to the wound.

Will raced back up the trail and pulled Dana to her feet. He checked her over and cradled her hand in his. "Are you bleeding anywhere else?"

She rotated to check her thigh where her already damp pants were now also coated in mud. "That's it as far as I can tell, but I'm sure my whole body's going to hurt tomorrow."

Adam inspected his mother's hand and pursed his lips. "Bet you wish we had a first aid kit, huh?"

She recoiled at the blinding headlamp. "Yeah, yeah. Hand over a Band-aid, and I'll worry about disinfecting it after I shower." She winced at her own insensitivity and bit her lip. Adam had been right all along, and she owed him an apology. "Hey, kiddo. I'm sorry. I should have listened to you and been more prepared. Thank you for having my back."

He smiled and applied the bandage to her hand.

A while later, the family reached the base of the mountain and crossed the road, but the campground was nowhere in sight.

Will walked ahead several yards. "This mountain is cursed. Or haunted or something. The campground should be right here." He was lucky he was out of reach because Dana would have smacked him on the back of the head for saying that in front of the kids after what they'd just been through.

Leah hugged her arms across her stomach. "I'm scared."

Dana pulled her close. "We're going to be fine. As soon as we get back to camp, we'll build a nice fire and get dinner going."

Adam handed out granola bars from his backpack. The emergency blanket hung off his shoulders. "Not on wet wood, we won't."

Nate greedily bit into the bar. "Dude, you should change your handle from Iron Robot to Bear Grylls."

"If Mom hadn't taken the neon flagging tape out of my bag, we could have marked the trail and not gotten lost in the first place."

Dana stiffened. "Well, if I hadn't taken stuff out, you would have fallen off the mountain hours ago because your backpack was way too heavy."

"We could've taken turns carrying it," grumbled Leah. Lies. She would have used her broken wrist as an excuse to avoid shlepping the pack.

Will called back to them, "Hey, I see a streetlight up here."

The boys jogged to catch up to their dad. Leah and Dana linked arms and followed at a slow clip to allow Harvey to keep up.

"I bet this dog doesn't even get out of the tent tomorrow. His feet are probably blistered," said Leah.

Dana cringed. She hadn't considered how hiking barefoot on gravel and rocks would affect the dog. She stooped to pat him. "I'm sorry, fella. We're almost home, and I'll give you a big treat."

Leah harumphed. "The tent is *not* home."

As they approached the light, disappointment washed over Dana. Instead of the campground, they'd happened upon a lone cabin with a light on a telephone pole at the end of the drive.

The kids talked over one another as panic set in.

"We're lost!" Adam's problem-solving mindset had reached its threshold.

Will held up his phone. "How are there no bars in this god-forsaken state?"

A light glowed from the cabin's window, and an ancient, two-toned Suburban sat in the gravel driveway. Dana glanced at her watch. "Let's just knock and ask for directions."

A hushed argument erupted among the kids as they debated the merits of seeking help versus the risks of stranger danger.

The porch light flicked on, and the front door opened. The kids ducked behind Will and Dana, and Harvey let out one warning bark.

A heavyset man in a flannel shirt stepped onto the porch. "Can I help you folks?"

Will held up his hand in a tentative wave. "Yes sir. We got caught in the storm up on Summit Trail, and we're turned around. Could you point us toward Silver Mountain Campground?"

The man scratched his head. "Silver Mountain, you say? You sure did get turned around." He pointed in the direction they'd just come from. "It's a little over a mile down that way."

Five Hardings groaned in unison.

"Why don't you let me give you a lift? I imagine you all are ready for dry clothes and a hot meal."

Five heads bobbed in unison.

The man waved them over as he walked to the Suburban. Will took the passenger seat while Dana and the kids squeezed into the middle row. Without the usual third row, an open space stretched behind them. Dana sent up a quick prayer, hoping it had been removed for hauling furniture, not body bags. Harvey stood alert in the back, his head resting on Nate's shoulder.

The man introduced himself as Tarence. "If you're staying at Silver Mountain, you'll have met Frances and Bonnie by now. The wife and I have known them for years. Rumor has it they're secretly billionaires, but you wouldn't know it to look at them."

Dana's ears pricked at the mention of fresh mystery surrounding the campground owners. "I guess that would explain their helicopter."

Will turned and cut his eyes at her, a warning not to pry.

"Bonnie and her chopper are legends in these parts," said Tarence. "If not for them, the mountains would claim many more victims than they do."

The Suburban bounced off the highway and onto the campground service road. "Here we are. Safe and sound. I can let you out at your—" He didn't finish his thought. The entire campground was shrouded in darkness, save for the owners' cabin and a group of people with lanterns and flashlights clustered on the porch of the visitor center.

Tarence put the SUV in park and rolled down his window. "What's going on?"

"Missing hikers," called a bystander.

The Hardings piled out, and Harvey leaped over the seat to join them.

"These the hikers you're looking for?" Tarence called.

Hunter pushed to the front of the group. "Thank you, Jesus. Where have y'all been? Bonnie's inside on a landline trying to get searchers out."

Dana's eyes grew round, and she grabbed Hunter's arm. "You didn't call my dad, did you?" The only thing worse right now than a search party convening to look for them would be upsetting her dad.

"Of course not. I wouldn't worry him unnecessarily."

Adam surveyed the parking lot. "Why is it so dark?"

"Storm knocked out the power," said Hunter.

Fueled by her urgency to get off the mountain, Dana's hand hadn't bothered her much. However, now that the family was safe, it throbbed. She flexed her fingers, eager to clean the wound and disinfect it with one of their multiple first aid kits. "How are Josie and the kids?"

"We've got a gas generator, so they're fine." Hunter lifted his trucker cap, scratched his head, and replaced it. "Jos isn't feeling great, but she'll be relieved that y'all are safe." He gave them an appraising look. "I'm going to head back now and give her the good news. See you there." Hunter jogged away, the beam of his flashlight bouncing with each step.

Will thanked Tarence for the ride and called off the rescue mission. "Folks, I apologize that you had to get out tonight, but my family and I appreciate your concern."

Bonnie stepped out with a kerosine lantern and looked them over with a careful eye. She pointed at Leah's cast. "You had that when you left here, right?"

The teen nodded. "Soccer injury."

"Missed the sign in the rain and crossed the pasture, huh." Bonnie hadn't phrased it as a question.

Will ran a hand over his damp hair. "We were watching for them, but the overgrowth and the rain got the better of us."

"I warned the Forest Service this would happen. If they won't get out here and do something about their signage, I'll have to take care of it myself."

Frances put her hand on her sister's arm. "The important thing is that everyone's safe." She turned to the Hardings. "Come in and let me make you some sandwiches."

The kids' faces lit up at the mention of food.

Dana tried to argue that they couldn't impose, but Frances ignored her protests. "Nonsense. The power's out, and you're gonna have a tough time getting a fire going on wet wood."

"I told you so," Adam whispered to Dana.

"Let me just fill their bellies and give you one less thing to worry about tonight." Frances even invited Harvey to come along.

The Hardings followed Frances to her cabin, which was unaffected by the power outage.

As they got closer, the whirr of a motor grew louder.

"Is someone mowing your yard in the dark?" asked Adam.

Frances laughed. "No, dear. That's the generator. They're a must for anyone living on this mountain year-round."

The log cabin was nothing like Dana had imagined after hearing about last night's cookie visit. She'd pictured a dark, small space with dated, rustic decor and animal heads mounted on the walls. Instead, the spacious interior boasted a stone fireplace between floor-to-ceiling windows. In the daylight, they would offer panoramic views of snowy peaks reflected in the meadow water, just like the photo featured on the campground's website. The sisters had spared no expense furnishing their mountain hideaway.

Sure enough, a stuffed bear guarded the dining area, but rather than the round table cluttered with cookie racks Dana had envisioned, it was a grand room with a long, custom oak table that would easily seat twenty. A modern highchair stood against one wall, awaiting a little one's arrival.

Everyone followed their hostess into the kitchen and washed their hands.

"Frances, your home is lovely," said Will. "I noticed your trophy bear. Did you or Bonnie shoot it?"

"Heavens no. It came with the campground. Its home was the old visitor center until last winter when a pipe burst. We moved it up here while the building was renovated, and it just stayed." She chuckled as she opened the fridge. "Sometimes I scoot it around the house on a furniture dolly and scare the tar out of Bonnie."

Dana took the cold cuts, cheese, and condiments Frances passed her and set them on the granite counter. "I'm surprised at you picking on your little sister like that."

"It's payback for all the rotten things she did to me when we were kids. She's a gem though." Frances took inventory of the sandwich fixings and set a stack of paper plates on the table. "Bonnie's been too busy saving the world to settle down and have a family of her own, but I've got plenty to share. We get along well until she tries to treat me like one of her military subordinates."

Leah spread mayo on slices of bread. "Is that when you scare the tar out of her, Miss Frances?"

"Oh no, dear. I save it until she least expects it." Frances giggled to herself. "One time I put the bear in her shower." After a beat, she added, "That one might have been pushing it. Since she's the only one who can fly the chopper, I don't actually want to give her a heart attack."

Dana winced. Two years ago, she'd walked in on her dad giving CPR to his neighbor Rita before paramedics arrived. The memory still haunted her dreams. "I can see why your daughter Valerie says you and Bonnie keep her on her toes."

Frances pulled snack cakes and chips from the pantry. "I adore my daughter, but she's a fuddy duddy. Thinks we're too old to live out here. If she had her way, we'd have signed this place over to her long ago and resigned ourselves to playing bridge in a retirement home."

Leah brandished the butter knife. "But you're not even that old."

Will and Dana both cast disapproving looks at their daughter.

"What?" said Leah. "Pops is older than Miss Frances, and he still lives on his own."

Frances patted her arm. "You're right. I'm old, but I'm

not *that* old."

Dana had grown accustomed to watching for changes in her dad's behavior that might show he couldn't live alone anymore, but she saw none of those signs in Frances or Bonnie. There had to be another reason Valerie wanted them off the property, and she intended to find out.

Chapter 16

Just as the Hardings left Frances's cabin, the rain began falling again. Dana had scarcely warmed up, her damp clothes still clinging to her, before they ventured back into the night. Adam donned his headlamp and wordlessly handed Leah back the glowstick he'd stashed before they'd gotten into Tarence's SUV. The only other light along the way came from the occasional camper window.

Dana tucked her head and jogged back to the campsite, not even bothering to try and keep up with her much faster family. Even Harvey raced back as though he'd had enough of the great outdoors for one day.

She arrived to find Josie standing in the Winnie's doorway, her face tight with worry. "You guys had me scared to death.'" Josie stepped down, wincing slightly before masking it. "At first, I thought you were pranking us since you said to call for help if you weren't back by dark." Her hand pressed into her side as though covering an injury. "Then I started to panic thinking Hunter and I might have to raise our kids by ourselves." Josie wrapped her arms around Dana before she could stop her. "I'm so relieved you're safe." She pulled back and wiped her wet hands on her sweats. "Soaked and filthy, but safe."

"I tried to warn you not to do that." Dana studied her friend's face. "Are you okay? You don't look like you're feeling any better."

"I'm sure I just need a good night's sleep. The triplets are finally down, and I'm going to turn in early myself." Josie smiled, but it didn't reach her eyes.

"Fine, but come get me if you feel worse." Dana's gaze followed Josie as she made her way into the camper, her movements slow and labored, each step up a visible effort. Dana said a prayer Josie would be better by morning.

Will instructed the kids to leave their muddy shoes on the enclosed porch rather than bringing them into the tent. "Just get the stuff you need to shower, and don't get the beds dirty."

Adam pointed at the wet dog nosing his way into the tent. "What about Harvey?"

Will chewed his lip. "We'll take him with us and spray him off. It's the best we can do tonight."

So much for those pristine living quarters Will was sure they'd keep. Maybe in the future, their vacations wouldn't have to include the furry child.

Dana handed out trash bags to keep their clean clothes dry on the walk to the bathrooms. "When you're done, drop your dirty stuff in, and we'll worry about it tomorrow."

Showering by flashlight would be a challenge, but Dana couldn't wait to scrub away the muck and mud. She turned on the faucet, waiting for the hot stream that never came.

"Mom, why won't the water heat up?" Leah called from the next stall.

"The water heater must be electric."

"Ugh! I hate camping."

Dana couldn't agree more. "Screw it. I'm going in." She plunged under the icy spray, her breath sucked away by the shock, and jumped right back out. She'd underestimated the frigidity of the mountain water. She shrieked as she stuck one arm beneath the stream and silently questioned all her life choices that led up to this moment.

A similar squeal emanated from the men's side of the wall.

After the briefest showers of their lives, Dana and Leah consolidated their belongings into one bag, and Dana improvised a rain poncho for Leah out of the second one. They raced back to the tent, shivering.

Leah hunkered down in her sleeping bag, teeth chattering. "Wh-what d-do you th-think is taking D-Dad and the b-boys s-so long?"

"Harvey." Dana dug through her suitcase for something less rain-drenched to put on. "You know the second he gets in here, he'll shake and get the whole tent wet." What would be harder to fall asleep to—the smell of wet dog, or the thumping of rain on nylon?

"I wasn't made to live without electricity. I miss the heater, and my phone's dead." Even muffled under a pile of blankets, Leah's frustration came through clearly. "It's bad enough not being able to text my friends or check Instagram, but now I can't even read or listen to music. We're going to freeze to death."

Dana sympathized. She'd been counting on a hot shower to relieve her sore muscles after the hike. Now they ached even more, but the solution was right in the Tahoe. She pulled Leah's garbage bag over her head and dashed outside. Moments later, she returned, dripping but victorious, lugging the generator tucked protectively beneath the garbage bag. She set it on her suitcase and quickly plugged in a charger, the overhead light, and—most importantly—the space heater.

"Mom, you're my hero." There was a phrase that didn't get spoken nearly often enough.

The guys made it back from the bathrooms, and Nate and Adam immediately dove under their covers.

"Ah," Will groaned. "You know what we forgot?"

When no one spoke, he answered himself. "The dog bowl and the ice chest." Of course they had. Nothing else today had gone right, so why would they have remembered the cardinal rule of the campground?

Will slipped on Dana's flip-flops and left. When he returned, he set the ice chest, with the food bowl atop the lid, just inside the door.

"You're not going to put it in the Tahoe?" Dana asked.

"It's raining, and my heels are hanging off the back of your shoes. I'm not walking any extra steps tonight."

Dana shook her head. "Why didn't you just put on your own shoes? You know that bowl is going to get knocked off, and dogfood will go everywhere."

Will's tone turned sharp. "No one touch the dog bowl."

The intensity of the moment was punctuated by the heater and the light both shutting off.

"What just happened?" whispered Adam in the darkness.

Will groused, "Who thought it would be a good idea to power a fifteen-hundred-watt heater and a bunch of other stuff with the solar generator that only has a sixteen-hundred-watt output?"

Dana bristled. "The same person who thinks you sound like a word problem on a fourth-grade math test."

The kids giggled.

"If you'd worked through this word problem first, we could have avoided blowing the motor out on expensive generat—" Will yelped.

Dana shone a flashlight on him.

His jaw flexed as he clutched his hand against his thigh. "Dana, if the screen on that space heater gets hot enough to burn skin, then it's a fire hazard in a tent. You should know that."

"Keep your voice down," Dana said through gritted teeth. She'd tried to give him grace for his bad mood after such a harrowing evening, but he was working her last nerve. "Hunter and Josie will hear you." She refrained from pointing out that he hadn't minded the heater last night or that the metal screen wasn't close enough to anything to *be* a fire hazard. "You should have known not to touch it."

"I bumped into it trying to get into bed in the dark."

Dana scooted out of her sleeping bag again and fumbled for the first aid kit. "Put some ice on it, and I'll get the burn spray."

The dog bowl skated off the ice chest's tilted lid, scattering kibble across the tent floor. Dana's nails dug into her palm as she fought the urge to blurt, "I told you so." For several seconds, the only sound was Harvey crunching dry morsels in the dark.

Will closed the ice chest and wordlessly zipped himself into his sleeping bag.

"Don't you still need the burn spray?" Dana asked.

"I'll stick my hand out, and the cold air will soothe it." After a beat, he snickered. Soon, the family erupted into laughter.

When they finally caught their breath, Leah spoke. "For everything that went wrong today, at least one thing was spot on. Adam and his backpack saved us from even worse disaster. He's the MVP."

"Mm-hmm. Good job, little bro," said Nate.

Adam sat up and shone his flashlight in each of their faces. "I hope y'all learned a lesson. I tried to tell you to bring survival gear and snacks. Duh."

Leah leaned across the void and yanked the light from him. "You're about to learn a lesson on the dangers of blinding people."

"Mo-om, Leah took my flashlight."

"Tattle tale."

A distant howl cut through their bickering. Harvey answered it with a warning bark.

"Was that a wolf?" Adam stage-whispered.

"Wolves don't live this far south. It's probably a coyote," said Nate.

"Oh great. Another apex predator that travels in packs."

Adam shuffled to the bottom of his sleeping bag and pulled it over his head.

While Dana couldn't help but be impressed by Nate's knowledge of population distribution, the idea of coyotes being nearby instead of wolves offered her no more comfort than it did Adam.

Once again, sleep proved elusive. Dana lay awake, reflecting on the time spent with the people who mattered most to her, gratitude warming her despite the lingering chill. She'd gotten what she prayed for—time with her loved ones, but God hadn't given it quite the way she wanted. Next time, she'd be more specific with her prayer requests. The familiar verse from 1 Thessalonians 5:18 settled over her like a comforting quilt. *Give thanks in all circumstances, for this is God's will for you in Christ Jesus*— even in the frigid, soggy ones.

Chapter 17

Josie

The next morning, Josie expected to wake up more refreshed than she had the day before. Despite the working heater and the extra space after she and Hunter swapped beds with the triplets, she never found a position that alleviated the discomfort in her belly. She'd spent most of the night curled in the fetal position and was already awake when the triplets breached the car seat barricade, causing a commotion that probably roused half the campground.

She got up to help change diapers and dress the babies, but she struggled to even stand upright.

"Jos, I think you should lie back down. I've got this." Hunter's two-day scruff gave off a rugged, sexy vibe that would have made her swoon if she'd felt better.

"No, I spent half the day in bed yesterday. I need to get up and move around." She pressed a hand over her tender belly. "Maybe I'm just really constipated."

He flashed her a grin as he slid a fresh diaper under Ben. "And they say romance is dead." His face turned from teasing to concerned.

"What's wrong?" Josie asked.

"You're very pale. Let me feel your head." He held the back of his hand up to her face.

She ducked out of his reach. "Gross. Wash your hands

first."

Outside, Nate and Adam shushed one another while noisily opening and shutting car doors.

"I'm sure Dana has a thermometer in that steamer trunk of a first aid kit, and it sounds like everyone's up."

"I told you, it's nothing, and I don't want to alarm Dana."

The dads cooked breakfast for ten again, and as the ache in Josie's gut continued to intensify, she was grateful to sit idly by watching as they coordinated their efforts between the campfire and the Winnie. She grinned at Harvey who rolled onto his back, soliciting belly rubs from the triplets. She lifted her coffee mug for a cautious sip, but the aroma turned her stomach.

"Dana, if I end up the subject of a *Dateline* special because I've died mysteriously in the San Juan Mountains, promise me you won't let my mom give them embarrassing footage of me practicing the viola with pigtails and braces. And no bare belly pregnancy pics."

Dana put her hands on her hips and tilted her head to the side. "You know pregnancy pics are inevitable. The most intriguing part of the story will be your status as a mom of triplets."

"I mean it." Josie drew a shaky breath and pointed at her neighbor. "I will haunt you."

"I feel like we keep having the same talk over and over—you can't say morbid stuff in front of your children." Dana glanced at Adam, whose wide eyes indicated he'd heard Josie's threat. "And I'd prefer if you didn't say it in front of mine either. They'll have plenty to discuss with a therapist as it is."

Josie pushed herself upright, hoping movement might

shake off the pain. Instead, a searing bolt tore through her side. Her legs buckled, and she collapsed back into the camp chair. Her hands trembled as she leaned over to set her cup on the ground. Even the slow, measured breaths she'd used to weather panic attacks were useless against the stabbing. A low, guttural moan escaped as she doubled over.

Dana crouched in front of her. "You're not teasing, are you?" She felt Josie's forehead and called over her shoulder, "Nate, bring me the first aid kit."

Plastic latches clicked open, followed by a digital beep as Dana ran the device over Josie's forehead. Another beep sounded. She kept her eyes squeezed shut as fire pierced her side.

A small, warm hand patted her cheek. "Mama, you okay?"

Josie wanted to reassure her child, but she leaned over the arm of the chair and vomited instead. All over her coffee cup. Ben began to cry.

Dana gathered Josie's hair into a low ponytail and asked, "Where does it hurt?"

Josie pointed to her lower abdomen on the right side.

Dana ordered Leah and Adam to take the triplets into the camper. "Tell your dad and Hunter to get out here now." She fixed her eyes on Nate. "Go to the visitor center and call 9-1-1. Run."

"What do I tell them?"

"Thirty-five-year-old female with 102 temp, abdominal pain, and vomiting. Possible appendicitis."

Appendicitis? Josie had been mostly kidding when she warned Dana to vet any footage used in her *Dateline* special, but now, real fear pulsed through her. Without medical attention, her condition could be fatal.

Hunter placed a cool washcloth on Josie's face. "Jos, you're gonna be fine, but we need to get you to the hospital."

How far away was it? If she couldn't sit upright in a chair without getting sick, she'd never survive a long car ride.

She shook her head. "The kids."

He leaned his head close to hers. "I can't hear you. What?"

She mustered her strength and fought through the agony to make her voice audible. "The kids."

"We'll take good care of them," Dana said.

Josie collapsed against Hunter and whispered, "Don't let me die."

He scooped her into his arms and placed her in the middle row of the Hardings' Tahoe.

Gravel crunched as a golf cart pulled up next to the SUV. Nate jumped off before it came to a complete stop and ran to his mom. "Bonnie saw me before I could get to the phone."

"I radioed for emergency services." Bonnie inspected Josie. "I don't like her coloring. My chopper can get her to Durango Mercy in a fraction of the time it would take to drive through the mountains." She patted Josie's hand. "Follow me to the helipad."

If Josie had had the strength, she would have protested. She could endure the forty-minute ride and spare everyone the hassle. Hunter slid into the seat next to her, cradling her head in his lap as Will turned the ignition. Each bump was torture, and she was certain they were pushing well past the campground's speed limit.

Will laid her on a leather bench seat in the aircraft and covered her ears with headphones. He sat across from her in a plush captain's chair that backed up to the pilot's seat. Josie had no other helicopter experience with which to compare, but it seemed fancier than any she'd seen on TV. A wave of nausea rolled over her. She clenched her jaw, squeezed her eyes shut, and prayed not to throw up all over the expensive interior.

The headphones muffled the pounding of the blades and allowed her to hear Bonnie's voice on the mic. "Hang tight, sweetie. I've already contacted the hospital staff, and they've cleared us to land on the helipad in just a few minutes. Don't you worry."

The only indication Josie had that they'd become airborne was morning sunlight briefly hitting her eyelids and disappearing as they turned in the direction of Durango. She didn't even feel them touch down, but as soon as the blades stopped, a swarm of hands transferred her from the chopper to a gurney. She may not have felt the landing, but every pebble under the wheels between the helipad and the hospital's double doors sent shockwaves through her.

A physician introduced herself, pressed on Josie's abdomen, then everything went dark.

Chapter 18

Dana

Dana checked her watch and frowned. How had it only been an hour? It felt like three. The triplets were in full chaos mode, scaling everything within reach, including the Winnie's rear bumper ladder. They hurled rocks and chased butterflies with reckless enthusiasm and pestered Harvey to the point of desperation. When the poor dog had finally had enough, he nudged open the tent's zipper with his snout and hid under a pile of blankets.

Time dragged even more slowly with the weight of worry. Josie might be fighting for her life, but without cell service, Dana couldn't even get updates. Her one comfort was that Will had driven straight to the hospital after dropping Josie and Hunter at the helipad and would stay until she was stable. If the triplets ever settled down, Dana could walk to the visitor center and call him.

"Livvie," said Leah. "Spit that out. We don't eat sticks." She poked a finger in between the framework of her cast and scratched at her skin. "I really wish we could childproof nature. These kids are wearing me out."

Dana nodded at Leah's arm. "Why do you keep doing that?"

"Doing what?"

"Messing with your arm. Let me see it." Dana examined the diamond-shaped sections of skin in between the lattices. She pressed Leah's bright red forearm and gingerly turned it over. "Let me see the other one."

Leah grumbled, but she produced her right arm for inspection.

"I think you're sunburned, but only under the cast." Dana frowned, trying to figure out the best way to treat it.

"That tracks. I was afraid to get sunscreen on it. The doctor never said which chemicals can deteriorate the material of the cast."

"Hm." Dana marveled at her brilliant daughter's diligence. "Good thinking, but maybe we risk deterioration to keep you from toasting yourself."

Adam jogged over to the picnic table where Dana was combing the first aid kit for a burn remedy. "Mom, can we go to the game room?"

"Sure, in a sec." She squirted a dollop of aloe into each section of skin. "You're going to have weird tan lines when this thing comes off."

"I don't care." Leah shrugged. "It's still better than the other kind of cast. Hunter told me horror stories about his and how his mom had to put his arm in garbage bags and seal them with duct tape just so he could shower. He said when they cut it off his mom threw up from the smell."

Nate unfolded the two umbrella strollers and strapped Olivia and Ben into the double. "Uh Mom, where's Connor?"

Dana scoured the campsite, heart racing. He wasn't in the tent or the Winnie. They fanned out, screaming Connor's name. Dana jogged up the road. She'd promised Josie they would take care of her babies, and one was already missing.

Two sites over, a woman rounded the front of a large fifth wheel camper leading Connor by the hand. "Looking for this?"

Dana scooped him into her arms and swayed back and forth as she hugged him fiercely. "You scared me."

"He just now showed up asking where his mama went." The woman pulled her jacket closed and crossed her arms. "I take it you're his mama."

"No, I'm his neighbor."

The lady cocked her head and shifted her stance. "Where *is* his mother?"

Dana repositioned Connor onto her hip. The last thing she needed was this stranger thinking she was a kidnapper and calling the cops. "She's in the hospital in Durango, appendix probably. Their dad and my husband are with her, leaving my kids and me on triplet duty. We're all staying in site twelve." She patted Connor's chest. "These guys are slippery little buggers." Dana clamped her mouth shut to put the brakes on her overshare.

The woman rocked on her heels. "Triplets? Wow, you've got your hands full!" The second-most popular response—after "bless your heart"—anytime someone learned about the toddler trifecta.

Connor squirmed. "I get down, Dana."

She kept a firm grip on him. "Oh no, I don't trust you. You ran away." She thanked the woman for bringing Connor back and waved. "Sorry we bothered you. We'll keep a closer eye on all of them from here on out." Dana turned to go.

"It was no trouble. I hope his mom's okay."

So did Dana.

Connor patted her face as she carried him to the campsite. "Where Mama go?"

The last time the toddlers had seen their mother, she vomited and could barely speak. Dana pressed her forehead to his. "Your mama got sick, so Daddy took her to the doctor. You have to stay here with Leah, Nate, Adam, and me until they come back. Do you understand?"

"Okay. Gimme down."

Dana followed the boys as they muscled the umbrella strollers uphill toward a stone building. Just inside, to the left, washers and dryers hummed softly in a narrow laundromat. A long table sat between them, its surface littered in stray dryer sheets and an abandoned sock. Dana blinked. If the website for this place had mentioned a laundromat, that detail had been buried under more looming amenities like *vaulted toilets* and *primitive campsites*. She made a mental note to return later with last night's hiking clothes, which were currently dangling from a makeshift clothesline to dry.

Beyond the laundry room, the space opened into a cavernous lodge. A pool table and ping-pong table dominated the center, while club chairs huddled around a fireplace. A low bookcase lined one wall, its shelves stocked with books and board games—though the only available playing surface was a too-small coffee table near the hearth.

Dana hesitated, fingers resting on a stroller buckle. The babies had been cooped up too long, but nothing about this room screamed toddler friendly. At least the fireplace wasn't lit. The clacking of billiard balls echoed through the space, indicating Nate and Adam were setting up a game.

Leah paced between the tables, fully absorbed in her phone. "I don't understand how those two ladies can afford a helicopter, but they don't bother putting in a cell phone tower out here. Or extending the Wi-Fi."

Dana pinched the bridge of her nose, the weight of the day's stress heavy on her. "I'm going to the visitor center to call Pops and to see if your dad sent an update on Josie. Baby Houdini's coming with me." She gripped the handle of the single stroller. "Can I trust you three to watch Ben and Olivia?"

The Harding kids nodded and mumbled vague agreement, but Dana wasn't taking any chances. "I mean it. Guard these two like it's your only job and don't let them out of your sight. We've had all the excitement we need for one day."

Her words seemed to hit home. Even the usually sullen seventeen-year-old muttered a resigned, "Yes, ma'am."

Adam shook off his backpack and handed Dana a walkie-talkie out of it. "Keep this on in case we need you."

She clipped it to her waistband. "What else have you got in there today?"

"Snacks and toys for the you-know-who." He pointed at the strollers.

His survival skills far exceeded what his informative essay had led her to believe. "Impressive, kiddo." She ruffled his hair.

Weariness, no longer dulled by the chaos of Josie's illness and Connor's disappearing act, settled into Dana's bones. "Connor, I think you've gotten heavier since the last time I pushed you in a stroller." Her calves burned as if punishing her for yesterday's hike, and her back ached from sleeping on an air mattress.

"Yeah. I big."

She grinned. Two was such a fun age, full of giggles, boundless energy, and the kind of mischief that kept life interesting. Then again, ten, fourteen, and seventeen had their own charm. Trading diaper changes for school pick-up lines wasn't the worst deal.

As they neared the log cabin, Dana's pocket vibrated wildly. She pulled her phone out, the screen lighting up with a flood of unread messages. Too many to process. Instead of sifting through them, she called Will.

"Hey, I guess you got my text."

She tucked the phone between her cheek and shoulder and pushed Connor to a table. "Actually, no. I just got a signal and called you first."

"They took her back for surgery. It's definitely appendicitis."

"How's Hunter?"

"Pacing and biting his nails. I'm going to stay here with him at least until Josie wakes up. Then I'll see what he wants me to do."

She nodded. "That's good. Do that."

Will cleared his throat. "Dana? There's something else."

"How bad is it?" She closed her eyes and braced for Will's next bombshell. Today had been dramatic enough already.

"How bad is what?"

"The something else."

"Depends on your perspective." He paused like he was gathering his courage to break the news. "Josie will have to spend at least one night here, maybe more, so Marie is on her way up from Albuquerque to help with the kids."

That made sense. When Leah broke her wrist, Dana had been frantic to get to her. She couldn't imagine how Josie's mom must feel with her daughter being airlifted to a hospital for emergency surgery. "Should we plan to leave and go home when Josie gets out?"

"I don't know what she'll feel like doing. Let's play it by ear and help however we can."

Dana agreed. They said goodbye, and she sat on a bistro chair to read her messages.

"Dana. I get out. Peez." Connor flashed puppy dog eyes and a toothy grin.

She lowered her phone and smiled. "Connor, if I let you out of the stroller, you may *not* run away."

He dropped his chin to his chest. "Oh-kay."

She bent to unbuckle his straps, and Connor pressed his hands to her cheeks. "I uv you."

"I love you too, baby." She hugged him and set him on

the ground.

The door to the visitor center opened, and Frances appeared with a paper cup and a carafe. "Just made a fresh pot, and you look like you could use a pick-me-up."

Dana was too exhausted to be offended. She accepted the black coffee, keeping one eye on her charge. "Thanks. I didn't get any caffeine into my system before mayhem ensued this morning."

Frances set the pot on the table and took the seat opposite Dana. "Your friend is the one Bonnie flew up to Mercy, right?" She scanned the patio, even though they were the only three people there. "Where are the rest of the babies?"

"My kids are watching them. I wanted to check on Josie and couldn't trust this one. He slipped past us and went looking for his M-A-M-A."

"Poor thing. My youngest used to disappear on me all the time. I'd have given anything for one of those leashes people are so critical of to keep up with him."

How long was Dana obligated to engage in polite conversation? She just wanted to finish checking her messages, chug this coffee, and get back to the kids before another incident occurred. "Connor, you're getting too far away. I'll be done soon, and we can go." Maybe Frances would take the hint and let her get to it.

"Why don't I entertain Connor for a few minutes?" Frances placed her hand on Dana's arm. "I promise I won't take my eyes off him."

Dana still hadn't talked to her dad since they left home, and she wouldn't be able to focus on the conversation while chasing the two-year-old. "Thank you. I'll just be a few minutes." She clicked on her dad's number and walked to the edge of the patio. Doing so gave her no privacy, but moving any further away would weaken her signal strength.

Frances picked up the coffee pot. "Hey Connor, let's

go see if we can find you a ball in the gift shop." The two entered the visitor center, and Dana followed them with her eyes through the window.

Her dad picked up after three rings.

"Hey Dad, how's it going?"

"Just fine. Patch escaped his collar at the park again. This time he accosted one of the senior citizens in the morning Tai Chi class. I'm sure there'll be a neighborhood petition to get us banned from the park. How's camping treating you?"

Frankly, if that was the worst trouble the two of them were up to, she could rest easy. "Fantastic. When we get home, I'm going to tie a string between two branches for hanging wet towels just so I can keep this pioneer spirit alive all summer."

"Then you better bring some trees back with you. The kids all doing well? How's my granddaughter's cast holding up?"

She returned to the bistro chair and positioned it to where she could see into the gift shop behind the lobby. Connor and Frances bobbed in and out of view, but he appeared to be supervised well enough since the place was still standing.

"The kids are good. Adam's a regular Cub Scout with a backpack full of survival gear." She stopped short of telling him just how much of that gear they'd used yesterday. "The cast was the right choice, being that we got caught in the rain. Hard to sunscreen though. Leah's going to look slightly reptilian when it comes off."

Silence filled the airways as Dana debated how to tell her dad about Josie. The Caraways treated him like an extension of their own family, and he acted as a surrogate grandparent to the triplets. "Dad, Josie's in the hospital. She woke up this morning with appendicitis, and she's in surgery now. I'm sure she'll be fine, but I thought you'd want to know."

He let out a heavy sigh. "When you see her, tell her I'm praying for her." He asked about the triplets and who was with Josie.

Dana explained the current arrangement. "Her mother is driving up to help with the kids late today."

"In that case, I'll be praying for you, too. I don't see Marie and the great outdoors getting along very well."

Through the window, she caught a glimpse of Connor dragging a walking stick. Any second now, that thing would become a sword or a bat and demolish half the gift shop. Where was Frances? "Dad, I better go. If you need us and can't get through, call the campground number, okay?"

"You're two states away. What could I possibly need from you?" He was probably rolling his eyes. "I'm a grown man, Dana. You don't have to keep tabs on me all the time."

She did, but he didn't need to hear it. They said their goodbyes, and she entered the building. "Everyone alright in here?"

Frances strode into view, a large sack looped in the crook of her elbow and Connor's small hand tucked firmly in her grasp. The toddler beamed, holding up a plush teddy bear dressed in a tiny shirt adorned with the campground's logo. His grip on the bear was fierce, as if he'd just won the grand prize at a carnival.

Dana squatted to his eyelevel. "Did you go shopping?"

"We sure did." Frances shook the bag. "Picked out three of everything so the little ones won't fight over who gets what. Put a few treats and souvenirs for *your* kids in here, too."

"Thank you." Dana patted her pockets, realizing too late she hadn't brought any form of payment. "Can you add it to our tab? I don't have my wallet on me."

Frances dismissed the request with a flick of her wrist. "On the house, of course. I wouldn't saddle you with a bill for stuff I picked out. Besides, we let all the kids choose a free memento. By the end of a week of camping, every family deserves a reward for getting out without killing each other."

Dana let out a hesitant laugh and accepted the bag. "That's really kind of you, but with the helicopter ride alone, I'm sure you're losing money on our stay."

"Oh, pish." Frances batted the comment away with both hands. "Between you and me, we're loaded." She made a sweeping gesture toward the visitor center. "We do this for fun."

If so, then why charge guests at all? In fact, why not pay guests to come? Dana said the least awkward reply that came to mind. "That's great. Thank you so much for watching him." She held up the bag. "And for the gifts. I really appreciate it, but I better get back before his siblings turn on the big kids."

Frances patted Connor's back. "You be a sweet boy now." Then she shook Dana's hand. "Don't hesitate to ask if you need anything."

Walkie-talkie beeps and static came over the line. "Mama Bear, this is Iron Robot, come in Mama Bear." Apparently, girls got call signs after all.

Frances's revelation only further piqued Dana's curiosity about the two sisters, but her sleuthing would have to wait. "This is Mama Bear." *Please Lord, no more catastrophes.*

"We have a diaper situation in the game room. Heading back to camp. Over."

Diaper situations she could handle. Dana secured Connor in the stroller and tied the bag of goodies to the handle. "Roger that, Iron Robot. We'll meet you there."

Chapter 19

Josie

"Josie," a muffled voice called from the distance.

Little by little, the thick fog trapping Josie's body lifted. Pain. Helicopter. More pain.

Awareness trickled back to her. She flinched from the bright lights overhead. Something cupped her mouth, echoing her words back to her as she tried to call for help.

"Don't try to speak yet." A woman's voice commanded and soothed at the same time. "You're getting oxygen to help you wake up. Just relax."

Josie's head swam, thick and heavy, like trying to think through molasses.

"You're going to be just fine, but you need to stop moving."

She wasn't moving. Her legs were paralyzed, while tubes and wires held her arms in place. The mask smothered her, pressing the stench of antiseptic plastic into her nostrils. She fought to pry her fingers beneath it and inhale fresh air, but comforting hands covered hers, and a voice she recognized cut through the remaining fog. "Jos, I'm here. Just rest."

Once again, harsh, fluorescent light burned past Josie's eyelids. "How long was I out?"

"A while. How do you feel?" Hunter asked.

Fine except for the fact that she'd abandoned her children in the Colorado wilderness. "You should be with the kids. Are they okay?"

"Dana and Leah are with them. I'm sure they're fine."

Her fingers found the bed controls. She blindly pressed a button, and something beeped.

"Jos, let me help you. What do you need?"

"To sit up." Her voice came out in a ragged whisper, her words scraping her raw throat.

Hunter pressed a button that inclined the bed. "How's that?"

She turned to face him, and a wave of nausea overtook her. "Not good. Lay me back down before I throw up."

A nurse entered and checked monitors near Josie's head. "I'm Annika. Are you in any pain?"

"My ribs hurt, and I'm gonna be sick." Josie's voice barely rose above a whisper.

"I'll give you a shot of Zofran. The surgeon used carbon dioxide gas to inflate your abdominal cavity during the procedure. That's what you feel in your ribs." The nurse fiddled with Josie's IV. "Hopefully we can get you moved into a room soon so your mom can see you."

Josie groaned. Her mother was the reason she'd ended up here in the first place. Maybe not *here,* as in the hospital, but in Colorado. No, that wasn't right either. They'd ended up here because Josie lied. They could've been at home right now, and maybe her appendix wouldn't have gotten infected at all.

"Hunter," Josie whispered. "Why is my mom here?"

"Babe, I had to tell her you were having an emergency appendectomy. What do you think she'd do if she found out later?"

Fair enough. "But why is she *here*?"

He stood straighter, and his mouth formed a thin line. "Come on. You really think she was going to stay in Albuquerque with you in the hospital three and a half hours away? Besides, I'm not leaving your side tonight, so It'll be good for the Hardings to have extra hands with the triplets."

Josie's stomach churned again. "That's not going to go well."

"She'll be Will and Dana's problem. You just worry about healing."

"When can I go home?"

"You'll probably be discharged tomorrow," said Annika. "You're lucky you got here when you did. If your appendix had ruptured, you'd be a guest in our fine establishment for a bit longer."

Josie pressed her head into the pillow and closed her eyes. She'd not only derailed her own family's vacation but the Hardings' too. She deserved whatever punishment God saw fit for her deception, but nothing Dana had done warranted having to deal with her mother unchecked for the next twenty-four hours. Or longer.

Marie Saldana had a knack for being the kindest, most helpful person in the room, until she wasn't. With the flip of a switch, she could morph into a hyper-critical control freak. And given that she wasn't one for roughing it—she'd never even stepped foot inside a camper before, let alone spent the night in one—Josie didn't have high hopes for her mother's best behavior at Silver Mountain.

Hunter pulled Josie's blanket higher on her chest. "I'm going to find Will and let him know you're awake."

Will was here, too? Poor Dana. She was stuck with six kids by herself, one with a broken wrist and three under three. Josie closed her eyes again. This was all her fault. Except the broken wrist. She had nothing to do with that.

When she opened them again, her gurney was on the move. A transporter pushed her to a private room where Josie's mother was already seated in the only chair.

She hopped up as Josie rolled in. "There you are, *mija*. I was so worried about you. You've had a rough day." She took Josie's face in her hands and kissed her cheeks.

"Hi, Mom. How was your trip?"

"Interminable. All I could think about was getting to you and the babies."

"Have you seen them yet?"

"Oh no. I came straight to the hospital. But now that you've come through the surgery and we know your appendix didn't rupture, I'm ready to get to work taking care of my sweet *nietos*." She clasped her hands together. "I'm sure they've grown a foot apiece since I saw them last." She came to Lubbock for Easter weekend, for Pete's sake. It wasn't like she never got to see her grandkids.

Hunter returned and took his place at Josie's bedside.

Her mother pulled a notepad and pen from her purse. "Before I go to the campground, what do you need? Tell me, and I'll go right to the store."

"Thank you, Marie, but I've already got Will on it," said Hunter. "You should stay here a while until he gets back, though. That way you can follow him out to Silver Mountain."

Marie scoffed. "I'm quite confident I can find my way without following your neighbor."

Oh yeah, she was definitely going to be a problem for the Hardings.

After Marie left, Josie pulled the front of Hunter's shirt until his nose touched hers. "You've got to get me out of here. My mother and Dana aren't going to last a day together."

He extricated himself from her grip and patted her hand. "Dana's tougher than you think, and your mom is usually very nice."

"I hope it's the anesthesia talking, but I don't think this is one of those times. She had that wild-eyed look about her that said stay out of her way. We need to rescue our friends."

Hunter adjusted Josie's pillow and offered her a cup of water. "There's nothing we can do about Marie or Dana. You could have died today, and your only responsibility right now is resting. Got it?"

Recovering from surgery on a camping trip would be bad enough. But doing so while her mother took charge of the kids? Dying might have been easier.

Chapter 20

Dana

Dana smiled through gritted teeth. She and Leah spent an hour trying to get the tiny monsters to nap only to have their grandmother arrive ten minutes after the last one finally closed his eyes.

Marie Saldana had barged into the Winnie with a flourish. "*Mis amores*, your Abuelita is here."

A startled Ben wailed. Dana bent to comfort him, but Marie beat her to it, bumping Dana with her hip in a move that didn't quite seem accidental. "I've got this." She offered no apology. "I can take it from here. If I need you, I know where to find you."

Dana hesitated, but Marie's clenched jaw left no room for negotiation. "Remember, there's no cell service in the campground."

"I'm sure I'll manage just fine." Marie shooed Dana and Leah out the door.

They ducked into the tent and collapsed onto air mattresses. Leah rolled onto her side. "That was weird, right?"

"You mean the way Marie treated us like we were in her way and a bother to her and her precious grandchildren? Yeah."

"She's always so nice to me when she comes to Lubbock. When I help her with the triplets, she makes my dinner and treats me like family. And when I leave, she overpays me. Today, no 'hi,' nothing. It was like I didn't even exist. Do you think she has what Pops has?"

Marie didn't exhibit the signs of dementia they'd experienced with her dad. She was, however, assertive to the point of rudeness.

Dana tried to be understanding. "Maybe she's just tired and worried about Josie. She wasn't banking on a trip to Colorado when she went to work this morning."

Leah threw her arm over her face. "Well, even though she was rude, I'm so glad to have a break. How does Josie do this all day every day?"

"No clue. Maybe she was so run down from trying to keep up with the triplets that her body couldn't fight off the infection, and that's why she got appendicitis."

Movement caught Dana's eye as a lizard skittered across the tent's crimson canopy.

Before she had time to process its presence, it plummeted onto her arm. She shrieked and ran out of the tent as if it were on fire, screaming for all she was worth.

Leah scrambled out after her. Harvey lifted his head at Dana's distress but followed lazily, showing no alarm whatsoever.

Their mother's howls sent Nate and Adam, who had been playing their portable gaming devices in hammocks, scrambling to their feet. "Mom, what's wrong?"

"Someone left the tent unzipped, and a lizard got in." She knew who the someone was. Harvey when he went to hide from the babies.

The Winnie's door flew open, and Marie stood with one hand fisted on her hip. "What on earth is going on out here?"

"Sorry, Marie." Dana painted on her brightest smile and turned toward the camper. "Just a little creature from the great outdoors getting too friendly in our living quarters."

"We'll catch it, Mom." Nate motioned for Adam to follow him and headed into the red nylon terrarium.

Marie scanned the campground from her post in the doorway. "Where is the play area for my grandbabies?"

Dana swept her arm over the landscape. "You're looking at it. They like walking down to the lake." She spotted the bag from Frances on the picnic table. "There are toys from the visitor center over there."

Marie held her position and pulled a face. "You shouldn't have wasted your money on gift shop garbage."

Dana said a silent prayer for the wherewithal to deal graciously with this woman who was quickly becoming a thorn in her side. "I'm sure Hunter and Josie packed some that are of higher quality than gift shop garbage, as you called it."

"Oh, I don't want to bring their toys out here." Marie flicked her wrist. "It's so unsanitary. But maybe I will peek in the bag and see if there's anything suitable to entertain toddlers."

Dana took a seat in a camp chair and watched the tent shake and pop like a bounce house at a five-year-old's birthday party. "Boys, how's the lizard abatement going?"

"Uh, did you know lizard tails come off?" Adam yelled.

Oh, she knew all right. A few years ago, Nate and a neighbor kid found out the hard way when they captured a house gecko in the garage. The tail popped right off. They set up a gecko convalescent home out of Dana's good leftover container and turned the whole fiasco into their middle school science fair project.

Leah's face twisted and her body shivered. "Don't you dare leave a tail in our tent."

The rustling came to a halt, and the door unzipped. An arm emerged, flicked an indistinct object, and withdrew inside. The door zipped closed once again, and the tent resumed quaking.

"I cannot with them." Leah stretched out on the bench beside her mom. "What's taking Dad so long to get back?"

He'd planned to stay at the hospital until Josie was out of surgery, but Dana hadn't had a chance to hike back to the visitor center to check her messages.

"Marie, did you go see Josie before you came here?"

Her indignation was likely visible from space. "Of course I did. You think I didn't make sure my daughter was out of harm's way before I drove to the middle of nowhere?" Defensiveness laced her tone as if she'd been accused of a crime.

Dana checked her watch. "Was Will there? I figured he would be back by now."

"I'm here to care for my grandbabies. I don't have time to keep up with your husband."

"Wow, Marie. I'm so sorry we're keeping you from those grandbabies." Dana folded her arms and turned to Leah, whose mouth was hanging open. "Why don't we go for a walk and see what's become of your dad?"

She clipped Harvey's leash onto his collar. "Nate, Adam. I'm taking Harv and Leah with me to the visitor center. Be back shortly."

Once they were out of earshot, Leah asked, "What is that lady's problem?"

"I don't know, but if we stayed another second, I was going to lose my temper."

When they'd gotten about halfway to the visitor center, Frances drove up in the campground golf cart sporting a Colorado Rockies baseball cap. "I was just coming to find you. My daughter took a message from your husband a little bit ago. He said Josie is doing well, but he will be later getting back than he thought. And his phone was about to die but he said to tell you he's bringing pizza for dinner. Hope he went to Sal's." She kissed her fingertips. "His New York-style pizza is legendary around these parts. It's the real deal."

Dana cocked her head. "Huh. Not something I would have expected in southwest Colorado."

Frances put her hand to the side of her mouth. "Rumor has it Sal was a mobster back east, and he came here to lay low. I doubt Sal's even his real name, but he sure can sling a mean pie."

Dana chuckled and thanked her for the update. "Do you normally track down guests to deliver personal messages?"

Frances tipped her cap. "Only when one of them has a medical emergency on our watch." She made a U-turn and tootled back up the path to her log cabin.

Leah's posture drooped. "Ah man. Now I'm hungry for pizza. Do we have to go back and deal with the triplets and the Wicked Witch of the West, already?"

Dana draped her arm around Leah's shoulder. "Don't call her that. And you left out the tent lizard. We get to deal with that, too."

"Yay."

They arrived back at site twelve to the boys and the triplets huddled together and Marie tensely pacing a tight line between them and the picnic table. "Thank goodness you're back. Your children are playing with a reptile and letting the babies touch it."

Dana peered over Olivia. The beast in question was a four-inch, stubby-tailed lizard, no doubt the same one that had dive bombed her earlier. The creature's flanks expanded and contracted rapidly—likely winded from running all over the tent, but it showed no signs of aggression as Nate held it close to the ground for the triplets to observe.

"How about we let the lizard go?" Dana suggested. "I'm sure it's traumatized after the adventure it just had."

Nate lowered his hands.

"Not there!" She pointed into the distance. "*Way* over by the trees. I don't want it wandering back into our tent."

The triplets took off after Nate and Adam, but Connor

fell and whimpered.

Marie rushed over and cradled him. "Shh, I've got you, baby. Are you hurt?"

If he'd gotten to nap for longer than ten minutes, and if Marie had left well enough alone, he would have popped right up and rejoined the chase. Instead, he wailed for several minutes, milking his grandmother's attention.

Marie rocked him on her lap at the picnic table. "Poor Connor. You miss your mommy, don't you?"

Dana waved her hand in front of her throat and pantomimed buttoning her lip to get Marie to zip it. "Let's steer clear of talking about M-O-M-M-Y. He's had a rough time processing…everything today." She conveniently left out the part where he'd gone on a quest to find Josie and went missing for a few minutes.

"I guess I can relate." Marie sat Connor upright and bounced him on her knee. "When Hunter called me this morning, I flew into fix-it mode. Threw some clothes in a bag and hit the road. Seeing her lying in that bed was a gut punch."

Dana softened toward the woman who'd been so snippy with her. "I get it. My kids haven't faced a life-threatening illness, but there's no worse feeling than seeing your kid sick or hurt and being powerless to do anything about it."

Marie let the squirming toddler down to join his siblings, who were busy poking the ground with twigs. "I can't help but wonder if she'd even have gotten sick if she hadn't followed your family out here on this silly adventure."

And just like that, the warm feelings disappeared. Dana shoved her hands in her pockets and scraped the dirt with the toe of her shoe. She bit back the urge to tell Marie that while she might be right, Josie and Hunter only came on this silly adventure because they were avoiding her. "You know appendicitis can occur at any time regardless of where a person is."

Marie stood and moved closer to her grandchildren. "True. But her medical care and recovery would have been much easier in a larger city with better hospitals. And in her own home, I could look after her and the kids more comfortably. Out here, she might as well be in a third-world country."

Dana managed a thin smile. "Maybe you're right." Conceding to Marie stung a little. Still, recovering from surgery almost anywhere else had to be better than sharing tight quarters with three toddlers and an overbearing mother. Poor Josie.

The boys resumed their stations in their hammocks, and Leah donned earbuds and tuned out the rest of the world.

"Now that my tent is reptile-free, I should try to get some work done." She had a sudden urge to write a scene where an old lady got eaten by a wild animal.

Dana lost track of time before tires rumbled into the drive, signaling Will's return. She stepped out to greet him, double-checking that she had zipped the tent securely.

He encircled her in a tender hug and planted a kiss on her lips. "It's such a nice afternoon. What are you doing cooped up in the tent?"

"Hiding. Where have you been? I thought you'd have come back hours ago."

"I picked up a few things in town for Hunter and Josie to make their night in the hospital a little easier." Will motioned for her to follow him to the SUV. He opened the passenger door, releasing the savory aroma of fresh takeout. He waited as she climbed in, then slid into the driver's seat. "I saw the weirdest thing in town. I wanted to video it, but I left my charger with Hunter, and my battery died."

"Go on." Dana urged him to get to the good part so she could vent about Marie before the whole crew caught on that they were trying to talk in private, which would only invite interruptions.

Will rotated to face her. "I think there's more to one of these campground ladies than meets the eye."

Really? There was more to the elderly helicopter pilot who snuck out of the woods carrying a rifle than a sweet spinster living with her sister? The sister who gave away free merchandise and claimed to be loaded, no less.

"You know the one who flies the chopper?"

"Bonnie."

"I saw her in town." Will's eyes were wide as though he'd dropped a bombshell.

"William. She flew the Caraways to the hospital. Did you think she would turn around and come back without running an errand or two?" She shrugged dramatically. "Or, I don't know, staying to make sure her guest was going to pull through before she took off again?"

He blinked, stone-faced. "Are you done? When I got to the hospital, I pulled up as the black chopper took off from the helipad. Figured Bonnie was heading back out here, but she flew off in the other direction."

Dana scratched her eyebrow. Will's tale of intrigue was turning into a real snoozefest. "Babe, land the plane." Or helicopter.

"Okay. Bonnie got out of an old green pickup truck across the street from the supermarket and into the back of a black Town Car. And then I saw the same green pickup parked at the pizza place, but no Bonnie. I know it's kind of nosey, but when I pulled in just now, I took a little detour past the campground helipad, and guess what wasn't parked there."

The helicopter. Dana would have heard it even though she hadn't seen it. The chopper hadn't returned since taking off with the Caraways this morning. "Do you think she met up with a secret lover?"

Will gave a nod of understanding. "I was hoping she was a spy, but I guess your theory makes more sense. Where do you think she flew off to?"

Dana hated bursting his bubble. She wasn't too keen on thinking about senior citizen trysts herself. "The kids did say she was an expert marksman. Maybe she earned the money to buy that chopper working as an assassin."

"That's probably it." Will chuckled and grabbed two pizza boxes from the middle row. The top of the box announced its origin—Sal's New York Pizzeria.

Dana hadn't had the chance to recount her afternoon with Marie or even to tell him what Frances had said about her and Bonnie's financial situation, but the smell of pizza was making her mouth water and her stomach growl. She'd catch him up later. "Oh hey, Bonnie's sister said that guy Sal is rumored to be a mobster in hiding, so you may be onto something. She could be working for him." She elbowed him playfully in the ribs.

He walked to the picnic table with the pizzas. "Yeah, yeah. You wait. If it turns out she really is an international woman of intrigue, you're going to feel bad for making fun of me."

She wouldn't. The likelihood of uncovering a salacious secret about the campground's elderly owner was about as high as the chances of her and Marie becoming besties.

Chapter 21

The Harding children clamored to the picnic table, but Dana planted her hand on the lid of the top pizza box to keep anyone from opening it. "No one touches the food until your hands are clean." She pulled a sanitizing wipe from its package and washed the table.

Will turned to the triplets' grandmother. "Marie, I got enough for everyone. Dig in."

Nate reached for the wipes, but Dana grabbed them. "Nuh-uh. Anyone who touched a lizard today must use soap and water."

"Ah, Mom. The pizza will be cold by the time I get back from the bathroom."

She crossed her arms. "Dad had to drive forty minutes to get it here. Five more won't make a difference."

Marie led Olivia and Connor by the hands. "Everyone can get washed up in the motorhome. You too, Adam, and Leah. Let's go."

The boys followed Marie and the triplets.

"We call it Minnie the Winnie, or just The Winnie for short," Nate informed her.

"That's cute. Did my daughter come up with that? She likes to give names to inanimate objects."

Leah hung back and grabbed her mom's forearm. "Did you see that? She was *nice*. I'm so confused right now."

Dana picked her own jaw off the ground and shrugged. The same Marie who had bitten her head off for asking about Will's whereabouts earlier was now grand-mothering the whole tribe. Nothing weird about that.

Will pulled paper plates from the dry-goods box and set them on the table. "What are you whispering about?"

"Not sure," said Dana, "but I think there are two different people living in Marie's body." It made sense why Josie didn't want her to come to Lubbock for the week.

Leah leaned in, poking at her casted arm again. "She's nice and all now, but earlier, she was really rude to Mom, and she didn't even say hi to me or anything."

Will set a slice of pizza on a plate and handed it to Leah. "Cut her some slack. She's worried about Josie." He lowered his voice to little more than a whisper. "And according to Hunter, Marie's never been camping, so she's probably freaking out."

"We haven't either, Dad, but you don't see me screaming at everyone."

Dana caught Will's eye over their daughter's head. Seeing the pot call the kettle black made her realize she may have been too hard on Marie. She wasn't a monster, just a teenager trapped in the body of a grandmother.

The Winnie's door flew open, and Nate lowered Olivia to the ground.

Will picked her up and plopped her on top of the table. "Livs, do you want me to cut up your pizza?"

"No." The toddler held her hands up like there was an invisible ball between them. "Big piece."

He proceeded to place a full-sized slice in front of her as if he had never met a toddler before.

Dana whisked it away. "How about we give her a piece more in line with the size of a two-and-a-half-year old's stomach rather than an adult serving?" She cut the slice down the middle and put one half on another plate before giving Olivia hers back.

Marie returned and insisted the triplets' pizza be cut into bite-sized pieces. "We've already had one crisis today.

Maybe we avoid a choking incident if we can."

Dana picked up Olivia's plate, inciting a tantrum. "Fair enough." She didn't have 'perform the Heimlich maneuver on a toddler' on her Bingo card anyway.

Marie cleared her throat. "Pizza isn't a healthy meal. Are there no fruits or vegetables around here?"

Dana crushed her lips between her teeth. The audacity of this woman to criticize the free meal she and her grandchildren were being served rather than showing the least bit of gratitude.

"Good point," said Will. He lifted the lid of the ice chest and pulled out a bag of grapes. "These have been washed, but I'm assuming you'll want to cut them for the triplets." He held the bag out to Marie.

She smiled curtly and took it. "Very well. I'm sure the camper has cleaner utensils and a proper cutting board." She marched off, then paused. "I trust you'll keep an eye on my grandbabies while I'm gone."

Fat chance that Marie trusted the Hardings to do anything. "Absolutely." Dana prayed her face didn't reflect the hostility she felt.

Olivia stayed right where Will had parked her— perched on the tabletop with a paper plate between her legs. He remained close to make sure she didn't tumble off. Ben sat next to Leah, his plate beside him on the bench, while Connor knelt between Nate and Adam, stretching to reach his food. Every triplet was accounted for, supervised, and safe.

Will's hot breath tickled Dana's ear. "She's a piece of work."

She turned to face him. "Five minutes ago, you were all about cutting her slack."

"Yeah well, I take it back. That was an uncalled-for amount of aggression on Marie's part. I sure hope Josie gets discharged tomorrow."

Dana did too, but then what? Would they all pack up

and drive home? Josie's health was the priority, but the kids would be so disappointed if their vacation got cut short and their babysitting duties ramped up while she recovered from emergency surgery.

Soon, Marie returned from the Winnie with two bowls. One held cut grapes that she spooned onto the toddlers' plates, and in the other, the remaining whole grapes Will had given her. "Leah, sweetie, I washed these for you and your brothers. You need some antioxidants with your processed carbs."

Never mind that Will had told her they'd already been washed. Dana folded her arms, once again fighting the urge to speak up against Marie's criticism.

Will nudged her shoulder. "You good?"

Dana nodded.

Adam piped up with a full mouth. "What're we doing after dinner?"

"Don't talk with food in your mouth, dear," said Marie.

That was it. She'd crossed a line, and Dana wasn't going to put up with it any longer. She opened her mouth, but Will clamped his hand over it.

"A walk down to the lake." Will removed his hand and turned to Marie. "We can all go. I bet you'll want to tire the little ones out before bedtime, won't you, Marie?"

She checked her watch. "I suppose. Then the triplets will be good and ready for bathtime."

Adam scrunched his face. "How are you planning to bathe them?"

Realization dawned on Marie. "Oh dear. There's no tub." She squared her shoulders and smiled. "No matter. I'll figure it out."

Will, ever the peacemaker, said, "Let us help, Marie."

Her countenance shifted from pleasant to hostile in a flash. "I'm sure I'll manage." She made it perfectly clear that she wanted no assistance from Dana or Will, but the reason for her attitude remained a total mystery.

Once everyone had their fill of pizza and antioxidant-rich grapes, Dana's family donned their jackets, and Adam handed out walkie-talkies and strapped on his backpack.

Dana wasn't opposed to another family member being the designated pack mule for a change since that job usually—always—fell to her, but she worried Adam was taking his preparedness philosophy to the extreme. "Buddy, we've walked to the lake several times already. It's five minutes away."

He cut his eyes at her. "Didn't you learn your lesson yesterday?" There was no point in trying to deter him, and with the triplets in tow, the backpack might be more useful than ever.

Will held Harvey's leash this time, and the old dog moved with surprising energy. He must not have gotten blisters from the hike after all.

Dana drifted to the end of the procession, which suited her just fine. From back here, she had the best view, watching her children interact playfully with one another while keeping eyes on the little kids. Not so long ago, Leah, Nate, and Adam were toddlers themselves. Time was a thief.

As they neared the lake, the rhythmic thump of helicopter blades swallowed the kids' cheerful banter. Trees bent and swayed wildly as the chopper descended.

"What on earth?" Marie's jaw hung open as it dipped behind the trees.

Nate tossed a grapefruit sized ball—one of the many items Frances had given the kids— in the air and caught it. "Every time we come to this lake, that thing is either taking off or landing. Weird."

Marie pressed a hand to her collarbone. "What kind of campground is this?"

"We don't really know," said Will. "But I wouldn't be surprised if the CIA had something to do with what goes on around here."

Dana slipped her hand into Will's as they left the lake. The only alone time they'd had together since leaving Lubbock two days ago had been those few moments in the Tahoe before dinner. "It's nice out here when no one's lost or dying. So far, I don't totally hate camping."

"Me too." Will squeezed her hand and pointed. "Look up there."

A red Tacoma with a business sign on the door panel turned off the main road and into the campground. It veered right, which led to the clearing with the helipad.

"That truck said, 'Sal's Pizzeria' on the side of it."

Dana's lips pressed into a thin line. "And?"

"And they don't deliver outside the city limits."

Okay, that was odd, but there was no way Bonnie was in cahoots with a potential mobster. "Frances told me today they were loaded and only operate the campground for something to do. She also mentioned Sal's rumored mob ties, but I doubt she would have brought it up if they were in business with him."

"Maybe she doesn't know."

Dana mulled over that scenario. "You're saying Frances doesn't know her sister and roommate is working with or for the mafia? And she never asks where all the money is coming from? I don't buy it. There's gotta be another explanation."

Will drew her hand to his lips and kissed her knuckle. "Maybe we've got it backward and Sal's working for Bonnie."

"Still leaves Frances out of the loop. Unless..." Dana tried to connect the dots, but there wasn't enough information to work with. "I've got nothing. Maybe tomorrow you and I can go for a walk a little deeper into the woods behind the lake, and we can try and find out what Bonnie was doing back there with the rifle."

"We need to put a pin in that until Josie gets out of the hospital. One of us should go to town and check on her tomorrow, and she and Hunter will need a ride back when she's dismissed."

Dana's shoulders sagged as guilt crept in. What kind of friend was she, wrapped up in unraveling a stranger's mystery instead of focusing on Josie's health? Of course, she wanted her friend to be discharged tomorrow—she needed her to be okay. But as the reality sank in, so did another selfish truth. She and Will weren't going to get another stolen moment together on this trip. They were just as busy in the wilderness as they were at home in the city. Something had to give before time completely slipped away from them.

Chapter 22

Josie

Lying in a hospital bed was its own form of torture—almost as bad as wrangling three toddlers with stomach bugs. Maybe the lingering PTSD from bed rest and the triplets' NICU days played a role, but Josie needed out. Now. She jabbed the call button for the nurse while Hunter dozed in the corner chair.

Her pulse hammered as a growing sense of anxiety pressed in. The blood pressure cuff tightened around her arm, and she clawed at the Velcro, desperate to rip it off. A shrill beep from the monitor sliced through the room.

Hunter bolted upright, his chin jerking from his chest at the noise. He was at her side in an instant, checking her over. "What's wrong?"

"Get me out of here." Josie's voice came in gasps. "I've never been away from the kids this long." Her chest constricted, each breath shorter than the last. "I can't—" She couldn't take one more second in this bed, in this room. The walls were too close. Sharpness settled into her ribcage. She couldn't move. Couldn't get enough air.

"Josie, stop." Hunter's firm but gentle hands guided her shoulders back onto the bed. "Inhale."

She dug her fingers into the sheets, forcing herself to

listen. One slow draw of air. Then another. It shuddered through her lungs, but it came.

"What five things can you see?" Hunter maintained eye contact with Josie as they continued the grounding exercise to help her stave off the panic attack.

"Window, TV, dry erase board, sink, you. I can touch your hand, the bed, railing, blanket…" Her eyes darted for another item as her matted hair fell over her cheek. "My hair. I'm better now. Thank you."

"I know you want to leave, Jos, but we can't rush it." He swept the stray tendril behind her ear. "For one, we don't have a ride. Also, if your blood pressure is elevated from a panic attack, the staff might think you're fighting infection from the operation and keep you here longer."

Josie squeezed his hand. Not only could she do nothing to care for her kids while she was stuck in this bed, but she couldn't even talk to them or text to see how they were doing. How did cellular dead zones still exist today? And more importantly, what kind of monster considered camping to be an enjoyable recreational pastime?

A chipper nurse entered and checked the monitors. "Good morning. How is our patient today?" She must've just come on shift. The last nurse was far less jovial.

"Ready to go home. Or at least back to the motorhome where my babies are. How soon can we make that happen?"

The nurse lifted the blood pressure cuff off the bed. "A lot sooner if you let us do our jobs."

"If you send me back to the woods, you'll have one less patient and less work to do."

Hunter patted Josie's shoulder. "Please excuse my wife. This is the first time she's been away from our triplets, and she's very concerned about them being in a campground without either parent."

That was good. Play on her sympathies. Josie gripped the bed rail and pulled herself into a seated position. "Yes, they're two, and my mother, who has never camped in her life, is taking care of them on her own. There's no phone service all the way out there." She pressed her lips between her teeth as though fighting back tears. "We really need to get back to our babies." She pleaded silently with her eyes.

The nurse fastened the cuff around Josie's arm. "Your vitals will tell us if you're ready to be released. Leave this alone, and I'll see what I can do about getting the doctor in here." She gave Josie a supportive smile and left the room.

Hunter stared at her with a mixture of disappointment and amusement. "Really, Jos? Your mom is not out there all alone."

She shrugged, staring at the ceiling. "I said what I had to."

"I'm not sure they're going to find you stable enough to leave this place. And to be honest, that may be for the best."

She leveled her eyes at him. "What? You want me to stay here?"

"Of course not. But hear me out. You just had surgery. Your body needs rest to heal."

Josie cut him off. "I'll heal faster when I can see my kids."

Hunter blew out a slow breath. "How much rest are you going to get in a twenty-two-foot motorhome with them, your mother, and me?" He rubbed the back of his neck, his gaze flicking out the window. "And if we drive home, you're going to be miserable sitting in one position for hours. At least here, I don't have to worry about you trying to lift toddlers or climb steps."

"Right now, my worry is for the kids and anyone who tries to keep me from getting back to them."

Another woman in teal scrubs entered. "You sure look like you feel better than you did yesterday." She washed her hands at the sink near the door. "Let's take a peek at your incisions and see about getting you out of here, if that's okay with you."

Josie had no recollection of seeing this woman before, but she just became Josie's new favorite person.

Teal Scrubs lowered the bed rail and lifted the edge of the blanket. She glanced at the two small wounds held together with Steri-Strips, then covered Josie again. "No redness, which is good. Keep the strips dry today and don't pull on them. Let them fall off naturally in the shower." She scribbled a note on her clipboard. "I'll have the nurse remove your IV, and you can get dressed to go home."

Josie fixed a stare on the back of Teal Scrubs's head until she exited and closed the door behind her. "Why doesn't anyone around here introduce themselves?"

"That was the surgeon who took out your appendix. She probably assumed you remembered her." Hunter opened a cabinet Josie hadn't noticed before and pulled out a bag with her sweatpants. "Do you need help?"

She lowered her legs over the side of the bed and pushed herself into a seated position. The pain was nowhere near what her C-section had been. Why was everyone making such a fuss over a laparoscopy? "I think I can handle it myself, but I don't remember even getting undressed. Yesterday is all a blur. Except my mother stopping by. Do you think she knew we only came to Colorado because I lied to her?"

"Of course not. She was worried about you is all." He shook the pants. "I thought you were in a hurry to get out of here."

She plucked them from his grip. "And I thought you said we had to wait for someone to come get us."

As if on cue, Hunter's phone vibrated. "It's Will. I'll let him know he can head this way." He swiped the screen. "Hey man. How is everyone holding up out there?" His eyes got big, and he nodded. After a long pause, he smiled at Josie. "Sounds good. We'll see you in a bit." A puzzled look crossed his face as he slipped the phone back into his pocket.

"Is he on his way?" Josie asked.

"Not exactly. Bonnie's picking us up in the helicopter. She insisted."

Josie winced as she tugged on her sneakers over the yellow hospital-issued grippy socks. Changing diapers was going to hurt, but she'd been through worse. "How are the kids and my mom?"

"They're all still alive, but your mom may block our phone number and move somewhere else after this."

"Oh no." Josie sat still with her other shoe still in hand. "What did they do?"

"Apparently, Ben pulled a camp chair over to Adam's hammock and made himself at home. He's so small though, no one saw him in it and thought he disappeared." He put his hand on Josie's arm. "Don't worry. Dana noticed the chair and found him right away."

"Great. If Will and Dana stop speaking to us too, I won't blame them."

A nurse knocked on the door and entered without waiting for an invitation. "Let's get you unhooked and ready to go. Your chariot is set to arrive in just a few minutes."

"I had no idea medevacs had two-way service," said Hunter.

"They don't. Miss Bonnie is our most generous benefactor, which affords her special privileges. You guys must be on her V-I-P roster."

Hunter and Josie exchanged confused glances.

"Her what?" she asked.

"All I know is that Bonnie has friends in high places." The nurse slid her thumb across her fingertips, indicating big money.

Hunter smirked. "Yeah, that's not us. After insurance pays its part, we'll be making twenty-dollar monthly payments to your fine establishment for years to come."

The nurse nodded. "That's fair. You've got triplets. Car insurance for three teenagers alone will probably cost you my annual salary."

Josie chuckled and regretted it. Her hand flew to her side. "Ow, don't make me laugh. Or cry."

"Since you folks aren't local, we had the outpatient pharmacy go ahead and fill your prescription for antibiotics and pain meds." The nurse set a small bag and a stack of papers on the rolling tray table. She gave them a few more instructions. "That stabbing in your ribs may spread to your neck and shoulders. It's normal and will resolve itself in a few days." She pointed to the paperwork. "There are some suggestions in here that may help if it gets too severe."

Yay, another misery to look forward to.

"Enjoy the rest of your stay in southwestern Colorado, but I hope we don't see either of you back here."

When the nurse left, Josie and Hunter waited in silence for whatever might come next. Hunter chewed his nails while Josie wrestled with her own thoughts. Nothing good could come from her mother crashing their family vacation. Then again, once her meds wore off, Josie might not be in any shape to care for the triplets. Maybe driving back to Lubbock was their safest bet.

The memory of yesterday's torment flared in her mind. Sitting through a road trip with that much discomfort would be even worse than enduring camping with her mother.

Hunter brushed his thumb across her cheek, his gaze searching hers. "Everything okay?"

She knew him well enough to know the same worries were torturing him, too. She arranged her features into a smile. "I'm just really looking forward to getting back to our children."

A transporter in brown scrubs wheeled Josie to the emergency center's exterior doors and paused as the black helicopter descended onto the landing pad. The moment he pushed her outside, the frigid air hit her face, and she shivered. Sweatshirt weather was completely overrated. The wind from the chopper's blades whipped Josie's hair around her face and wound it into a mass of fiery red tangles that would take forever to brush through.

The door opened, and Bonnie stepped out to greet her. "Welcome aboard. I'm happy to see you alert and with some color to you."

Josie stood and tried to lift her foot onto the step bar, but she couldn't quite manage it. She winced as her foot connected with the ground. Hunter hopped in and reached out for her hand as the transporter hoisted her by the waist. She stumbled, but Hunter caught her and lowered her onto the bench seat.

A well-dressed man sat in the captain's seat where Hunter had ridden yesterday. He adjusted his cuffs and brushed away invisible lint from a suit that no doubt cost more than Josie and Hunter's mortgage payment. His mouth turned up, and his eyes crinkled in a George Clooney kind of way, but it was far from a real smile. It mirrored the grimace airline passengers displayed whenever someone with a baby sat next to them.

A woman occupied the other captain's seat, head down, engrossed in her phone. She wore her headset under her chin rather than over her platinum blowout, which fell over her face, obstructing it from view. She didn't so much as glance at Josie or Hunter, let alone acknowledge their presence. Poor things.

"This isn't weird at all," Josie muttered to herself. Not

that anyone would have heard anyway. She cautiously scooted across the bench seat to make room for Hunter. He handed her a set of headphones and rested an assuring hand on her thigh. Weird or not, they would be with the kids shortly, and that was what really mattered.

Bonnie's voice came through the headset. "Alrighty, folks. We'll be taking off shortly. Please make sure your seatbelt is fastened, and let's have a great flight."

No one spoke again until Bonnie touched down on Silver Mountain's helipad. "Thank you for flying with us. Please be cautious when exiting."

The other two passengers stepped out first and didn't bother offering to help Josie, not that she expected them to, but their manners were atrocious. If her mother had been aboard, she likely would have told them so.

The Hardings' Tahoe pulled up as Hunter lowered Josie to the ground. Dana hopped out and gingerly hugged her friend. "I'm so glad you're back."

"Ex-CUSE me," said the chopper's other female passenger. "I believe that SUV is for us." She stepped in front of Josie and made a grab for the Tahoe's rear side door handle.

Her companion put his hand on her back to help her into the vehicle.

Dana rushed to block the two intruders from entering. "Excuse *me*, but I'm not your Uber. I'm here to pick up my friends, and you're being rude." Dana's assertiveness surprised Josie and made her proud.

The couple started to argue, but Bonnie cut them off. "Yoo-hoo." She lugged two high-end designer carry-ons and pointed with her chin at a golf cart coming up the path. "Your ride is over here." She dropped the bags onto a seat. The cart's driver, a woman in her early forties whom Josie had never seen before, motioned the couple over.

The two walked away from the Tahoe grumbling about poor service and how insulted they were to be remanded to an open-air golf cart while a bunch of nobodies got picked up in a town car.

Josie scooted herself onto the passenger seat, minimizing any movement that hurt. "Who is she calling 'nobodies?' At least we're observant enough to know the difference between a town car and a stranger's SUV."

Hunter hopped in the middle row. "They sure didn't seem like the camping type. I mean, who wears a suit in the woods?"

Dana put the vehicle in gear and turned toward the campground. "A lot of things don't add up around here. But enough about that. How are you?"

"I guess we're about to find out," said Josie. "I feel better today than I did yesterday. What about my mom? How have things been with her here?"

A muscle in Dana's face twitched. "Great." Her voice came out high and strained.

Hunter let out a low whistle. "That good, huh?"

Dana's shoulders drew in. "She's great with the kids. Not a fan of me though, but it's fine."

Josie sagged against the headrest and said a silent prayer. *Lord, please forgive me for lying to my mom, even though I tried to make it right by coming here. Thank you for keeping my appendix from rupturing, and I ask you to please keep the peace for all of us.* The Tahoe came to a stop in front of the campsite just as she said 'amen' in her head.

Hunter helped her out of the car, and tiny arms engulfed her legs.

"Mama. Hi. Up peas."

Hunter lifted Olivia so Josie could hug her. "Mommy can't hold you. She has an owie."

"But I can give you kisses, Livvie Lu. I missed you so much." Josie planted dozens of kisses on a giggling Olivia before Hunter set her down and scooped up Ben and Connor, one in each arm.

Josie kissed them both with the same fervor as she had Olivia. "My boys. I missed you too." She ruffled Ben's auburn curls. "I heard you pulled a little escape stunt."

Dana's head swiveled to her friends. "He didn't get far. Just a couple of sites over, and we found him in less than two minutes, I promise." She ruffled Connor's hair. "Isn't that right?"

Hunter and Josie exchanged wild-eyed looks.

"I was talking about Ben climbing into the hammock this morning." Josie's heart pounded, and she fought to keep her tone light. There were five Hardings and three toddlers. Dana had no excuse for losing two kids. What else had gone on while she was away?

"That one's on Marie. I was down at the bathrooms with Leah and my boys, and Will was walking Harv—you know what? Doesn't matter. Come sit down."

Josie's mother hurried over. "*Mija.* Oh, I'm so glad you're back." She planted her hands on Josie's cheeks and pulled her face down to kiss her.

Josie bit back a whimper. She was several inches taller than her mother, and stooping sent a red-hot twinge through her gut. "Hey, Mom. You survived your first night of camping, I see."

Marie flicked her wrist. "No worse than staying in a one-star motel, which I have done a time or two. Come, come. Let's get you off your feet."

Will and Hunter each took one of Josie's arms and lowered her into a camp chair. Her kids flocked to her, vying for her attention and showing off their new toys. "Did Abuelita buy you those?"

"Bita no toys," said Connor. He gestured and jabbered, but the only word of his story Josie understood was 'Dana.'

Marie parked herself on the picnic bench and pulled Ben onto her lap. "Bita didn't have time to buy toys on the way here."

Olivia turned to her grandmother and shook her finger.

"Bita say 'no toys aside.'"

"Oh, for goodness' sake. I wouldn't let them bring their toys from home out of the camper to get filthy. But Dana bought them plenty of outdoor toys at the gift shop before I got here."

Guilt pricked Josie for the thoughts she'd had about Dana's negligence. She was a good friend and a terrific aunty who spoiled the babies as if they were her own. "Dana, that was so thoughtful. But really, Mom. We brought those toys to use outside. Anything to keep them from destroying the campground or plummeting to their deaths from scaling a rock face."

Will put his hands on Dana's shoulders. "The toys came from the campground lady."

"Bonnie?" asked Hunter.

"No, the other one. I want to say Edna."

Dana pinched the bridge of her nose. "Frances. Her name is Frances, and how are you so terrible with names?" Frustration was etched into the lines on her face. "I'm going to check on my kids." She pulled a walkie-talkie off her hip and walked up the road.

"Is she okay?" Josie asked. She'd only been here five minutes and was already hyper-aware of her mother's abrasive demeanor. Without her or Hunter as a buffer, Dana had likely absorbed the brunt of her mother's barbs.

Will followed Dana with his eyes. "The kids are hiking Summit Falls Trail again, so she's a little tense."

Josie stiffened. "What? The death trail where y'all got lost? Why are they unsupervised? Someone has to go after them." Everyone stared at her like she had two heads. Why weren't they more worried about them?

"Josefina." Her mother leaned forward and grasped her hand. "They're teenagers. They're allowed to be on their own a little bit."

"Sure," said Will. "Besides, Adam and his backpack are better supervisors than Dana or I."

Dana returned with a little more bounce in her step. "Kids are fine. Heading down. So, how about those people on your flight? What was up with them?" It was like the tension she'd stormed off with melted away. Josie would have to wait until her mother wasn't there to find out why the instant shift, but if she were betting, she'd say it had more to do with her mother than Summit Trail.

"I know, right? They didn't acknowledge us at all on the flight. Granted, it was like ten minutes or less, but we were certainly beneath them. You don't think they're camping here, do you?"

Dana bent to scratch Harvey's neck. "Definitely not. No one goes camping in a suit or with Louis Vuitton luggage."

Marie rested her chin on her fist. "Tell me more about these people."

Hunter clapped Will on the back. "What do you say we take the babies on a little walk while they spill the tea?"

"Oh no." Her mother sat up ramrod straight. "Spilling the tea is a polite term for spreading gossip, and that is a sin. I merely want to hear my daughter tell me about her trip from the hospital." She smiled sweetly until the men had rounded up the babies for their walk. "Now, what about these awful people with the fancy luggage?"

Josie recounted her transport in the luxury craft and gave her mother the rundown on her travel companions, though "companions" felt like a stretch. They'd been anything but friendly. The poor things had to suffer the indignity of flying alongside mere peasants.

"But here's the weirdest part. I watched in the side mirror when we drove up here, and the golf cart took that couple *away* from the campground. They disappeared into the woods. That makes no sense, though." If there was a secret business venture that took rich folk into the woods, it might account for the inexplicable wealth of the campground owners.

Dana leaned forward, eyes wide with curiosity. "This morning, when I went to call my dad, I googled that helicopter. I mean, I don't know for sure it was the exact one, but close enough." She opened her phone and showed Josie and Marie a screenshot. "New ones cost almost ten million dollars. So, Frances wasn't exaggerating when she said they were loaded."

Josie let out a low whistle, a habit she must have picked up from Hunter. "I just wish I could figure out what Bonnie's secretive trips into the woods are about, and why she's flying rich people who are *clearly* not campers out here."

Her mother waved her arms. "Back up. What's this about secretive trips?"

"We saw her come out of the woods behind the lake with a shotgun," said Josie.

"Rifle," Dana said. "You know the lady driving the golf cart? That's Frances's daughter. I met her a couple of days ago, and she got cagey when I asked her why her aunt was traipsing around with a high-powered weapon."

"I bet they have a pot farm back there." Marie clapped like she'd solved a mystery.

Josie shifted in her seat. She was too tall to be comfortable in the folding chair for long, but too sore to stand up. "I can't imagine growing marijuana would be lucrative enough for them to buy a ten-million-dollar helicopter. And why would she bring snooty people with luggage to a pot farm?"

Her mother shrugged. "Well then, maybe it's a cornfield with a lion in it like in that movie where the eccentric uncles have more money than they know what to do with."

"And the snooty rich people are lion food." Could have been the pain meds talking, but Josie liked this game. "They were jerks, so maybe they're bad people, and no one will bat an eye if they disappear in the woods."

Dana chuckled as she swept her hair into a ponytail and wrapped it with the hair tie from her wrist. "It's an intriguing mystery for sure. I'm dying to find out more."

Josie winced from both the verbiage and the crick in her shoulder. "Don't say 'dying.' We've had all the close calls we need for one vacation."

Chapter 23

Dana

Dana bit her tongue to keep the peace. No one had come close to dying. Dana found both missing toddlers within moments of their disappearances, and Josie's appendix hadn't ruptured. Things could have been so much worse.

Marie put her hand on Josie's arm. "You look uncomfortable. Wouldn't you like to go lie down?"

Josie cocked her neck to the side and massaged her shoulder. "Not right now. That's all I did in the hospital, but I would like to stand. Help me up?" Dana hopped out of her seat and grasped Josie's arm. Marie followed suit, and they pulled Josie to her feet.

Marie folded her arms and watched her daughter as if she might fall over any second. "You've got that post-laparoscopy gas pain, don't you?"

"How did you know?"

"My gall bladder surgery. Turning my head hurt worse than the incisions." Marie scurried to the Winnie and returned with her purse. "I may have some Gas-X in here. That's supposed to help." The black hobo bag rivaled Adam's backpack, but after much rummaging, Marie came up emptyhanded. "Sorry, *mija*. I can go to town and get you some."

Dana put her hand on Marie's arm, half-expecting the

woman to recoil. "First let me see if there's some in my first aid kit." She ducked into the tent and returned with the box."

"Ay, that thing's the size of a mobile clinic!" Marie rested a hand on her hip. "I've seen pharmacies with less medical supplies."

Josie snorted.

Dana ignored the teasing and located a packet labeled "simethicone." She tore it open and dropped two pills into Josie's palm.

As she tipped her head to swallow them, Josie's balance faltered. She swayed, and Dana reached out to steady her.

"Back in the chair, friend." With a hand on Josie's back, Dana guided her down again.

Marie slung her purse onto her shoulder, switching to an all-business tone. "We need to talk about getting you home. Now, I can follow you back to Texas in my car and stay as long as you need me."

Josie's cold, trembling fingers wrapped around Dana's hand. A fleeting grimace crossed Josie's face before it vanished, replaced by a placid expression. "Not today, Mom. I just want to take it easy and see how I feel after tonight, okay?"

"You don't have to stay out here just to satisfy Dana and her family." Marie jerked her head toward Dana without taking her eyes off Josie. "Your health comes first."

"Mom, stop." Josie's grip clamped tighter with every strained sentence. "We're here because we want to be, and I don't know yet if leaving is the right call. At least out here I can lie down, and there isn't a seatbelt digging into my tender spots while toddlers scream behind me for ten hours."

The grim picture Josie painted made Dana's side hurt too. She couldn't imagine the difficult position Josie was in, no matter what she decided.

Marie scuffed at the dirt with her toe, arms hugged tight across her chest. "Do you even need my help? If not, I guess I'll go home."

Josie inhaled a slow breath, likely staving off an impending anxiety attack. "Mom, I do need your help. And if you'll stay here tonight, we'll figure out how to make the camper work for all six of us. But I need to do this my way. Please."

Dana couldn't take it anymore. She patted Josie's hand as though tapping out of a UFC fight and racked her brain for a reasonable excuse to escape. The kids? No, they were still on the trail, and using them as her reason for leaving would send Marie and Josie into a panic. Claiming she needed to make a call wouldn't work either—she'd already spoken to her dad that morning, and everyone knew it.

"I'm just gonna…" Dana mumbled, gesturing vaguely toward the vaulted toilet before bolting away at a brisk pace, relief washing over her as she put some distance between herself and the mother-daughter tension. Then she caught a whiff of the outbuilding and veered in the opposite direction. Her encounters with that place would remain limited to emergencies only.

Mercifully, Will and Hunter appeared up the road with the triplets in tow. Will carried a giggling Olivia on his shoulders, her tiny hands gripping his forehead for balance. Hunter had Ben perched on one hip, the boy's head bobbing as he fought off an impending nap. With his free hand, Hunter half-dragged Connor, whose ear-piercing screams shattered the camp's peaceful quiet. Mud streaked his face, clumped in his hair, and coated his clothes.

Dana hurried to meet them. "What happened?"

Hunter tipped his head at Connor. "Someone didn't listen and got too close to the lake."

Dana opted to help by taking the clean child from him so he could better deal with the soggy one. She held her arms out to Ben, but he responded by clinging to his dad's shirt. Surely, she could outsmart a two-year-old. "I'm going to see your mommy. Want to come with me?"

"Mommy? Yes. I go see." Ben leaned out of Hunter's grasp and let Dana carry him to camp.

She walked ahead of the guys, Hunter's pace slowed by Connor's state. "What did you see on your walk?"

He patted Dana's cheek. "Kickin. Water. Bug." She loved how often the toddlers touched her face. It reminded her of Leah, Nate, and Adam at their ages. Back when she was the center of their worlds, and *they* were the ones embarrassing *her* in public and not the other way around.

"Are you sure you saw a chicken?" These kids were obsessed. "Your parents need to teach you about other kinds of birds besides chickens." Dana hefted him higher on her hip. She wasn't used to walking more than a few feet at a time carrying babies. "You sure are getting big."

He spotted his mother and lost interest in small talk with Dana. "Mama. Mom. Hi." Dana lowered him to the ground, and he bolted toward Josie and plowed into her legs.

"Oof." Josie winced at the impact. She bent with visible discomfort and patted his back. "Hey Benny. How was your walk?"

"He says he saw a chicken." Dana bit her lip, swallowing her concern for Josie, and put on a playful smile. "I think you're going to have to break down and give the kids what they want."

Josie chuckled, her brows knitted together. "Bird poop and flies are exactly what I was hoping to add to my life."

No one asked what was wrong with Connor. His screaming was impossible to ignore, but maybe Josie and Marie were so accustomed to upset toddlers they were unphased.

The men strolled into view.

Marie spotted Connor and sprang into action. "*Mijo,*

que sucio! Why are you so filthy?"

"When we don't listen to Dad, we fall in the mud." Hunter offered no further explanation.

Marie took Connor's hand. "Let me get him cleaned up." She turned back to Josie. "That is, if no one has any objections."

Dana froze and held her breath. Marie's comment was meant to poke the bear and see what would happen next. A bold choice.

"Be my guest." Josie pointed her open hand at the Winnie and watched her mother and son make their way inside. She turned to Hunter and opened her mouth to speak, but Leah, Nate, and Adam clomped up the road, bickering.

"I found it, so I should get to hold it." Adam whined.

Nate turned his shoulder away from his brother, an unidentified round object clutched in both hands. "No way. You pulled the lizard's tail off."

"I don't know why either of you are holding it after it peed on Adam," said Leah.

"To show Mom. She'll think it's neat."

Adam thumped his chest. "But *I* found it first."

Dana girded herself to see the creature her kids couldn't wait to show her. Nate's hold on it gave her peace of mind that it probably wasn't a snake. "What did you find?"

Nate held out his hands. "A turtle. Didn't you have one when you were a kid?"

Dana grinned at the reptile withdrawn into its shell, hiding from its captors. "Not that kind, but yes, I had a pet turtle until it got too big for its tank. Then Pops took it to the lake and turned it loose."

Adam peeled off the straps of his backpack and let it fall to the ground. "That's what we're gonna do with this one. It was in the road, and I saved it so a car wouldn't hit it."

Dana picked up the abandoned backpack and ruffled

Adam's hair, receiving a wet hand in return. "Got a little sweaty out there, I see." She wrinkled her nose and wiped her hand down her jeans. "I'm glad you kept the turtle from getting hit, as long as you weren't putting yourself in danger by running into the road."

Leah rolled her eyes. "He's not a baby anymore, Mom. He's probably the most careful of all of us now."

"Glad to hear it." Dana jammed her hands into her pockets. "That's not a water turtle though, so let's not drown it in the lake. Maybe turn it loose in the woods where it can find bugs and will be safe from vehicles."

Olivia sidled up to Nate. "Ina see."

He lowered his hands so she could get a better look.

Ben scurried up to see as well. "Tutto!" He poked his finger at the opening in the shell where a nose peeped out.

Nate pushed his little hand away. "No touch. Turtles can bite." He'd clearly been trying to protect Ben, but the message got lost in translation.

Ben threw his head back and wailed. "Mine. I touch."

Nate lifted his hands out of reach and backed away. His heroic efforts were rewarded with more reptile urine.

Hunter picked up Ben and took Olivia by the hand. "Let's go, you two. It's time to eat and N-A-P." He set them inside the camper and helped Josie up the steps.

"I have an idea." Will jogged to the supply trunk next to the picnic table and pulled out a Costco box of granola bars. He shook its contents into the bin and held up the empty box. "You three wash up, get a snack, and relax. Mom and I will set the turtle free in a safe area."

How had she gotten roped into that job? Then again, she'd been praying for time alone with her husband. Maybe this was as good as it was going to get. "Y'all keep an eye on Harvey and don't leave the food open. Oh, and keep the tent zipped all the way."

Nate eased the turtle into the box.

Will closed the flap over the top, tucked it in a football

hold under his right arm, and offered Dana his left elbow. "Mi'lady."

She slipped her hand through his arm and called over her shoulder. "I've still got the walkie if you need us."

They strolled in companionable silence until they neared the lake.

Dana squeezed Will's arm. "Hey hon. I was serious when I told the kids this isn't a water turtle. Its feet aren't shaped for swimming."

His eyes twinkled despite the downward angle of his eyebrows. "Oh, we're not going to the lake." He was up to something, and Dana wasn't sure it was legal.

She struggled to keep up with his longer stride anyway, but in his excitement to enact whatever devious plan he had in mind, Will walked at an even faster clip.

She pulled her hand away from his arm. "I'm not sure how I feel about this sinister vibe you're giving off."

He tapped the granola box. "I know it's a flimsy plan, but I thought we could use this guy as a viable reason to cut through the woods to see what's hidden behind the lake."

Dana pressed her lips together. She liked that he shared her curiosity about Bonnie and her passengers, but the turtle wouldn't be much help with their caper. "What do you have in mind?"

The turtle scratched inside its cardboard prison.

"I've been thinking about those wildlife cameras. I did some reading on them at the hospital, and I'm willing to bet they surround these woods and act as security cameras, protecting whatever's located in the middle."

Will wasn't usually one for conspiracy theories. Although, given the unusual activities they'd witnessed the last couple of days, she was inclined to agree with him. "Why would someone go to the trouble instead of just installing a regular surveillance system?"

"You've gotta have an internet signal to transmit data from most cameras. They're also not as durable when it comes to weather or curious creatures." All good points.

They crossed the meadow adjacent to the lake and approached the tree line. Dana still hadn't figured out Will's plan, but scoping out the woods with him had to be better than enduring any more drama with Marie.

"Where did you see the camera when you were walking Harvey?" he asked.

'In the woods' probably wasn't the answer he was looking for. She surveyed the lake and tried to remember where she and Josie had been standing when they saw Bonnie that day. She had retraced the path as best she could with Harvey. "I think about twenty yards to the right of the fishing dock."

"Then we will cut through way over here and see if we can bypass the cameras." Will took the turtle out of the box and tried to hand it to Dana.

She pulled her hands back. "Oh no. I'm not carrying it. Why did you take it out?"

"If we do show up on a trail cam, it'll look like we just found it and are looking for a safe spot to put it down." He dropped the box and crushed it with his boot. "But if we're carrying a food container, we'll look suspicious, especially if Bonnie IDs us. After all, she knows we know about the helicopter passengers." What did they actually know about them, though?

With one hand, he picked up the flattened box and tucked it into his waistband, concealing it under his shirt.

Dana felt a twinge of guilt for not being more helpful—but not enough to risk getting peed on. "I still don't get it. If the cameras aren't connected to any signal, how do we know anyone will even see us on them?" She swatted at a fly buzzing her face. "We could be home in the eight-oh-six by the time the footage is even checked."

"Maybe. But I suspect someone who walks around with a rifle, flies a high-end helicopter, and associates with rumored mobsters takes security more seriously than that."

"So, we look for clues and act like we're rehoming an animal that walks around with its home on its back?"

Will's face brightened. "What? No. This is just a smokescreen to get away from camp without the kids wanting to come along. If I'd said we were going to hunt for rich people hidden in the woods, we'd have an entourage." He gave her a crooked grin. "But letting a turtle go was a surefire way to get you alone, Mrs. Harding."

She stood on her tiptoes and planted a kiss on his lips. "So, we can put that poor thing down now?"

"Let's at least get it to the tree line so another set of little hands is less likely to find it."

They pushed a few yards into the thicket and paused to let their eyes adjust to the dim light.

Will crouched and set the turtle at the base of a tree. It poked its head out, then scurried away into the undergrowth.

Dana scanned the trees for wildlife cameras camouflaged in the foliage like the one she'd spotted two days ago. "See anything?"

Will shook his head. "Let's go a little deeper and cut to the right." He slipped his hand into hers.

She ignored the thought of animal germs clinging to his skin and focused on the warmth of his touch, savoring the moment.

They had barely gone forty yards when Will gave her hand a light tug. "Look over there."

Another trail cam was strapped to a tree, three feet off the ground, angled to cover the area just beyond the one she'd already spotted.

"Should we keep going?" she asked, caught between curiosity drawing her deeper into the woods and the nagging fear of being shot for trespassing.

Will let go of her hand and slipped his arm around her shoulders. "Why not? What have we got to lose?"

Our heads.

Chapter 24

Dana and Will pushed further into the dense brush, dodging bushes and stepping over fallen trees as they tried to maintain a straight line through the disorienting forest.

Dana focused on her footing, but her thoughts drifted to Adam's backpack. Once again, they'd left camp intending to be gone only a few minutes, bringing no provisions. If they ended up lost out here, she'd never forgive herself.

Will stepped over a sapling with ease. "Remember that M. Night Shyamalan movie where the families live in the woods and scare their kids with fake monsters, so they won't leave the village?"

Dana's eyes widened, and her lips parted in disbelief. Who even brought up something like that in a creepy forest? "Is there something wrong with you?"

"Probably," Will said with a grin. "But why do you ask?"

"You're trying to scare me." She checked her watch. Barely ten minutes had passed since they'd left the clearing. But with no trails to guide them, finding their way back would be difficult.

"No, I was thinking maybe there's a secret compound out here. Bonnie could be the leader of a cult or something."

"I think Marie's idea of a pot farm is more realistic than that." Even the *Secondhand Lions* suggestion beat Will's hypothesis.

The walkie-talkie clipped to Dana's waistband crackled to life. "Mom?"

Her heart plummeted. Adam hadn't used her call sign or any silly CB talk, which meant the kids were in trouble. She stopped cold and pulled the radio to her mouth. "I'm here. What's wrong?"

Will edged closer, his brow furrowed.

Adam said, "Don't freak out, okay?"

Dana glanced at Will, eyes wide with fear. "Use more words, son, and do it quickly." She couldn't bear a drawn-out depiction of whatever awful incident had occurred.

"So, we were messing around, and Nate fell. He skinned up his leg and got some cactus thorns in it. Leah got out the first aid kit, but we need a grownup."

Will and Dana turned back the way they came—at least she prayed it was the same way. The filtered sunlight and heavily wooded surroundings offered few distinguishable landmarks to guide them.

Will took the two-way radio from Dana. "Hey, buddy, go get Josie's mom. She can look at Nate's injuries and take care of him until we get there."

Dana glared at the back of his head, as he was a step ahead of her. "What good will that do? Marie's an accountant, not a nurse, and she didn't raise boys."

He slowed his pace and took her hand again. "Hon, you know kids just need a mom when they're hurt. Josie can barely move, so Marie is the only other option. She'll know what to do."

Even though Will was right, Dana had serious doubts about Marie's ability to comfort Nate. Or anyone, for that matter.

Will helped Dana hop over a log. Had that been there before? "We should talk about something else to distract ourselves from worrying about Nate. How many cameras did you spot today?"

They were moving at a faster clip trying to get back to their kids than when venturing into the woods. Dana had to concentrate to keep her footing while gasping for air. "Just the one."

"Same. Then we can assume they have a wide angle and can capture images at great distances." Will paused to look around. "I think we came this way."

Lord, please don't let us get lost. Not again. They had to be heading in the right direction for their kids' sakes.

Will panted. At least Dana wasn't the only one winded.

"I read the good trail cams can detect motion up to a hundred feet away," he said. "The wide angles vary, but it's safe to assume these ladies would have installed state of the art equipment out here."

She tried to push her worry about Nate out of her mind by mulling over Will's theories. "You know, Leah asked why they didn't install a cell phone tower on their property. I told her that's not how phone companies worked, but money makes the world go round. If they can afford that helicopter, I'm sure they could get service out here."

"If they wanted it." Will pointed toward a dense stand of trees, where just beyond the trunks, light glinted, reflecting off the surface of the lake, no doubt. Water on their left meant they were heading in the right direction. "Maybe they're old school and think folks should enjoy the great outdoors without the distraction of their screens."

"Or they're trying to keep prying eyes off their land." She pinched the bridge of her nose. "You know what? I can't sleuth anymore. Right now, I don't care about Frances and Bonnie and whatever drug cult they're hiding back here." All that mattered was reaching Nate.

He gave her hand a reassuring squeeze. "You're right. I'm sorry. Let's go take care of our boy." Without another word, he led her forward until they emerged in the clearing. They came out closer to the lake than where they'd entered, but for the most part, they'd managed to stay on track.

Dana sent up a silent prayer of thanks that they hadn't gotten lost, then broke into a sprint—or at least, as close to one as a middle-aged mom with a desk job could manage.

A breathless Dana and Will hurried into the campsite to find Nate stretched out on his stomach atop the picnic table, surrounded by his siblings, the dog, and Marie.

"Hold still, baby," Marie said gently. "I know it hurts, and I'm sorry."

Dana's gaze swept over Nate. The leg of his shorts was pushed up, revealing a patch of road rash speckled with cactus spines. She placed a comforting hand on his back. "How are you doing, sweetie?"

Nate lifted his head from his folded arms and managed a lopsided smile. "Fantastic."

Marie held out a pair of tweezers to Dana. "You've got younger eyes than me. I poured antiseptic over the scrapes. Now we just need to remove the needles." She patted Nate's ankle.

Dana lifted her hands in protest. "I need to wash up first. Are the triplets already asleep, or is it okay to use the sink in the camper?"

"Go ahead," Marie said, though her tone was sharper than her earlier kindness toward Nate.

Dana nudged Will's arm. "You too, turtle hands."

She tapped on the Winnie's door. The kids chattered inside, so she cracked it open. "We've come to wash hands. Everyone decent?"

Hunter rinsed a dish in the sink. "Welcome. How's the latest patient?"

Funny. Ill and injured people were piling up around here at a rate proportional to Dana's mounting irritation with Marie. "As well as anyone with a thigh full of cactus spines can be," Dana said with a small smile. She stepped inside.

"Better his thigh than four inches north."

She chuckled. "I guess that's right." The triplets perched on their knees at the dinette table eating diced apples, cubed ham, and cheese. "Isn't it a hassle to transform the bed into a dining room for meals?" She leaned over Connor to make room for Will to squeeze in behind her.

"Yeah." Hunter rolled his eyes and whispered, "But my mother-in-law thinks the outdoors are unhygienic, and this is the best we could do."

As she dried her hands, Dana caught a glimpse of Josie lying on the back bed. "How's she doing?"

He shrugged. "She says she's fine, but I see the pain in her face. I'm glad she's getting a little rest."

"We're here to help," said Dana. "Just let us get Nate squared away and then we're all yours." Marie would love that.

"Thank you. We appreciate everything you guys have done for us and the babies. Jos would tell you that herself if she were awake."

Will and Dana stepped out of the Winnie and back into the fire with Marie Saldana.

Leah stood over Nate with her good hand on her waist. "I can get the tiny ones."

Nate arched onto his elbows. "No! Don't let that she-witch near my wound."

His sister whacked him on the back of the head.

"Hey," yelled Dana. "You two knock it off." She turned to Josie's mom. "I can take over."

Marie slapped the tweezers into Dana's hand with more force than necessary. "Fine by me. If you kept a better eye on your kids, stuff like this wouldn't happen." She stomped to the Winnie mumbling in Spanish.

Dana's own silent expression of disbelief was mirrored

on Will's stunned face.

Leah's jaw dropped. "What crawled up her bu—"

"No, ma'am," Dana cut her off. "We do not repay disrespect with disrespect." She might've wondered the same thing about Marie, but Leah needed to see her modeling turning the other cheek. *Lord, please heal Josie before I run out of cheeks to turn.*

Will high-fived Leah.

"You're not helping, William."

Nate waved his hands. "Ma, my leg."

"On it." Dana leaned over the table and plucked thorns until her back hurt. She stood erect and stretched. "Almost done, Nate."

"Ah man, I was hoping to be stuck on this table the rest of the day." His sarcasm leaned toward petulance rather than playfulness.

"I'm not the one who fell on a cactus because I was acting a fool with my little brother."

He cut his eyes at her. "No fair. You don't even have brothers or sisters, so you don't know what it's like."

"Touché, but my neighbor's mom never had to pick thorns out of me either." Dana slathered his thigh in antibiotic ointment.

Nate rolled over and hopped off the table. "Better my thigh than my 'touché.'" Everyone was a comedian.

"Do me a favor, kiddo. Stay out of trouble until dinner." She leaned in and whispered, "I'm already on Marie's bad side, and I don't think I can deal with any more criticism from her."

"You got it, Mom. Why do you think she's so mean?"

If Dana had the answer to that, she could rule the world. "Maybe she's just stressed about Josie's surgery." Stressed or not, Marie was targeting Dana, and the abuse was getting harder to take. Nate didn't need to know that, though.

Will clipped Harvey's leash to his collar. "You guys feel like doing a little fishing?"

Adam and Nate gave simultaneous yeses and went to gather gear.

"I'm going to the visitor center to salvage my Instagram campaign," announced Leah.

Dana pulled her laptop from its padded sleeve. "And I'm going to catch up on my word count." While she hadn't accomplished much writing so far this week, Nate had been right about the trip inspiring a whole crop of new ways to commit crimes.

Will handed a walkie to Leah and another to Dana. "With our current track record, let's stay incommunicado."

"That means the opposite." Dana clipped the radio to her waistband once again.

"The opposite of what?" Husbands were as annoying as children.

"Of 'in communication.'"

Will held up the radio in his own hand. "Whatever. Everyone, stay reachable."

She opened her laptop on the picnic table but changed her mind about working out in the open and relocated to her air mattress in the tent. While the thin nylon walls offered nothing in the way of noise privacy, Marie would be less likely to criticize Dana if she was out of sight.

More than once, Dana had fantasized about running away from her responsibilities and whiling away her days on a tropical seashore where no one asked her to find their missing articles of clothing or keys. She opened a new document and titled it "Incommunicado."

Her fingers flew across the keyboard as she made notes about a mom who escapes to paradise with no phone service only to discover she's trapped in an off-the-grid resort with a serial killer. She saved it and returned to her manuscript in progress with reinvigorated fervor. She didn't know how much time had passed when the walkie-talkie startled her out of her literary trance.

"Is this place famous or something?" Leah asked.

"This is your captain speaking. Come in, Cleats."

A pause followed so long that Will repeated himself. "Cleats, do you read me? Come in, Cleats."

Leah's eye roll came through the airwaves loud and clear. "I guess I'm Cleats?"

"Sure," said Will, "it's more fun this way. Over."

"Great. Glad you're having fun. *Over.*" Leah emphasized the last word. "I just want to know if this place is well known. Over. Because I used the campground's name in a hashtag and got thousands of likes. Over. And a celebrity commented, 'Bonnie is the best.' Over."

Celebrities could camp too. Although Dana didn't know why they would want to.

Nate's voice cut through the static. "This is a blatant misuse of the term 'over.' Over."

Leah growled. "Next year, we are vacationing where real phones actually work."

As entertaining as her family was, Dana was on the cusp of a plot twist that demanded her undivided attention. "Leah, was there more?" If the child could get to the point—provided there was one—Dana could get back to writing before fish, toddlers, or some other camping conundrum befell her.

"Yeah, someone else commented, 'That place saved my life. Hashtag wellness.' And I thought that was weird, so I went on a deep dive, and there isn't like an official Silver Mountain Insta page or anything. But people use it as a hashtag for spiritual enlightenment posts and all kinds of mental health and wellness stuff."

If Will was right about there being a cult in those woods, there would be no living with him.

Leah kept talking. "Is that why y'all booked this place?"

Dana was glad no one could see her face right now. Was Leah serious? Not once in their marriage had she and Will even discussed spiritual enlightenment, to say nothing of planning a vacation with it in mind.

"Folks, this is your captain again. I chose this place for the running water and flushing toilets. Plumbing in these here parts is a campground luxury."

"And we're thankful you did, captain," said Dana.

"Oh yeah, and I talked to Pops. He said, 'Tell your mom not to worry, but I need to talk to her about something.' Over or whatever."

Dana's heart pounded out of her chest. Turns out, telling someone not to worry or freak out doesn't guarantee they won't do it anyway. This family had entirely too many close calls for her not to.

Chapter 25

Josie

After a dose of meds and a nap, Josie felt almost human again. The constant sear in her shoulder reminded her she must be. Even though she hadn't attempted to sit up yet, in theory, she was ready to rejoin their so-called great family vacation.

Her mother and Hunter 's hushed argument drifted through the camper.

"I don't buy it," Marie snapped. "I know my daughter. There's no way she'd agree to this trip on her own. What's really going on?"

"Marie," Hunter said, exasperation lacing his words. "For the hundredth time, Josie and I are fine. Better than fine. There's no grand conspiracy, no cracks in our marriage, and I didn't drag her kicking and screaming into the woods. Can we please let this go?"

Josie eased out of bed, trying to ignore the burning above her collarbone. She shoved her feet into sneakers and made her way to the front of the camper. The triplets were splayed across the dinette-bed, tangled in blankets and napping in odd angles, but her mother and Hunter weren't inside.

She teetered at the stepwell and braced herself against

the edge of the counter. Mustering her strength, she cautiously exited the Winnie and followed the direction of her mother and Hunter's voices around the far side of the camper.

Hunter jumped when he saw her and quickly pulled her to him with an arm around her waist. "You shouldn't be climbing stairs by yourself."

"I walked down, not up. I'm fine," she said, brushing him off. "What's going on out here?"

Hunter scratched his jaw, then pointed toward Marie. "I'm explaining to your mother why we chose to go camping."

Josie's stomach dropped. Did he confess that they'd come here to legitimize the claim she'd made to her mother over the phone?

"No one is here under duress, and we're not trying to salvage a failing marriage, are we, babe?" He gave her a playful wink that let her know he'd kept her secret safe.

Marie's jaw flexed, her glare laser fixed on Hunter.

Josie laughed, though the movement sent a fresh wave of pain through her. "Can you imagine anyone resorting to a camping trip to save their marriage? Camping is where bad marriages go to die, and good ones either get stronger or hit the rocks."

Hunter bumped her shoulder with a smirk. "Depends on the number of life-threatening events, huh?"

"And power outages." Josie ticked items on her fingers. "Broken heaters. Most importantly, it depends on the number of toddlers tagging along."

Marie shook her head. "You make jokes about how miserable camping is while trying to prove you agreed to this for fun. Why?"

"No, I have a question." Josie's smile vanished, and her tone took on an edge. "Why do you care so much about what we're doing when Laurel does outdoorsy stuff all the time? You don't bat an eye when she gets a wild hair to cross-country ski and sleep in a tent in the dead of winter." She crossed her arms, but they wouldn't stay folded. Fueled by rising anger, her gestures grew more animated with each word. "So why are you giving Hunter and me grief about a family camping trip at a nice RV park, in a motorhome that's nicer than some motels?"

Hunter kept one hand on Josie's back while tapping his lip with a finger on the other. "I've been wondering that myself. Why are you so convinced we ended up here through some sinister means, yet you fully support your other daughter roughing it in far worse conditions?"

Marie threw her hands up, exasperation etched on her face. "It's so out of character. All I've ever heard is Josefina complaining about the activities Laurel does. There's no way she'd voluntarily bring the babies all the way out here. She would've told me."

"I did tell you." Josie's voice barely rose above a whisper, guilt pressing heavy on her chest. She had told Mom, in a moment of panic, just to keep her from coming to town. Who did that?

Stirring inside the camper halted any further discussion. Her mother had to know about the lie, and she was dragging it out, waiting for them to crack. It wasn't enough that Josie had made good on the excuse she gave for why Mom couldn't come visit. Marie Saldana wouldn't be satisfied until Josie came clean.

She rubbed her shoulder as she turned back to the Winnie. A weary smile played at her lips. Her children might drain her energy, but they filled her life with joy, and no pain would ever be so severe she wouldn't attend to them. She stepped into the camper and came face-to-face with one of her sons standing in the sink.

"Benjamin, how on earth did you get up there?" Josie reached for her little mountain goat, but Hunter stopped her.

"You aren't supposed to lift anything over ten pounds

for two weeks." He edged past her and hoisted Ben into his arms. "What are you doing, kid?"

Ben pointed at a high cabinet. "Fishies."

The drawer beneath the stove stuck out, partially open. Josie pointed to it. "Benny, did you climb up that?"

He pulled back his lips showing all his teeth and nodded proudly.

Hunter glanced at the open drawer and then at the sink. "How?" He set Ben on the floor and said, "Show me how you got up there."

A wave of dread pulsed through Josie. No good could come from letting Ben repeat his climb, but her curiosity won out. While Olivia, Connor, and both their parents looked on, Ben gripped the edge of the sink and used the drawer as a step. Next, he planted a foot on the handle of the cabinet below the sink until he could leverage his body weight to get into the sink.

"Ay!" No one had noticed Marie enter the Winnie. "What kind of parents let their toddler scale the kitchen cabinets for training purposes of the other two kids?" Hunter lowered Ben to the dinette-bed and admonished all three kids at once. "Do not climb up there again. The stove is hot and will burn you." He turned to Marie. "Happy now?"

She rolled her eyes. "They won't believe you. Ben's already climbed it twice. The kids run the show around here, and I honestly don't understand it." She wagged her finger between Josie and Hunter. "You're both just as bad as those two out there. No discipline." She pulled her purse off the bed above the cab and stormed out griping in Spanish about unsupervised children and ignorant parents.

Hunter called after her. "Marie, please stay. We don't want you to leave like this, and I could really use your help with the kids until Josie has had a little more time to recover."

Josie followed intending to apologize, but before she

had a chance, her mother waved a manicured hand over the campsite. "I need a break from all this, and the kids need something more nutritious than campfire food. I'll be back."

With that, Marie hopped into her Camry, backed out, and drove away as angrily as one could at seven miles per hour.

"Geez, what's her problem?" Hunter pulled the goldfish crackers out of the cabinet and poured some into three bowls.

"I think she knows I didn't want her to come stay with us." Josie sat next to Olivia and smoothed a dark curl out of her eyes.

"Jos, there's no way. Besides, she's been very vocal with her opinions and disapproval today, and I imagine if she thought that, she'd have come out and said as much."

Olivia poked a goldfish cracker into Josie's mouth. "Eat, Mama."

"Thank you, baby." Josie sagged against a cushion. "Why does my mother make me feel like I'm in trouble when I'm a thirty-five-year-old adult? She still treats me like a petulant child." *Lord, please don't let me become my mother.*

"Even so, she dropped everything to come help us. She would do anything for you." Hunter dipped his head and gave her that crooked half smile. "So would I."

"I hope she comes back in a better mood."

"Do you feel like walking up to the game room? We can throw Connor's muddy clothes in a washer and let the kids play with all the outside toys we brought that your mom won't let them use."

Josie pushed herself upright, assessing her body's limits. The game room sat less than a hundred yards away—manageable, even if she had to take it slow. After being cooped up all yesterday, the movement would do her some good.

"I'm game." She grabbed a few toys, stuffed them into a cinch bag, and slung it over her good shoulder.

Hunter carried out a bag of dirty clothes. "You shouldn't push a stroller, so why don't we let the kids walk?"

Every chance for the triplets to burn excess energy was good, but if they took off in opposite directions, she would be little help corralling them. The campsite had been eerily void of Hardings since she awoke. "Where do you think Will, Dana, and the kids got off to? Their car's still here."

"I dunno. I hope if they're hiking again, they've got Adam's survival bag. I would've felt better if they'd left a walkie-talkie with us just in case."

Josie pushed the thought away. "Surely no one's unlucky enough to get lost hiking twice in one week." She clamped a hand over her mouth. Bad luck had led to Connor and Ben slipping away from their supervisors. It had caused her appendicitis. If anyone was that unlucky, it was definitely the Site Twelve crew. Either that, or they were cursed.

Olivia reached up and slipped her small hand into Josie's. Ahead of them, Connor and Ben rambled along the path, uncovering bugs and picking up sticks. For once, neither tried to dart off.

Though Josie tried to savor the sweetness of the moment, her mother's words gnawed at the edges of her joy. She turned to her husband, voice barely above a whisper. "Hunter, are we bad parents?"

He squinted, clearly thrown by the sudden change in topic. "Of course not. Why would you even ask that?"

She wrinkled her nose. "My mom thinks we let the kids run wild and don't discipline them."

Hunter scoffed. "I'm not taking parenting advice from the woman who forced her daughters to play instruments they hated and pushed them into degrees they didn't even want."

Josie opened her mouth to argue but hesitated. Laurel had genuinely loved political science and helping college students prep for law school, but Hunter was right. Josie had wanted to be a hairdresser for as long as she could remember, but her parents had refused to let her take the high school career courses that would have earned her a cosmetology license. Instead, she'd followed their plan—college, a business degree, and a path she never wanted.

"You're saying we won't be forcing our kids to join the school orchestra."

His lips pressed into a thin line, his gaze distant. After a pause, he asked, "Jos, do you resent your mom for the way she dictated your life?"

She'd spent plenty of nights wondering how things might have turned out if she'd followed her own path instead of the one her mother meticulously laid out. But in the end, the answer was simple. "If I hadn't gone to college, I never would've met the cute guy who was way too obsessed with his trucker hat—even when they weren't in fashion—and we never would have had three kids together. So no, I don't resent her for plotting the course that led me here with you."

"We might have met anyway," he countered.

Josie chuckled, reaching up to flick the brim of his cap. "Right, because regular haircuts are so your thing."

"That's on you, babe." His grin was lazy, unbothered, but he wasn't wrong. These days, she was the only one who cut his hair, but between his long hours in construction and the chaos of raising three toddlers, those trims were sporadic at best.

Olivia let go of Josie's hand, her tiny legs carrying her after a butterfly flitting above a grass. Josie's own childhood had been far more structured, tidy, and controlled than the messy, wild freedom her children lived in. And yet, she wouldn't trade it. Not for anything.

"Now that you mention it," Josie said, a wry smile

tugging the corners of her mouth. "I do kind of resent her for raising me in a sterile bubble. My friends' parents said things like 'go play outside' and 'don't come in until dinner.' My mom was the opposite. She wanted us inside where she could monitor our activities. I can only imagine the punishment I would have gotten for emptying a bookshelf the way our kids do daily."

Marie believed in order and structure. Free play, chaos, and disarray had no place in the Saldana home. Maybe that explained why her father left. Why her sister rebelled, trading polished shoes and pressed blouses for hiking boots and flannel.

A different kind of ache twisted in Josie's gut—not from her surgery but from the creeping thought that her mother's overbearing nature had driven their family apart. Her hand flew to her belly.

"Jos, are you okay?"

"Yeah, it's noth—"

Olivia's blood-curdling scream cut Josie off.

Her discomfort all but forgotten, and with no regard for her post-op restrictions, she lunged for her daughter and scooped her off the ground. "What's wrong, baby?"

Olivia hugged her arm to her chest.

A small thorn protruded from the reddening skin on the back of her hand.

Hunter lifted Olivia out of Josie's arms. "It was a bee. See if you can pull out the stinger."

Josie grasped the tiny wrist and pulled it closer to her face. She pinched the stinger between the nails of her thumb and index finger and plucked it as Olivia screamed even louder. "What if she's allergic?"

"I'm sure Dana's got a bee sting kit and Benadryl in her first aid supplies." He rubbed Olivia's back and shushed her. He turned to the boys who had ceased their exploration and stood frozen in wide-eyed alarm at their sister's cries. "Come on, guys. This way."

Josie corralled them and followed Hunter back to camp as Olivia continued to wail. Thankfully, they hadn't gone far, so the return trip was short. She dropped the bag of toys, hurried into the camper, and returned with ice cubes wrapped in a towel. "Here, Livvie. Put this on your hand."

At first, the toddler resisted Josie's attempt to apply ice to her wound, but she finally settled in Hunter's arms and let him soothe her hand with the cold pack.

Josie lingered at the Harding's tent entrance. "Should I just go in?"

"We don't have a choice. Her hand is swelling."

His words cut through her hesitation about barging into someone else's living quarters. She yanked the zipper up and ducked inside. The white box the size of a small suitcase adorned with a red cross was impossible to miss. She carefully stepped over an air mattress and grabbed it. "Oof." Heavier than expected. She winced, pressing a hand to her side, silently praying she hadn't popped a stitch. Back at the picnic table, she set the kit down and flipped open the latch.

Her own mother couldn't have organized the contents any better. Bandages, antiseptic wash, and a variety of medical supplies were arranged for easy access. Josie pulled out a zippered pouch emblazoned with the words "bite and sting extractor." She held up a cylindrical tube with short handles on either side. "What does this do?"

Hunter took it from her and positioned it over the bee sting. "It sucks out the venom." He drew back the plunger, leaving a red circle in its place. Olivia's eyes widened as she took a ragged breath.

He held out the tube to Josie. "We should wash that before we put it back."

She traded him for an ampule labeled "sting swab."

Olivia simpered as Hunter dabbed medicine on the red bump.

"That feels better, doesn't it?" He kissed her fingers,

eliciting a giggle in between hiccupping sobs.

Josie measured out a dose of liquid antihistamine, handed it to Hunter, then trudged up the Winnie's steps to wash the sting extractor and retrieve four popsicles. She paused to steady herself before descending again. "Who wants a popsicle?"

"Me," Olivia and Hunter sang as they held their hands up to receive their grape-flavored rewards. Ben and Connor scrambled onto the bench, eager for their own treats. As they swung their legs and licked their popsicles, purple juice running down their chins, the last of Josie's reserve faded. In its place, dull soreness pulsed in her gut while gas pains pierced her shoulder once again.

She picked up the discarded bag of toys and set out the bowling pins and balls. "Where did you put the dirty clothes?"

Hunter smacked his forehead. "I was so worried about you lifting Livvie that I must have dropped it."

"How did we not notice that?" Keeping eyes on small humans meant their gazes stayed focused at ground level.

"Injury blindness?" Hunter gave her a sheepish shrug.

Josie tilted her head. "Is that the same thing as tunnel vision?"

"Probably, but worse because parents with a hurt child can't see beyond their kid's suffering."

A flicker of understanding settled in Josie's chest. Was that how her mother felt when she found out Josie was sick? Maybe she hadn't realized how rude she'd been because she had her own form of injury blindness.

Hunter lifted Olivia off his lap and deposited her on the bench next to her brothers. He set off to recover the jettisoned laundry bag and called over his shoulder, "No heavy lifting."

What would her mother have to say about their parenting when she returned and discovered one of her precious *nietos* had been stung by a bee? There would be reproach and a litany of helpful hints on how it could've been avoided if only Josie and Hunter had made better choices. One thing was certain, Josie was definitely going to hear about it... possibly for the rest of her life.

Chapter 26

Dana

Whether from the mountain altitude or worry, Dana's heart pounded as she hurried to the visitor center to return her dad's call.

Endless scenarios of the trouble he might've gotten into raced through her mind. A skipped dose of his medications could've triggered a memory lapse, leaving him vulnerable to a car accident, getting lost, or falling. Her one comfort was that he had spoken to Leah and hadn't mentioned an emergency.

For the second time today and the thousandth time this week, Dana offered up a pleading prayer. *Lord, please take care of Dad. Let him be okay. And his little dog, too.* Patch Johnson was a vital member of their clan.

At a low point after his neighbor passed away, her dad found the pup, filthy and emaciated next to a gas station. Patch had become his reason for getting up in the mornings and for keeping a schedule. That dog was his primary form of exercise and entertainment, and if anything happened to Patch, her dad would likely decline rapidly. Again.

A car approached from behind. Dana kept to the edge of the pavement, well out of its way, but the driver tapped the horn. She turned and saw Marie at the wheel. Dana waved, assuming the honk was a friendly greeting, but Marie drove on, eyes locked on the road, and didn't so much as give Dana a passing nod. She dropped her hand and clenched her fist to keep from acting on the intrusive thought that tempted her to offer up a far less Christ-like gesture.

As Dana neared the patio, her phone dinged to life with a barrage of text messages, the most recent one from her dad.

Everything's fine but call me when you can.

Her editor and friends from her mentor moms' group at church also left messages, but all she cared about was checking on her dad.

She clicked on Edward Johnson's name in her favorites list.

Through the picture window, Dana locked eyes with Frances's daughter, Valerie, at the desk. They exchanged polite waves as Dana pressed the phone to her ear, a lesson in common courtesy Marie Saldana could have used.

Her dad answered on the first ring. "That was fast. I told my granddaughter there was no rush."

Dana lowered herself onto a bistro chair. "Hello to you too, Dad. And her exact message was 'tell your mom not to worry, but I need to talk to her about something.'"

"But you freaked out anyway."

Patch emitted a single bark as if to let Dana know he was fine.

"No, I didn't, Dad." It was only a half-lie. The worry that spurred her to rush to the visitor center simmered to mild concern now that she'd heard his voice. "What did you want to talk about?"

"Did I give you my bank card?"

Her dad insisted Dana use his card to pay for his prescriptions or buy gifts for the kids, but she couldn't remember when the last time would have been. "No, why?" Even as she asked it, the sinking feeling in her gut told her she already knew the answer. "Where did you use it last?"

"I got gas and went to the store last week. Haven't seen

it since."

A thought struck her, and she tightened her grip on the phone. "You didn't give it to Leah, did you?"

He liked to think he was slick, sending his grandkids on shopping sprees on his dime behind her back. Dana had caught onto his game long ago. The jobless leaches were either shoplifting or getting spoiled by their Pops. When she grilled them as to which, they sold him out every time.

"Not that I know of. I'm starting to think it's been stolen."

Dana rested her forehead on her hand. "How would it have gotten stolen?"

"I don't know, but it's not in my wallet. And I wouldn't have taken it out and laid it down somewhere."

The line got quiet, and Dana pulled the phone away from her ear to check the signal. "Dad?"

"You know what? I bet Maggie took it."

"The cleaner?" If so, she wouldn't have been the first dishonest employee, but she also worked for his neighbors across the street, and they hadn't had any complaints about her.

"Yeah, she's in and out of every room. She would have had access to it."

"You think the woman who makes sandwiches for you stole your debit card. Is anything else missing?"

"Now that you mention it, Patch's rope toy and his favorite ball have both disappeared."

Dana pinched the bridge of her nose. "Dad, they're probably under the sofa or his bed. As for your card, did you call the bank? They can tell you if there have been any purchases made that you didn't authorize and turn off the card." She thought of something else and sat up straight. "And for the love of all that is good, do NOT confront Maggie unless you have irrefutable evidence she stole and used it. Otherwise, let's assume you lost it, okay?"

"Fine." His voice was flat, drained of any fight. "Do

you have my account information?"

"Not on me, Dad. Didn't think to bring your financial records to Colorado." Of all the contingency plans she'd packed for, her dad's missing debit card wasn't one that crossed her mind.

"I'll go to the bank in the morning."

Something in his tone gave her pause. "Dad, are you sure you're okay?"

"Of course, I am. Why wouldn't I be?"

Maybe anyone could've misplaced a debit card, but when that person had a history of memory loss, it became a red flag. Dana softened her tone. "Because it's my job to check, that's why."

A sleek black Town Car turned into the campground and took a right toward the helipad. Valerie stepped outside, taped a sign to the door, and locked it behind her. "Your daughter's the one in the space cast, right?" she whispered. "You just missed her."

Dana put her hand over the mic on her phone. "She caught up with her dad and brothers down at the lake."

"Ah." Valerie hopped onto a golf cart with three rows of seats and took the same path as the car.

"Dana, are you still there?"

"Sorry, Dad." Imagining the scene playing out beyond the tree line distracted her from the conversation. "You're taking your meds and eating, right?"

"No, I'm trying out a new diet where I eat nothing but Cheetos and candy bars."

"Funny." Dana edged as far off the patio as she dared, lest she lose the Wi-Fi signal. Based on what happened this morning at the helipad, odds were high the Town Car's occupants would hop onto Valerie's golf cart for their own trip into the woods. "Listen, I've got to go, Dad, but keep me posted on your card situation. And I mean it, don't confront the sandwich lady."

She itched to take off running to catch a glimpse of the

passengers and where they were headed. "Don't forget, I taped a list of contacts to your fridge in case of an emergency."

"How could I forget? You wrote it in giant letters on lime green paper."

"I love you, too, Dad." She clicked to end the call and jogged across the driveway and down the road that led to the helipad. Crunching gravel alerted her to an oncoming car's approach. Should she stay the course and pretend she was merely out for an afternoon stroll or duck into the thicket to avoid being seen?

Before she could decide her next move, the car rounded a curve and came into view. She lowered her head, pretending to focus on where her feet would land with each step. The black Town Car slowed, and the limo tint of the passenger window lowered to reveal none other than the campground owner and helicopter pilot extraordinaire.

Dana feigned surprise. "Hey there, Bonnie."

"We have better walking trails on the other side of the campground." Her face gave nothing away. The set of her mouth was neither welcoming nor warning. "The roads in this area aren't well-maintained for foot traffic." Yet they were maintained enough for golf carts.

Beads of sweat rolled down Dana's face as her mind raced to formulate a reply. "Right, but my family is also that direction, and I needed a beat before I slip back on their radar."

Bonnie chuckled. "Camping trips will do that to ya. Family togetherness is a blessing and a curse."

"It's a blessing more than anything." Aside from the disastrous hike, family bonding had been scarce since they arrived at Silver Mountain.

Sure, they were all together when Dana plucked thorns from Nathan's leg, but crouching over him with tweezers while he winced didn't exactly scream quality time. Will had lingered on the sidelines, hands in his pockets, offering little more than the occasional "Hang in there, champ."

Now, Dana was the one ducking out, swapping fishing poles for her laptop, checking on her dad, and embarking on a reconnaissance mission in the woods. A better mom would already be at the lake, watching her kids cast lines and reel in memories.

"Don't wander too far into the woods. Guests tend to lose their bearings and get lost." Bonnie scratched her jaw. "And what with your track record..." She let the rest of her statement hang in the air.

Dana understood the sentiment, but suspected Bonnie's warnings were less about protecting directionally challenged guests than about keeping her private dealings from coming to light. She masked her suspicion with a polite smile. "Yes, ma'am."

As soon as Bonnie drove away, Dana cut through the brush and attempted to retrace the path through the thicket Valerie had taken this morning with the couple from the helicopter. The hum of the golf cart grew louder as it headed her way. This time she ducked behind a tree, pressing her back against its rough bark.

Valerie wouldn't accept the flimsy cover story Dana had used with Bonnie since she already knew Dana had been at the visitor center when she drove away. As the crunching of gravel waned, Dana peered out from behind the tree just enough to make out the tops of four heads bobbling on the cart. That meant Valerie was transporting three more visitors to a hidden location.

She jumped at the distinctive bleep of the radio at her hip. "Mama Bear, this is Thor. Come In."

Dana pulled the radio to her lips. "This is Mama Bear. What's up, Thor?"

"We caught some trout, and we need you to google how to clean and cook them. Over."

Was he serious? "Absolutely not. Put them back in the lake."

"Come on, Mom. Please."

Dana stood for a moment with the radio poised at her mouth. If there was any chance of avoiding this caveman ritual, she needed to think fast. "You know cleaning a fish means scraping off the scales, slicing it open, and taking out the guts." A shudder ran up her spine.

There was a long pause before Nate answered. "We know."

"Who's going to do that? Because it sure won't be me."

"Dad says he will, and to remind you he used to be a chef."

"Then why do I have to google the directions?"

After a beat, Will's voice came over the static. "The captain just needs a refresher."

She hung her head in resignation. With her family tethered to her through these ridiculous radios, she'd never get the chance to uncover what lay hidden in the woods. "Fine." Spinning on her heel, she trudged back toward the visitor center, already dreading her search for ways to turn poor, unwitting trout into dinner.

Dana took her time reading and returning emails and texts, delaying the inevitable fish slaying as long as possible. She even searched the campground on Google Earth. The clearing north of the lake showed a vivid image of the helipad and metal building. She zoomed in on the path leading into the woods, but there was nothing but trees and grainy brown and green pixelations. Whatever was hidden in the forest was meant to stay that way.

She turned her attention to learning more than she ever wanted to know about the catch of the day. Armed with screenshots on trout cleaning and cooking, she made her way back to the campsite.

"Get a load of these bad boys," said Adam as he held up a stringer with four fish hooked through their mouths and gills. He pointed out two in particular. "I caught these. The tiny one on the bottom is Leah's." He waved his hand dismissively. "And the other one's Nate's."

"How can you tell them apart?" While the trout seemed identical, Dana only asked to be polite. The less invested she got in them, the better.

Adam pressed his lips together like he was explaining the world's simplest process to a dolt. "Dad strung them in the order they were caught."

Those fish barely met the minimum size requirement, and according to Dana's research, they wouldn't come close to feeding their family, let alone the Caraways and Marie too.

Will led the way to a metal table on the side of the bathroom building and removed a fish from Adam's stringer. A sign over the table reminded anglers to thoroughly wash all tools and surfaces and to dispose of unused fish parts in the fast-moving current of the stream to prevent bears from coming into camp.

Leah wrinkled her nose. "Gross. Is the stream full of fish guts?"

"Duh," said Nate. "Where do you think the bears and racoons get their dinner?"

"Nice old ladies like Miss Frances. I don't know. I've literally never thought about it." She fidgeted with her cast.

Dana took a step toward her daughter. "Your sunburn bothering you again?"

"Either that, or I have flesh-eating bacteria from the lake water."

Now Dana had the urge to run back up the hill and look up water-born skin conditions. On second thought, she already couldn't close her eyes and unsee the fish cleaning instructions. Imagining a bacteria devouring her child's limb would give her nightmares. "You know what, we'll pour some bacitracin over it and hope for the best."

Will eyed Leah over the top of his sunglasses that slid down his nose. "Are you going to be cool with eating your catch?"

"Dad, don't say 'cool' like that," said Leah. "And it's not like I bonded with the fish or anything. I'd just rather not watch you hack it to pieces."

Dana was right there with her. She wordlessly handed her phone, loaded with gutting and filleting instructions, to Nate and took Harvey's leash in return.

Leah picked at her arm. "We have a backup plan for dinner, right?"

"Peanut butter and jelly sandwiches?" Dana shrugged. They might be eating fish *and* PB and Js.

"Okay, good." She waited until they were out of earshot of the guys and added, "I know Dad was a chef and all, but I have no confidence in this meal."

"Not sure I do either. After googling the instructions for him, I have serious doubts about this whole catching your own food thing."

"Could be worse, Mom. What if this was our fulltime way of life?"

Outwardly, Dana laughed, but inside she shuddered. She already knew one week was her absolute threshold, and they were only on day four.

Chapter 27

Josie

Though the evening sun still shone high above the mountain, a chill crept into the air. Josie eased into the camp chair, careful not to jostle her sore side, and wrapped her hands around a steaming cup of cocoa. Nearby, the triplets played in the dirt, crashing toy trucks into one another.

Hunter arranged twigs into a low platform in the fire ring. Next, he whittled wood shavings into a tinder pile and overlayed them with twigs. Then he constructed a teepee of split logs over kindling. His effort had to be the most meticulous campfire preparation known to mankind. At last, Hunter doused the wood in lighter fluid.

"Babe, the kids." Josie nodded her head toward the trio plowing over stacks of pebbles with a dump truck hauling a dinosaur and a tennis ball. "You can't light that with them so close. It'll flare, and they could get hurt."

Josie could have corralled them into the camper, but moving too much would hurt her abdomen.

"Not a problem." He picked up Connor and set him on the bench in front of the picnic table. "You guys sit here while Daddy lights the fire." He placed Olivia and Ben on either side of their brother. "Nobody move."

"Kay, Daddy." Olivia swung her legs.

Hunter returned to the fire ring, struck a match, and

dropped it onto the wood. Just then, the tennis ball flew from the direction of the picnic table and pegged Hunter in the groin, doubling him over. Sure enough, the fire flared dangerously high as he crumpled to the ground clutching his soft parts.

Josie rose from her seat. "Hunter! Are you okay?"

He whimpered in reply.

Olivia shrieked. "Daddy, you okay?" Her lip trembled.

"Oh, my ball." Ben, obviously the culprit, slid to the ground.

Josie glared with her sternest mom face and pointed at the bench. "Get back to your spot. Daddy will be okay." With no thought to her own pain, Josie knelt beside Hunter. "What can I do to help? Ice?" The acrid scent of burnt hair accosted her nose. It was an odor that periodically reared its ugly head in beauty school, but Hunter's hair was covered by his ever-present trucker cap.

He shook his head almost imperceptibly.

She pulled off the cap to survey the rest of his face. Half of his right eyebrow was singed to white ash. "Are you burned?"

"I don't think so," he whispered.

"Wee-uh!" Connor heralded his favorite Harding's arrival.

Dana and Leah rushed to Josie's side. "Oh no, what happened?"

Josie gingerly laid her hand on Hunter's hip. "Taken down by Ben's pitching arm."

"Wee-uh, gimme dat ball." Ben pointed at the fuzzy green grenade lying innocuously between the firepit and the picnic table. "Peas." He flashed his teeth and crinkled his eyes.

Leah picked it up and flicked it a few inches into the air, catching it in her palm. "Are the trips in trouble, or can I play with them?"

"Hunter parked them out of the danger zone, but

they're fine to go play," said Josie. Her eyes cut to the fire. The blaze that moments ago incinerated her husband's facial hair now simmered to a smoky glow.

Hunter pushed himself into a sitting position and clenched his fists on his thighs. "Maybe don't give the ball back to Nolan Ryan."

"Who?" asked Leah.

"A famous pitcher for the Texas Rangers." Even Josie, who'd never watched baseball, knew who Nolan Ryan was.

Leah's lips pressed together, and her eyebrows arched. "He's gotta be like a million years old because I've literally never heard of him."

This must be how Dana felt when she dropped references Josie didn't get—like she'd aged out of the group chat without warning. The blow to her gut had nothing to do with her appendix this time. No, this sting came from somewhere deeper, the undeniable realization she was officially old. She turned to tell Dana as much, but her friend had vanished.

Josie used Hunter's shoulder to push herself up. "Babe, I don't mean to kick a guy while he's already down, but you uh…" Her words trailed off. She pointed to her own eyebrow.

He traced the charred real estate where thick, brown hairs should have been and mumbled a word Josie hoped the kids didn't catch.

"Look on the bright side. If Ben hadn't hit you, the fire might've burned your whole face under that hat. He saved you, really."

He responded with an icy glare.

The unmistakable *zzrip* of the tent's zipper cut through the moment. "What the—" Dana stepped out and planted her hands on her hips. "I could have sworn I put that first aid kit right here after the cactus extraction. What if this is the start of early-onset dementia?"

Josie smacked her forehead. "Oh, my bad. Livvie got

stung by a bee, and we borrowed it for the sucker thing." She turned to the picnic table. Where was it? Maybe her memory was the one slipping. "You'd think such a large kit would be impossible to lose."

Hunter pointed to the supply trunk at the end of the table. "On the ice chest behind that box." He staggered to his feet and collapsed onto the bench like a man twice his age.

Josie hefted the kit onto the table and sat beside Hunter. "Sorry, Dana. I meant to put it back."

"Thank goodness. At the rate we're going, we should leave the medical supplies out here anyway." Dana sifted through the box and produced burn spray and a cold pack. She held both out to Hunter.

He put up a hand in protest. "I think I'm good. Save it. Odds are, someone will need both before the night is over."

"God forbid!" Josie mentally tallied the number of injuries the group had incurred that day alone. "Between the cactus, bee, and the fire-ball double whammy, I can't imagine what's left."

"Well." Dana drew the word out. "The guys are cleaning fish by the bathrooms, so the suture kit might get put to use." She pulled out a bottle of bacitracin. "Leah, heads up." She tossed it to the teen who caught it and squirted a glob onto a patch of skin beneath her cast.

"It's the curse of the lie," Josie whispered. She'd already known her appendicitis was divine payback for lying just to dodge quality time with her mother. But now, thanks to her, the whole crew was collateral damage.

"What are you talking about?" Dana tucked a stray strand of hair behind her ear. "You think all these mishaps are God's punishment?"

Josie rubbed circles on Hunter's back. "Of course. Think about it. Leah breaks her arm. Your whole family goes missing on a one-mile walking trail. I get sick and have to be airlifted for emergency surgery." She paused to rub her own shoulder, still tormented by gas pockets. "And what about all the other disasters today? How could it be anything but an Old Testament-style curse?"

"Jos, Leah fractured her wrist *before* you told your mom you were going camping." Dana lowered herself onto the bench. "And aside from the appendicitis, which was simply bad timing, the rest of that stuff comes with the territory when you venture into the wild. It's why mankind invented shelters in the first place—to keep nature from trying to kill us."

Dana's tone took on a defensive edge. "And that *hiking* trail was a lot longer than a mile with unmarked forks. Anyone could have gotten lost on it, but we found our way back, didn't we?"

"Yeah well, we've had a lot of misfortune. Even Murphy's Law can't account for the last forty-eight hours at Campsite Twelve."

"It has been a lot. Will also burned his hand on our space heater, and Leah's sunburned on her casted arm," said Dana. "And I scraped up my hand pretty good on the hike." She held up her palm with the scabby evidence.

Josie's eyes widened. "See? Either we're the unluckiest campers ever, or God's punishing us."

"No one's been mauled yet, so things could be worse," Dana said. "Besides, true bad luck would be falling off the mountain or accidentally ingesting toxic plants."

Josie glanced behind her at Leah and the triplets sitting on the ground in a circle, their outstretched legs connecting to one another's feet.

"Now you roll the ball to me, Connor." Leah tsked. "Put it down and *roll* it." She waited for him to follow her instructions. "That's right. Good job!"

Hunter tipped his chin in their direction. "Where was she when Ben landed that line drive right over home plate?"

"Ah, babe," Josie rested her hand on his knee. "You

might have lost both eyebrows and blistered your face if you hadn't collapsed when you did."

"Or worse," said Dana. "You could have ended up back at Durango Mercy in the burn unit."

Josie nodded. "Next time ease up on the lighter fluid."

The lingering soreness in her gut turned to a fresh stab, reminding her it was time for another pain pill. With the kids supervised, now would also be the perfect time to take a long overdue shower. At least with her mother out and Hunter recovering from his unfortunate mishap, she would have a little privacy without them hovering. She snuck away and let the silence of the Winnie and its mediocre water pressure restore her.

By the time she stepped out, laughter echoed through the thin camper walls. Will and the boys had returned from cleaning their catch, their voices weaving together with the triplets' delighted shrieks. The easy camaraderie, warmth of family, and simple joy of the evening folded over her. Cursed or not, they were meant to be here.

Josie reached up, attempting to twist her damp hair into a bun, but the pull on her muscles sent a twinge through her side. She dropped her arms letting her hair fall loose, its cool strands brushing her shoulders. She pulled on a zip-up hoodie over her long-sleeve tee, bracing herself for the crisp evening air, and stepped out of the Winnie, drawn toward the life buzzing just beyond the door.

Adam was regaling the group with a story about carrying fish guts to the creek. "It was so funny. Dad dropped the bag in the water, and he tried to get it with a stick and almost fell in. I had to jump on a rock to grab it."

The rumble of her mother's approaching Camry rose above the campground chatter. Josie prayed she was returning in a better mood than the one she'd left in, for everyone's sake.

Her mother stepped out of the car and called, "Nate. Adam. You guys want to give me a hand?"

The boys jogged to the car to retrieve grocery bags from the trunk.

"Where should we put them?" asked Nate.

"Take them into Minnie the Winnie. Isn't that what you boys call the camper?"

Marie slung her purse onto her shoulder and looped her arm through a plastic shopping bag. "I'm going to whip up a feast and top it off with cake for dessert. What do you say, fellas?"

"Well," said Adam. "We were just about to fry up the trout we caught." Nate elbowed him, and Adam winced. "But unless Jesus shows up and multiplies them like He did when He fed the five thousand, we're gonna need more food."

"Sounds good, Ms. Saldana," said Nate.

She held the door open for him. "You can call me Abuelita or Bita like *mis nietos* do."

Josie's jaw dropped. She prayed for her mother to be in a better mood, not body snatched. What happened to the woman who stormed off to buy groceries because her daughter wouldn't take her advice?

"Hunter, will you be a dear and help me put the dining table up so I can have a place to chop vegetables?" Her voice dripped sweetness, and even though Josie had never seen her mother drink alcohol even once, she had the urge to smell her breath.

Will set a skillet on the camp stove next to a metal tin of raw fish. "Marie, I'm about to batter these fillets, but there's plenty of room if you want to share this table with me."

Her eyes widened in horror. "Absolutely not!" She cleared her throat and regained her composure. "That's alright. This really isn't a sanitary place for food prep, now, is it?" A pang of embarrassment rose in Josie but was quickly overtaken by relief that her mother was not an imposter after all. And probably not drunk.

Hunter and Josie followed her to the door of the Winnie. Hunter held it open and stepped aside for the Harding boys to exit.

Josie's mom gasped. "Good heavens, Hunter. What did you do to your face?" Instead of waiting for an explanation, she turned to her daughter. "And you, Josefina Camille, what are you doing outside with wet hair? Are you trying to catch a cold to go with your bad appendix?" She marched into the Winnie muttering about adults acting like children.

"At least she didn't see Livvie's arm," Josie whispered out of the side of her mouth.

Hunter urged her with his eyes to be quiet. Josie didn't blame him for fearing the wrath of her mother, but it's not like she could ground them or sentence anyone to viola lessons.

"Hunter, that bed's not going to convert itself into a table."

Oh, Marie Saldana was back alright, and Josie kind of preferred the body snatcher version.

Chapter 28

Dana

Dana awoke to Harvey's cold nose nudging her cheek.

"Go back to sleep, Harv. It's the middle of the night."

Undeterred by her command, he whimpered and licked her nose.

"Ugh. Do you really need out?"

He stood at the door waiting. Dana weighed her options. She could ignore him until he woke up someone else or brace against the cold and darkness to take one for the team. Harv was getting up there in dog years, and he couldn't wait forever.

"Fine. I'm coming." She stealthily rolled off the air mattress so as not to jostle Will. As her eyes adjusted to the predawn haze, she slipped on her hiking boots and down jacket. She plucked the leash off the ice chest, clipped it to Harvey's collar, and grabbed her phone for a flashlight.

Will awoke to her unzipping the tent. "What's wrong?"

"Harvey needs out."

He shuffled in his sleeping bag. "I'm on it."

"I'm already up. Go back to sleep." Why couldn't he have awakened before she crawled out of the warm bed?

At home, Dana was a morning person. Waking before the rest of the family to write or read her Bible fortified her before diving into the chaos of the day. But getting up early at home meant padding to the kitchen in her slippers, pressing a button on the Keurig, and sipping the elixir of the writers in peace. Out here, not only was she cold and un-caffeinated, but the creatures still lurked, searching for food while she paraded herself as an easy snack.

Harvey meandered through the campsite, nose to the ground, taking his sweet time choosing the perfect spot. Dana shifted from foot to foot, the chill biting through her jacket and her patience.

Morning twilight cast the mountain in purple and silver hues. The scene, though veiled in shadows, stole her breath. For a moment, her fear of predatory wildlife faded, replaced by a quiet warmth that spread through her chest. Only God could create something so majestic, and in this stillness, Dana felt as though He had painted it just for her.

The leash jerked tight, breaking her reverie as Harvey charged toward a scent, emitting a low growl of warning to the creature who dared trespass. Dana flinched as a pungent whiff of skunk hit her a second before a white streak darted under the Tahoe.

"No, no, no, no." Her voice wavered, half a plea to the skunk, half to Harvey. "Everybody's calm. No need to spray."

Harvey lunged, straining against the leash. Dana dug in, using every ounce of strength to haul him back. By the time he finally gave in, she was pretty sure her leash arm had stretched so much her knuckle would drag the ground for the rest of her life. Avoiding a skunk spray was worth whatever disfigurement it caused. The odor would cling to the tent and permeate every article of fabric inside.

"What is wrong with you?" she hissed through clenched teeth.

Harvey paced and sniffed as Dana's heart raced. Neither of them would settle back to sleep easily, so they may as well take a walk and enjoy the sunrise.

Dana kept to the road, using her flashlight app to warn

away creatures more than to see where she was going. As they neared the lake, a faint glow beyond the trees captured her attention. What else could it be but the mysterious destination in the woods? If Dana had any chance of discovering where Valerie deposited her golf cart passengers, it was now.

Propelled by adrenaline from the skunk encounter, Dana moved quickly through the thicket. She kept her light pointed low, praying the darkness would conceal her long enough to finish her quest. She shrank at the notion of slipping past the trail cameras. If Will was right about their quality, they had night vision capabilities, and avoiding detection would be useless. She could only hope no one checked the footage.

The first rays of sunlight illuminated the sky at last. Dana turned off her flashlight and noted twenty-five minutes had passed since Harvey first tore her from the warmth and safety of her sleeping bag.

The old dog looked up with a whimper. At home, he did well to walk a mile through their neighborhood on smooth sidewalks.

Dana reached down and patted his neck. "Keep going, big guy. You can do it." When she glanced up again, a roof emerged from behind a dense row of pine trees, its surface gleaming with solar panels. Nestled behind the branches stood a two-story stone building similar in style to the game room in the campground.

"What did we find, Harv?"

They approached slowly, listening for people or sounds that might hint at the building's purpose. So far, the only detail that stood out was the lack of a door.

"This must be the back side," Dana whispered to the dog.

A row of college dormitory-style windows lined the first floor. Massive panes revealed a second-floor fitness center where the red glow of an exit sign illuminated silhouettes of a treadmill, stair climber, and rack of free weights.

Dana crept in the shadows of the tree line with Harvey's flank against her thigh until they reached the building's edge. What she found around the corner stunned her. The front side of the edifice was an unexpected mixture of rustic charm and classic elegance. It featured a portico with cedar pillars and a wide terrace above it furnished with wooden rocking chairs draped in plaid blankets. Valerie's six-seater golf cart was parked beneath the portico.

If Dana had uncovered a hidden hotel in the middle of the San Juan Mountains, why was the only road leading into or out of the property a single path barely wide enough for a golf cart?

Several smaller structures dotted the property as well as a garden and a fenced in doghouse on stubby stilts. Dana squinted. *Chicken coop.* Maybe Bonnie was running a next-level homesteading operation. Like a compound.

"Harv, don't tell your dad he was right about this place," she whispered. Even though the dog likely understood none of her words, talking to him gave her comfort that she wasn't alone. A noise under the portico made her freeze.

"Grab the rifle, Enzo." The voice came from a man. A heavy door closed, and footsteps echoed under the covered porch.

In her book research, Dana had visited a shooting range and learned to fire many types of firearms. While she was no enthusiast, the scrape of a rifle bolt sliding into place was unmistakable. Her throat clenched. She plastered herself against the side of the building and wound the leash around her wrist. She squeezed her eyes closed and held her breath as the footsteps grew closer. The dog, sensing his master's unease, growled.

"What the—" The same man spoke, only he wasn't around the corner anymore.

Dana opened her eyes and came face-to-face with a man with a gun. The barrel angled toward the ground, but it may as well have been pointed at her head.

Chapter 29

Josie

Josie slept better on the queen bed in the back of the Winnie than she had on the cramped dinette. Sharing it with her mother, however, had been less than restful. Every movement stirred her awake, triggering the same flurry of questions each time.

"What's wrong? Are you in pain? Do you need anything? Should I get up?"

"Nothing, Mom. Go back to sleep." Lather, rinse repeat.

Frantic knocking awoke them at dawn.

"Why on earth are those people banging on your door at this unholy hour?" Josie's mother barked loud enough to be heard two sites over.

Josie struggled to sit up. "Mom, shh. They'll hear you."

"Maybe it'll teach them some manners."

Josie glared at her in the dim morning light. Her mom always been strict, demanding, and obsessively neat. But outright rudeness was new for her. Josie wrapped a blanket around her shoulders and shuffled toward the front of the Winnie. Hunter had already climbed down the loft ladder and was unlocking the door. He opened it to a wild-eyed Will still in his pajamas.

"Have you seen Dana?"

"No, man," said Hunter, rubbing his eyes. "We just

woke up."

Will dragged his hands through his hair. "She left to walk Harvey around five and never came back."

Josie glanced at the clock on the microwave, and her neck prickled. Dana had been gone for over an hour.

Hunter reached out and put his hand on Will's shoulder. "We'll find her, I promise. Let me throw some clothes on."

"I'm going with you," said Josie. She pulled jeans and a hoodie out of the wardrobe and tossed them to Hunter.

He took her by the arm. "No, you have put too much strain on yourself already."

Her mother rose and had the good sense to look alarmed. "What happened to Dana?"

"I don't know, Mom." Josie rubbed her forehead. "She didn't come back from taking the dog out over an hour ago."

"I'll help look for her. You stay with the triplets." Her mother slung her travel bag onto the bed and began rifling through it. "I can't imagine what kind of trouble she could have gotten into. Surely Harvey would come get help or bark at least." The sharpness in her voice was gone, replaced by genuine concern.

In less than five minutes, Hunter, Marie, and Josie were dressed and standing outside the camper. Will and Leah had already checked the bathrooms and that he'd jogged to the lake with no sign of Dana anywhere.

Adam handed out walkie-talkies, and Hunter led a prayer for Dana to be found safe. Then the group dispersed in pairs. Josie stayed in camp with the triplets who were now wide awake and jumping on their bed. She left the Winnie's door propped open as she went inside.

"Good morning, my loves."

"Mama, where Daddy go?" asked Olivia.

Ben held his palms up. 'Bita go bye-bye?"

"Daddy and Abuelita went to look for Da—" She stopped herself. How would she explain Dana's disappearance to toddlers? "They'll be back later. Let's get you changed and eat breakfast."

Time stood still as Josie dressed and fed the triplets. The only radio chatter had been disappointing reports. "Not in the game room." "Not at the visitor center either."

Josie stood in the doorway picking her cuticles. What if Dana's worst fear had come true, and a wild animal had…Josie shook her head. The thought was too gruesome to even finish.

Chapter 30

Dana

Dana's body tensed, and her breath caught in her throat.

The man swore. "Who are you and what are you doing out here?"

"I-I-I…" Dana stammered, but no words formed.

"I didn't mean to frighten you. Thought your dog was the coyote that's been killing our animals." He paused, but Dana remained frozen. "Would you like some coffee? It's the least I can do for scaring the daylights out of you."

He turned and waited for her. Harvey pulled at the leash, urging her forward. She blindly followed the stranger with a rifle into the building. Her fight or flight instinct must have been broken. He held the door and led her into a lobby with a deer head mounted on the wall.

"What is this place?" She found her voice at last.

"This here is the hidden jewel of southwest Colorado." He crossed the room to a counter. A young man not much older than Leah hopped off a stool.

"False alarm, Enzo." The first man released the bolt and let the ammunition fall to the counter. "Lock this up, would ya?" He motioned for Dana to follow him, and once again, she inexplicably obeyed. This was probably what led to many a victim's downfall.

They stopped in a cozy nook with oak bookcases, plush

leather armchairs, and another stone fireplace. It had Bonnie and Frances's stamp on it, for sure.

"Make yourself at home. I'll be right back."

If Dana had any common sense left in her, now would have been the time to run, but the oversized armchair wrapped her in a hug. Even Harvey splayed on the fur rug and let out a weary sigh. They'd already made themselves at home.

A door swung open at the far end of the room. The gentleman who got out of the helicopter with Hunter and Josie stumbled through. He had on the same designer suit from the day before when he and his companion tried to get into Dana's Tahoe, though his shirt was untucked and rumpled now.

He called to someone inside. "Be sure you put my winnings in the safe. I'm going to bed." He didn't bother holding the door for the woman trudging out behind him.

Before it shut, Dana caught a glimpse of a green table and a man in a suit talking to a woman in a crisp button-down and black vest. In a casino, these uniforms would have denoted the pit boss and dealer.

The pieces clicked into place, and a chill ran up Dana's spine. She tugged her phone out of her jacket pocket. Still no signal, but "Wellness Wi-Fi" network didn't require a password to connect as a guest. She leaned forward in her seat and scanned to see if the coast was clear before googling "casinos in Colorado." Her heart pounded. The only legal gambling in the state was in three towns hours north of here or on tribal lands.

The man returned with a tray holding a carafe, mugs, and creamer. "Here we go." He set it on the table between the chairs and offered his hand. "Martin Wilkens. I'm the manager here."

She shook it. "Where is *here*, exactly?" She'd asked once already, but his answer hadn't cleared anything up.

"You're in the lobby of Silver Mountain Wellness

Retreat."

Martin's weathered face made it hard to pin down his age, but Dana guessed late fifties. His rugged attire—boots, jeans, and a well-worn Carhartt jacket—screamed rancher. Maybe cowboy. But manager of a wellness retreat?

"I know what you're thinking." His eyes twinkled as he grinned. "I have that quintessential hotel manager look, huh?" He had a relaxed, likable manner that put Dana at ease when she had no business being comfortable around an armed stranger running a secret casino in the woods.

Instead of bolting for the nearest exit, she ran her fingers over the supple leather of the armrest, wondering how much of Leah's college fund she'd have to dip into to buy a chair like this.

"And you are?"

She pressed her hand to her chest. "Oh, sorry. Dana Harding." She motioned to the heap of fur sprawled at her feet. "And this lump is Harvey."

"You're the writer." Martin's knowing smile deepened. "Bonnie warned us you might be a problem." He poured coffee into a mug and handed it to her.

Dana savored its warmth. Alarm bells should have been blaring in her head, but they were more of a distant hum. "How did you know I was a writer?" Her one novel wasn't exactly a bestseller.

"Bonnie checks out all her guests. Can't be too careful these days." Martin stirred his coffee, then took a slow, deliberate sip.

Dana told herself that if he'd meant her harm, he would have acted by now. Unless, of course, he was the type who enjoyed dragging things out. She blew lightly over the rim of her mug, as if that would also cool her nerves. "Did Bonnie say why she thought I'd be a problem?"

"Writers are naturally curious. You see a campground with helicopters coming and going and golf carts shlepping celebrities into the woods, and you can't help but wonder what's going on."

Dana blushed. "Can you blame me?"

"Not really, but we cater to a very niche clientele who values privacy. Outsiders—or neighboring campers, even well-meaning ones, pose a risk to that."

Her hand shook, and she set the mug on the tray to keep from sloshing it. If Martin and Bonnie viewed her as a threat, what did that mean for her safety?

Martin crossed an ankle over his knee, leaning back with an easy confidence that only made her warier. "Fortunately, you and Harvey showed up at the right time. Wellness activities for the rich and pampered don't start till late."

Dana latched onto the chance to lighten the conversation. "Have you always been in the hospitality industry?"

"No, ma'am. Used to work on an oil rig down in the gulf. Then my aunt talked me into being her business partner. Bonnie can be persuasive like that."

Dana's jaw dropped. "You're one of Frances's kids?"

"That I am."

Valerie said she came out to keep an eye on her mom and Bonnie. Odd, considering her brother managed the property. Unless Martin was the one she was really watching. The thought sent goosebumps skating up Dana's arms.

"I don't recall seeing anything about the wellness retreat on the campground's website."

"That's by design. The campground is for families and outdoor enthusiasts. It's meant for all to come and experience what the San Juan Mountains have to offer."

"But the wellness retreat isn't?"

"Definitely not," he scoffed. "This hidden gem's reserved for the well-connected, where luxury remains untouched by tourism." He paused, lifting his coffee. "It's an off-the-map sanctuary for people with way more money than sense. They come to recenter and connect spiritually with nature." He smirked. "Think Sedona, minus the gawkers and wannabes."

Dana had been to Sedona once. This lodge was lovely, but Silver Mountain didn't hold a candle to Sedona's landscape and renowned spas. Maybe the real attraction was the casino, though Sedona had plenty of those as well. "Is this place by any chance on tribal land?"

Martin nodded toward the closed door where the obnoxious man had boasted about his winnings. "You saw that in there, huh?"

Her shoulders drew up in a sheepish shrug.

"We aren't a casino, if that's what you're asking. There are occasions when friends of ours gather for a reunion of sorts and have a social game. Nothing more."

Right. Social games didn't need dealers, pit bosses, or safes to hold winnings. And she doubted too many of them lasted all night.

She cleared her throat and changed the subject to avoid raising Martin's hackles. "What sets this place apart and makes it a destination hot spot?"

"You can't just get online and book a reservation. You won't find the retreat in brochures or on any travel blog. In fact, we don't advertise at all."

A hotspot that no one knew about. What kind of marketing plan was that? "Then how do you attract customers and grow the business?"

"It's simple." Martin flashed a self-satisfied grin. "You ever shared a juicy tidbit of gossip prefacing it with, 'don't tell anyone?'"

She barely nodded, embarrassed to admit her moral corruption.

"Same premise. Gossips gotta tell. Snooty folks love to boast about their unique finds, and most people want what they can't have. So, the word about our sacred hideaway gets around. It's the bread and butter of the whole operation. Well, that and the yurts.”

Dana's eyes danced. Yurts were the romanticized royal bloodline of the common tent.

“They're out past the stable. Five-star amenities and a personal butler. Can you believe people book a year or more in advance and pay a king's ransom to stay in little more than a canvas hut?”

“I saw the chicken coop, but there's a stable too?” This place just got better and better.

“Absolutely. It houses a couple of horses, a llama, and some pygmy goats. The guests seem to love goat yoga.”

Dana shuddered. If anything with hooves stood on her back, she'd probably faint. “Goat yoga is a hard pass for me.”

“Smart. They're cute, but not exactly potty trained.”

Cute was… debatable. “My daughter's fifth birthday party was at a petting zoo. A baby goat headbutted me in the shin and glared at me with those rectangular pupils, like it was proud of the bruise it left.”

Martin snickered behind his coffee cup.

“Let one stand on me like it just won a game of capture the flag and I'm now its conquered land? No way.” She might've kept ranting if not for Martin's wide-eyed stare, fixed on something—or someone—just behind her.

Chapter 31

Josie

Connor patted his mother's leg. "Go aside, Mama. Peas."

"Good idea. Let's all go." Josie stepped out and led Connor by the hand to the lowest step. "You're going to have to jump. Mama can't hold you, remember?"

He didn't need to be told twice. With his mom gripping both his hands, he hopped down and hurried to the soccer ball the Harding kids had left out.

Josie repeated the process to extract the other two kids as the crunch of tires on gravel alerted her to Bonnie's morning rounds.

"You folks are up and about early this morning. You recovering alright?"

Josie rubbed the back of her neck. She hadn't given a thought to her own discomfort this morning. "Dana got up to walk her dog at five and never came back. Everyone else is out looking for her."

A knowing look crossed Bonnie's face. She pulled a radio from the golf cart and spoke into it. "We've got a missing camper, woman, mid-forties with a large black and brown dog."

A voice on the other end responded. "Yes ma'am. They're here."

"Thanks, Enzo. Drive 'em back, would you?"

"Yes, ma'am," replied the male voice.

Dana was safe. Josie sagged with relief and pulled the walkie-talkie Adam had given her off her hip. "Everyone, come back. They're fine and on their way."

The obvious follow-up questions choked out one another as three radios tried to talk at once. "Where…"

"What happened…"

"Just come back," Josie said into the radio. She looked to Bonnie for clues to Dana's whereabouts. "Who's Enzo?"

"An employee." Bonnie pointed vaguely in the direction of the lake. "Your friend wandered over to a secluded part of the property where we have another facility."

"How did you know that?" Josie eyed the proprietor with suspicion.

"A hunch. Ran into her out that direction yesterday. I could see the wheels turning behind her eyes."

"Does the other facility have anything to do with the couple on the helicopter?" Josie nudged the rogue ball back to Connor with her foot. "I couldn't help but notice they weren't exactly the camping type."

Bonnie tipped up the brim of her cowboy hat, her gaze drifting to the horizon before settling back on Josie, as if weighing how much to reveal. "Besides this top-tier campground, we run a spa retreat for guests who want a high-end, luxury outdoor experience."

Some of the tension in Josie's shoulders eased. "So, no secret pot farm guarded by snipers with high-powered rifles?"

"Heavens no." Bonnie threw her head back and laughed. "Just a few wild animals that terrorize the horses and kill the chickens, hence the weapon. Your friend was lucky not to happen upon a bear or mountain lion at that time of the morning."

"Pretty sure it was the dog that forced her out of the tent." Josie cast a quick glance at her kids, silently thanking

God the wildlife had stayed away from their campsite.

"We get the occasional lost hiker in these parts, but losing the same one twice in as many days? That's a first."

Josie huffed a laugh and gestured toward the triplets. "Apparently, two of these guys staged their own great escapes while I was stuck at Durango Mercy. If we stick around much longer, we're likely to set all kinds of records for campground mishaps."

"God forbid." Bonnie lifted her eyes heavenward. "You Texans sure do like to make a splash."

Chapter 32

Dana

Dana turned to see what had captured Martin's attention behind her.

The kid from the front desk coughed. "Sir? There seems to be a missing camper across the way." He nodded at Dana.

She looked at the time and jumped up. "Oh goodness. Will you please tell them I'm heading back now?" She jiggled the leash. "Come on, boy."

"It's okay, ma'am. I've already spoken to Bonnie. She's with your group and said I'm supposed to drive you back."

"It was lovely to meet you, Mrs. Harding. Again, I'm sorry about the rifle." Martin stood and extended his hand once more.

Dana shook it. "No hard feelings. After all, I was—" she hunted for the right word.

"Trespassing? Let me remind you that our guests value their privacy and pay a premium for it. We would appreciate your discretion."

"Of course." She nodded and followed Enzo to the door.

Dana's visit to the wellness retreat left her with more questions than answers. She climbed into the passenger seat of the golf cart, ready to pump Enzo for information, but Harvey refused to get in. With a sigh of resignation, she gave up the front and plopped onto the second row, Harvey settling in beside her.

They rumbled along the pebble path for a few yards before she spoke. "How long have you been working at the retreat?"

"This is my second season," Enzo said over his shoulder.

"Is it only open in the summer months?" Dana lobbed softballs to keep from spooking him.

"No, ma'am. The campground's only open from May to September, but the wellness retreat never closes. My mom won't let me drive out here during the school year though, so I work at my uncle Sal's pizza place until summer vacation starts."

She fought the urge to grill him about Bonnie's venture. "That's nice. How much longer until you graduate?"

"Just did. I got accepted into Arizona State, so I'll be moving to Tempe in August."

A bump in the path knocked Harvey's front paws off the seat. The old dog sat on the floorboard and laid his head on Dana's lap like that was his plan all along.

"My bad," Enzo said.

Dana gripped the metal handle beside her. "No worries. Sal's your uncle? I saw a truck with the pizzeria sign on it out here a couple nights ago."

"Oh, yeah. When I'm working the overnight shift, he lets me drive it." He pointed to the helicopter field where the same red Tacoma was parked next to the metal building. "See?"

"You worked all night?"

"Yes, ma'am. I get off at seven. I do three nights a week out here and deliver pizzas for my uncle another three."

"Wow, you're very busy."

Enzo slowed as they neared the visitor center. "Saving all I can for college."

Frances stepped outside and waved. Enzo stopped the cart.

"You gave us quite a fright, Mrs. Harding."

"Sorry about that." Dana pointed at Harvey. "*Somebody* woke me for a bathroom break and decided to chase a skunk. After that, our adventure snowballed."

"Well, get on down there. Your husband's anxious to see you. And we appreciate you not publishing a tell-all about our little forest refuge." Frances winked at her and gave Enzo a side hug. "Tell your mama I said hello."

"Yes, ma'am." He waited for Frances to wave them on before driving away.

"Why is everyone so concerned about the privacy of this place?" Dana asked.

He swiveled his head to the back seat. "You know who that guy in the suit this morning was?"

"No, but he sure could use a lesson in manners."

"Have you ever heard of a little movie called *Saharan Extraction?*"

She wasn't a fan of war movies, but it had been the summer blockbuster a couple of years back. Hard to not hear of it. Her eyes widened. "That was Chet Rustin?"

Enzo merely nodded.

"What is Chet Rustin doing in the middle of nowhere in southwest Colorado?"

The teenager spoke with a confidence beyond his years. He kept one hand on the wheel, the other drumming idly against the side of the cart. "Bonnie's turning this little corner of Colorado into the new Aspen for the rich and bored. The major players think they're getting a cutting-edge experience tailored just for them. Really, it's the same package deal anyone would get at an ecolodge." He turned back and smirked. "Rich people will pay anything to sit in a sauna and look at farm animals."

Dana arched a brow. "An ecolodge?"

"Yeah, they're eco-friendly hotels with sustainability

features." He grasped the steering wheel with both hands and scanned the landscape.

"Like solar panels and a vegetable garden?" she asked.

"Exactly."

She wrapped an arm around Harvey. "Are the chickens part of the sustainability model too?" The triplets would have lost their minds over them. Bonnie should consider adding a small petting zoo to the campground.

Enzo chuckled. "Yes, ma'am. They provide the eggs we serve." He scratched his chin. "Most of them anyway. There's been a problem with a predator lately."

Maybe a petting zoo out here wasn't a great idea after all. "And this ecolodge rakes in enough to pay for that fancy helicopter?"

Enzo shifted in his seat, his easygoing demeanor faltering for the first time. He pressed his lips together, hesitated, then turned onto the last stretch of road. "I don't think that's what paid for it," he admitted.

The golf cart slowed to a stop in front of Campsite Twelve. He tapped the wheel lightly. "Here we are."

She hopped out and thanked Enzo for the ride as both the Harding and Caraway clans descended on her, looking like they'd seen a ghost.

Chapter 33

Josie

Josie leaned against the Winnie's bumper as she watched for Dana to return. The sharpness in her shoulder and ribs had dissipated somewhat, but keeping up with the triplets in the great outdoors was taking its toll.

Will broke away from the group as the golf cart, driven by a teenager, rolled to a stop beside the Tahoe. He scooped Dana into a bear hug and buried his face in her neck.

Harvey stepped off the cart and ambled to the picnic table. He plunked down without acknowledging his humans.

"Haw-vee!" Olivia ducked her head and squatted to pet her fur neighbor.

Hunter flashed Josie a grin and slipped his hand into hers. She glanced over his shoulder to see her mother pressing her hand to her heart, bottom lip quivering.

"You okay?" Josie mouthed.

A single tear rolled down her mother's cheek before she swiped it away and regained her stern composure. "Fine."

"I'm sorry, everyone. I'll cook to make up for scaring you so early." Dana turned to her chauffeur. "Enzo, Bonnie, can y'all stay for a campfire breakfast?"

The young man shook his head. "No ma'am. I need to get back and finish my shift." He dipped his head. "It was nice to meet you, Miss Dana." He darted a glance at Leah, who bit her lip and smoothed her hair over her shoulder.

"Likewise, Enzo. Good luck at college. What about you, Bonnie?"

"I appreciate the offer, but I've got to get to my rounds." She climbed into her golf cart and shifted into reverse. "Mrs. Harding, the operations at the wellness retreat are entirely above board, but I'd greatly appreciate it if you'd keep it under wraps for the sake of my employees and our guests."

Dana laughed. "That's a gross overestimation of my influence. Your secret's safe with me, but social media's another story. Silver Mountain's clandestine sanctuary is trending. I had nothing to do with that."

"Yes. We've had to implement a password when people call the unlisted booking number." Bonnie held up her index finger. "Which, by the way, only fueled demand all the more."

Josie's head swiveled as she tried to make sense of their exchange. Dana would probably fill her in later, despite Bonnie's pleas for confidentiality.

Bonnie tapped the brim of her hat and drove away.

The group remained still, all eyes fixed on Dana. "The big secret in the woods is a wellness retreat?" Will still hadn't let go, holding her like she might vanish again if he did. "Why so cloak-and-dagger about that?"

Josie had been wondering the same thing.

"I'm starving. I'll explain while I cook," Dana said. She slipped out of Will's arms and hugged each of her children on the way to the fire pit.

The group trailed after her, except for Josie's mother who hung back.

"You talk. I'll cook." Will instructed Nate and Adam to unload the ice chest and food bin from the Tahoe. He arranged logs in the fire ring. "Go ahead, honey."

Dana sank into a camp chair. "I didn't mean to scare everyone." She tilted her head toward Harvey, who had crept out from under the table, angling himself just enough for Olivia to keep petting him. "It's his fault. If Harv hadn't tried to pick a fight with a skunk, we would've crawled back into the tent and gone to sleep instead of wandering into the woods."

Josie settled on the bench and drew her knees to her chest, shivering against the morning chill as it replaced the anxious energy coursing through her limbs. "But then we still wouldn't know what you found out there, so spill it."

Her mother inched toward the center of the campsite as Dana recounted her journey to the point where a stranger with a rifle led her into the lodge.

Will muttered a curse under his breath, drawing a sharp rebuke from Josie's mom. "Language! There are children here."

He struck a match and held it to the tinder, his jaw tight. "Sorry. I just didn't expect my wife to put herself in such a vulnerable position. Anything could've happened." His expression flickered with raw emotion—anger, fear, or maybe both. Dana's decision had been reckless, and the thought of what could've gone wrong sent a chill down Josie's spine.

Dana's eyes flashed with annoyance. "Do you want to hear the rest of the story or not?"

Hunter lifted Connor onto his hip. "We know everything turned out fine, so let's let her finish." He would have reacted the same way Will did if the tables were turned, and Josie had been the one to encounter a rifle-wielding man.

"So, after he unloaded the gun and handed it off to the kid who drove me back, he went to get coffee for us, and I saw that guy from the helicopter come out of a room where there had been an all-night poker tournament." Dana rotated in her seat to look at Hunter. "Do you know who he was?"

Hunter shook his head. "There was something familiar

about him, but I was focused on Josie." He winked at her from across the table. Even with the singed eyebrow, he was handsome. "Besides, he was pretty irritated that we were crashing his ride, so I avoided eye contact."

"That was Chet Rustin the actor." Dana's hands flew up at her own announcement. "Of course, I had no idea until Enzo told me afterward."

Josie's mouth fell open, her feet thudding to the ground. "Oh, wow. That means the woman who yelled at me was—Elara Finch!"

Leah gasped, blurting the name at the same time. "Jinx! No way! You met Elara Finch *and* Chet Rustin? Why can't I post about this right now?"

Dana wagged her finger. "You can't post about them at all. Bonnie and Frances were both clear about keeping the retreat under wraps."

Marie eased onto the bench next to Josie, arms folded across her chest. "I don't get it. Is this place like the North Pole? Will it lose its magic if common folk discover it?"

"Pretty much. Their clients pay a premium for an unattainable, luxury getaway," said Dana. "I just wish I'd gotten to see the yurts. They each come with butler service. Can you believe it?"

"Someone should let these people know they can toss a blanket on the ground and get an outdoor experience for free." Josie got up to help Will, who was listening more than cooking. Multitasking clearly wasn't his spiritual gift. At this rate, they'd be eating breakfast for dinner.

"Martin, Frances's son, said their whole business model is centered around exclusivity," said Dana.

Hunter dropped onto Josie's vacated spot and set Connor on his knee. "But what about the illegal gambling? I'm sure they'd get shut down in a heartbeat if the gaming commission, or whatever Colorado has, found out."

"I don't know." Dana's gaze flicked to Nate and Adam who were hanging on her every word. If only she could bottle their attention and take it back home. "I mean, millionaires don't always play by the same rules as the rest of us. If it wasn't just a friendly game among friends, like Martin said, someone would have to prove otherwise. I'm betting Bonnie and her employees go to great lengths to keep that from happening. No pun intended."

"Your conscience is okay with not reporting illegal activity then." Marie's self-righteous glare bore into Dana.

Josie put her hand on her mother's arm. "Mom, stop. An investigation into something that might not even turn out to *be* illegal would harm Bonnie and Frances's livelihoods, and for what?"

"For what? Because God does not delight in wickedness, and He doesn't condone His people concealing it." Two lines etched deep furrows between her brows as a scowl settled over her face.

Josie fought to keep her tone in check. "The Bible also says, 'let he who is without sin cast the first stone.' I can't see that there was any harm done by some rich people gambling away their own money voluntarily, can you?"

Her mother threw her hands up and stood. "I guess anything goes in the woods as long as no one gets hurt."

"Mom, where are you going?"

"To cut up some fruit. We may turn a blind eye to the sin happening right across the lake, but these kids won't get vitamin deficiencies on my watch." She stormed inside the Winnie mumbling in Spanish about the slow fade of society into total anarchy.

Dana thumbed over her shoulder at the camper. "Should I go talk to her?"

"No, she's my mom. I'll go." Josie dropped her head with a resigned sigh. "But if I don't come back, don't believe any story about me going into the woods alone. I didn't have it in me before the appendectomy, and I definitely don't now."

Chapter 34

Josie opened the camper door and came eye-to-eye with the woman who raised her viciously ripping the peel off an orange. She almost turned and walked right back out, but behind her mother's fury was a glimmer of pain that softened Josie's resolve.

"What is it, Josefina? Are you here to help, or is there something else?"

"I'm here to help, Mom." Josie pulled back the cushions that made up the triplets' bed and removed the table.

Marie took it from her. "*Mija,* you're not supposed to lift more than ten pounds." She flipped it over to unfold the legs and set the table upright at its full height.

"Mom, I could have done that."

"You want to be useful? Cut these up."

Josie took the apples her mother thrust in each hand. "I fed the babies while everyone else was searching for Dana. And yes, they had strawberries." Heaven forbid one meal not include a fruit or vegetable. Josie didn't dare hand out Pop-Tarts without pairing them with something nutritious—not with her mother nearby.

"I'm more worried about those big kids. I doubt Leah would have broken her arm if her parents paid the slightest bit of attention to her diet." She handed off a knife and cutting board and returned to peeling oranges over the sink.

Josie pressed her fingers to her temple to ease the throbbing that began the moment her mother called her by her given name. "Mom, those kids are not malnourished." A little voice in the back of her head urged her to let it go and stick to slicing apples, but she ignored it. "What's gotten into you anyway? I haven't heard you say a kind word about the Hardings since I left the hospital. In fact, you've been very critical and rude."

Her mother spun to face her with fire in her eyes. "I am *never* rude. Rude is waking up the whole camp because you decided to go for a walk in the dark without telling anyone. Rude is leaving your children unattended so they get hurt and have to depend on another adult to care for them. Rude is—"

"That's enough! Everyone can probably hear you out there." In her irritation, Josie narrowly missed nicking her thumb with the knife. "Everyone was curious about what was going on behind the lake. Dana saw an opportunity and took it. That's not rude because she had no idea it would affect anyone else. As for Nate getting hurt, weren't you the one who saId the kids were old enough to hike without their parents? He could've fallen on a cactus even if they were with him. Like how that bee stung Olivia right in front of me last night."

Her mother's mouth dropped open. "You let a bee sting my grandbaby, and you didn't even tell me?"

Josie set the knife on the cutting board and tilted her head back, trying to draw patience from the fiberglass ceiling. "You mean how you didn't see my son carry a chair over to a hammock and climb into it? Or how you thought he ran off, but Dana found him?"

"You're right." Her mother's shoulders drooped, and she sagged onto the banquette. "They don't call it the terrible twos for nothing. A single toddler is hard. Triplet toddlers in a campground is impossible. I don't know how you do this all the time." She squeezed Josie's wrist. "It's impressive really."

"Then what's your deal with Dana and Will?"

She withdrew her hand. "You mean other than them ratting me out for Ben's vanishing act?"

Josie shot her a warning look.

"They dragged you to the sticks on their ridiculous paupers' vacation, which made you get sick and have to have surgery." Paupers? Maybe camping enthusiasts *became* paupers after buying all the required gear.

"For the hundredth time, no one dragged me to Colorado. I came up with the plan all on my own." Josie bit her lip. There was no going back now. She would have to come clean.

"That's absurd. You hate camping! Laurel vowed after one trip that she would never take you anywhere outdoorsy again for as long as you both shall live."

"That's not true. We had a great time together. We cracked each other up until we were both in tears."

"Well…" Her mother drew out the word and scrunched her face like Connor did when he wanted something. "The thing is, she gave you one of her leftover prescription painkillers from her wisdom teeth surgery. Your great time only lasted until the drugs wore off."

A forgotten image flashed in her mind of slipping while crossing a narrow creek. Not only had she fallen in the water and soaked her clothes, but she twisted her ankle and bruised her leg.

"Laurel drugged me?" The throbbing in Josie's head grew. That trip occurred almost twenty years ago, but her sister's betrayal stung, nonetheless.

"Oh sweetie." Her mother reached across the table and patted her arm. "You were eighteen, and you happily popped that pill of your own volition. But then you didn't remember it when you got home." She shrugged. "It was sweet that you had such a great time with your big sister, so we thought it best to let you remember it that way."

Josie's lips twitched. If not for Laurel's medication, the trip would have been a bust, and Josie would never have advised Dana to get on board with this big family adventure. A laugh slipped out, squelching any residual hard feelings. "What other skewed memories from my past should I know about?"

Her mother chuckled. "All parents lie to their kids every once in a while. The only way I got you to eat broccoli was by telling you it was the favorite food of those boys on that *Home Improvement* show. It was much easier to get away with small fabrications before the internet." Lying to kids was okay, but failing to report gambling wasn't. Interesting double standard.

Josie rubbed her sweaty palms down her thighs. "Since we're confessing, I need to tell you something."

"Oh?" Her mother squared her shoulders and folded her hands on the table.

"The Hardings invited us to come to Colorado with them, but we declined at first. I thought camping with three toddlers would be too much work." She shrugged slightly. "Turns out, it is."

"What changed your mind?"

"You did." Josie scratched the back of her head. "See, we... I..." She fidgeted, searching for the right words.

"You changed your mind the minute I called and told you I was coming to Lubbock. It was your out."

Josie slumped against the seat. "How did you know?"

"I didn't. Your talk about confessing and the way you hem-hawed gave you away, *mija*." Marie stood and busied herself with the fruit at the sink. "You could have left it at that. Why go to the trouble of actually going all the way to Colorado in a motorhome?"

"Mom, come on. You would've checked on us and asked about it later. We would've had to keep lying to cover our tracks, and that's not who I am."

"No. Who you are is a woman who doesn't want her mother around. But instead of speaking up like an adult, you lie."

Josie's shoulders sagged. How could she argue when her mother's words were spot on? "You're right. I'm so sorry. I should've been honest with you."

Her mother added the sliced apples to the bowl of orange wedges and gave Josie a tight-lipped smile. "What's done is done." She stepped out of the camper, leaving Josie alone with her guilt.

Marie had always been hard on her daughters and had impossibly high expectations. But without her frequent trips to Lubbock in the babies' first year—always with meals to stock their freezer—Hunter and Josie would not have survived. Not wanting her mother to live nearby was selfish and insensitive.

Josie carried the knife and cutting board to the sink, asking God for wisdom and patience, anything to mend the rift with her mother, as she scrubbed the tools. Steeling herself, she stepped outside to join her family and nearly collided with her mother coming back in.

"Mom, are you okay?"

Her mother froze mid-step, her expression reminiscent of Chet Rustin's forced smile. "Everything is perfectly fine, Josie."

The sound of a pan clattering onto the table jolted Josie from her shame spiral. She turned to see her husband slack-jawed, a skillet dangling from his hand.

"What did you do?" He punctuated every syllable.

"She knows," Josie mouthed.

Nearby, the triplets kicked pinecones, calling for Harvey to fetch one. Their laughter barely registered through the haze clouding Josie's thoughts.

"Did I miss something?" Will asked, scooping eggs onto Nate's plate.

Hunter set the skillet on the table. "Marie called her 'Josie,' not 'Josefina.'" He rushed to Josie and rested his hands on her shoulders. "What can I do?"

Josie rubbed her forehead, still dazed. "I don't know. Maybe we give her some space for a bit."

"I'm sure it'll be fine."

Josie appreciated his support, even if neither of them believed his platitude.

He slid his hands down her back and wrapped her in a hug. "In all the commotion this morning, I didn't even ask you how you're feeling. Are you in much pain?"

"A livable amount. Until just now." She lowered her voice. "I'm so used to cringing every time she says my real name that I had a mild heart attack hearing 'Josie' come out of her mouth."

He snickered. "Same. Forgot I had a pan in my hand."

"Yes. The crash it made jolted my heart back into sinus rhythm like defibrillator paddles."

"Come on," he said, slipping his hand into hers. "Let's eat." When they were seated at the picnic table, he leaned close to her. "Did you just blurt it out?"

Josie shoveled a bite of scrambled eggs into her mouth and shook her head. "She was blaming…" She tilted her head toward the Hardings. "For me getting sick all the way out here. I came to their defense and flubbed coming clean, but she guessed it. Now I'm the one she's mad at."

A thud preceded a cry from Ben.

Josie jumped up and winced from the strain on her abdomen. She knelt in front of Ben who was clutching his face. "What happened, baby?"

"Saw-we." Connor patted his brother's back.

Hunter squatted next to them. "Connor, did you hit Ben?"

Connor shook his head. "I no hit, Daddy."

"He frow dis." Olivia held up a pinecone.

"Oh, I bet that hurt." Josie gently pulled Ben's hand from his face. "Let me see."

A red patch bloomed on Ben's cheek but no blood.

"I think you're okay." Josie kissed his face. "Shake it off."

Three toddlers flapped their arms and wobbled their heads. After several seconds, they ran off giggling.

"You trained the kids to dance to Taylor Swift songs?" asked Leah.

Josie stiffened under the weight of judgment in the teenager's eyes. "Just this one. Listen, when you have three preschoolers constantly injuring themselves and each other, you teach them to cope in any way you can. Otherwise, the crying would never stop, and I'd spend the whole day coddling them. Ain't nobody got time for that."

Leah threw open her hands. "And you couldn't have shared that trick with me any of the times I've babysat?"

Hunter glanced behind Josie, stood, and pulled her to her feet. "Marie?"

Josie followed his gaze. Her mother closed the Winnie's door and hefted her travel bag onto her shoulder.

"Mom, you're leaving?"

"I am. I'll say goodbye to the kids after I put my stuff in the car."

Josie grabbed Hunter's hand. "Do something."

He raised his eyebrows questioningly. "Like what?"

How was she supposed to know? Letting her mother leave in a huff wasn't the right call though.

Marie returned from her Camry and tugged down the hem of her top. "I need to get back to Albuquerque, and you all are doing just fine here."

"Mom, I don't want you to go. You've been a great help with the kids, and I still can't lift anything over ten pounds, remember?"

"Yeah, Marie, we're glad to have you." Hunter gave

Josie's hand a supportive squeeze. "It would be good to have extra hands with the kids a while longer."

She motioned toward the Hardings. "Oh, you have plenty of hands. And I still have a realtor coming to my house, even though I'll be revamping my retirement plans." Her mouth pulled into a thin line. "Now, *nietos,* come and kiss your Abuelita goodbye." She knelt with her arms open.

The triplets ignored her and continued playing until Leah intervened. "Hey, go hug your grandmother." She pointed toward Marie with a firm 'I mean business' expression.

Olivia ran into Marie's arms. The boys followed suit, dragging plastic bowling pins behind them.

Never had the kids fallen in line so fast, and Josie silently vowed to take a lesson from the teenage expert. She studied Leah's face, noting the firm set of her mouth and narrowed eyes. Josie would have jumped to attention too if Leah had given her that look.

The Hardings gathered round, each taking a turn hugging Marie, even Dana, who had more reason than anyone to celebrate her departure. Josie clung to Hunter, rehearsing the words she might say when her own turn came to face her mother.

Hunter let go of Josie to embrace Marie. "You'll call and let us know when you make it home, won't you?"

She rolled her eyes. "You can't get calls out here, but sure. I'll let you know."

Josie inhaled a fortifying breath. "Mom, thank you so much for coming. You have been a huge blessing this week."

Her mother swiped away her praise. "That's what moms do." She planted her hands on Josie's cheeks and drew her head down to kiss her. "*Mija,* you'll always be my little girl."

"I love you, Mom." Josie blinked back tears.

"I love you, too." With that, Marie slid into her Camry

and backed out. She waved as she pulled away, but she didn't look back.

Josie stood rooted to the spot, hugging her chest as she watched the taillights inch away at what she was sure was exactly seven and a half miles per hour. She swiped her cheek and turned to face the others. "Well, what's everyone standing around for? The day's young, and adventure's calling." The corny line broke the awkward silence and got everyone moving again.

"Can we go fishing?" asked Nate.

Adam folded his arms. "You just wanna beat my record."

"Here's a thought," said Leah. "Maybe we stick to catch and release because I sure don't want to eat trout two days in a row."

Dana appeared at Josie's side. "You okay?"

She shrugged. "I'm a terrible person for hurting my mom's feelings."

"It'll work out. You two have weathered worse, right?" Dana hugged her.

Had they? This was uncharted territory—lying to keep her mother from visiting, then fleeing the state to cover her tracks.

Josie stuffed her hands into her pockets, eager to change the subject. "Oh hey, Leah's got an impressive bossy streak. The next time the triplets are out of control, I'll just have her come over and straighten them out. Where did she learn to assert her authority like that?"

"I think it's hardwired into firstborn daughters' DNA. The ones who end up with multiple little brothers develop an extra helping." Dana checked behind her and angled her head close to Josie's. "Sometimes she scares me a little."

Josie laughed and nodded. Leah scared her too, but she didn't dare admit it aloud.

"Hey, Jos," Hunter called from the open door of the camper. "How long has this red light been blinking?"

Her chest tightened. Blinking like the timer on a bomb? Of course. This morning alone, they'd faced a missing person and sent her mother packing. What was one more disaster? "What red light?"

Chapter 35

Josie pressed her hands together. "Say a prayer for me. I'm going in."

"You've got this," Dana said. "What's the worst that could happen?"

"Seriously?" Josie trudged toward the Winnie to investigate Hunter's discovery.

He pointed to a control panel, where a small red light blinked steadily. "The gray water tank is full. We need to drive up to the dump station and empty it."

She squinted at the blinking light, not entirely sure what a gray water tank was. Emptying it, though, didn't sound like anything she wanted to take part in. "Go right ahead. I'll stay back and watch the triplets while you drain the tank." She snickered to herself.

He narrowed his eyes. "I've never done it before and might need help, especially with parking the Winnie."

She threw her head back with a moan. "Fine." She stepped out and called to Dana. "Can the trips head down to the lake with y'all, and we'll catch up after we dump the gray water?"

"Of course." Dana wrinkled her brow. "Are you sure that's something you should do two days post-op?"

Josie grinned. "Ooh, good point." She spun back toward the camper. "Sorry, babe. I forgot I can't lift anything. Wouldn't be safe for me to help." She held up her hands in an exaggerated shrug.

He hopped out of the Winnie and yanked the cord from the site's electrical box. "Fine, but we'll have to pay for any damages out of the preschool budget." A low blow, but an effective one. The triplets would age out of Parents' Day Out in the fall, but their spots were secured for preschool in September. Without that lifeline, Josie would never make it through cosmetology school.

"Alright, you win. I'll help you if I don't have to lift anything."

"It's just attaching hoses and turning valves, Jos. Should be fine."

Josie followed behind Hunter as he disconnected the water and reeled in the awning. Then she stood outside to make sure he didn't hit anything driving away.

As they pulled beside the sign that read "dump station," she turned to Hunter. "Now what?"

"Now we hook up the hose and open the valve." He said it like he'd done it a dozen times. He dragged a big orange tub of hoses out of the cargo bay, set it by the rear wheel, and fished out a fat blue one to hook underneath the camper. "Can you put the other end in the waste hole?" He pointed to a metal lid in a concrete slab.

Josie bit her lip as the process of draining the tank became clear. "I don't think so."

"Please, babe. The sooner we get this done, the better."

She tried to flip the lid open with the toe of her shoe, but it didn't budge.

"You just gotta get in there," Hunter called, a safe distance away from the sewage hole.

Josie took a deep breath and held it, wrested the lid open, and connected the fitting over the hole. She took two wide steps away and exhaled. "Now what?"

The answer became obvious with a gurgling noise that made her jump.

"It's just shower and sink water, babe. Not a big deal." Hunter's reassurance had barely left his mouth when he yelped, stumbling backward. His face scrunched tight. "It got in my eye!"

Her gaze whipped to the valve, where a fine spray shot from the loose connection.

"Help me, would ya?" Hunter scrubbed his lips against his sleeve, panic rising in his voice. "I need to disinfect...everything."

Josie bit the inside of her cheeks to keep from laughing. "It's not a big deal, remember? Just sink water."

Hunter stood and felt his way down the side of the camper. "I could go blind, Josie."

She rolled her eyes, thankful he couldn't see her do it. She wrapped her arm around his waist and walked him to the Winnie's door.

Once inside, Hunter slid his fingers along the countertop.

Josie grabbed a container of wet wipes, pulled one out, and put it in his hand. "Here."

"Thanks, babe." He scoured his eyes and held his hand out for another wipe. "These don't have disinfectant in them."

"They're good enough for your children's bottoms. Now, let's get back out there."

He squinted and blinked rapidly as if testing his vision. "I need soap and water."

"Go use the sink in the bathhouse. We'll never get the tank drained with you running the water in here."

"Good idea. Can you finish up while I wash my face?"

"So we can both be blinded? I'd rather not."

"Please, Jos. It should be drained by now, so there won't be anything else spraying. Just push in the valve handle and unhook the hose. Then use the black water hose to rinse out the blue one while it's still in the waste drain. It's not that hard."

Her earlier amusement at his overreaction gave way to irritation. "I love you, but you should know I'm having a really hard time liking you right now." So much for not putting a strain on herself. Weren't those his exact words to her?

"I wouldn't ask if I thought it was going to be too much for you."

"Fine. Whatever. I'll do all the work while you wash your face."

Josie tackled the waste tank like a seasoned RV pro—draining, flushing, and stowing the hoses. She even managed to avoid touching anything too disgusting. But resentment simmered beneath her composure. Lugging the bulky tub—definitely over her ten-pound post-op limit—had her gritting her teeth, not that Hunter cared.

She jerked the cargo door open with more force than necessary. It smacked against the camper with a hollow thud. Only after she hefted the tote inside and slammed the door shut did she notice the problem—the key Hunter had left in the lock now bent at an unfortunate angle.

Fantastic. The mangled key refused to budge.

After a beat, she flipped the door open again, carefully this time, and pulled a black toolbox to the edge and located a pair of pliers. Straightening the key would be Hunter's problem, if she could get it out of the lock first. She clamped the tool around the key, braced her hip against the cargo door, and pulled.

"Jos, what are you doing?"

Josie startled at Hunter's voice, and the key snapped clean off.

Hunter dabbed his ear with the towel hanging around his neck. His shirt dangled from the other hand.

"You showered?"

His damp hair stuck up in unruly spikes. "Had to. Contaminated water got in my hair, and there's no telling where else." The mist from the loose hose fitting was so fine, there was no way it doused his entire upper body like he claimed. He'd have had to lie directly under it—and maybe roll around a little.

Josie waited as he ducked into the camper to grab a clean shirt, praying all the while for God to give her patience.

Hunter stepped out of the Winnie pulling a cap over his hair. "Much better."

"I'm glad you're decontaminated now because we have a new problem." She held up the pliers with the camper's keyring dangling from its jaws.

"What the— How did— Seriously, Josie?"

Heat rose up her neck. "Don't start with me. You're the one who left your wife who had emergency surgery TWO days ago to deal with waste removal unsupervised. You're lucky all I broke was a key."

They drove back to Campsite Twelve in silence except for the cargo door slapping open and shut as Hunter drove over speed bumps. Josie got out to direct him into the spot and left to catch up with the Hardings and triplets at the lake.

Dana danced with Connor who was laughing as he bounced on her hip. "Hey, how was it?"

"Don't ask." Josie eased herself onto a boulder near Ben and Olivia.

"That good, huh?"

She ducked her head for Olivia to tuck a dandelion into her hair. "Thank you, baby."

Her daughter beamed. "Mommy, you boo-ful now." She ran off to pick more flowers.

"Who knew I only needed one flower to make me look like a Hollywood starlet?"

Dana set Connor on the ground. "Where's Hunter?"

"Hopefully fixing the lock on the camper." Josie described the ordeal at the dump station. "I swear, Dana, he was a bigger baby about getting dirty water on his face than I was about having appendicitis or the after pains from being inflated with carbon dioxide."

"That's not saying much. You were quite stoic when you felt bad. Other than planning for a TV special about your demise." Dana put one hand on her hip and tilted her head. "Come to think of it, you haven't complained at all since your surgery. Are you sure you're human?"

"I've had three babies cut out of me and routinely survive on less than five hours of sleep a night. At this point, not much rattles me." It wasn't entirely true, but like most moms, she pushed past her own discomfort to take care of everyone else. Hunter could take a lesson.

Olivia held a flower out to Dana. "You wan be boo-ful too?"

"Absolutely!" Dana plopped on the grass to give Olivia access to her hair.

"You know," Josie said, "I've heard stories of selfish husbands who ate in front of their wives during labor or wore earplugs so the baby's cries wouldn't disturb their precious sleep. And I was so thankful I dodged that bullet. Until today."

Dana patted Josie's leg. "Cut him a little slack. I would've freaked out too if I got that on my face or in my eye."

"It's his attitude about it, though. If the tables had been turned, I feel like he'd have accused me of overreacting and told me it was nothing to get worked up about." She gestured vaguely toward the dump station. "And I'm pretty sure I wouldn't have made him help me in the first place— two days post-op."

Dana smirked, stretching her legs out in front of her. "No, if either one of our husbands had emergency surgery, I'm sure he'd be milking it for as long as possible."

"Hunter might still be in the hospital, hooked up to a pain pump." Josie traced a divot in the rock with her fingertip before glancing back at Dana. "How have you and Will been getting along this week? It can't be easy sharing tight quarters with your kids."

"Except for him biting my head off about the space heater when the electricity was out, we've actually been having fun together." Dana leaned back on her palms, tilting her face toward the sky. "The only alone time we've had was releasing that turtle into the woods, but he's been really involved with the kids, and I love that."

After a while, Leah joined them from the fishing pier. "Can we go back to camp? The boys are getting on my nerves, and my arm needs more aloe."

Dana rose. "Sure thing. Josie, do you and the littles want to head back with us?"

"Yeah, I should fix the mess I made—sooner rather than later." Her stomach knotted. She meant the broken key, technically, but the image of her mother driving away, hurt and blindsided, haunted her. When they arrived at camp, Hunter held out the jagged half of the key he'd wrestled from the lock.

"How'd you get it out?" Josie asked.

"Tweezers and WD-40. Now I'm gonna head up to the store and get some duct tape to keep the bay closed until we can figure out a better plan. Care to join me? You probably have a ton of messages since you haven't touched your phone in a couple of days."

"Okay, if we take our time, maybe my mom will get home and call while we still have service." She grabbed her phone out of the Winnie and switched it on.

"I'll push the double stroller, and one kiddo can walk. They'll take turns." He loaded the boys and instructed Olivia to stay by Mommy.

The trip to the lake had wiped Josie out. Well, that and all the day's drama before it, but she painted on a smile. "I'm sure I can push the single stroller. It's gotta be less strain than lifting that tote full of hoses."

Hunter matched his stride to Josie and Olivia's relaxed pace. "You should have waited and let me put it away."

"You took so long in the bathroom, I lost hope you

were ever coming back."

His mouth hung open. "Is that why you broke the key-to punish me?"

"Of course not! It was an accident, but being mad at you probably didn't help."

"If the tables were turned, you'd have done the same thing." Surgeons weren't as thorough scrubbing in as Hunter was cleaning a little gray water off his face.

"Whatever you say, babe." In almost three years of parenting, Josie had gotten plenty of undesirable substances on her. There simply weren't enough hours in the day to shower after every incident. "How about we agree that we both could have handled that situation better and move on?"

"Fine by me." Hunter's clipped tone only grated on her nerves more.

As they neared the visitor center, Josie's phone buzzed in her pocket. She pulled it out, and her screen lit up with messages from well-wishers back home. Clearly, Hunter or Dana put the church prayer ministry on alert about her appendicitis.

Another, less encouraging message caught her eye. Glad you're ok but what did you do to Mom???? Her sister Laurel wasn't known for her superfluous punctuation, so she must have been upset.

Josie turned the screen to Hunter.

He leaned in to read the message. "That's going to be a fun conversation. Want me to give you some privacy?"

She put her hand on his arm. "Don't you dare." If a scolding was coming, she at least wanted Hunter and the kids nearby as an excuse to hang up quickly—a ready-made escape route. Heart thudding with trepidation, she tapped her sister's name.

Laurel picked up on the first ring, as if she'd been waiting for Josie's call. "You almost die and don't even tell me? Are you taking after Dad now?"

Josie lowered herself onto a bistro chair. "No." Their dad had kept his cancer diagnosis a secret for months before they found out. "One minute, I thought I had a mild stomach bug. The next, I'm being airlifted to the hospital. And it's not like I have cell service out here."

"Yeah, Mom filled me in. And for the record, I'm glad you're okay, even if I had to hear it third hand and after the fact."

Josie ignored Laurel's dramatization. Hunter had called their mother, whose job was to relay the news to the rest of the family. She hadn't done anything wrong, and the comparison to Javier Saldana was a low blow.

"Mom also said you don't want her to live in the same state and that you took off to Colorado to hide from her," said Laurel. "You'd rather sleep on the ground—which I happen to know you hate—than let her come visit." At least she came by her theatrics honestly.

Josie tipped her head back, searching the sky for patience. "I'm *not* sleeping on the ground. It's a very nice motorhome. And I never said she couldn't live in Texas. I just don't want her around the corner, popping in whenever she pleases to criticize my parenting. She disapproves of everything I do with the triplets. And sure, I'm not as good a housekeeper as her, but no one is."

Hunter unbuckled Ben and Connor, and they raced off to join Olivia in a raucous game of toddler tag. Josie stuck a finger in her free ear, trying to muffle the chaos enough to hear Laurel on the other end.

"Fix this, Josie. Mom's really hurt." The line got quiet until Laurel added, "I don't want her to move to Boulder because *you* don't want her around. At least you have three little reasons for being a terrible housekeeper. I don't have an excuse."

They said their goodbyes, and Josie turned her attention to Hunter and the kids.

"Everything okay between you and your sister?"

"Just peachy. She's afraid if I don't patch things up with Mom, she'll become a thorn in Laurel's side."

Hunter swung Ben onto his shoulders. "This is why I'm glad I have brothers. Throw a couple of punches when Mom's not looking, and we're back to a clean slate. No emotional baggage."

She tilted her head, incredulous that the father of her children would say such a thing. "You're telling me you'd have your sons duke it out whenever they have a problem?"

"I mean, if the options are between swift justice or prolonged hard feelings…"

"Uh-huh." She stood and shoved her phone into her pocket. "Ready to buy some tape?"

Bonnie greeted them as the Caraway troop filed into the visitor center. "How can I help you folks?"

"We had a mishap at the dump station, and the key to the external doors of the camper broke off. We need a way to secure the cargo door and keep it from flapping until we can get to a locksmith."

"Well, that's a new one. Mind if I take a look at that key?" Bonnie walked around the desk.

Hunter set Ben on the floor and fished in his pocket. He held his palm up with the two broken pieces of the key.

Bonnie picked up the end that had been attached to the key ring and turned it over. "Fun fact about Winnebago. They only key about ten different locks for everything but the deadbolt. So, getting a replacement is easier than you think."

Josie met Hunter's eye, which mirrored her own confusion.

"I'm not following," said Hunter.

Bonnie held up the end of the key. "See these four-digits? You need a copy of a key with the same code, which anyone who sells Winnies should have on hand. You get yourself to the dealership in Durango, and I bet they can make you a new one on site." She ducked into the room with the store and motioned for them to follow. "And here's your tape."

Hunter reached for his wallet, but Bonnie waved him away. "On the house. Don't think a roll of duct tape is going to bankrupt us."

Olivia pulled a plush bear off a low shelf and held it up. "Daddy, I need dis."

"You already have one. Didn't Miss Frances give it to you?"

She looked up through her long lashes. "Peas, Daddy. I need two."

He pointed at the top of her head. "Meet the thing that's going to bankrupt *us*."

Josie took the bear and set it back on the shelf. "That's our cue to go. Everyone back to the strollers."

Josie led a screaming Olivia outside while Hunter scooped the boys into football holds and followed her out. Ben and Connor kicked and arched their backs, resisting being buckled into their seats.

"Want toy!" Olivia screeched.

The boys joined her angry pleas. "Git dat ball!"

"Go get toys!"

Josie kept a firm grip on Olivia's hand and raised her voice to be heard over the tantrums. "So, I was thinking. I can ask Dana and Will to borrow their Tahoe to go to town and replace the key while you feed the kids and put them down for naps."

"Oh, you were just thinking that?" Hunter wore a dubious smirk.

She shrugged. "Yeah, I mean, there's no reason to go to the trouble of buckling in car seats and taking squirmy kids all that way. I'll take one for the team and go by myself. The key was my fault after all." Two hours to herself without screaming toddlers would be heavenly.

"Nice try, Jos, but you can't drive on narcotics. I'm all in favor of paying the Harding kids to babysit though."

She held out her hand to him. "Deal."

Hunter shook it. "When you need some time to yourself, all you have to do is ask."

"That's easier said than done when so many tiny humans count on me to keep them alive."

He stopped pushing the stroller and turned to her. "You aren't in this by yourself, you know."

"I know."

"It doesn't feel like you do. You had surgery two days ago, and you're already overdoing it because you don't trust anyone else to help."

She bristled. That wasn't true. She *wanted* help. Okay, maybe she didn't *want* it, but she needed it.

"I'm just saying," said Hunter, "maybe you wouldn't be so desperate for a break if you'd eased up on jumping straight back into full mom mode. And maybe—just maybe—you wouldn't have driven your mom away if you'd let her take charge and actually accepted her help."

Josie's glare could have melted steel. She accepted help just fine. It wasn't *her* fault her mother got her feelings hurt so easily.

A trio of kicking, screaming toddlers dragged on her patience like anchors, and she silently prayed the Hardings would be up for babysitting. How did she go from missing her children so fiercely one day to needing space from them the next?

Hunter's words held more than a sliver of truth. If she'd stayed in bed and let her mother handle the triplets without interfering, she wouldn't have confessed the lie that sent her back to Albuquerque. Guilt pricked her. She'd pushed her mother's help away so hard she might never get it back.

Chapter 36

Dana

"Ready?" Dana perched on the edge of Nate's hammock as Will did the same on the other side. They rolled toward the center, the fabric swallowing them. After a minute of concerted shifting, taking great pains to keep from tumbling out, Dana curled into Will. Even though he assured her it was rated for five hundred pounds, she sent up a silent prayer that it held. "I pictured this as more romantic in my mind."

Will rested one arm behind his head while his free hand traced lazy trails along her arm. "I think it's nice. We haven't had much time just the two of us since we left home."

It was true Dana wanted more quality time with Will, but their hanging retreat came with an irritating soundtrack—triplets fussing in the Winnie while Leah, Nate, and Adam tried in vain to get them to nap.

"Why didn't we go to town to replace the key and leave Hunter and Josie on kid duty?" Dana carefully adjusted her hips to a more comfortable position without either of them being hurled to the ground. "We could've gone to lunch together. Maybe done a little sight-seeing."

"We got the better deal right here."

A toddler's demand broke the sound barrier. "No, Wee-uh. I no sweep. I pway wif toys."

"How is this better?" Dana pressed her cheek against Will's chest to muffle the piercing screams.

"Are you kidding? Winding mountain roads make you mean and carsick."

Dana lifted her head just enough to squint at him. "Carsick, sure. But how do they make me mean?"

"Have you forgotten accusing me of trying to drive us off the side of the mountain on the way up here?" Will swept her hair off her neck. "You threatened to get out and walk."

"That was the nausea talking."

The camper door flew open, slamming against the Winnie with a dull thud. Adam stomped down the steps, fists balled at his sides. "I can't do it anymore." He flopped crossways into his hammock, feet still planted on the ground as he rocked back and forth. "I need a break from the triplets. They're so intense!"

"They're in a camper, not in tents," Will quipped.

"Very funny, Dad."

"Three kids are a handful, that's for sure," said Dana.

Adam let out a dramatic moan and tilted his head back. "Dad, can we do something fun on our last day tomorrow?"

"Are you not having fun now?" Will asked.

"I want to go somewhere away from camp." Adam dragged a hand over his hair. "Without the babies."

Will stood as Dana clung to the sides to keep from being rolled onto the ground. He pulled up a screenshot on his phone and held it out to Adam. "It was going to be a surprise, but I booked us a white-water rafting trip."

Adam's wide-eyes mirrored Dana's. Only where hers held sheer terror, his were filled with excitement. "No way! Thanks, Dad." He jumped up and clapped his hands. "This is going to be epic."

Why did everything have to be epic? Dana had no

desire to traverse an icy river in an inflatable boat. It was bad enough sleeping on a blow-up bed in a frigid tent. "I hope you booked that trip for four because I'm not going."

Will took her hands and helped her rise out of the hammock. "Come on, Dana. It'll be fun. A core memory before Leah goes off to college, and the boys get too busy to hang out with us." He bent his face close to hers. "The more fun stuff we do with the kids, the more likely they'll be to come back and visit when they're grown."

She saw what he was doing—guilting her into another adventure. This time though, she wasn't having it. "William, I would be too stressed out to have fun. Besides, someone has to stay with Harvey."

"I'm sure the Caraways can keep an eye on the dog for a few hours. But if you're dead set against it, I guess I can see if Hunter wants to go in your place." He furrowed his brow and cocked his head. "What happened to the thrill-seeking girl who went cliff diving with her cousin on Spring Break?"

She clenched her jaw. "That was a long time ago." Her high school body had shrugged off stunts that would send her forty-five-year-old self straight to the chiropractor. Or the hospital. Hard pass.

He tapped his index finger on his chin. "Or better yet, where's the adventurous woman who snuck off to investigate that secret hotel operation in the woods this morning? *She* would try rafting."

Dana paced an angry path between the hammocks and the firepit. "I try new things all the time. I'm here, aren't I? Two weeks ago, I *tried* taking our child to have her broken arm set by an orthopedic surgeon. Just yesterday, I tried picking splinters out of our son's leg. I tried dealing with my friend's medical crisis." She took a step closer to Will and whispered, "I even tried really hard to be nice to her overbearing mother."

"She has a point, Dad." Adam settled back in his

hammock and folded his hands behind his head. "Abuelita, I mean, Mrs. Saldana was a lot."

Dana propped her elbow on her crossed arm and held in a laugh with her palm over her mouth.

Will turned to Adam with his hands on his hips. "Mind your own business, kiddo."

"You're in my area." Adam pointed toward the center of the campsite. "Go talk about grownup things over there if you don't want me to be in the conversation."

Dana crossed to the picnic table so as not to disturb the ten-year-old's downtime. "I even tried hiking in the rain."

Will rolled his eyes. "It wasn't raining when we started the hike."

She put up her hand. "Whatever. The point is, I don't have the emotional bandwidth for another death-defying activity this week."

"Okay." Will placed his hands on her shoulders and touched his forehead to hers. "I should have asked you if you wanted to go before I booked the excursion. Are you sure you don't mind us going without you?"

Mind it? She preferred it. An afternoon to write in peace without having to break out the first aid kit or set reptiles free in the woods. It was her ideal vacation scenario. The only missing piece was a waiter delivering frozen concoctions to her poolside cabana.

At last, quiet settled over Site Twelve as the triplets succumbed to sleep. Nate slipped out of the Winnie, careful not to let the door slam. He tiptoed to the table and plunked down next to his mom. "I'm never having kids."

Dana bumped him with her shoulder. "Hey, at least you're getting paid for your troubles."

He propped his elbows on the table and rested his head on his arms. "I know. And I know Josie and Hunter really needed the help this week, but I kind of wish they hadn't come. Their kids are too little to do much, and they're getting on my nerves."

"Then you'll be happy to learn that—" Will's words were cut off by Adam, who made a mad dash from his hammock.

"Nate, guess what? Dad's taking us rafting tomorrow! And I bet it's going to be rough waters because the snow is melting out of the mountains."

"Seriously?" Nate sat up straight. A grin spread across his face. "That's awesome!"

"What's awesome?" asked Leah. No one had heard her approach.

"White water rafting. We're going tomorrow." Adam tapped Will with the back of his hand. "Show her the pictures."

Leah nodded. "Cool." She reached into the ice chest, grabbed a soda, and returned to her babysitting post without the slightest show of emotion.

"I'm sure she'll be excited when she gets there," Dana assured Will. If the teen shared her mother's aversion to rafting, she would have protested right away.

Dana sat in the Winnie's shade, laptop balanced on her knees, typing away when Josie and Hunter returned from Durango that afternoon.

Hunter tossed the Tahoe keys to Will. "Thanks, man."

Josie held up a paper bag with Sal's logo on the side. "To show our appreciation, we brought dinner. Hope everyone likes spaghetti and meatballs."

Dana glanced at her watch. Dinner at 3:00? The kids would be hungry again long before bedtime.

As if reading her mind, Josie said, "We'll put everything in the fridge and reheat it tonight." She handed the bag to Hunter and reached into the back seat for another one.

Reheated spaghetti did sound better than hot dogs again. Campfire meals were fun for about a day and a half. Then the charm wore off, along with any motivation to scrub pots and pans without a kitchen sink.

"What made you choose Sal's?" Dana asked. Durango had plenty of restaurants. Funny they'd unknowingly picked the same place Will had.

"Frances," Josie settled into a camp chair and held Connor's hand as he climbed onto her lap. "We stopped at the visitor center to load the directions to the RV dealer and asked her for a lunch recommendation." She stretched her legs out with a satisfied sigh. "The food was so good we just had to share."

Ben trotted over, holding out a plastic bowling pin. "Come on."

Connor slid down and followed Ben to a grassy patch where they batted a ball back and forth with the pins.

"Be careful, boys," Josie called after them, then turned back to Dana. "You'll never guess who we saw at Sal's."

"Bonnie?"

Josie's brows lifted. "How'd you know?"

"Really?" Dana tilted her head. "She's the only other person you know around here besides us and Frances—who you already said was at the visitor center."

"It was weird, though." Josie lowered her voice slightly. "She came out of a back room with two men in suits. Then they all got into a black car together."

Dana closed the laptop and leaned in. "Will saw her get into a black car at Sal's the night you had surgery too. And Sal's nephew is the one who drove me back this morning." She frowned. "Something doesn't add up, but I can't quite put my finger on it."

Josie shook her head. "Might be best to let it go. You got lucky this morning, but you don't know what kind of ties Bonnie has. Her sister said she was a marksman—sharpshooter or whatever—in the military. Snooping could get you into real trouble.

Dana pushed down the flicker of defensiveness. Josie meant   well. "I'm too tired to snoop. I've been up since five, remember? And that air mattress isn't exactly conducive to a full night's rest." She smothered a yawn. "I cannot wait to sleep in my own bed again."

"I hear ya. I'm ready to park my kids in their cribs where they can't escape and get into mischief."

Dana's mouth fell open. "You mean Ben can't climb out of his crib yet?" That kid scaled the picnic table at least three times a day. He had no trouble getting into the hammock by himself, so surely he could get out of a baby bed.

"Mercifully, not yet. But I know it's coming."

"Connor and Livvie will be right behind him, I'm sure." Dana glanced at her watch again. "This has been the longest day ever. Did your mom get home okay?"

Josie's expression tightened. "Yeah. She called Hunter while we were in town to let him know." She sighed. "Wouldn't even talk to me."

Dana reached for her hand and gave it a reassuring squeeze. "She just needs a little time. You two will work it out."

"Thanks." Josie squinted at the boys playing in the grass. "Excuse me." She sprang out of her chair, sending it toppling backward, and snatched the bowling pin from Connor's hand. "No sir. We do not hit." Gone was any hint she'd had emergency surgery only two days ago.

A single bark rang out from the tent's entrance. Harvey's tail wagged as he waited to be let inside.

Dana pushed up from her seat and unzipped the tent door. Inside, Leah lay on her stomach, feet kicked up behind her, eyes glued to her phone. Harvey hopped onto Dana and Will's air mattress, turned two circles, and flopped down with a dramatic sigh.

"You know it's bad when even the dog needs a timeout," Leah said without looking up.

Dana pressed a finger to her lips. "Shh. You'll hurt Josie's feelings if she hears you." Since the hundred-pound mongrel took up her bed, she sprawled on top of Nate's sleeping bag with a groan. "But why can't he take his timeout on his own bed?"

Leah cupped her hand around her mouth and whispered, "After putting up with the triplets for so long, Harvey deserves the best bed in the place."

"Don't we all." Dana threw her arm over her eyes. She loved the Caraways like they were her own family, but even she was at her limit. Toddlers in the woods were far more work than she imagined.

Dana awoke to a symphony of rapid tapping on the exterior of the tent. Oh good. More rain. She scanned the space, shivering against the cold. Leah was gone, but Harvey lifted his head and huffed, clearly sharing her opinion of the weather. She pulled on her jacket and unzipped the tent. Will and Hunter stood beneath the Winnie's awning, steaming mugs in hand. She tugged her hood over her head, zipped the door behind Harvey, and hurried toward them.

Will slipped an arm around her waist, drawing her into his warmth. "How was your nap?"

"Great." She relaxed against him, inhaling the comforting mix of rain, coffee, and the buttery garlic aroma wafting from the camper. Inside, her kids' voices mingled with toddler chatter. "I was so tired, I—" Her stomach growled loudly, cutting her off.

Hunter chuckled and held the Winnie's door open. "Good timing. Dinner's just about ready."

Dana hesitated on the bottom step. The camper offered retreat from the dreary weather, but the sheer number of people inside its narrow walls made it feel more cramped than cozy.

Inside, the triplets and Adam were seated around the banquette while Josie shuffled dishes from the oven and microwave to the table. Nate and Leah stood in the narrow walkway, passing paper goods over Ben's head.

Josie sucked a stray glob of spaghetti sauce off her finger and smiled. "Come on in and make yourself at home. Or would you rather I make you a plate to eat outside?"

Ultimately, the Winnie enticed her with its comforting atmosphere and trumped her middle-aged claustrophobia. "If there's space for me, I'll come in."

Adam patted the cushion beside him. "There's plenty of room."

Josie set toddler-size portions of spaghetti and garlic bread in front of each of the triplets. "If I'd known we would be eating inside tonight, we'd have gotten something less messy." She instructed Leah and Nate to serve themselves and find a place to sit.

Leah opted for the edge of the queen bed, Nate for the floor in front of the bathroom door.

Once everyone else had their dinner, Will and Hunter squeezed into the camper. Hunter climbed into the cockpit and balanced his plate on his knees in the passenger seat while Will stood in the stepwell holding his over the sink.

Adam cleared his throat loudly. "Hello. Didn't we forget something?" He folded his hands and bowed his head.

"Would you like to offer grace, Adam?" asked Josie.

He twisted his face. "Offer grace? No, I just thought we should say the blessing."

"Same thing, doofus," Leah said.

Adam narrowed his eyes in a death stare, bowed his head again, and prayed. He'd scarcely said "amen" before they all dug in.

Will moaned and his eyes rolled back. "This is delicious. That Sal sure knows his way around a kitchen."

Obviously. Otherwise, his restaurant wouldn't be successful. Dana kept this thought to herself.

"I'm impressed," added Josie. "After seeing Bonnie and an entourage leave his place, I was beginning to think it was just a front for money laundering or illegal gambling."

Dana's throat seized mid-swallow, and she clapped a hand to her chest as a meatball lodged in her windpipe. Eyes watering, she coughed and sputtered, desperate to clear her airway.

Will set his plate in the sink. "Hon, are you ok?" He patted her back until she regained her faculties.

She nodded and took a sip of water.

"Why would you put money in the washing machine?" Adam asked with a cheek full of food.

Dana almost choked again. "Don't talk with your mouth full." She gave Josie a warning glare. "This isn't really dinner conversation."

Maybe Josie spent so much time with toddlers, she forgot how to censor herself. Sooner or later though, she'd regret her loose lips and grow a filter. Hopefully, that moment would come before Dana had to explain organized crime to her son.

Will resumed his position in the stepwell and picked up his plate. "Josie, how are you feeling? You're getting around a lot better than I would have expected so soon after surgery."

She shrugged. "I'm alright, I guess. Still sore, but this is nothing compared to having a triple C-section."

So help me, if Adam brings this up too, he's spending the night in here. Dana pinched the bridge of her nose. "Another topic not suitable for the dinner table."

Dana's mind churned over the link between Sal and

Bonnie. Frances had said there were rumors about his ties to the mob. That in conjunction with the clandestine poker tournament at the wellness retreat couldn't be a coincidence. There had to be a connection, but was finding out the truth worth the risk?

Chapter 37

Dana poked her head into the driver's window. "Remember, leave your phones in the car so they don't end up in the river." She gave Will a quick peck. "That goes for you, too. Oh, wait." She pulled a Ziplock bag from her pocket and handed it over. "For the key fob. Make sure you put it in a pocket it can't fall out of."

Will took the bag with an exasperated smile. "Honey, I don't need you to mother me." He tapped her forehead lightly with his finger. "We'll be fine."

Leah leaned forward from the back seat. "Don't worry, Mom. My shorts have a hidden pocket that zips."

Will passed the sandwich baggie to her over the headrest. "See? I already have a backup mom."

Dana rolled her eyes but couldn't help smiling. "Okay, have fun. Love you." She stepped back, waving as the SUV pulled away.

Josie reclined against the side of the camper, arms crossed loosely over her chest. "Thanks for letting Hunter go in your place. He was so excited about rafting. And I haven't exactly been much fun this week."

"Nonsense." Dana tugged a camp chair to the shade of the awning. "He got to ride in a very fancy helicopter because of you." She quirked a teasing eyebrow. "Not to mention his close encounter with a Hollywood A-list actor and his supermodel girlfriend."

Josie let out a chuckle. "That's true. I do make his life

more exciting. Speaking of which, how did you and Will convince him to leave me on my own for a few hours?"

"I'm here too, so you're well-supervised."

"Funny." Josie pulled her phone out of her pocket and drummed her fingers on the back of it as if lost in thought.

"Want me to keep an eye on the triplets while you go use the Wi-Fi?" Dana picked at a cuticle, trying to keep her face from giving away the fact that she only offered herself up as the babysitter tribute out of politeness. The words had slipped out when she saw Josie's expression, but wrangling the toddlers at the campsite all on her own had the potential to be more treacherous than coursing down rapids.

"Thanks, but I was just thinking I might actually have time to start this novel I downloaded last week while the little beasties nap." She bit her lip. "Please don't tell anyone I called my children that. I'll be so thankful when they get past the terrible twos in a couple of months."

Dana smirked. "Good luck with that."

"What's that supposed to mean?"

"Oh, sweetie." Dana had the urge to wrap her friend in a comforting hug before she broke the news to her. "There's a reason people call them 'threenagers.'" She gave Josie's arm a gentle squeeze. "Three-year-olds test every boundary with greater skill and obstinance than they did at two. Like teenagers. They're meaner and more capable of getting into things, they get more embarrassing in public, and somehow their sweetness fades in the process."

Josie rubbed her temples with both hands. "So, this is just the warm-up act?" Her vacant stare gave her the look of a war-weary soldier.

"There will be plenty of fun times to make it worth the extra work." Dana dipped her head to look Josie in the eye. "You'll get through it, and when they're four, you'll wish they were three again."

"Dear Jesus, come back quickly."

Dana bit back a grin, a smidgen of guilt clouding her amusement. Slowly dawning horror dawned on Josie's face.

Fifteen years ago, Dana had confidently informed her mother, "Either Leah's a toddler prodigy, or the terrible twos are a myth."

Carolyn Johnson had beamed with grandmotherly pride and agreed that Leah was indeed exceptional—right as the two-year-old dunked her entire hand into her grandmother's tea glass, sending its contents splashing squarely into the woman's lap.

"Try not to think about it. They're your children. You'll be enamored with them at every stage, even the actual teenage years." Dana rose from her seat. "I'll leave you to your book."

Josie still hadn't moved, frozen in place as Dana clipped Harvey's leash and started up the road toward the bathroom. She shouldn't have said anything. Bursting her friend's bubble after such a hard week was cruel—especially when sometimes, just *believing* better days were ahead was the only way to survive the ones that weren't. Josie would figure it out soon enough. All moms did. Time with her kids was short, even when they were actively draining the will to live.

Dana intended to tie Harvey's leash to the leg of the fish cleaning table while she ducked into the women's room. Then they would take a little walk before she got to work on her manuscript. However, as they approached the building, movement caught her eye about a half second before Harvey let out a low growl.

Dana tightened her grip, praying they weren't about to have another skunk encounter. A black head popped up and sniffed the tabletop. The thing she'd feared most about coming to the mountains locked eyes with Harvey. The bear dropped onto all fours and rounded the legs of the table. Dana's mind raced as she tried to recall whether she should stay still or get loud. Even Harvey seemed not to know what to do. He continued to growl but pressed himself so tightly to Dana's leg that she struggled to remain upright.

A memory from freshman Biology crept into her panicked thoughts. "You don't have to outrun the bear," her professor had joked. "Just be faster than your hiking buddy."

"Harvey, don't you dare let this bear get me," she hissed.

Tires skidded to a stop behind her, but Dana kept her eyes on the predator in front. An airhorn blared, startling both her and the dog. The bear, not so much.

"Get out of here. Go on, get!" A female voice shouted as the airhorn sounded over and over.

The bear turned and ambled back into the woods.

Dana swallowed hard against her dry throat. The fear that paralyzed her finally eased enough for her to turn and thank her savior, who had maintained a safe distance behind her the entire time. There stood Valerie and Martin, who once again had a rifle in his arms.

"Pretty sure that's the same one," Valerie said, lowering the airhorn.

Martin nodded. "He wasn't even fazed. We're gonna have to call Parks and Wildlife to relocate him." He carried the weapon to a pickup truck blocking the road.

Dana switched the leash to her other hand and flexed her cramping fingers. "I thought bears were supposed to be scared of dogs."

"They usually are," Martin said. "But this guy's gotten too comfortable around people and pets. That makes him dangerous."

"How did you know he was here?" Dana asked.

Valerie held up her phone. "Tracked him on the trail cams."

Heat crept up Dana's neck. She'd been banking on those cameras going unchecked until she was back in

Texas. "H-how often do you review those?"

"They're connected to our network," Martin explained. "We get immediate motion alerts. Like when someone tromps through the woods carrying a turtle." He gave her a wink.

"So, you saw Harvey and me on our early morning walk yesterday, too?"

Martin shook his head. "Got the alert, but the signal was too weak to access the footage. Which is why I came at you with a rifle." He winced. "Again, sorry about that."

Dana held up her hand. "I was the one in the wrong place. At least you weren't aiming it at me."

Valerie reached into the truck and pulled out a can of bear spray. "Keep this with you until we get this guy off the property." She pushed the can into Dana's hand. "And don't let your kids go off on their own." Maybe she saw the fear in Dana's eyes because she placed a reassuring hand on her shoulder. "There's nothing to worry about. The bear was too curious, which is a problem. But if he'd been aggressive, my brother would have shot him."

By now the airhorn had attracted the attention of other campers.

The woman who had found Connor when he wandered off approached. "Everything okay over here?"

"Yes, ma'am," said Martin. "Juvenile male bear in the vicinity. Had to scare him off."

"In the middle of the day? That's not normal," the lady said.

"But not unheard of." Valerie pointed toward the metal table. "Especially if he caught a whiff of fish guts." She gave the newcomer another can from the truck. "Keep this on you for now, just as a precaution." She hopped into the open door of the passenger seat. "We need to report this and alert the rest of the campground."

Martin waved as he pulled away. "You folks stay safe."

The woman turned the can over in her hands. "Do you

just spray it like wasp spray?"

"I think so." Dana examined her own bear spray. "I just hope we aren't all so spooked that we accidentally mace one another."

The woman gave a perfunctory chuckle and headed down the hill.

Dana led Harvey back to the campsite. The triplets were seated at the picnic table where Josie divvied up apple slices and graham crackers.

"That was the world's shortest nap. Did you get any reading done at all?"

Josie shook her head. "Nope, some fool with an airhorn woke them up before I got through the first page." She pointed at the bear spray, a silent question forming on her face.

"You heard Frances's kids scaring away a bear that was eying Harv and me." Dana held up the can. "Valerie gave me this for protection."

"I guess that's a good reason to wake the living dead. And my kids." Josie wiped her hands on the back of her leggings. "I'm glad you weren't hurt. But don't you have a can already?"

"Two actually, but I wasn't about to walk back empty handed after the way that thing moseyed off without a care in the world. It's just biding its time before it comes back."

Alarm flickered in Josie's eyes. "What should we do?"

Dana sat the can on the table in front of Josie. "You keep this one. I'll grab another from the tent."

Josie pinched it between her thumb and forefinger as if it were a soggy tissue. "No thanks. The kids are the ones most likely to spray this—right into each other's eyes. We'll take our chances with a bear."

"That's what I said!" The whole reason Dana had ventured to the bathroom in the first place had been forgotten for a time, but now the urge to go returned. "Will you watch Harvey while I go back to the bathroom? I was so scared I forgot to go earlier."

"Just go in the Winnie."

Dana feigned horror. "And be the reason you or Hunter gets another face full of sewer water? Never." She grabbed the bear spray and dashed off.

As she exited the bathroom, she ran into Valerie again, this time on a golf cart.

"Back already?"

Valerie leaned over the steering wheel and peered up the mountainside. "Keeping an eye out until the wildlife guys get out here, just to be sure."

Dana followed her gaze. "Think it'll return to the scene of the crime so soon?"

"Hmm?" Valerie sat back seeming to snap out of a reverie. "I dunno. Dude's on his third strike though, so I don't want to take any chances." After a beat, she added, "Too bad they don't tranquilize humans and haul them away on their third strike, too."

Even though Dana ought to get back to help Josie, curiosity called louder than obligation. What human was she referring to? "Hypothetically, or were you thinking of a particular person you'd like to shoot with a tranq dart?"

"I'm sorry." Valerie dragged her hands down her face. "I shouldn't vent about my problems. I don't even know you."

Dana rested her hip against the side of the cart, crossing her arms as she listened. People had a way of unburdening themselves to her. Maybe it came with the territory— middle-aged, unassuming mom types were safe, trustworthy. The kind of person you could confess your secrets to without fear of judgment.

Valerie hesitated only a moment before spilling her guts. "It's Martin," she said, her voice tinged with frustration. "We already have our hands full out here between the wild animals and Aunt Bonnie's dealings. Then he goes and pulls his usual stunts."

She turned in her seat, locking eyes with Dana, as if deciding how much to reveal. "I know you saw the poker game yesterday. And you probably know gambling's illegal here."

Dana studied the dirt beneath her shoes. "Martin said it was a friendly game among friends." The words tasted like a weak excuse even as she said them.

Valerie scoffed. "That's his problem. He thinks he can get away with stuff like that because Aunt Bonnie's connections offer a fair amount of immunity."

Dana tipped her head, curiosity burning a hole in her restraint. Bonnie wasn't just a wealthy eccentric, that much she had already figured out. "Do Bonnie's connections have anything to do with black cars and meetings in the back room of Sal's?" Her throat tightened the moment the words left her mouth. No turning back now. She'd just put all her cards on the table.

Valerie's jaw tightened. She exhaled sharply through her nose, then nodded. "Yeah. But Sal's not in the mafia like my mother believes."

Dana arched an eyebrow. "Why does she think he is?"

"Small-town rumor mill." Valerie glanced toward the tree line, lips pressing together like she was weighing how much to say. "Aunt Bonnie doesn't share much about her real job with Mom because she'd worry too much."

"But she does with you?"

"Only on a need-to-know basis," Valerie admitted. "And Sal falls under that category."

Dana's mind raced to fit the puzzle pieces together. "So, he's more than a restaurateur but less than a mobster." The picture forming in her head was murkier than ever.

Valerie let out a dry chuckle. "He's a facilitator for strategic intelligence operations, which I think is Bonnie's way of saying his level of security clearance precludes her from divulging the true nature of their relationship to us mere mortals."

Dana let out a slow breath, her pulse thrumming in her ears. What had she stumbled into? "How does your brother factor in?"

"On occasion, the folks with diplomatic immunity make requests that aren't entirely above board."

"Like poker tournaments?"

"Exactly. Martin finds ways to grant those requests, even when they're risky and could attract the wrong kind of attention." Valerie twisted to look behind her and lowered her voice. "Which is what happened today when a high-profile guest made a viral post about her boyfriend's winnings. A boyfriend that shouldn't have even known about the tournament, much less been invited to play in it."

Elara Finch must have violated the ecolodge's confidentiality agreement.

Dana swatted a fly away from her face, her stomach knotting. "Oh no, is anyone in trouble?"

"Not this time. One of Sal's specialties is throwing the press off our scent." Valerie rubbed her forehead, stress etched in the lines around her mouth. "But mistakes like that—allowing the game in the first place, not the model's predictable social media indiscretion—come at a steep cost. It's not just about legality. They could compromise the security of nations." She shook her head. "But all my brother cares about is money."

This was far beyond what Dana had envisioned. Poker games and shady business deals were one thing, but global security? A different beast entirely. "Wow, I don't even know what to say. I'm sorry."

Valerie's jaw tightened. "It's why I want to get my mom and Aunt Bonnie out of here. Martin keeps putting them in unnecessary predicaments like this. They don't need the money."

Dana glanced at the woods, the bear a minor inconvenience compared to the threats Valerie had just divulged. "Please don't take this the wrong way, but why did you share what seems like very sensitive information with me?"

Valerie let out a humorless laugh and rubbed her temples as if trying to ease the weight of her thoughts. "My husband isn't a huge Martin fan, so confiding in him about stuff that happens at the retreat only causes marital friction." She traced the seam of her jeans with her thumb. "You already knew things I haven't been able to talk to anyone else about, and you walked out of that bathroom at the exact moment I told God I needed a sympathetic ear."

"You can thank the bear for that." Dana chuckled. "I hightailed it back to camp before I had a chance to go to the bathroom earlier." She touched Valerie's arm. "But I get it."

"You have an ambitious, opportunistic sibling too?"

"Not that part. I'm an only child." Dana fidgeted with the can of bear spray. Deep conversations with virtual strangers ranked right up there with rafting and bear encounters. "I meant needing to get things off your chest and praying the right person comes along to listen." She offered a small smile. "And just so you know, your secrets are safe with me."

The bigger concern was whether Dana was safe with Valerie's secret.

Chapter 38

The intrepid rafters rolled into camp just as Dana began stacking logs for the evening fire. She met the Tahoe as a scowling Leah stomped out, wet hair plastered to her head and dragging her backpack by one strap.

"Water is stupid. I'm going to take a very long shower."

"Showers have water, genius," Nate said.

The stare his sister gave him could have melted steel. She stormed into the tent without another word.

In contrast, Will, Hunter, and the boys wore wide grins and reeked of sweat and sunscreen.

"Y'all smell like you had fun." Dana thumbed over her shoulder. "What happened to her?"

Will stepped out and planted a peck on her forehead. "We hit a rapid, and the boat folded in half like a taco."

"Yeah," said Adam. "Leah went flying. It was awesome!"

Dana's eyes widened in horror. "Was she hurt?"

"Not at all. Just stunned by the cold." Will leaned down to pet Harvey. "A brawny guy on our boat reached into the river and yanked her up by the lifejacket."

"I'm sure she loved that." She chewed the inside of her cheek, torn between checking on her daughter and risking getting her head bit off or giving Leah some space until her mood improved. Parental obligation won out over self-preservation. "I'm going to see if she needs anything."

Dana hovered at the open tent door, scanning for

anything with a tail or wings that might have breached the unzipped fortress. "Sounds like you had quite the adventure this afternoon."

Leah dug through her suitcase. "Yeah, other than narrowly escaping hypothermia, it was great."

Ah, like mother, like daughter. "So, you don't hate water after all?"

"I hate freezing water. And at the moment, all boys." Leah slung a fresh towel over her shoulder and grabbed her toiletry bag. "Everyone had a good laugh at my expense, even Dad and Hunter, who should've had my back."

Dana clenched her jaw. Watching someone fall into treacherous waters, especially your own child, wasn't funny at all. "I'm so sorry. Maybe letting you go rafting with a broken arm wasn't the best call."

"Mom, no. That's not why I fell out. It was amazing! I can't wait to go again next time."

"Next time?" Dana's stomach dropped. Another rafting trip would mean camping again. She wasn't sure she had it in her. "You, uh, *want* to come back here?"

"Maybe. I would like camping better if we had a motorhome instead of a tent, but it's fun." Leah edged past Dana.

"Wait, take this." Dana grabbed a can of bear spray off her suitcase. "On second thought, I better go with you."

Leah's face twisted into that singular grimace of disdain that only a teenager can pull off. "Why are you being weird? It's still daytime. I can handle showering alone."

"Right after y'all left, there was a bear sniffing around the fish gutting table. Miss Frances's son scared it off, but I think it's still roaming the area."

Leah froze as though weighing her options. "Okay, you can come with me." She stuck close to Dana as they made their way to the bathrooms. "This is another reason a camper beats a tent—no hikes to the bathroom, and, more importantly, shred-proof walls.”

Dana threaded her arm through Leah’s and arched a brow. “You know what would be even better than that?”

“You’re going to say a beach resort.”

“Think about it.” Dana held up the spray can. “Fewer predators, warmer water.”

“True, but then you’ve got sharks. And sand gets everywhere. I prefer to enjoy nature without taking half of it home with us.” Leah pulled away from Dana and shifted her shower caddy. “Plus, we always end up sunburnt and grumpy. This was a nice change.” She must not have counted her own grumpiness or her current sunburn.

“I’m just saying, there are vacation options we haven’t properly explored.” Dana let out a wistful sigh. “We’ve never been to a Caribbean resort.”

“Mom, I really think you should give rafting a chance. It was exhilarating.”

Dana opened her mouth to compliment her daughter on the five-syllable vocabulary word but clamped it shut as a Parks and Wildlife truck rumbled past. It was hauling an enclosed metal trailer, the kind that looked like a dinosaur enclosure in *Jurassic Park*.

Valerie jogged over panting. “They got him!” She bent forward, hands on her thighs.

Dana’s eyes darted around, searching for Valerie’s signature mode of transportation, but she didn’t see the golf cart anywhere. “Did you run all the way from the visitor center?”

Valerie shook her head and pointed down the road. “Parked over there. I’m just winded from helping the team load a 250-pound bear into the trailer.” Dana would’ve gladly run a mile—maybe two—before volunteering to shove a bear into a metal box.

Leah’s mouth dropped. “There’s a bear in there?”

“Yup.” Valerie stood and pressed her hands into her back. “He’s going to be relocated to an area farther away from civilization."

"How did they catch him so fast?" Dana asked.

"The wildlife guys had the idea to lure him out with fish guts, which is probably what keeps him coming back here anyway." Valerie wiped her hands on her shorts, grimacing as if she could still smell the bait. "We're going to have to move that table or train our campers to clean it better."

The towel slipped from Leah's shoulder. She wound it around her casted arm. "I'm sure getting the pants scared off of them by a bear would teach them a lesson."

"Except I'm the one who had the close encounter," Dana said. "And I didn't even fish, let alone cut into one."

"I guess it's safe for me to shower alone now?"

"Of course. Try and get the river water out of that cast." Dana smiled as she watched Leah disappear into the bathroom. She turned back to Valerie. "Have you had time to think about what you're going to do about your brother?"

Valerie shoved her hands into her pockets, eyes downcast. "There's no easy fix. I'm going to start with a conversation with Aunt Bonnie, but if she won't listen, I don't know what comes next."

"I'll be praying it all works out. And if you need moral support, you can always call or text me."

A flicker of relief softened Valerie's face. "That means more than you know. It's hard to open up when all of Durango gossips about my family. Bonnie's famous around here, which puts the rest of us under a microscope."

"I don't know what that's like, but I can imagine it's very isolating." Dana saw the way people whispered behind Josie's back when the triplets were babies. For months, she was so self-conscious, she avoided going anywhere with them.

Valerie didn't have a stroller the size of a freight train, but the attention from having an aunt with a multi-million-dollar helicopter and secretive pizza-parlor meetings couldn't be easy.

Dana fidgeted, the itch to ask a probing question winning out over politeness. "So how exactly did Bonnie end up with such a remarkable helicopter? It doesn't seem all that practical for search and rescue in the mountains."

"Oh, she has a different one for that." Valerie swiped her hand dismissively, as if everyone kept multiple choppers on hand for various tasks. "Your friend just happened to need a medevac when the luxury one was on hand."

"Two helicopters?" Dana's jaw dropped.

"The rescue chopper's at the municipal airport right now. There's not exactly room for both out here. But that didn't answer your question." Valerie motioned across the lake. "The one you saw, when a certain movie star's girlfriend mistook you for her Uber driver, was a gift from a Middle Eastern sheikh. A little token of appreciation for Aunt Bonnie saving his son's life."

Dana searched Valerie's face for any hint of a joke. "You're messing with me, right?"

Valerie didn't so much as twitch her lip. "Unassuming old ladies can get into places no one else can because people don't expect much of them. Underestimating Aunt Bonnie's been the downfall of many. But the ones who know what she's capable of and trust her? Let's just say they're very grateful for her skills." Valerie glanced at her watch. "I need to get going. Can't show up to my daughter's birthday dinner wreaking of bear fur." She wrinkled her nose and waved as she trotted toward the golf cart.

Dana traipsed back to Site Twelve, a spring in her step. This week had been packed with more adventure than she could have dreamed. If she tried to sort the good from the bad, she wasn't sure which column would win—but the excitement in Leah's voice as she gushed about rafting left little doubt. The fond memories outweighed the rest.

As if reading Dana's mind, the boys' laughter rang out as they rehashed their white-water adventure.

"We came at just the right time," Nate said. "By August, most of the mountain snow will have melted, and the water won't be nearly as rough."

Adam, sprawled across the picnic table with his feet dangling off the edge, grinned. "I don't know about all that, but isn't it awesome how God put the boulders in just the right places to make the river move faster?"

"Adam Harding." Dana strode into the group where three adults lounged in camp chairs, listening to Nate and Adam ramble on like seasoned river guides. Not one of them had told the kid to get down. She planted her hands on her hips. "You're covered in who knows what, and your rear end is sitting where we put our plates."

He slid to the ground, rolling his eyes so hard Dana was sure he could see his own brain. "Mom, you *do* realize squirrels, marmots, and raccoons climb all over the table, right? Do you really think I'm dirtier than them?"

"Yes."

"You let Nate lie on the table after he fell in a cactus. And *he* hadn't even been rinsed off by river water." His logic was getting harder to argue by the second.

"That was different. It was the only surface we had for an operating table." She pointed to the bench next to him. "*You*, on the other hand, have plenty of other places to sit that *aren't* where we eat."

He muttered a resigned, "Yes, ma'am," before turning back to Nate. "About the rocks, don't you think God does that just for our enjoyment?"

Dana scanned the faces of the other adults. All eyes were on Nate.

"I guess so," he said. "I hadn't really thought about it before, but it does seem like God designs some things just for our enjoyment. Like letting Leah be the one to get flung out of the boat because it was way funnier than if you or I had fallen."

Will and Hunter pursed their lips in silent agreement.

Josie shook her head with a small smile. "I don't know about God making your sister fall out just for laughs," she said, "but I *do* believe everything in nature proclaims Him. It reminds me of that Psalm, ninety-eight I think, that says, 'Let the rivers clap their hands, let the mountains sing together for joy. Let them sing before the Lord.'" A profound reminder that all of creation was made to worship the Creator.

Adam furrowed his brow and tilted his head. "I don't get it. Rivers can't clap, and mountains can't sing." Apparently, it was a more profound reminder for some than others.

"It's not literal. Or probably not." Dana sat beside him. "But in the New Testament, when the Pharisees told Jesus to make the people stop worshipping, he said if they did, the rocks beside the road would cry out."

Had Dana spent more time this week praising or complaining? She took in the mountains stretching against the horizon, their quiet majesty wrapping her like a familiar embrace. The week had been full of laughter, adventure, and more chaos than she cared to admit, but sitting here now, gratitude washed over her. She hugged her arms across her chest.

"You look cold, hon." Will stood. "Let me get the fire going."

"What's for dinner? I'm starving," Adam announced.

That kid was always starving. Proof that all was right in Dana's world.

"Everything," Dana said. "We're clearing out the last of the groceries, except for breakfast, so we don't have to haul it back." She got up to help Will. "Was camping everything you hoped for?"

He struck a match, holding it to the tinder pile. "Oh yeah." When the flame licked the kindling, he rose and slid an arm around her waist. "What about you? Did your first camping trip live up to the hype?"

She leaned into him, inhaling the faint scent of pine and smoke. "I didn't know what to expect."

"Imminent death, if I had to guess."

She elbowed him, and he responded by tickling her ribs. She shrieked, laughing as she tried to escape.

"Hey! No roughhousing around the fire," Nate called.

Still giggling, Dana melted back into Will's arms. "I wasn't finished. I didn't know what to expect, but camping was so much more than I could have imagined."

Will rested his chin atop her head, pressing a kiss to her hair. "So, what I hear you saying is, you can't wait to do it all again next year."

She smiled, the answer coming easier than she expected. "If it means seeing you and the kids light up like this? Then yeah. I can't wait."

And the best part? She actually meant it.

Chapter 39

Josie

Josie pulled a stray toy from beneath the picnic table and tucked it under her arm. The camper was packed, and the Caraways were almost ready to hit the road.

Hunter stepped outside. "The car seats are buckled in. Let's round up the rugrats and dump the tanks one more time."

Josie groaned. The worst part of the trip, save for the little detour to the hospital.

He rested his hands on Josie's hips. "I'm going to miss this place. How about you?"

She rotated to take in the view and pressed her back to his chest. "I'm going to miss the mountains and cooler temperatures, but I'm looking forward to a long bath and putting the kids to bed in their cribs."

He nuzzled her neck and let out a low growl. "I'm looking forward to that, too."

"Hunter, mind giving us a hand?" Will called. He was crouched on his knees shoving the folded tent into a duffle bag.

Hunter jogged over. "How can I help?"

"We've got to cram all this stuff back into the cargo carrier and strap the boxes back on the hitch."

"On it." Hunter got to work helping the Hardings load up while Josie coaxed the triplets out of the dirt and into the camper.

"Come on, guys. Are you ready to go home and see all your toys again?"

"Ina see Bita," said Connor.

Olivia echoed his sentiment. "Yeah, Bita!"

Josie took each of their hands in hers. "We'll see Abuelita soon, I'm sure." Even as she said it, she hoped it were true. The women in her family loved fiercely, but they held grudges with equal fervor. Her mother might stay away for months now that she knew the truth about Josie's feelings. She pushed the thought aside before it could settle in and ruin her day. There was still plenty of time for the car ride home to take care of that. She patiently guided Connor up the steps, careful not to lift him and aggravate her incisions.

Behind her, Leah scooped up Ben and hitched him onto her hip. "You shouldn't lean over the table to buckle them in. I've got it."

Josie straightened with a grateful sigh. "Thanks. You're a good egg."

"Yeah, yeah." Leah rolled her eyes. She climbed the steps behind Olivia and settled Ben into his car seat. "Aside from getting lost on the mountain in the rain and thrown off a raft into a freezing river, I had a really good time out here."

Josie blinked, momentarily thrown. "You did?"

"Yeah, and don't tell my parents, but the limited access to my phone was actually good for me."

Josie's jaw dropped. "You're kidding."

Leah fixed her with a flat, unimpressed stare. "Obviously. I can't wait to get back to civilization and use my phone again. But I did have a good time. It was nice seeing my parents get to hang out together without soccer games or band concerts. No schedules, no taking care of my Pops for a change. Just being in the moment."

Josie studied her, recognizing the honesty beneath Leah's sarcasm. Maybe this trip had done more for all of them than she'd realized. "Aside from my near-death experience and hurting my mom's feelings, I had a good time, too."

"Do you think y'all will make up soon?" Leah adjusted Olivia's straps while the toddler patted her cheeks.

"I hope so." Josie absently twirled one of Connor's curls around her finger. She had so many regrets about the way she'd handled her mother. Knowing how much she'd hurt her was worse than lying to her in the first place.

"Can I ask you something?" Leah didn't wait for permission. "Why was Marie so rude to Mom and Dad this week? She's sweet when she comes to Lubbock."

Josie winced. She was hoping the kids hadn't noticed her mother's terrible attitude. "In her mind, your parents were the reason we decided to come to Colorado, and she thinks that's why I got sick."

"Your mom thinks my parents gave you appendicitis?"

Josie chuckled dryly. "Essentially, yeah. Ridiculous, right?"

"Grown-ups usually are."

"Tell me about it," Josie said. "I'm no therapist, but I'd bet my mom's anger was really displaced fear."

Leah frowned. "Huh?"

"She was worried about me, scared of what could've happened. But instead of facing her feelings, she buried them under anger. It was easier to blame someone else than to admit she was afraid." Josie's gaze drifted to the triplets. "She probably even worries she'll end up raising the kids if something happens to Hunter and me."

Leah's brows pulled together. "Why would she think that?"

"That's just how her mind works. She always jumps to the worst-case scenario."

A flicker of understanding crossed Leah's face. "Ohhh. Like when my mom bought that mondo first aid kit."

"Exactly!"

"Don't y'all have other family members who would help with the babies?" Leah asked.

"Yes, but Hunter's parents have their hands full with his grandparents, and my sister is… well, not a kid person."

Leah huffed. "I've noticed."

Of course she had. Leah had witnessed it firsthand two years ago, when Josie's mother and sister blindsided her over a misunderstanding surrounding Laurel's wedding. Laurel didn't even know how to pick up a baby. She had all the maternal instincts of a goldfish.

Hunter returned to the Winnie lugging the dry-goods box with Dana's first aid kit balanced on top. He scooted them under the table. "All set."

"Where's Leah's suitcase?" Josie asked.

"We made space for it over there in case she needs it before we get back." His crooked grin was suspicious.

"Good thinking." Leah planted a kiss on top of each toddler's head. "See you at home."

Josie watched the teen skip out of the Winnie and eyed Hunter with her hands on her hips. "What are you up to?"

"Nothing, babe. I'm just ready to go. Aren't you?" He bolted the door and climbed into the driver's seat without meeting her gaze.

As soon as the Winnie merged onto the highway, Josie nestled into a cocoon of pillows, adjusting them to ease the lingering discomfort. She shut her eyes, knowing her window of peace was short. Before long, the triplets would demand snacks, freedom, or both, but for now, she let the hum of the road lull her to sleep.

Chapter 40

Dana

As the family piled into the Tahoe, Dana turned to Will with a pointed look. "New road trip rule: no driving off until we confirm everyone is in the car. Agreed?"

Will rolled his eyes. "I only left you once."

"And that's all it takes."

Leah and Nate wasted no time plugging in their earbuds and reclining against their windows. Adam's gaming device dinged to life, his head disappearing as he became absorbed in what was on his screen. Even Harvey settled in with a contented sigh.

"Anyone need motion sickness meds before we hit the road?" Dana asked.

"I'm good," Adam called from the third row.

Dana popped a pill into her mouth as Will buckled his seatbelt. "At the breakneck speed of seven and a half miles per hour, the Dramamine should kick in before we even hit the main road." Gravel crunched beneath the tires as he pulled away. "Goodbye, Site Twelve. Until next time."

"Until next time." Dana smiled, her laptop resting on her knees as her fingers tapped impatiently against the lid, itching to start writing. She exhaled slowly, letting the warmth of the trip sink in. "I hate to admit it, but this might've been one of our best vacations yet. Definitely the most memorable."

Will cocked an eyebrow. "Even with the bear and the outhouse?"

"And the lizard in the tent. Don't forget nearly losing an arm trying to keep Harvey away from that skunk."

Will chuckled. "You had quite the week of wildlife encounters."

"Yep. Like one of those drive-through zoos where the animals aren't caged. Except I wasn't in a car."

"So, more like a petting zoo?"

She grinned. "With rifles and helicopters."

Will pulled the Tahoe to a stop in front of the visitor center, leaving the engine running. "I'll go settle up."

Dana pushed open her door. "I'll come say goodbye, too." She hopped out, stretching her arms overhead before letting them drop to her sides. "I think I'm really going to miss Bonnie, Frances, and her kids."

Will waggled his eyebrows. "Especially Martin?"

Dana rolled her eyes and caught his arm. "Ugh. Come on."

Inside, the scent of old coffee lingered in the warm air. Bonnie looked up from behind the desk and beamed. "It's going to be awfully quiet around here without you guys."

"I'm sure you'll have plenty of interesting guests across the way to keep you entertained," said Dana.

Bonnie's mouth twitched, a knowing glint in her eyes. Instead of responding, she reached into a drawer and pulled out a book. She set it in front of Dana. "Before you go, would you mind signing this?"

Dana blinked at the familiar cover. *Dying to Donate.* Her book. She traced a finger over the glossy title before meeting Bonnie's gaze, warmth spreading through her chest.

"Well, I'll be," Will murmured.

Dana took the pen Bonnie held out to her and flipped open the front cover. "I'd be honored." She wrote a thoughtful note about how she would always remember

Silver Mountain and the family that ran it. She closed it, set the pen on top, and pushed it slowly across the desk.

Bonnie folded her hands. "I'll be looking forward to your next book. Perhaps one day you'll consider loosely basing a novel on our little neck of the woods."

"There's an idea," said Will. "You could stock it in the gift shop."

The door flew open, and a breathless Frances entered. "I was hoping I'd catch you." She pressed one hand to her heart and with the other held out a plastic leftover container to Will.

"Fran, did you run over here?" Bonnie stood and helped her sister into the seat she'd vacated.

Frances waved off the concern. "Couldn't send those kids all the way to Texas without a snack for the road."

"Chocolate chip cookies?" Will lifted the corner of the lid and inhaled. "They're still warm."

"Fran bakes for her grandkids and the wellness center almost every day," said Bonnie.

"Don't cookies defeat the purpose of a wellness retreat?" Will asked.

Dana shot him a warning look. After everything they'd been through this week, offending the owners as they rolled out was a bad move.

Frances raised her chin proudly. "My ingredients are locally sourced and of the finest quality."

Bonnie nodded. "Some VIPs have paid a pretty penny for my sister's baked goods."

Will pulled out his wallet and flipped it open. "Speaking of payment, what do I owe you for the six days?"

Bonnie lowered herself back into the office chair. "It just so happens that Site Twelve was on the house this week."

Dana and Will exchanged glances.

"How can that be?" Dana asked, brow furrowed. "We

were probably your most high-maintenance guests."

"Let's just say your company was payment enough." Bonnie winked, her face otherwise giving away nothing.

Back in the Tahoe, Will twisted in his seat, hopefully making sure everyone was accounted for. "That was wild, right? I can't believe they comped our whole stay."

"Even though they didn't say it outright, I have a feeling it was their way of reminding us how much they value our silence about… everything we learned."

Will pulled a cookie from the container in his lap and took a bite. "Fine by me. My silence is cheap." He turned up the radio and sang along to the rock and roll of his youth.

Dana opened her laptop to a new document, a familiar thrill running through her. Her fingers flew over the keys.

Deep in the woods, hidden from prying eyes, was a casino catering to the elite, outdoorsy types who preferred to gamble without the neon excess of Vegas. But in this exclusive retreat, where fortunes turned on the river and secrets lurked behind every cabin door, the real high stakes game didn't involve cards. It was about survival.

"Aren't you going to check that?" Will pointed to the cupholder where Dana's phone buzzed wildly as it regained a signal. She picked it up and skimmed to be sure none of the incoming messages were from her dad.

Leah shrieked from the middle row, and Will jerked the wheel, swerving just enough to make Dana's stomach flip.

"Don't do that!" Will snapped, steadying the car.

"The cast company has been reposting all my camping pics. I have like two thousand new followers!" Leah practically vibrated with excitement. "Are we *sure* I have to get this thing cut off next week?"

Dana turned in her seat. "You have a follow-up

appointment, but whether the cast comes off is up to the doctor." Part of her hoped it wouldn't. The extra layer of protection gave her peace of mind, like packing for every contingency did. But as her thoughts drifted to Adam's fully stocked backpack, conviction settled in. There was a fine line between planning wisely and overpreparing out of a lack of trust in God's provision. Will had pointed that out before they even left home. There was no way she would tell him he'd been right all along.

She reached back, giving Leah's knee an encouraging pat. "You know, sweetie, I think you're going to be glad to get that thing off. You'll have your full range of motion back."

Leah groaned dramatically, but Dana caught the flicker of relief in her eyes. "You're right. I'm sure I'll find new ways to build my Insta following."

One more thing for Dana to worry about.

Chapter 41

Josie

The rumble beneath Josie stilled, and the sudden silence jolted her awake as the Winnie rolled to a stop—in front of her childhood home. She blinked against the sunlight, her groggy mind scrambling for answers. Behind her, three little heads lolled to the side, still lost in sleep. She turned to Hunter, her voice clipped. "What are we doing here?"

Hunter cut the ignition. "We're making amends."

"Did you wait for me to fall asleep to change the GPS?" Then it hit her—Hunter's earlier weirdness was premeditation. "No, this was your plan all along."

He grinned, completely unapologetic. "I couldn't think of another way to get the two of you to make up." He nodded toward the house. "We've been spotted. Come on."

Josie groaned and looked out the window. Her mother stood on the porch, arms folded, expression unreadable. Great. With one last glare at Hunter, Josie unbuckled her seatbelt and climbed out.

"Surprise." The word landed flat in the thick air separating them.

Her mother didn't budge. "Shouldn't you be on your way to Lubbock?" No warmth, no hug, just a cool stare.

Josie swallowed and forced herself forward. "I don't like

how we left things."

Her mother's silence was louder than any argument.

Fine. Josie would have to do the heavy lifting. Ironic since she was under doctor's orders not to pick up anything over ten pounds. "I shouldn't have deceived you about the camping trip." The words tasted foreign, but she meant them. "I had a gut reaction without thinking things through, but the truth is…" She exhaled, glancing toward the Winnie. "I need you, Mom. We need you. I— we would love for you to live in town, to be there for us and the triplets."

Her mother stared past her, avoiding eye contact.

Lord, I don't know what to say. How do I fix things with her if she won't let me?

Before Josie could find the right words, the Winnie's side door flew open.

"Bita!" Ben's voice rang out as he barreled across the yard, his little legs pumping with all the force of a child on a mission. He flung himself into his grandmother's arms, clinging to her like she was his favorite person in the world.

"Benny!" Marie's face transformed, softening into a radiant smile as she hugged him tight.

Olivia and Connor tumbled out of the Winnie and ran past their mom, giggling as they joined the pile-on.

Hunter sidled next to Josie, lacing his fingers through hers.

"Well, don't just stand there. Come in, come in!" Marie herded the triplets inside, leaving Josie standing on the walkway, her mouth slightly agape.

Hunter gave Josie's hand a steadying squeeze, his grin downright triumphant.

She'd give him his moment for now, but how the scene played out once they were inside would determine how long she held his little detour against him. "How does she do that?"

"Do what?" Hunter asked, his tone too amused for her liking.

She clenched her jaw. "Flip from icy and imperious to warm and welcoming in two seconds flat."

Hunter slid his grip from her hand to her elbow, steering her toward the house. "The magic of grandbabies."

Inside, Marie was already rummaging through the kitchen cabinets. "If Abuelita had known you were coming, she would have gone shopping." She produced a package of Oreos and held them up. "How about some cookies?"

"Mom, I don't think they need sugar before they have to sit—"

Her mother's scornful stare cut her off mid-sentence.

"We'll all have cookies," Hunter declared smoothly. He lifted the triplets onto dining chairs and pulled one out for Josie. "What can I do to help, Marie?"

"Oh, I'm guessing you've helped plenty already," she said, her tone dry. "But you can cut up some strawberries."

He pulled a bowl from the fridge and raised his eyebrows at Josie. "Say something," he mouthed.

"Mom, I'm sorry."

Her mother poured juice into sippy cups. "Yes, you've said that."

Of course she wasn't going to make this easy. Josie gritted her teeth. They'd come all this way, so she may as well dive headfirst into the deep end. "Sometimes you can be... a little intense. And judgmental. And it hurts my feelings."

That got her mother's attention. Her nostrils flared as she set the carton on the table. "Oh?"

Josie pushed on before she lost her nerve. "But you mean well. No one takes care of us like you do. And the babies adore you."

Her mother's face softened just enough for Hunter to step in. "It's true," he said. "All we've heard for two days is, 'I want to see my Abuelita.'"

Olivia mimicked her dad. "I see my Bew-wita." It sounded like "burrito."

Josie bit the inside of her cheek-giggling right now would have been in poor taste. "Mom, we would be really happy for you to move to Lubbock."

Marie's mouth formed a taut line as she passed out the cups. "Please don't patronize me. You've already made your feelings about my move well known."

Josie swallowed. "No. I was caught off guard. I didn't have time to process the news before I reacted."

Her mother's unyielding gaze locked onto hers. "You mean before you lied."

"Yes. But I really do want you to be close by." Josie crossed her legs, winced, and uncrossed them. "The kids would love to have sleepovers at your house, and you could give them all the junk food you want without us knowing."

As though considering the idea, her mother's eyes lit on each toddler, a smile playing on her lips.

Hunter scooped a small pile of berries onto each of three paper towels. "I think Josie was concerned you might pop by and get upset by the state of the house. As I'm sure you can understand, we have a hard time keeping it clean with these three."

Josie appreciated him taking half the blame for the chaos they lived in, though she doubted her mother held him to the same impossible standard she reserved for Josie.

"After two days in a camper with them, I have a better understanding of what you guys deal with."

So, the nearly three years of triplet pandemonium in the Caraway house wasn't the eyeopener a single camping trip was. Josie held her tongue.

"I used to think staying organized with the triplets would get easier for you as they got older. I can see now that as soon as you have them figured out and think you're one step ahead, they learn a new trick and throw the whole system out of balance again. What you do is impressive, really, and I should've told you so before now."

Hunter caught Josie's eye and winked. "Honestly Marie,

most days we're just thankful everyone survived."

"Well, if our girl is going to get out of cosmetology school and open her own booth, you guys are going to need a backup to help with preschool pick up."

Josie's pulse skipped. She pushed up from her chair, taking a cautious step toward her mother. "Does that mean you'll move to Lubbock?"

Her mother nodded as tears welled in her eyes.

Josie barely had time to blink before Hunter wrapped both women in a tight hug. Emotion clogged her throat, and she fought to keep it together, but when Connor stood in his chair and threw his little arms around all three of them, she lost the battle. A teary laugh bubbled up as she pulled back, wiping at her damp cheeks.

Her mother cleared her throat, her voice thick with emotion. "I owe Dana and Will an apology for how I treated them. I just… I—"

"It's okay, Mom," Josie said softly. "I think I understand. And I'm sure they will, too."

Her mother gave a small nod, then squared her shoulders, regaining her usual composure.

"So, we're good now?" Hunter asked, glancing between them.

Marie sniffed and waved a hand. "We are—so long as I never have to spend another night in that rolling tin can."

"Hey!" Hunter gave her an offended look. "I'll have you know that is a very nice tin can."

Josie smirked. "What happened to 'I've stayed in motels worse than this?'"

Marie arched a brow. "Just because I *have* doesn't mean I *ever* intend to do it again."

Chapter 42

Dana

Dana clacked away at her laptop's keyboard, making the most of her time in the orthopedist's waiting room.

Beside her, Leah scrolled through her phone. "What do you think I should do to keep my Instagram followers engaged once this cast comes off?"

Promote your mom's books. Though Dana doubted Leah's audience had many avid readers. "I don't know, sweetheart. You'll think of something, I'm sure."

Leah sighed dramatically. "Maybe I'll use my platform to expose the hypocrisy of doctor's offices—charging no-show fees, refusing to see late patients, yet making us wait for hours."

Dana looked up from her screen, realizing with amusement and only mild horror, she and Leah had officially become Edward Johnson and her.

"Let's swing by and pick up Pops for lunch when we get out of here," Dana closed her laptop and sent a text to her dad. She'd talked to him plenty since they got back, but somehow, they kept missing each other in person. How had a grandfather with mild dementia managed to develop a more active social life than she had?

"Sure. Feels like we haven't seen him in forever."

A few more minutes passed before a technician finally

called Leah's name. He led them back, took an X-ray of her casted arm, and then ushered them into an exam room. "Dr. Graham will be with you shortly."

As he closed the door behind him, Leah scoffed and pulled out her phone. She set the stopwatch and held it up. "Let's show the world what 'shortly' means in a doctor's office."

Dana opened the laptop, eager to get back to work. The world? Since when did two thousand followers make up a global sampling? Before she could even finish crafting a section of dialogue, a knock sounded at the door, and the doctor stepped in.

Leah shot Dana a look and discreetly tilted her phone screen toward her. "Shortly," in this instance, was seven minutes.

Dr. Graham washed at the sink and shook Leah's good hand. "How'd that cast work for you?"

"Great. Definitely the right choice for a camping trip."

He scanned his badge on the computer and pulled up the x-ray on the monitor. He leaned his face close to the screen, brows knitted together.

Dana's stomach twisted. Dr. Graham had seen something that concerned him.

He spun on his stool to face Leah. "Show me that arm."

She extended it, and the doctor threw his head back with laughter. "I love the beading, but that image sure threw me for a loop." He pointed to the X-ray, where white circles formed a line along her knuckle. "Now that I'm sure we aren't dealing with abnormal growths, let's look at the scaphoid."

Dana blew out a sigh of relief and smiled to herself remembering how just a few weeks ago she had mistakenly believed that tiny wrist bone to be a skull plate.

"You're a fast healer, Miss Harding. I don't see any reason for you to keep the cast on."

"How can you be sure?" Dana asked, trying to keep the

worry out of her voice. The last thing she wanted was for the cast to come off too soon and lead to another injury.

He pointed to the screen and explained in excruciating detail how he could tell it was healed. "I'm sending you to physical therapy to help you regain your strength and range of motion."

Leah's face lit up. "Can I get back to full soccer workouts now?"

"Not for two more weeks." He tugged on surgical gloves and took out a pair of scissors from a drawer. "The second-best thing about this cast, next to being waterproof, is how easily we can cut it off. No saw." He snipped through the lattice, one piece at a time, until an opening ran the length of it. He pried it apart, and Leah lifted her arm out.

She turned it over in the light, inspecting the diamond-shaped tan lines covering her skin. "I look like Aquaman."

Dana stifled a laugh as Leah tested her wrist, rotating it cautiously. A flicker of discomfort crossed her face, but she didn't complain.

Dr. Graham gave her a knowing look. "Sore?"

"Weak and stiff," she admitted.

"That's normal. Give yourself time. Meanwhile, sunscreen is your new best friend."

Dana pulled into her dad's driveway, eyeing the unfamiliar sedan parked beside her. He hadn't mentioned having company when she asked him to lunch.

Leah hopped out and bounded toward the front door. Before she reached it, it swung open, and a woman stepped outside. She wore a red tee shirt under a denim button-up with the sleeves rolled to her elbows. Laidback but put-together. Comfortable here.

Dana crossed the lawn at a measured pace, her senses on

high alert. "Hello."

The woman's face brightened with an easy smile. "You must be Dana and Leah. I've heard so much about you. I'm Maggie."

"It's nice to finally meet you." Dana had a laundry list of questions for Maggie about her dad's behavior and anything out of the ordinary that would point to a decline in his mental faculties. But before she could ask, her dad stepped onto the porch, pulling Leah into a bear hug.

Dana swallowed the lump in her throat and forced a smile. "Thanks for looking out for my dad."

"It's my pleasure. He's a delight." Maggie dipped her head and made her way to the car next to Dana's Tahoe.

"Dad, she's pretty." Dana lifted her hand to wave as Maggie backed out.

Her father snorted. "She's also married and about ten years too young for me."

"Did you find your bank card?" She hugged him, inhaling Polo cologne and Icy Hot ointment.

"I did. It had fallen between the seat and the center console in the car."

"No man's land," said Leah in a knowing tone. "When something slips down there, you might as well buy a new one because it's lost forever."

"Aren't you glad you didn't accuse Maggie of taking it?"

Casually avoiding answering the question, he clapped his hands. "Now, are we going to lunch, or are we just gonna stand around yapping about my cleaning lady?"

Leah gave her Pops the passenger seat and climbed in behind Dana. "Notice anything different about me?" She held up her arms and wiggled her fingers.

"Hey, you got your cast off! Looks like you took a nap under one of those orange construction fences."

Dana glanced back in the rearview mirror. "Don't listen to Pops. It looks like you had a fun vacation is all." She turned back to her dad and shot him a warning look. Had he completely forgotten how sensitive teenage girls were about their appearances?

She felt her dad's scrutiny as she turned out of Mesquite Village, his retirement community.

"You look happy and relaxed. You had a good vacation too, didn't you?"

She smiled. "It was epic."

ABOUT THE AUTHOR

Stephanie King writes humorous contemporary Christian fiction and nonfiction articles about God refining chaos into connection. She and her husband have raised three children in Texas, where they currently live with the youngest and an opinionated German Shepherd.